FREEDOM ROAD

A THRILLER

Other Titles by William Lashner

A Filthy Business

The Four-Night Run

Guaranteed Heroes

The Barkeep

The Accounting

Blood and Bone

The Victor Carl Novels

Bagmen

A Killer's Kiss

Marked Man

Falls the Shadow

Past Due

Fatal Flaw

Bitter Truth

Hostile Witness

Writing as Tyler Knox

Kockroach

WILLIAM LASHNER

FREEDOM ROAD

A THRILLER

THOMAS & MERCER

Text copyright © 2019 by William Lashner
All rights reserved.

Published by Thomas & Mercer, Seattle

www.apub.com

Amazon, the Amazon logo, and Thomas & Mercer are trademarks of Amazon.com, Inc., or its affiliates.

ISBN-13: 9781503904460
ISBN-10: 1503904466

Cover design by M. S. Corley

Printed in the United States of America

For Alison Dasho,
who always had more faith in Oliver
than Oliver had in himself

We have been cursed with the reign of gold long enough.

Eugene Debs
January 1, 1897

I. Revolver

1

LIGHT MY FIRE

Chicago, 1968

Oliver Cross took a commuter train to the revolution.

It was the same train his father took to work every weekday morning and the occasional Saturday, the Chicago & North Western from Kenosha to the Loop. His father boarded the train in Highland Park, the seats already filling with suited men briskly turning the half-folded pages of the *Tribune* or the *Wall Street Journal,* first checking the prices of their stocks, and then the Cubs score, and then maybe the national news if they could stomach it. Oliver expected he would take that same train each weekday morning and the occasional Saturday after he finished law school at the University of Michigan. Maybe he'd catch it from Evanston or Winnetka for a few years at the start of his career before he'd be able to afford the high-priced house by the lake or country club in Highland Park that was his ultimate goal. Oliver's father, a LaSalle Street lawyer, dealt in debentures; always the rebel, Oliver had his eye on the more rough-and-tumble world of mergers and acquisitions.

But the commuter train wasn't loaded with its normal contingent this day. It was a Sunday, late in the summer, a few weeks before Oliver would have to return to Ann Arbor for his second year of studying the law, and he rode the train with his great pal Finnegan, heading into the city to see the freak show.

"None of it matters," said Finnegan, also a law student, though at Loyola, which meant a lesser job and a lesser future, which gave Oliver a prickly sense of satisfaction. "They can huff and puff all they want but Humphrey has the nomination."

"Unless Lyndon steals it back," said Oliver. "I wouldn't put it past him."

"Johnson would definitely steal it if Kennedy were still around, the way he hated him. Too bad about that California thing," said Finnegan, making a no-ice-cream-for-you face.

"I'll never get over it," said Oliver.

"Me neither," said Finnegan. "Let's get a dog before we go to the park. I'm starving."

Being a child of his generation, Oliver was vehemently against the war, which meant staying in school to beat the draft and arguing over beers with retrograde assholes in the pubs in Ann Arbor. He had been an avid McCarthy supporter until Kennedy got himself shot in California, whereupon Oliver suddenly switched his allegiance to the dead man. It seemed the right thing to do. And there was something about McCarthy supporters that ate at him. They were a little too preppy, too sure of themselves, cold-blooded like their candidate, the former monastery student turned senator; they all smiled at you with the self-satisfaction of the recently ordained. Oliver knew all about McCarthy support- ers, since he had been one for so long and fit the mold so well. But now, with the 1968 Democratic National Convention set to open in Chicago, the ghost of Robert Kennedy had his heart.

Better a dead man as president, Oliver figured, than Richard Milhous Nixon.

The commuter train that Sunday was filled to standing with the young, the restless, the earnest, the curious, and Finnegan, who was going for the girls. Oliver would have been content to sit out the noise and spectacle with a cooler of beer by the family pool, but Finnegan had convinced him this was a once-in-a-lifetime opportunity. "What about free love don't you understand, Cross?" Finnegan had said, which, all in all, was a pretty effective argument. And so Oliver sat on that train as it snaked through the tenements and industry of the northern part of the city. The fringed leather satchel of some longhair standing in the aisle banged into Oliver's shoulder with every turn.

"Sorry, man," said the longhair without doing anything about it. Probably a McGovern supporter.

The train emptied at Clybourn, and a jaunty, smoke-wreathed parade headed east over the bridge on Courtland toward Lincoln Park. There would be a concert, speakers, Yippies and hippies, and girls with loose shirts and flowers in their hair. The sky was high, the day was perfect, and Lincoln Park was the place to be, as long as you left before eleven because Mayor Daley had decreed that the park was to be emptied by eleven.

"The last train back is at ten fifteen," said Finnegan, looking over a printed schedule as the two waited for a couple hot dogs at a shack on Armitage with a VIENNA BEEF sign overhead.

"I don't expect I'll last that long," said Oliver. "Let's catch something about five."

"Unless we catch something else."

"Syphilis?"

"Don't be such a killjoy."

"Unlike you, Finn, I have a girlfriend."

"In Michigan, man. What's that got to do with anything?"

"When's the first train after five?"

"Five thirty-seven."

"Let's shoot for that. The festival should be over by then and Florence is making a ham."

"What happened to you, Cross? You're like an old man already."

The franks came freshly grilled, with long slivers of pickle, hot peppers, and tomato slices, along with onions and that peculiar Chicago relish that is so green, it looks like a traffic light signaling go, eat, enjoy. Oliver splatted mustard on top—no ketchup, thank you—and took a bite. Through the soft bun and garden loaded on top he could feel the casing snap between his teeth and taste the spurt of grease. Suddenly there was no war, no politics, his mother was still alive, his father still knew how to smile, his brother was home from Vietnam, and Ernie Banks was back to playing shortstop at Wrigley Field.

Was there anything better in the whole wide world than a Chicago dog?

◆ ◆ ◆

Oliver Cross missed the five-thirty-seven north to Kenosha. He also missed the ten-fifteen. Instead of being asleep in his bed at midnight with a stomach full of Florence's ham, he found himself on Clark Street, just west of Lincoln Park, holding hands with strangers on the front lines of a war.

On his left stood a red-haired, freckled girl with a bandanna stretched over her nose and mouth to protect against the expected fusillade of tear gas. On his right stood a tall man with glasses and a beard shouting out a string of obscenities. They were part of a line that fronted a writhing mob of youth facing off against a row of helmeted, blue-shirted police intent on clearing the roadway with all deliberate violence and speed.

And right then, in the middle of the madness, Oliver couldn't have told you how he got there.

He had lost sight of Finn in the afternoon hours, during the short-lived so-called Festival of Light, where slithering guitars and unintelligible lyrics had been blasting through the crowd and across the lagoon in the middle of the park. Everyone had been pressing forward because the band wasn't on a stage and no one could see a thing, and in the melee, the two friends had lost contact. Oliver was actually relieved to be alone; he wanted to dig the brave new world in which he found himself on his own, without Finn's judgment or sarcasm. The music was loud, the mob was dancing. There were balloons in the trees, and hats of every variety, and Mary Jane was being passed freely from hand to hand as if the drug itself were an integral part of the festival.

That Abbie Hoffman sure knew how to put on a show.

Oliver wasn't much for drugs—he was his father's son and would have preferred a martini—but somehow, there, it had felt wrong to give his usual "No thanks, I'm cool." The crowd itself told him he wasn't so cool after all. There were kids within the throng, high schoolers still, with so much natural defiance in their bones that he felt suddenly defensive. Pulling back would be to somehow deny his generational membership. So you could say he was shamed into it—peer pressure, yes!—but Oliver had spent his day so far as a tourist gawking at the young stoned hippies, so filthy their scented message had to be purposeful, as well as the bearded beatniks with their fisherman's caps, the organizing Yippies with their special white jackets, the black kids with their cowboy hats and berets, the hip girls with their slouch bags and blazing eyes. Oliver had spent so much of the day, so much of his life, being ever so careful that maybe it was time to cross a fucking line.

And that was how, in the midst of a cataclysmic swirl of mediocre rock, he had found himself seriously stoned when the city abruptly cut the power to the amplifiers, the crowd surged, and all hell broke loose.

For Oliver, in the midst of the craziness, things suddenly had become distant and unfocused, unconnected by acts of his own will. He drifted through a wild landscape divorced from any reality he understood, like the Hieronymus Bosch painting his mom used to show him at the Art Institute.

He could remember a young man, shirtless, tall and thin, flailing his arms and legs to a wild drumming before falling into the lagoon and swimming off. "Revolution," he called out when he reached the island in the middle of the water and waved his arms like a madman. "Bravery. No retreat."

He could remember sitting within a wide circle on a beach and chanting *Om Namah Shivaya* with Allen Ginsberg. Allen Howling Ginsberg!

He could remember kissing a girl with a white headband beneath a tree in the dimming light of dusk, a pretty girl who disappeared as suddenly as she had arrived. Oliver called after her but he didn't know her name. "Hey, Headband!" Five other girls turned around.

He could remember wandering the green fields after darkness fell, making his way by the flickering lights of trash fires, stumbling across lovers in the shadows, listening to the strum of folk guitars, being offered and accepting more hits from more joints, and all the time being carried forward by the drums, the drums, the pounding drums, beating out a secret message sent from one relay to the next in a line that surely spread across the whole of the continent.

He could remember great beams of light prowling through the park, followed by news teams with their heavy, hungry cameras.

He could remember watching a rousing charge toward a row of toilets surrounded by police, the chargers being chased away by raised batons in what felt like a wild game of capture the flag. Instead of joining in, he had unzipped his fly and drowned a small tree.

He could remember a young kid sitting on someone's shoulders, waving the Vietcong flag and shouting, "Stay in the park! The park belongs to the people!"

He could remember the people's strategy delivered calmly through bullhorns by the Yippie marshals, "Break up, don't bunch," even as a helicopter flew just above the tree line, the blinding oval of its search-light slithering across the ground.

And he could remember the official city car with a speaker on its roof announcing that the park would close at 11:00 p.m. and all journalists and demonstrators who refused to honor the curfew would be arrested. As a phalanx of police began its sweep westward from the lake, and the Yippie leaders urged all to leave, the mob ignored both and made a stand with cheers and chants.

"Fuck the marshals."

"Revolution."

"This is now Che Guevara National Park."

"It's five minutes to eleven."

"Red rover, red rover, send Daley right over."

"Here they come."

"Onto the streets. Onto the streets."

And suddenly, without any force of intent, Oliver Cross found himself in the great confrontation of the night, of the week, of his generation, part of a groundswell fueled by youth and drugs and a righteous fury at an unjust and barbarous war. The protesters joined in battle lines against rows of police with their helmets and their batons, public servants who believed they were the final defense against an anarchy that was enveloping their city and threatening to destroy the very fabric of their nation.

To be honest, even at the vanguard of this epical clash, standing there with his high being burned away by raw fear, Oliver was still playing the tourist. Like any true student of the law, he found himself in sympathy with both sides. The police were not the enemy, nor were the demonstrators. Something was tearing the country apart, and that something was the root of the problem. They should be joining arms, the police and the young; they should be marching together against the malign powers that sought to divide them, whatever they might be.

"Hell no, we won't go."

"Ho, Ho, Ho Chi Minh."

"Oink, oink, fascist pig bastards."

The police moved forward in rank. Spotlights reflected off helmet and baton. Cameras whirred as name tags were unpinned from blue police shirts and slipped into pockets. A plume of smoke rose from down the street.

"Prague, Prague, we are Prague."

"The streets belong to us."

As Oliver gripped the other protesters' hands and stood against the harsh formation of authority, a strange moment of stillness arose, when the shouts subsided and the police stopped their advance and the night seemed to hinge between ferocity and solidarity. A few angry calls from the rear of the crowd were swallowed by the quiet. A few white-shirted police among the rows of blue worked to keep the troops calm. A woman stepped forward from the crowd and offered an apple to one of the policemen, who grabbed hold of it and took a bite.

And Oliver imagined just then that he could see the future, that the massing police and the massed demonstrators would become one, an American collective working together to take control of the streets and, eventually, the nation. This was the America Oliver Cross believed in then, a sane land of brotherhood and equality where disputes over things as meaningless as a park curfew, as fraught as race, and as serious as war could be dealt with intelligently, humanely, with the forces of decency and law. And as a lawyer, Oliver naturally imagined himself at the epicenter of this great reconciliation. The hope of that reconciliation, and the image of his own great future riding astride that hope, was filling his heart when the red-haired woman next to him shouted out in a voice so sharp, it cut through the night like a scimitar:

"Your mother sucks dirty cock!"

Later there would be accounts of rocks and beer bottles thrown at the police from the back of the mob. Later it would be reported that packs of demonstrators rushed the fierce blue wall in a futile attempt to make it back into the park. Later all manner of incident would be put forward as the spark that started the riot, but Oliver Cross would never doubt that the words shouted by the protester standing beside him were the instigating factor, as if the police had just been waiting for an excuse and that fearless, reckless woman, releasing the hounds of her righteous fury, had given them exactly what they wanted.

The police charged. Batons flashed. The lines broke and there was a brutal to-and-fro when, in the middle of the battle, came the blow, a strike on Oliver's head so hard that it permanently creased his skull even as it knocked the world right out of him.

He drifted sweetly on the edge of consciousness. He had no name, no past or future, and the present, with all its chaos and violence, was only a distant babble. He raised his hands and fell to his knees and sank into the ground as if it were made of taffy. All was white static, a television left on without a signal. And out of that whiteness came the chanting—"*Om Namah Shivaya, Om Namah Shivaya*"—as figments of the world emerged: a beach, a park, a circle, a bearded man with glasses and little finger cymbals. "*Om Namah Shivaya.*" Within the staticky now there was no must do, no can't do, no ambition or fear of failure, no right or wrong, up or down, yes or no. There was for him, just then, only freedom pure, filling every cell in his body. He felt himself expanding until he was about to explode with joy, every particle of his being joining with the great indifferent flower of the universe.

Later, Oliver Cross would say that this was the moment that changed everything, where he stepped out of one kind of life and into another, but that would not be the entire truth. Because when the next blow came, shattering his collarbone and deadening his left arm, he wasn't changed at all, just knocked right back into the world exactly as he always had been.

Except the world was now in flames.

◆ ◆ ◆

Oliver Cross, kneeling helplessly on the street, looked up into the uneven darkness of the city sky and saw above him, amidst the fury and chaos, a dark-brown baton rising to slam again into his skull. It would kill him this time, the baton, he was certain, yet still, in his daze, he waited for the blow as if it were some sort of benediction.

Until a bright light fell on the cop gripping the baton, who immediately spun around and swung his cudgel at a television camera, shattering the lens into shivers, and then went on to smash the light and the cameraman, too.

Amidst this slashing and banging, someone grabbed at Oliver from behind, pulled at him and dragged him back, all the while shouting at him to get up, to get going. The next thing Oliver knew he was staggering past the paddy wagons being loaded with body after body, past the cop cars with their sirens blaring, staggering through the crowd, but not on his own. He kept his deadened left arm tight to his body while he was pulled away from the battle by a woman in a dark coat with a blue bandanna over her face—the same woman, in fact, whose hand he had been holding just a few moments before.

She pulled him through the chaos and onto a side street, past a pack of kids straining to roll a car onto its side. One of the kids caught him staring.

"Barricades, man," the kid said. "Power to the people or some such shit."

"Keep going," said the woman, and that's what he did, lurching with her into the guts of Old Town.

Half a block later she tugged him into an alley and around a dumpster with Daley's name printed on it in white block letters. They ducked into an entryway lit by a single yellow bulb over the door.

"Sit down," she said.

Oliver dropped onto the entryway stoop.

"You're bleeding like a pig in a slaughterhouse." She leaned forward and moved her hands through his hair and across his skull. "Chicago, hog butcher for the world."

"What?"

"Carl Sandburg."

"Who?"

"Read poetry much?"

"Why?"

"You have a two-inch-long gash in your head. Here."

She pulled the blue bandanna down off her face and reached back to untie the knot. After wiping the blood off her hands she wadded the bandanna into a ball and pressed it onto the wound. Then she gently took hold of his right hand and placed it on top of the bandanna to keep it in place.

As she did all this, Oliver found himself staring at the most beautiful woman he had ever seen. He had noticed her striking green eyes before, in the line of protesters, evident even with her mask, but now that he could see her entire face, long jawed and sharp, with the slight sardonic twist of her lips, he was stunned.

"Hey, you," she said, snapping her fingers as if to wake him from a hypnotic trance. "Are you with me?"

"Yes . . . fine . . . yes . . . I am . . . okay."

"That cut needs to be looked at," she said. "You'll be getting stitches. And what's with your arm?"

"I think . . . my collarbone . . . they broke—"

"What were you thinking, rushing at them like a fool?"

"Rushing at who like a what?"

"You don't remember? They must have beat the memory right out of you. Three of them had some kid up against a car and were taking their whacks when you charged like a maniac. As they were banging at you, the kid got away. It was pretty stupid, but it was also, in a way, almost heroic."

"Right now, considering I'm a bloody mess sitting on a stoop, I'd go with stupid."

"Yeah, me too."

"I can't get arrested."

"Do you have a record?"

"No. I . . . I just can't."

She took a step back and looked down the alley toward the street. "Those kids will keep the cops busy for a while. If we get rid of the light, you can hide out here until it's safe for you to find a hospital."

She unslung the bag from over her shoulder and swung it high. The yellow bulb shattered with a pop, plunging the alleyway into darkness.

"If any cops come down the street, they'll just pass us by," she said, before sitting next to him. "I'm Helen."

"Oliver."

"And why are you so afraid of getting arrested, Oliver? It could be a badge of honor. 'What did you do in the war, Daddy?' 'I fought my war in Chicago.'"

"I'm in law school," he said.

"Ah, I see, and the bar association might not be so impressed. What's a law student afraid of being arrested doing on the streets of Chicago, today of all days?"

"I don't know." He thought about lying, coming up with some noble gibberish to impress this Helen, maybe by talking about his brother, and the war, and his determination to make the politicians in Washington listen to the voices of his generation. But there was something about this woman's manner, and the way her beauty so startled, that squeezed out the truth. "I came with a friend, Finnegan. The thing was just something to see, I guess. All the freaks and the music. Allen Ginsberg. And maybe we thought we'd find some girls."

She laughed. "I admire the shallowness. This whole day I've been rubbing up against such saccharine earnestness that my teeth ache."

"And my brother's in the war," Oliver added because he couldn't help himself.

"I'm sorry."

"But he's not why I came. He volunteered. He wants to go into politics himself and looks at the war as an opportunity."

"But still."

"Yeah."

"And how did the girl thing work out for you?"

"Not great."

"I'm sorry I can't help alleviate the situation, but I'm engaged."

"Really?"

"Getting married in the spring."

"Good for you."

"Isn't it?"

"You don't sound convinced. Is he here?"

"He's in med school, on rotation in New York. But I'm at Bryn Mawr and I thought it was time to make history instead of just reading about it in books."

"Bryn Mawr, huh? Preppie little Philly school. I suppose that means you're here for McCarthy."

"I'm not here for anyone."

"So what are you? Yippie? Hippie? SDS?"

"I'm Helen," said Helen.

"I was for Kennedy."

"It's amazing how popular he became after they killed him. But they're all just politicians. I'm not for any of them. I'm for anarchy, mayhem, liberty, and art. I'm for singing naked on the rooftop. I'm for a freedom that sinks into your bones until the itch drives you crazy."

"Sounds like being married to a doctor to me."

"I'm going to be an artist and I've read my Virginia Woolf. But marriage is what you make of it, Oliver, just like life."

"And what are you going to make of it?"

"Something that's mine. I read somewhere that the key to making a great painting is to free our minds of the jargon and limitations imposed on us from the past. Proper perspective, proper use of color, proper theme, propriety itself, the so-called natural order of things. What does the world look like when you strip that all away?"

"I don't know."

"Neither do I, but I intend to find out."

"I like Picasso."

"Picasso is everybody's favorite artist, and he works so hard to be exactly that. But he just hops from one set of rules to the next. Cubism, neoclassicism, surrealism. What about no rules? What about looking at the world as if you're the first person to ever see it and putting that on a canvas? That's how I want to paint. That's how I want to live."

"Sounds exhausting."

"But think of the freedom. No rules, no laws, nothing but the beat of our own hearts. We toss off whatever they try to foist on us and build our own structures. That's part of what we're doing here. Did you see Ginsberg?"

"I joined his chanting circle."

"How experimental for a good Episcopalian."

"How did you know?"

"It's like we're following in the footsteps of the Beats, sure, but not chained to their male-centric, macho Buddhist crap. We'll make our own rules."

"Our own crap."

"At least it will be ours. What do you want out of life, Oliver?"

"Respect, money, I don't know. A job worth doing. A house on the beach or by the golf club."

"Do you like to golf?"

"Hate it."

"Do you like the beach?"

"Not really. The sand, you know. It chafes."

She laughed.

"Love," he said.

"Well, that's original. But what kind, Oliver? The kind they tell you to want in the movies and in poems?"

"Sure."

"The kind that follows their rules, uses their ceremonies, the kind that enslaves you, and makes you spend a life of drudgery supporting the house and kids and backyard pool even as the love sours from all that dire responsibility?"

"Does that sound so bad?"

"It sounds like my mother's life, without the pool. We could never afford the pool."

"You can use ours."

In the darkness he could feel her move closer and then, suddenly, on that step, she was kissing him.

He pulled back. "Why are you doing that?"

"You like Picasso."

"You said everyone likes Picasso."

"But not everyone is here now, bloodied and broken in heroic battle."

"Is that what it was?"

"And not everyone has a pool."

She put her hand on his cheek and kissed him again. Her mouth felt soft, electric. He could have happily fallen into the moist warmth of it. He wanted to reach out and grab hold of her, but with his broken collarbone screaming in pain and his right hand still pressing the bandanna over his wound, he was unable to execute his normal movie clinch. So instead he just sat there, passively letting her kiss him and kissing her gently back. And as he kissed her he felt something rise up from his heart. That might have truly been the moment, the moment that changed everything.

Or maybe it was the moment he felt her hand undoing his belt buckle, and then the button of his pants, and then the zipper. When she had pulled him out of his underwear and had him in her hand, gently stroking him as her mouth explored his and their tongues danced one with the other, he pulled back again.

"What about the med student?"

"He likes this, too," she said.

Or maybe the moment that really mattered was a few moments after that, when his lips shivered on hers and his breath caught and she laughed in surprise before wiping her hand on his shirt.

She gave him a quick peck on the lips before standing and heading into the darkness. By the time he figured out what he wanted to say to her, she was gone.

Hours later, in the dim morning light, Oliver stumbled back onto Clark Street, where the survivors of the night's battles wandered dazed among overturned cars, strewn trash, and pieces of discarded clothing stained red with blood. He was immediately led by a white-jacketed Yippie marshal to a theater on Wells Street, where protesters stood behind iron gates within an ornate stone arch, holding the latch shut until they determined that he wasn't a plainclothes cop faking his injuries to slip through their defenses.

In the mob scene inside the theater, his head was bandaged and he was given a sling for his useless arm, along with a snort of something that didn't quite deaden the pain but made it something distant. He fell asleep for a few hours on the theater's roof, before waking in excruciating pain and setting out for the hospital to get his collarbone and head taken care of.

But no matter how powerful all those moments truly were for Oliver Cross, the moment that actually might have changed everything happened two weeks after that night, half a world away, when elements of the Eleventh Light Infantry Brigade of the United States Army, participating in Operation Champaign Grove, engaged an enemy force while sweeping an area four miles west of Quang Ngai City. The eighty-minute battle, which resulted in sixty-one enemy deaths, also resulted in two infantry soldiers killed in action, one of whom was Second Lieutenant Fletcher Cross of Highland Park, Illinois.

After receiving word of his brother's death, Oliver Cross left school suddenly and took a bus from Ann Arbor, with transfers in Detroit, Cleveland, and Baltimore, on his way to Philadelphia and a very different future.

2

THE BEAST IN ME

Fifty Years Later

The small brick house at 128 Avery Road is dark as death on Halloween. Up and down the street jack-o'-lanterns twinkle on walkways and spotlights illuminate front-yard gravestones decked with cobwebs pulled from plastic bags. Children dance along the sidewalks with their masks and blood-drenched fangs, hitting house after house in their devilish protection racket, but the gloomy door of 128 receives not a knock.

In truth, the trick-or-treaters would have passed it by even if it had been lit like a firecracker. The younger children are steered away by the firm hands of their parents, and the older children scare one another with stories and dares, but none has the courage to tempt the fate that resides behind that door. Later, when lights are dimmed and most of the children are inside, dazed by sugar as they count their haul, eggs will be thrown at the dark house at 128 Avery Road and yolks will drip down the front door like sallow tears.

The little monsters, they'll get theirs, sooner than they can imagine. Carrying home candy hiding the razor blades of truth. Spoonfuls of sugar to help the capitalist poison slide down their sad, deluded throats.

Yellow stains still mark the door of 128 Avery Road on Christmas morn, the yolks having hardened like unruly dribbles of atomic sludge. On the plots surrounding the house, colored lights are blinking and plastic reindeer stand guard. A blow-up Santa waves to passersby from inside a great plastic ball. Through picture windows you can see trees, some of them even real, decked gaily with lights and tinsel and bright, shiny ornaments. Stacks of presents lie undisturbed until the rooms come alive with shouts and laughter as the wrappings are torn off with joyful abandon.

But there are no shouts or music within the darkness of 128 Avery Road. The only sign of life is a slight *whoosh* of the curtains in the front window, as if some brooding ghost were floating back and forth, forth and back.

Celebrate what? Pull away the colored paper and all is bitterness and death. The only gift worth having is nothing. Let them laugh now, the little families in their little bubbles, it won't be long until the tears fall.

The first blizzard of the season descends on Avery Road a week after the New Year's parties and fireworks. Children fall backward into the snow, making angels with their arms, and build forts to withstand fierce tactical assaults. Parents shovel their own walks and the walks of their neighbors, working together to clear driveways of heavy drifts caused by the plows. But the snow on the sidewalk in front of 128 remains pristine, untrammeled by shovel or boot. Neighbors visiting one another for hot chocolate and gossip glance nervously at the dark house as they veer into the street. The yellow stains still on the wood seem shameful somehow, a reminder of something best forgotten. A young boy starts in on shoveling the walk and the curtain twitches over the front window of 128 Avery, but the boy's mother calls him home and that is that.

A few days later a pink notice from the township about the unshoveled walk is taped to the door at 128 Avery Road, giving the occupant thirty-six hours to clean the way or be cited. But the next day is warm, and the snow is already melting, and soon a narrow meandering path of wet cement appears within the banks of the dissolving snow. Yet the notice remains taped to the door week after week, month after month.

Shovel what? I've been shoveling their crap my whole life, and what did it get me? The more you shovel, the more they dump until you're neck-deep in their crap. The only thing I'm shoveling now is the mealy dirt of the graveyard.

Spring sweeps onto Avery Road like a hawk chasing a barn mouse: the days lengthen, daffodils pop, children in Little League uniforms play catch with their parents on the street. Lawns fertilized to within an inch of their lives spurt before being mowed and edged with ruthless savagery. Even the lawn of 128, more weed than grass, grows wildly in that early spring. The neighbors talk among themselves about the unruly patch, but none dare march to the door, with its yellow stains and pink notice, to make the general displeasure known.

Late on a Thursday, with the approach of dusk, a sight brings all activity on Avery Road to a halt. Gardeners stop mid-dig, ball players stop midthrow, dogs freeze midpee as an angular old man, broad of shoulder, bent of back, and bald as a grapefruit, pushes a rusted reel mower back and forth across his ragged patch of yard, his long jaw working all the while. No one shouts a hello or raises a hand in greeting. As the rusted blades spin, chewing more than slicing the sprouting leaves of weed and grass, the residents of Avery Road retreat, slowly but inexorably, into their own cozy houses, parents to check on their children, children to huddle in front of the televisions. And all the while, all anyone on Avery Road can hear is the spinning of the rusted blades as Oliver Cross curses aloud and pushes the infernal machine back and forth, forth and back.

Make way for the mower. I scythe, I seethe, I destroy. Make way for desolation. Make way for bitterness and tears. Make way for Yama, son of Surya and Saranyu, for I have mixed his poison and become like him a walking death.

On the Monday before Memorial Day, a bright, shining day with all the promise of the summer season to come, the police appear on Avery Road.

3

CRYSTAL BLUE PERSUASION

Oliver Cross sits in his unlit living room a mile west of the Philadelphia city line, drinking Lone Star from the bottle and staring at his old television set, the volume off because the inanity that pours out of the speaker is too much to bear. In the silence he tries to hear the voices of the past, the calls to arms, the chants and songs, the steely, righteous riff from a Fender, but all he hears is silence. All is silence, all is waste and regret. Who are those fools with no regrets? The only thing that keeps him warm through this winter of his life are his regrets. He should have fought in the war, he should have stayed on the farm, he should have screwed that girl with the mole on her cheek freshman year, he should have just said no. No. What could have been simpler?

But he could never say no to her.

Oliver Cross sits in his faded, cloth-covered recliner in the fading afternoon, drinking and stewing, the only two pleasures left to him in this bitter world. He drinks and he stews and lets the silence wash through him like truth, until above the silence he hears the authoritarian sound of car doors shutting—*slam, slam-slam*—and he knows, as sure as he knows the fist of pain twisting in his spine, that the police have come for him.

The knock on his door is delivered with the same fascist rhythm as the slammed car doors. Oliver lifts a huge gnarled hand and scratches at the dent in his bald head. Maybe they'll go away, he thinks, or maybe they'll knock down the door and have to clean off the dried raw egg before replacing it; either option seems preferable to him getting up and answering their damnable knock. He imagines the door bursting open with a great clash and clatter as an army of police charges in amidst a cloud of splintering wood, only to find him in his chair, grinning like a hyena. Guns trained on his face, he'd calmly tell them to piss off.

"Oliver," comes a familiar voice from his porch. "Could you open the door, please? We need to talk to you."

"Do I have a choice?" Oliver shouts back. His voice is the ratchety croak of a ticked-off bullfrog, a seventy-two-year-old bullfrog with an indolent lymphoma that is suddenly becoming industrious and a wrenching arthritis in his back.

"Not really, no. Please, Oliver. We won't be long."

Oliver sits for a moment more, scratching again at his head—itchiness being one of the symptoms of his condition—and nodding at the sad facts of the moment, before he straightens the chair and pushes himself to standing. She's right, he doesn't have a choice; he wonders when he ever did. Everything in the stream of his past seems like it happened without his choosing, because if ever he had chosen anything, how did he end up here? It takes half a minute for his back to go through the pains of straightening as far as it can straighten. He is at what now constitutes his full height when he opens the door.

Jennifer Post stands in the doorway, flanked by two uniformed police officers, men with jaws jutting like they're expecting trouble. A non-uniformed woman with a briefcase stands behind them, and behind her is the cop car, its blue and red lights spinning. Jennifer is smiling; the two cops and the woman aren't. Jennifer's familiar eyes are brown and kind; the cops' eyes are covered with gray sunglasses that match the color of the guns on their hips.

"Are you going to invite us in?" says Jennifer, African American and young, or what passes for young to Oliver these days, plump and forty or so. Her frizzy hair is bound into a ponytail, and a scarf, as always, is at her throat. Oliver stands in front of the four uninvited guests and scratches at his head like he is figuring the odds at a craps table. But what is there to figure? When do the odds ever not favor the moneymen? He steps to the side.

"Gosh, it's so much cheerier than the last time I was here," says Jennifer once inside. "Is that a new stain on the carpet? I think it is. I must say, Oliver, it adds just the right touch of hominess. And everything smells like . . . like . . ."

"Old socks," says Oliver.

"I didn't know Glade made that scent. Maybe you should open a window. It's a beautiful day in the neighborhood. Let's air this place out."

Her cheeriness grates as always, but with Jennifer he senses that it is a true reflection of her inner self and not some act, and that stops him from vomiting his disdain onto her scarf. One doesn't shout at a lame girl for her limp, or upbraid a blind man for his lack of sight. She is entitled to her disability.

"The officers need to search your house and your truck," she says.

"Why?"

"We'll talk after. In fact you can count this as an appointment, so I won't need to see you on Thursday. But for now it would be better if you just sat down and let them do their work."

"Maybe I should call the lawyer."

"That's your choice." She takes out her phone. "If you want, I could call Donald for you. But they're still going to search."

Oliver feels anger and frustration rise within him. That they should be allowed to treat him like this is intolerable. He knows the

Constitution, he knows his rights, he went to law school after all. True, it was for only a year, but you learn everything first year anyway. As his anger rises, he closes his eyes and lets the emotions build until they fill him with an exploding hate before overflowing and splashing like raw sewage onto the carpet. And she wonders about the stains. When he opens his eyes again, he is outwardly as calm as toast. This is a trick he learned in San Francisco and used much at Rockview, the craphole they sent him to after the farce of a trial.

"Put the phone away," he says. "I hate the lawyer almost as much as I hate your meddling."

"This shouldn't take long."

"Whatever you say." He walks slowly to his chair, falls backward into it, puts his hands on the armrests, and stares at the television. "You're the boss."

"I like to think that you're the boss, Oliver, and I'm just here to facilitate good decision-making."

"Then get the hell out."

"Well, when you put it that way," she says with a light laugh.

One of the cops says, "We'll need the keys to your vehicle, sir."

"They're in the kitchen. On the table."

"I'll stay here with Mr. Cross," says Jennifer.

As the officers and the woman with the briefcase begin rummaging through his house, Oliver stays silent and seated. Jennifer walks about inspecting the living room as if she were thinking of getting into real estate. Oliver isn't worried about what they will find, because there is nothing to find. There is no illegal drug, no porn, not even any hard alcohol, just a case of beer in the fridge, which doesn't count because it is only beer. Let them waste their time searching; wasting it is all their time is good for anyway. Everyone's time, when you get down to it.

"I realize now I've been a little lax in visiting the homes of my clients," says Jennifer.

"I'm not a client. Clients can walk away."

"I'm finding your house very revealing. You haven't done a thing to it in two years. It's as depressing as the day you came home."

"It fits my eye."

"It could use some work. Do you happen to know a carpenter, Oliver, hmm? And why didn't you put anything on the walls after the renters left? I know your wife was a fine artist. Wouldn't her paintings look lovely in this room?"

"I don't need paintings to remember her," he says. "She still talks to me. Every damn day."

"What does she say?"

"Take out the garbage."

"And is that Fox News on the television? Why are you watching Fox News?"

"I like to keep my eye on the enemy."

"Are the police going to find anything?"

"No."

"I told them they wouldn't."

"Then why are they here?"

"There's a child missing. The father voiced a concern."

"Damn crank."

"The police chief promised the father he'd check it out. It was considered advisable to bring me in when they did."

"It's a neighborhood of cranks and they all hate me."

"How does that make you feel, Oliver?"

"Like I've finally done something worthwhile."

"How long have the egg yolks been on your door?"

"Since Halloween."

"And you didn't think to clean the mess off?"

"I thought about it. Then I rolled over and went back to sleep."

"Keeping the notice to shovel your walk taped to the door is a nice touch, too."

"That way they won't have to put another one up next time it snows. Which brat is missing?"

"Let's wait until they finish the search."

"Fine," says Oliver. "I'll be here."

It doesn't take long. Two of the bedrooms are completely bare, and the closets are mostly empty. Only the basement is crowded with crap. When Oliver rented the house during his term at Rockview, he moved all his stuff into the basement and covered the pile with a tarp. When he returned, most everything stayed right there. He brought up only a table, a couple kitchen chairs, the recliner, a bed, the television; what else would he need?

"It's clean, Ms. Post," says the tech when the search is completed.

"Thank you," says Jennifer. "I'll stay with Mr. Cross for a bit after you leave."

"Are you sure that's advisable, ma'am?"

"Oh, Oliver's a sweetheart. Aren't you a sweetheart, Oliver?"

"Sweet as dirt."

They wait as the cops and the tech shuffle out of the house. Through the closed front door they can hear the car doors slam and the cop car drive away. With the cops coming up empty, the sound is not quite so authoritarian. Oliver, thinking of the show they are putting on for the neighbors, almost smiles and then catches himself.

"If this is in place of our next appointment," says Jennifer, "I suppose I should ask how things are going."

"Peachy."

"Did you join any of the community groups we talked about last time? Have you been in touch with friends? With family?"

"No."

"How about your son? Has he tried to get in touch with you?"

"No."

"Have you tried to get in touch with him?"

"No."

"Don't you think you should?"

"Why?"

"Maybe because you're his father?"

"We all make mistakes."

"You can't give up on your child."

"He gave up on me."

"You're breaking my heart, Oliver."

"Yeah, well, life breaks your heart, and then it just keeps slamming away. Come back to me when you're seventy-two and tell me about the party. Anything else? I've got my day to finish."

"Any specific plans?"

"Sitting here, stewing. There are beers in the fridge."

"You need to get a life, Oliver."

"I had one. It died."

"The child who's gone missing?" says Jennifer. "She's your grand-daughter Erica."

Oliver sits as still as a rock, trying not to let anything show. Jennifer is looking for a reaction, and on principle he never gives the system what it wants. So he sits in his chair, as immobile as Lincoln within his monument, thinking through the implications of what Jennifer has just said.

Erica is his eldest granddaughter. He has not seen her since before the trial. She was thirteen or fourteen then, with Helen's shocking green eyes. What is she now, seventeen, eighteen? And missing? It's all falling apart. Every step was wrong; every decision was disastrous. He starts into rubbing his head and keeps rubbing until his big old hand falls over his face. The realization is dawning. His mind doesn't work as fast as it used to, but eventually he catches on.

If Erica is the missing child, that means the father who has accused him to the police chief, the crank who has sent the cops scuttling through his house, is . . .

"So, Oliver," says Jennifer. "Any plans now?"

4

MR. BIG STUFF

After Jennifer leaves, Oliver sits and waits as his emotions rise within to choke him. Just once he'd like to taste something other than his own bile when the world intervenes in his misery. He used to wonder whether the problem with his life was the hard heart of the world or the damaged heart inside himself, but he stopped wondering when he realized it didn't much matter. It isn't one or the other, just the two rubbing together like flint and steel. There is no place left for him in this world, and that's a problem with a single solution.

When he figures Jennifer has finally given up idling at the end of Avery Road to spy on him, he waits another ten minutes before pushing himself out of the chair. He manipulates his back as he walks into the kitchen and grabs the car keys. A few moments later, a brown-and-tan 1990 Ford F-250 diesel, racked with rust and wheezing all the while, bounces out of the driveway and onto Avery Road.

Thirty-six years ago, when Helen and Oliver Cross escaped back to the world with their seven-year-old son, Fletcher, in tow, they chose this house because it was close to Helen's ailing mother. It was also barely habitable and cheap as dirt, a convenient factor since dirt was about all they had to their names. But by that point Oliver had done enough carpentry at the farm not to be daunted by the rehab. That the house was smack in the middle of a multiracial, working-class neighborhood was not just a positive feature; it was a prerequisite.

Oliver, raised in affluence, had turned his back on the values of his upbringing. He and Helen were committed to joining the ranks of the Lumpenproletariat that would rebuild the nation, one child taught and one nail hammered at a time. At least that was the plan, which showed just how little Oliver knew then of the Lumpenproletariat. While he viewed the neighborhood as the model for a new age of American egalitarianism, his neighbors viewed it as suburban.

Now as he drives through these streets, he sees only a sty of dead-eyed swine, force-fed fast food and fancies, trusting their fate to plutocrats who have nothing for them but disdain and a designated slot in the line to the slaughterhouse. He should have left decades ago, found a place more amenable to his yearnings and worldview, maybe someplace high in the mountains, or in Costa Rica. But there was the boy and his school friends, there was Helen's teaching job, there was his failing furniture shop and Helen's chemotherapy and his own treatments. There was life. And then there was death.

But even with all the bitterness he holds toward his neighbors on Avery Road, they are still his people, struggling each day to scratch a living out of the barren fields of capitalism. As he drives out of the neighborhood, away from the city and into leafier environs where houses compete ever more feverishly in their ostentation, he feels he is driving through a foreign land peopled by cannibals. If his truck stalls, which it has been known to do, and he steps out of the cab to see what is what, he will no doubt be set upon by the worst kind of brutes, the unrepentant wealthy. That his son, for whom he and Helen reentered the world so long ago, has ended up living here, among the savages, is either an inevitability or a betrayal, and Oliver chooses to believe it is the latter because that pisses him off more and these days being pissed off is when he is his most authentic self.

Oliver parks his truck across the street from a stone monstrosity with turrets and buttressed walls and a worshipful arched entrance-way. Two stained-glass windows flank the great oaken door, behind which Fletcher lives with his wine collection and his big white teeth. It didn't much concern Oliver when his son fulfilled Oliver's own youthful expectations and headed off to law school. The world needed lawyers on the correct side of things: Darrow and Marshall, Kuntsler and Ginsberg and Weinglass. Even Paul Robeson had been a lawyer.

But instead of fighting the system, Fletcher embraced it. What kind of labor lawyer doesn't represent labor? That was a question Oliver asked, loudly and gibingly, over numerous Thanksgiving turkeys when Helen was still alive and the family still celebrated holidays together. Fletcher would stammer out a response, but the answer was evident: the kind of lawyer who aspires to nothing nobler than to live in a Gothic cathedral and nibble partridge bones.

Before the truck has even stopped rocking, Oliver scoots out and begins his mad hobble up the wide lawn. His back is bent, his work boots land splayed on the grass, his unbuttoned flannel shirt trails behind him like the plaid cape of a lunatic in a Scottish asylum. He bangs at the door with the bottom of his fist, twice, thrice.

"Fletcher, you bastard," he calls out before banging again.

Oliver knows what has happened. His son's precious little daughter has taken a hike out of the morass of sick consumerism that Fletcher has bathed her in for eighteen years, and Fletcher's response is to sic the police on his father. How dare he?

"Come out here and face the music for once, you little coward." *Bang, bang.*

When the door finally opens, it is Petra, Fletcher's wife, standing in the doorway. There is something in her face that stills the anger inside him for a moment, a moist redness on cheeks that are always proudly pale. She is holding a glass of wine. And she is smoking.

The sight of a cigarette, held vertically in her long fingers, causes Oliver to take a step back. Petra doesn't smoke, Petra doesn't drink, except for a fine wine at dinner, and Petra doesn't laugh or mess her makeup with tears; Petra is cold as cash. But here is his daughter-in-law with her cheeks red, her eyes moist, and a cigarette in her hand. The scene is so out of beat with his expectations that it quiets his rage for a moment. But he doesn't want his rage quieted and so he bulls through as if Petra's evident distress doesn't exist.

"Where's that son-of-a-bitch son of mine?" he barks.

Petra glances behind her for a moment, before stepping outside onto the stone of the front portico and closing the door behind her. "You're upset about the police," she says in her breathy German accent.

"I'm pissed as hell. He had no right."

"I asked him to send them."

Oliver cocks his head. He has been so filled with a fierce, joyful rage at his son's betrayal that he doesn't want to imagine the possibility that what happened to him was anything but personal. "You might have asked him to do it," he says trying to maintain the comfort of his anger, "but he's the one who did it. The parole officer said as much."

"People were talking. You had become part of the story."

"I'm not part of anything in this house anymore."

"You're right," she says calmly, before taking hold of the cigarette and putting it between her lips. She inhales like she's done it before and blows out a thin line of smoke. "And now everyone else knows, and they can get back to finding my daughter."

Oliver never much cared for Petra; her hair always done, her clothes always stylish and pristine, the tense smile she always gives him—but he also never felt the heat of animosity from her that emanates every second from his son. When he finally lets go of his anger and fully registers her condition, he feels enough shame to turn and look away.

So concerned over his own humiliations, he has missed sight of the big screen.

"I assumed Erica ran," he says, "like any normal kid forced to live in a frigid stone cathedral. Is it something else?"

"We don't know."

"Was she kidnapped? Is there a note?"

"No note, no communication of any kind. But her phone is off, which is not like her. She feels naked without her phone. Even if she only ran away, we don't know where she ran to, so forgive us if we are scared."

"She'll turn up, they always do."

"Except when they don't."

"Was there any indication of trouble?"

"There were constant indications. She is not an easy child. But you haven't been around, so you wouldn't know."

"It wasn't my choice."

Petra shrugs and takes a sip of wine.

"I thought she was still a sweet little princess," says Oliver.

"They're all sweet little princesses until they're not. When was the last time you saw her?"

"The last time you let me. Before the trial."

"She changed. There were drugs. We found marijuana."

"Oh no," he says. "Not marijuana."

"Spare us your wild past."

"Have you talked to her friends?"

"Of course. They say they know nothing."

"It's hard out there. These kids don't know how hard. She'll get hungry, come home, put back on that prep-school skirt."

"Let's hope so," she says. "Erica would look so—"

Before she can finish, the door is yanked open and Fletcher looms in the gap, red tie loosened, white shirtsleeves rolled up, a glass of liquor in hand. Chunky and freckled, with wispy red hair, he is already half in the bag. As Oliver takes in his son's middle-aged softness, whatever anger he feels dissolves and he is flooded with emotions that he doesn't completely understand because he can barely remember when he felt them before.

This is the boy who slid into the world and into his arms on a river of blood in the old stable at Seven Suns as Helen lay screaming, surrounded by what seemed like a coven of witches. This is the swaddled boy he rocked to sleep every night as he softly sang "Who'll Stop the Rain," the sweet boy Oliver tossed high in the clean mountain air, and crawled alongside in the seeding grass, and ran with through the fields, arms outstretched, screaming at the sky as they chased away the rabbits. The boy he taught how to hunt with the bow and arrows they had made together in the shop, how to weed with a short-handled hoe, how to plane a piece of wood flat as slate, how to swing the Ernie Banks signature bat he had brought him from one of his visits to Chicago. This was the boy he coached in Little League when they returned to the world, the boy he watched run track in high school, still chasing those rabbits.

"I'm sorry about Erica," says Oliver, softly.

"And that's why you came banging on the door, calling me a bastard?"

"The police came to my house," says Oliver.

"Good."

"They searched my house."

"And what did you expect me to do? The police are helping look for her; I needed to tell them everything. What you did was part of it. I had no choice."

"You had a choice. You chose to poke me in the gut."

"I did what I had to do. Now do me a favor and haul your rotting carcass off my property." Fletcher grimaces at Oliver with those straight white teeth of his, an exhibition that allows Oliver to shake away his misty-eyed remembrances and clutch at the one emotion that never lets him down in the sunset of his years.

"Piss off," Oliver says, slapping the air with one of his big palms before he turns and starts shambling back down the front lawn. As he retreats, he turns his head in an act that echoes from his past and yells behind him, "Go choke on your money."

"I bet you choke on my money every day," says Fletcher from the safety of his porch. "Every damn day."

"Damn right I do." Oliver stops, turns around. "You should have told me you were having problems with Erica. Maybe I could have helped."

"What were you going to do, poison her, too?"

"I ought to bust you in those choppers of yours."

"Erica used to talk to Mom all the time," says Fletcher. "Later she kept on telling us how much she missed her. Maybe if she still had Mom to talk to, she wouldn't have left."

"What about you?" says Oliver. "Why couldn't she talk to you?"

"I was too busy selling out."

Fletcher backs into the house and slams the door behind him. Oliver, his teeth clenched so tightly his jaw hurts, looks at Petra, who coldly takes a drag from her cigarette.

"He go to the dentist much?" says Oliver.

"Like clockwork," says Petra. "Four times each year."

"That's my boy," says Oliver Cross.

5

SHE SAID SHE SAID

Oliver Cross rages, but not against the dying of the light.

The light can't die soon enough, as far as Oliver is concerned. He has even considered turning it out himself on more than one occasion, but he doesn't want to give the bastards the satisfaction. He can't tell you for sure exactly who the bastards are, but they know who they are and that is good enough for him. So he soldiers on, ignoring the Prozac™ prescribed against his will, but taking his Aleve™, his Lipitor™, his Warfarin™, his Flomax™, his Rheumatrex™, his Benicar™, eating the vegan slop he prepares twice a day, exercising by pacing back and forth like a leopard in his cage, back and forth, forth and back, raging all the while.

He rages because the people don't deserve their country and proved it by electing a racist orange glob of hair coughed up by the Russian cat. He rages because the politicians have elbowed their way to the trough and will wreak whatever havoc necessary to keep their faces in the slop. He rages because those politicians he votes for are just as lily-livered as those he opposes while the real beasts march ever forward, biting off heads and sucking blood. He rages because everything he fervently believes with his heart and soul has been discarded as useless weight slowing down the great capitalist machine that is devouring mouthful by mouthful the entirety of the earth.

But most of all he rages because his wife is dead and his son despises him and his life has lost all purpose and he is old and cold and the pain in his back is like a corkscrew ever turning. And when his rages reach a point that boils his brain, it seems only his wife's sweet voice can bring him back from the abyss of his torment and fury.

"Oliver, dear," she whispers into his ear, and from the first word the song of her voice begins to wrap around him like a blanket of calm. "You finally saw him, our son."

"Yeah, I saw the bastard," he says to her out loud.

"How did he look, our darling boy?"

"He looked . . ." Oliver hesitates a moment, not wanting to break his dead wife's heart. "He looked well fed."

"He always had an appetite," she says. "Did you kiss him for me?"

"I didn't kick him, so there's that."

"You didn't fight with him, did you, Oliver? Oh, Oliver, of course you did. Why can't you forgive him?"

"I don't want to forgive him. And he doesn't want to forgive me. It's the only thing we have in common, that and blood on our hands."

"Oliver, stop. He was always just like you. A mini-Oliver."

"He has a better smile."

"Are you still on about his teeth?"

"We never should have left. That was our big mistake."

"We had no choice."

"He left us no choice, and he's the one who paid the highest price. Even his daughter can't stand him. She ran away."

"Erica?"

"She took off. I'm almost proud."

"Why did she leave?"

"She hit the road to find herself, like we did, and good for her. Against all odds, even in a mausoleum like that house, Kerouac lives. Remember when we took off for the west. San Francisco or bust, hitch-hiking the whole way."

"We gave up everything just to go."

"You gave up everything."

"True. The deposit on the wedding dress was nonrefundable, as my mother never stopped reminding me."

"I remember taking peeks at you in the back of the truck that picked us up outside of Pittsburgh. You were so beautiful in the morning light that I was afraid to look at you for too long. You'd see through me and I didn't want you to know how scared I was."

"I knew."

"The richest moment of my life," he says. "When everything was still in front of us."

"Traveling hopefully."

"Who said that? Vonnegut?"

"No, not Vonnegut. His son, maybe."

"So I was right."

"Yes, you were right."

It might just be his imagination running off with him, these con-versations with the voice of his dead wife that fall loud and clear as a summer rain in his head, but it doesn't feel like his imagination. Whenever she comes to him it is as if the great crack in the universe has widened to let her voice slip into his heart.

Reality first cracked for him in a sweat lodge in the mountains of New Mexico, in a ceremony replete with song and drum and a gray sludge passed hand-to-hand in a hollowed gourd. This was three years after Chicago. Helen had stayed on in San Francisco, organizing an art show in Golden Gate Park, as he sat cross-legged on the dirt with a Carlos Castaneda paperback in his back pocket and his heart open to all the possibilities of the multiverse—including extreme nausea. His stomach was twisting fitfully from the foul concoction, while young men danced in a circle, pounding on water drums and singing ancient chants. It had seemed wildly unpleasant and a bit ridiculous when, suddenly, the mud-covered roof of the sweat lodge tore open, letting in the light of an infinite stretch of stars that split the sky in two. He turned into a bird and flew high over the landscape, and then the heavens themselves cracked apart, letting in a light so pure that it burned like fire as it poured into him through his little bird eyes. It seemed as if the light were full of truths, impossible truths, truths he couldn't quite grasp or relay because of his own ignorance, truths that were unknowable but still somehow known. They burned his brain, all the perfect truths in that light, and filled him with all the wonder of this world and the next and the next and the . . .

It took him months to recover.

When he did, finally, when the mania had passed and he could focus on the simple tasks of bathing and feeding himself, when he could have a conversation without his words shooting off into the cosmos, the world had been altered irrevocably and he saw things ever more clearly. But as an aftereffect, there was now a fault in the dome of the universe, and it is through that fault, from the other side of things, that Helen speaks.

"You don't sound worried about our granddaughter," she says.

"I'm happy for her," says Oliver. "She got out, like a bear cub from a trap."

"You know better."

"Do I?"

"She could have been taken."

"There's no ransom note, no demand. She left on her own."

"Then she could be lost."

"You can't be found until you're lost. Our goal was exactly to get lost, remember."

"I remember the Haight."

"We shared a room with a drummer from that band—what was its name?—and a puppeteer from the Diggers, and spent our days plaiting flowers in the park."

"And I remember all the lost children," she says.

"Eyes like marbles, dancing naked like zombies."

"They had gone west to find themselves, too."

"It's not for the fainthearted, we learned that. It's hard work. At the farm, starving through the winters. But wasn't it worth it?"

"To us. Yet some never came home. What if Erica ends up one of the dazed, one of the lost?"

"She's too tough for that. She always reminded me of you."

"I wasn't so tough, not without you."

"You were our strength."

"We were only strong together."

"I know that now."

"Do you miss me?"

"You don't let me, you keep talking and talking."

"Do you love me still, Oliver? Enough to do anything for me, enough to move the world?"

And there it is, the lilt in her voice, the tell that says to him as sure as there is fire in the sun that she wants something. Helen never just comes to bear love and companionship, there is always some deeper purpose to her visits. *Take your medicine, Oliver. Get to the doctor for your back, Oliver. Eat something, you're getting so thin. Shouldn't you have the bump on your neck looked at? Don't forget your appointment with the parole officer. Take out the garbage, Oliver, the kitchen is beginning to smell.* During their life together, he loved that she was in charge; it left his mind free to soar. But he has grown to resent that she is still in charge even after her death.

"What do you want?" he says.

"You know what I want."

"Fine. I'll take my medicine."

"This is bigger than that, Oliver."

"Bigger than Flomax?"

"We had our hard times, didn't we?"

"Yes, we did."

"And you blame yourself."

"Who else would I blame?"

"Then think of this as making it up to me, darling. Think of this as clearing the slate."

"What do you want, Helen?"

"Find her, find Erica. Wherever she has disappeared to, whatever she thinks she is looking for, find our granddaughter, Oliver, and bring her back to our son."

6

SOMEBODY TO LOVE

Oliver Cross sits in his truck drinking coffee, waiting for some absurd rich man's car to leave its driveway, which is well down the street. That Oliver's son will be driving the car on his way to his white-shoe corporate law firm only makes the acid in the convenience store coffee burn more bitterly in his throat, but bitter is how he likes things now.

He can read Helen's maneuvering like he is reading a map. She knows there is no way he can find a missing girl. He has no computer, no fancy cell phone, no sources in law enforcement to tap into, other than a parole officer overseeing his every move. You might as well send a blind man into the desert after a missing goat. But Helen has been trying to get him back into the good graces of his family ever since he was released from Rockview two years before, and she surely sees this as an opportunity to finally get it done. Already he has seen his son for the first time in years. Glorious day! Now she is sending him out to find Erica, knowing just the fact of his asking questions could change the toxic familial dynamic. Helen was always too clever for her own damn good, but it is hard for Oliver to say no to the voice of a dead wife he loved more than life itself.

So he sits in the truck and slurps his bitter Wawa coffee. He needs the coffee because he was up early and he needed to be up early to catch his son leaving, and he needs to catch his son leaving because the questions Helen wants him to ask Petra can't be asked with Fletcher's virulent hatred coursing through the house. The only flaw in the plan is the coffee.

He eyes the neighboring shrubbery, wondering which plant he can piss on for the five painful minutes it will take for him to unload without getting waylaid by a property owner or a dog, when he sees a black Mercedes sports car roll down his son's driveway. Fletcher's puffy face bobs behind the windshield, looking like it belongs to an inflatable punching doll, one of those you hit as hard as you can and still it bounces back with that same infernal smile. The Mercedes turns away from where Oliver is parked, headed toward the train station.

Oliver finishes his coffee, tosses the cup atop a pile of trash on the passenger seat floor, starts the engine, and drives down the road, up the long driveway, and around the back. He bangs on the kitchen door.

Petra is a mess when she answers his knock: her face undone, her hair askew, wearing a blouse creased by a fitful night's sleep. She looks like she drank herself unconscious on the couch the night before.

"I need to pee," he says, barging past her in a bent-back waddle.

"There's a bathroom down here," she calls after him as he starts pulling himself up the wide stairway to the second floor. He knows there is a toilet on the ground floor, but his wife has set him on a task, and what is he going to learn in a first-floor powder room?

In years past he would sweep into that house and up the stairs and grab the girls in his arms and rub his rough face on their cheeks. He would play dolls with the baby, and read picture books to Erica, and teach them both protest songs. "If I Had a Hammer" they would sing, or "Blowing in the Wind," or, when he was feeling particularly pessimistic, he would try to teach them "Eve of Destruction," though that never went well. Too many words.

He even began showing Erica some simple chords on the small guitar he and Helen had bought for her. "The D is like this, then stretch your fingers for the G, and then press these three strings right here for the A, and then you go back to the D," which was all you needed to play "This Land Is Your Land." And while she strummed the song, taking interminable time for each chord change, he told her the story of Woody Guthrie and his beat old guitar with the sticker that read, "This Machine Kills Fascists."

"What's a fascist, Grandpop?"

"It's like a banker, sweetie, only worse," he said.

"Is Daddy a fascist?"

"No, your father's not a fascist."

"Good."

"He only works for them."

After his piss, he puts on his reading glasses and checks the plastic prescription bottles in the medicine cabinet. Adderall™. Ativan™. OxyContin™, two bottles, both empty. All prescribed to Erica Cross. She was stuffing into her craw almost as many drugs as he does, and he could guess exactly why they had been prescribed. Adderall to keep her studying hard enough to get into an Ivy League college; Ativan to keep her smiling while she danced at the debutante ball; OxyContin to keep her numb enough to follow all the rules and ask no questions. Fletcher had been worried about Erica's marijuana use, but all the while he was pumping her full of ever more powerful poisons whose main purpose is to fill the pockets of the pharmaceutical companies—the same companies Fletcher undoubtedly represents in their labor negotiations.

No wonder she ran. Oliver would have been disappointed if she hadn't.

In Erica's room he scans the smiling photographs of friends and family taped to the wall among the posters and magazine covers of singers and sallow-faced celebrities whom Oliver has never heard of. On the wall behind him is a mural of a smiling zebra on a carousel that Helen painted when the girl was still a baby.

The photographs are like a timeline, showing Erica as the young girl he remembered and then growing ever taller and ever more beautiful, often with her sister. What is her name, the sister, Oliver's other granddaughter? Christ, he is getting old. Too many bonks on the head, too many drugs. Or maybe not enough. It hurts to look at the most recent pictures because of Erica's resemblance to a dream: red hair, green eyes, a splash of freckles across her nose and high cheekbones, she is the girl behind the dumpster, the girl he left his life for, she is Helen to a tee.

On the table by the bed, like a memorial, sits a framed photograph of Oliver's wife. Helen's hair in the photograph is no longer red but gray, her nose no longer as sharp as it was, her chin pointy with age. You can see the resemblance between grandmother and granddaughter still, but unless you saw Helen then, young with that mouth ready to devour the world, the haunting resemblance won't punch you in the gut like it punches him.

He doesn't see his own picture anywhere, though there are places where photographs have been obviously yanked from the wall, montages of times before Helen died, when he was still part of the family. That's where he lives for Erica, in the gaps. That she hasn't put other photos over the empty patches on the walls is a victory of sorts.

"What are you doing, Oliver?" says Petra.

Petra, standing now in the doorway, has put herself back together, regaining her sheen of plastic perfection, but Oliver can see the cracks beneath the surface. Sometimes the best things about a piece of porcelain are the flaws. He imagines the scene that morning before he knocked: Fletcher dressed to steal in his suit and tie, coming down the stairs and seeing his wife collapsed on the couch, the wineglass upended on the carpet. Fletcher must have left without waking her, without making sure she was all right or giving her a kiss goodbye. For some reason, the dark resonance of the moment makes him a little happy, which pisses him off. And he feels a bit sad that he never truly got to know his daughter-in-law before it all went to hell.

"Our little girl grew up," he says as he peers at her over his glasses before turning back to the photographs.

"They tend to do that."

"Who's this?" He points at an African American boy in one of the photographs on the wall, the boy standing with his arm around Erica.

"That was her boyfriend, Adam. They broke up a couple months ago."

"Is he still around or is he missing, too?"

"He's still around. He plays baseball for the school."

"Adam who?"

"What do you want, Oliver?"

"Why did you tell Fletcher to have the police search my home?"

"I already explained."

"Yeah, you explained. But your explanation sounded fishy. Instead, it felt like you just wanted me to know. Fletcher was leaving Erica's absence to the police and nothing was happening and you wanted me to know."

Her lips twitch into a wry smile. "You look good, Oliver."

"I look like crap. And you could have just called."

"Would you have answered the phone?"

"No."

"His last name's Morgan. Adam Morgan."

Oliver yanks the photograph off the wall. "Now which of these little pixies would she most likely have confided in?"

Petra walks past Oliver and pulls off a picture of Erica and three other girls. "These are her closest friends. The girl on the left is Carly. They've been together since the first grade."

Oliver stuffs the pictures in his pocket. "I'll be in touch."

"Oliver?" she says. "I followed Fletcher's lead regarding your relationship with our family because it was his mother and you're his father and I just thought it should be up to him, but I was wrong in that. I should have fought to keep you in our lives, at least in our daughters' lives. I'm sorry."

"Sorry doesn't win the peach," says Oliver.

"I'm not saying what you did was right, but at least you did something. Fletcher's just sitting around and drinking Scotch and waiting for someone else to save his daughter. But I can't bear the sitting and waiting. Something needs to be done. My baby needs to be found."

"And you think I'll find her?"

"At least you'll do something."

"Yeah," says Oliver. "That's always been my problem."

Just then he sees her, on the other side of Petra, walking down the hall in blue pajamas, rubbing her eyes. The other granddaughter, what is her name? Elisa, that's it. What is it with all the *E*s? He remembered her as a roly-poly three-year-old with fat cheeks. Now she's a seven-year-old beauty, with Petra's blonde hair. When the girl looks up and sees Oliver in her sister's room, she instinctively leans into her mother's hip.

"Who's that?" says the girl.

"That's your grandfather, dear," says Petra. "Daddy's daddy. Grandfather Oliver."

"The one who killed Grandmom?"

"That's right," says Petra.

The girl shies away from him, slinking back, using her mother as a shield, so that only one eye peers out at Oliver from behind her mother's hip. She is too cute for words, blood of his blood. This is what Helen has been after, this moment, why she set him on this chase. It won't be long before Helen is all over him for details of her youngest granddaughter. He leans forward and puts his hands on his knees and stares at her over his glasses for a long moment, soaking her in, before he says,

"Boo."

7

I Heard It through the Grapevine

The way Elisa looked at Oliver was the most brutal of mirrors. His youngest granddaughter's eyes were wide with fright and her lips trembled before she buried her face in her mother's hip. The laughter that he had intended from his harmless little joke choked in his throat.

So this is what he has become, a ghoul to frighten the innocent young. Maybe Helen sent him on this quest to change that, to change him in his last rancid years, but could any effort be more futile? Whatever he might once have been, whatever he might have been able to become, he has aged into this bitter piece of human jerky with no purpose other than to send little girls shrieking into the night. Despite all his good intentions, all his spiritual yearnings, all his right thinking, left-leaning politics, he has fulfilled his destiny by becoming a monster.

But maybe, just maybe, that's exactly what Erica needs.

The area between the preppy private school where they stashed Erica and the sports fields is thick with boys and girls in their uniforms and practice jerseys, lugging around equipment bags and walking with that youthful, athletic lope to join their compatriots running around the track or smacking the ball back and forth with their field-hockey sticks.

They are all so beautiful, so full of promise that Oliver Cross can't help but feel sorry for them. Ahead of them they have the dreamworld of college and then, they all hope, a good forty years of selling their souls day by day for bits of paper with pictures of pallid-green politicians. They think money will buy them safety, but he knows the truth. Their lives will fail, their loves will die, their children will turn, their grandchildren will disappear. And they will look back, one and all, at these shining days and wonder what the hell happened.

"I can't now," says Adam Morgan, brushing past the old man on his way to the baseball diamond. Oliver had been standing with a photograph in his hand, the one with this boy standing with his arm around Oliver's granddaughter, and eyeing the athletes passing by until he spied Erica's old boyfriend making his way to the fields. He is tall and thin, in full uniform, with hair spilling out of his blue cap. A bat bag hangs from his shoulder. "I have a game."

Oliver grabs a fistful of bag and yanks.

The boy jerks backward, his arms flailing, before successfully stopping himself from falling. He instinctively lifts a fist, but when he looks into Oliver's eyes the fist stills its progress, hovering in the air for a moment, suddenly a useless thing, before the fingers open and it disappears.

"You know who I am," says Oliver.

"Yes, I know who you are."

"Then you know you have time to talk to me."

The boy looks at him, glances away, and then back again. "Okay," he says, gesturing Oliver off the path between the school building and the fields to a spot with a bit of privacy.

"I don't know where she is," says the kid.

"But you know something."

"Yo, Adam," calls a teammate. "We've got to get going."

Adam waves him on and turns back to Oliver. "We have a game. Look, I don't know anything, I really don't."

"Why did you break up?"

"One of those things, I don't know."

Oliver shoves the photograph in front of the boy's face. "Look at her."

"I know what she looks like."

"Look at her."

The boy takes the picture and stares and his face grows darker.

"So?" says Oliver.

"I don't know."

"You say that a lot."

"What do I say a lot?"

"I don't know."

"Because I don't. I have to go."

"Tell me what you do know."

"That picture was taken in the fall last year, before her injury. She busted up her knee playing field hockey and started in with the Oxy after the surgery. She wasn't ready to quit when the prescription ran out, so she didn't."

"Where'd she get her supply?"

"It's high school, man. Everything's available. The stuff that passes around in our hallways would blow your mind. But where she got it isn't the point. The point is she changed. She stopped caring about things, school, friends, herself even, the way she looked. She wasn't fun anymore."

"She needed help."

"What was I going to do?"

"Help her."

"Yeah, well maybe I tried. What did you do?"

Oliver looks away, spits. "So you broke up with her because of the drugs."

"She broke up with me."

"With you? Why?"

"I don't know. There was someone else, what do you want me to say? She was screwing someone else. How's that, Grandpa?"

"Who?"

"I don't know."

Oliver stares.

"She didn't tell me," says the boy. "She didn't even admit it, but I knew. I could tell. It was the way her kisses felt different, you know. Like she was just trying to get through it. The way everything felt different. And then she told me it was over."

"And you don't know who it was?"

"No."

"Who would?"

"I don't know. By then she had become something of a loner. Sometimes she told me she had been at Carly's, but then Carly didn't know anything about it. So she might have fessed up to her."

Oliver takes out the photograph of Erica with the three girls. "Which one?"

"That one, there." He points to the same girl Petra pointed to. "Carly Brackin. Are we done?"

"One more thing," says Oliver. He pauses a moment, stirring up his courage. "What was Erica like before? What was my granddaughter like when you two were still in love?"

For a moment the boy's face is an abacus, tabulating all the things horrific and strange that Erica told him about her grandfather. They must have added up to something because he looks again at the picture in his hand.

"She just saw everything differently, you know. Everything was new to her, nothing was a cliché. She saw colors no one else could see. Yeah,

I know, it was a high school thing, so what. Everything was richer with her. And you know, I still miss it. I miss her. I look around and all I see is drab."

Oliver nods, remembers. "You know what you need to do?" he says.

"What's that?"

"Snap out of it."

The boy smiles and nods before walking away, toward the ball field, and then a moment later starts to run.

"So how's that, Helen?" says Oliver Cross out loud. "I've been chasing you since '68 and now I'm as good as chasing you again."

8

LYIN' EYES

Oliver Cross puts his old boom box on the hood of the truck and slips in a cassette. The tape player is the size of a bread box, which, along with Oliver and boom boxes, is another thing no one has much use for anymore. He found the player in the mess of old crap piled in his basement. The cassettes were beside it in a water-stained cardboard box that hadn't been opened in years. That box is now on the floor of the truck's cab, along with empty plastic clamshells that held the new batteries.

He presses "Play;" the dulcet tones of "Take It Easy" slip through the speakers, soon followed by Glenn Frey's rasp of a voice. He turns the volume up as loud as it can go. Too bad there isn't an eleven.

Oliver once met Glenn Frey and wasn't much impressed with him or the Eagles, a bunch of sellouts playing pabulum for elevators and dentist offices, complaining about how hard it was selling out, and warning the huddled masses about the great tripartite plagues of money, drugs, and pussy, even as they grabbed as much of each as possible.

Every time he hears the Eagles, what is left of his teeth start to grinding, which perfectly fits his mood as he leans against his truck on the wide suburban street outside of Carly Brackin's house, a flashy, overwrought piece of crap, sitting amidst a slew of other such pieces of crap in a new development on the outskirts of the township. Welcome to Capitalist Acres, the sign should read, where nothing matters other than the size of your wallet and your supreme lack of taste. These are the kind of houses he hated working on when he was still taking outside jobs to keep his furniture shop up and running despite an alarming lack of demand. If he is going to be pissed off, he figures he might as well go whole hog and piss off everyone else in this stinking development. The Eagles are the perfect weapon.

He tried to play it polite with the girl, knocking lightly on the door, faking a smile like a doting grandfather just looking out for his missing granddaughter's welfare. Maybe the smile was more fearsome than kind, but it didn't matter, this Carly knew too much about him to be fooled. She had a squinty face, young and pretty and squinty. Maybe she needed glasses, or a glass of Scotch.

"I can't talk to you," she said.

"All I want to know is his name," said Oliver.

"Go away, please," she said. That "please" was a nice bit of politeness before slamming the door in his face. Maybe they taught the well-mannered door slam in finishing school now.

He kept knocking until it was the mother who answered. Tall and gaunt with fluttering hands, she looked like she was flinching the whole length of their short conversation. As far as Oliver was concerned, the only good thing about his having a reputation was that it was a bad one.

"My daughter doesn't want to speak to you, Mr. Cross."

"I'm just looking for Erica."

"She's not here, I promise you."

"She was with a new boy. Tell your daughter all I want is a name."

"She's already talked to the detectives. I was with her when she did."

"Did she tell them who the new boy was?"

"She told them she didn't know if Erica was seeing anyone new, and I believe her, so there is no use continuing with your badgering. This is our property. You are trespassing. Are you still on parole, Mr. Cross?"

"What the hell does that matter?"

"I wouldn't want to have to call the police."

"I bet you wouldn't," said Oliver Cross.

Right after that he went home and burrowed in his basement for the boom box. Now, with his truck parked in front of the house, and the Eagles playing as loudly as the stereo allows, he leans against the side of the truck, stares at the door with his arms crossed, and waits. When the tape snaps to a stop, with no response other than a curtain twitch from the house, he opens the bay, turns the tape around, and presses "Play" again. There is a cassette of Hendrix in the cardboard box, of Creedence, of Janis Joplin, but why give them the satisfaction of something worth listening to when he can subject the bastards to "Witchy Woman?"

A kid walks by on the sidewalk, short hair, glasses, tattoos on his arm. He lifts a fist in solidarity. "Eagles. Going old school. Rock on."

"Eagles suck," says Oliver.

The kid stops and looks at him. "Then why are you playing them?"

"I'm in the mood for suck," says Oliver.

"I get you, man."

"No, you don't. And you never will."

The kid laughs. Oliver hadn't been trying to be funny.

It isn't long before the police cruiser, lights flashing, pulls up behind his truck. Two uniforms step out. The woman comes up to him, smiling. The man stays back, a hand resting on his wide belt, talking softly into the microphone hanging over his shoulder. Both are wearing armored vests. He supposes they're worried things could get out of hand, he'd start in to playing Jackson Browne, and then all hell would break loose.

"Is there a problem here, Mr. Cross?" says the woman cop over the music.

"No problem," says Oliver back.

"It looks like a problem to me," she says. "What are you doing, sir?"

"I'm standing here in a public street, listening to music. The street is public, am I right?"

"Yes, sir."

"And it's not a crime to listen to the Eagles, is it?"

"No, sir."

"Though you might want to rethink that."

"We're going to have to ask you to leave."

"I think I'll stay. You know, First Amendment and all. Power to the people."

"We're not asking, Mr. Cross."

"You just said you were asking."

"You're disturbing the peace and harassing the homeowners of this property," says the male officer still standing by the police car. "Get in your damn truck and go home."

"Does he always handle your situations by barging in like that?" says Oliver to the woman cop.

"He likes to assert himself."

"Tell him to assert his ass back to the precinct." The woman laughs as Oliver pulls a business card from his shirt pocket.

"Before you do anything, you should give her a call."

By the time Jennifer Post joins the party, the police are sitting in their car, lights still flashing, and there is a small crowd of kids and a few oldsters watching from the other side of the street. Oliver notices Carly Brackin keeping an eye on things from an upstairs bedroom while Mrs. Brackin watches from behind the curtains downstairs. A few in the crowd sing along with Don Henley, though they don't seem to know many of the words other than "Desperado." About right.

Jennifer parks behind the police car, talks a moment to the female cop, and then makes her way to Oliver. She leans against the truck and listens for a bit.

"I love the Eagles," she says.

"I'm not surprised."

"What are you doing, Oliver?"

"I'm taking your advice."

"When did I advise you to make a spectacle of yourself and harass law-abiding, taxpaying homeowners with classic rock?"

"It's only classic if you mean old, and it's only rock if you mean not rock."

"Oliver."

"You told me to get a life."

"And this is your new life?"

"The girl in there knows something about my granddaughter."

"You're looking for your granddaughter?"

"Somebody has to."

"Does your son know?"

"His wife knows."

"That's a start. Look, I'm glad you're reconnecting with your family, Oliver, it warms my heart. But the girl already spoke to the police."

"She didn't tell them the name of the boy Erica ran away with."

"And she knows?"

"Yes."

"You're sure?"

"She knows. I could see it on her squinty little face. And she lied to the cops about not knowing there was someone new."

"Interesting."

"That's a crime, isn't it?"

"It could be."

"But the police are here to bust me for playing the Eagles. I love the criminal justice system."

Just then the tape player shuts off. Oliver opens the bay, flips the tape, and presses the "Play" button. Dulcet tones and then Glenn Frey running down that road. Again. And again. For all of eternity. Talk about the damned.

"You think this little exhibition of yours is going to work?" says Jennifer after the song mercifully ends.

"There's only so much Eagles anyone can take."

"You're going to get me fired," she says. "Another half hour, that's it."

"Fine."

"Welcome back to the world, Oliver," she says before she pushes herself away from the side of the truck and walks to the police car.

A few moments later the police car drives off, the male cop in the passenger seat giving Oliver one of those hard-cop looks that Oliver always finds so amusing. He checks his watch. The boom box blasts out "Already Gone." Oliver spits.

Before the tape spools to the end again, the door of the Brackin house opens and out steps little Carly, with her squinty, pretty face. She glances behind her as she descends the front steps and then walks slowly toward Oliver, her eyes cast down, a folded piece of paper in her hand.

"Please turn that off," she says. "I'm begging you."

He shuts off the tape player.

"Erica told me she hates you," says Carly.

"Dog bites man."

"And that she'll never forgive you."

"I'll never forgive myself."

She looks up at him then. She isn't squinting now, and her eyes are wet, which frightens Oliver.

"Do you think she's in trouble?" she says.

"I don't know. That's the point."

"I wouldn't be surprised." She hands over the paper. "This is his name and his address. I went there once. He's an idiot with tattooed arms and a scar on his face, but she talked about him like he was the second coming. I had never seen her like that before. It was like she was lost in him." Pause. "And there were drugs."

He nods as he opens the paper and gives it a scan. Frank Cormack. The very sound of it has a shifty quality. "Did this Frank person go to school with you?"

"No. She met him at a coffeehouse when we were performing one of my songs. He was working the deck. He's some sort of folk singer."

"Did you know she was leaving?"

"She didn't tell me. Something must have happened all of a sudden."

"When it happens, it tends to happen just like that."

"Good luck finding her, and, please, don't come back."

She starts walking to the house and then she stops and turns around. "Erica said she'll never forgive you, but that she still misses you."

Oliver Cross doesn't say anything back. He just watches as the girl retreats into the safety of her house and then he almost smiles. So Erica misses him. Who would have imagined that? Talk about your peaceful, easy feeling.

9

BLACK DOG

The address Carly Brackin gave him leads Oliver to a second-floor unit in a duplex next to the railroad tracks. When Oliver bangs on the apartment door, he hears the barks and growl of a dog, which gives him hope. Maybe she is in there. Maybe this will be easier than he thought.

"Cormack," he calls out. "You there, Cormack?"

He hears no answer to his bang and call but for the wild howling of the dog. He thinks of knocking on the downstairs apartment to see what the neighbors might know, but figures that would make too much cautious sense. Instead he pulls a crowbar from his brown Carhartt jacket.

It is too warm for the jacket but he wears it anyway because with the slit he cut into the lining, he can easily slide a crowbar into the inside pocket. There was a time he was part of a crew refreshing apartments for new tenants and he was often required to bust into the units. It never hurt to have a crowbar at the ready: it could lever open a locked door; it could pick up a discarded piece of crap-stained clothing too filthy to touch; it could crack the head of a mad and half-starving dog when it leaped at your throat.

Before working on the doorjamb, he looks behind him, sees only a girl lolling by the train tracks, and then wedges the bent claw of the crowbar into the gap beneath the dead bolt. It takes only one swift yank, and a single painful bark from his back, to splinter the wood and free the bolt.

He raises the crowbar high as he pushes open the door, expecting a snarling rush of dog meat, but instead of a crazed pit bull, what comes at him is a medium-size mutt with matted hair and soft eyes. It wouldn't have taken much of a blow to crack its little skull, but despite his reputation on Avery Road, Oliver Cross is not a violent man. He dislikes even stepping on a cockroach—the frantic, futile retreat, the crack of shell, the white guts spurting. So when the dog attacks, he doesn't smash its crown with a swift blow. Instead, he lifts his boot and, none too gently, shoves the thing's jaw.

The dog is so shocked at the calm rebuke that it retreats from the room, yelping and spinning as it goes.

Oliver looks around, smelling the stink of the place, and feels the dawning of a fierce worry that makes his scalp itch. With the crowbar raised and his eyes focused on the doors off the front room, he takes a step forward. Something squishes beneath his boot.

"Little fucking mutt," he growls.

At the sound, the dog dashes back into the room and barks as if to say it serves Oliver right for shoving a boot in its face. Oliver cleans his boot sole on the cushion of the couch and keeps moving forward.

The worry comes because Oliver recognizes this scene. Not this exact scene, but the mise-en-scène. This is an abandoned apartment, one left in great haste and one step ahead of physical eviction. The clothes scattered, the drawers dumped, the furniture tipped. Useless objects are strewn across the floor as in the aftermath of a hurricane, along with a pet left behind to crap all over the floor before it withers and dies.

But this time he isn't interested in the details of the desolation: the holes in the walls, or the cracked sink, or the carpets ruined by the dog. With his crowbar he picks up a lank bowling shirt from the floor. He recognizes it from the photograph of Erica and that Adam Morgan kid. It is hers; she was here. Did she race away with this Frank Cormack asshole? Or, more frighteningly, did he race away from something he had left behind?

Oliver calls out his granddaughter's name as he wades through the apartment, the dog nipping at his heels. He feels like a monster on the loose, searching for something large and inert, a girl in trouble, a girl attacked, mutilated, left for dead. The images that flit through his brain are enough to choke him, but when he scours the place, every room, every closet, every space beneath bed and bureau, he finds nothing. Sweet nothing.

For a moment the terror eases, but then it floods back in. He has been going through the motions in his search for Erica, trying to satisfy his dead wife's whim without too much struggle. It was all about the show. He figured his granddaughter had run off to see the world and find herself, just like he and Helen had run off after the radical events in Chicago made their staid paths seem obsolete. That's what kids are supposed to do when they're suffocating in conformity. Life is too important not to take the wild leap.

But now the terror has risen again, even in the face of finding nothing in the apartment, and it will stay with him, sitting like a rider on his back, jabbing its spurs into his sides at every turn, every pause. Because once he has imagined the worst, he won't stop looking until he can put Helen's fragile mind at ease. And his own.

In the bathroom, in the filthy toilet, he finds two cell phones leaning up against each other, unable to fit down the hole. He rolls up his sleeve and reaches in. As he washes his hands and the phones in the sink with water hot enough to scald, the dog rams Oliver's leg with its head.

Oliver pushes it away again with his boot. Oliver doubts there will be anything of use in these waterlogged bricks, but you never know.

Finished with his search, he heads to the door and, as he does, the dog's yapping suddenly stops. The quiet startles Oliver, who turns and looks at the pup's eyes, wet and pleading. There were hounds at Seven Suns, prideful things that sprinted across the landscape after hedgehogs or lay like kings of the earth in the afternoon shade. Free and feral, as dogs were meant to be. It's why they never had a dog on Avery Road; it seemed wrong to keep such an animal locked up in a house.

"You hungry?" says Oliver to the dog. "You thirsty? You want to get the hell out of here and go crap in the woods?"

For a moment Oliver thinks of just letting the thing out, opening the door and watching it flee into the wild. Go, little hero, and be free.

But dogs like this mutt aren't meant to be free. Perhaps someone will find it, take it in, brush its matted fur and feed it and give it a loving home. But most likely not. Most likely it will starve in the woods, or be run over by a train, or be eaten by a fox, or, even worse, get picked up by the animal cops and be gassed. It's a pity about the dog, but what the hell is Oliver going to do about it? What the hell indeed?

He slips the crowbar back into his jacket and finds a mostly empty bag of kibble in the kitchen. The dog follows him and sits down by his two metal bowls, both empty. Oliver fills one bowl with water and the other with food and then stands back to watch the dog eat.

It doesn't just go at it, wolfing its meal. Instead, the dog takes a mouthful of food and scurries away, drops the kibble onto the hallway floor, and eats it there. Finished, it comes back to the bowls, works a bit at the water, and then takes another mouthful into the hallway. Oliver finds the whole act somehow touching. When it is finished with the food, licking the bowl for any final microscopic bits, the dog walks over to Oliver and stands in front of him, waiting.

Waiting for more? What a greedy bastard. Oliver admires that.

He stoops down as best he can and checks the dog's collar. Its name is Hunter. It has had some shots. There is a number to call, probably the number of one of the cell phones that were in the toilet. Oliver rubs the dog beneath his chin and Hunter stretches his neck.

"You're going to help me find him, aren't you, Hunter, you little beast? That's right, you're going to run him down like a hound from hell."

The dog licks Oliver's wrist.

A few moments later, Oliver is climbing down the steps of the building with Hunter on a leash and the near-empty bag of dog food under his arm, two metal bowls tucked inside.

"Hey, mister," says a girl leaning against an electric pole across from the building. It is the same girl he saw before out by the tracks. Up close she is older than he thought, but still almost young enough to be in school with Erica. Beautiful black skin, a ring in her nose, long tight curls of dark hair, and a smile that looks like a permanent feature, as if she were born to smirk. "Is that your dog?"

"Would I be taking him if he wasn't?" he says.

"Can I pet him?"

"Sure," he says.

The dog pulls him toward the girl. She stoops down and scratches his head. "Hey, little doggie," she says as the dog leans in to her. "He's filthy, mister, and he smells like crap."

"He gets into things," says Oliver. "Do you know my nephew who lives in that apartment up there? Frank? He was watching him for me."

"Frank?"

"Frank Cormack."

"Yeah, I know Frank. I live over there." She nods toward a clutch of rickety houses on the other side of the tracks. "I watched you break into his apartment."

"I had to get my dog and he didn't give me a key. Have you seen him lately?"

"No."

"There was a girl with him, red hair. You know her?"

"Erica?"

"Yeah, that's her."

"Sure, Erica. Who's she to you?"

"Any idea where they went?"

"No, man, no idea. You got a cigarette?"

"You shouldn't smoke."

"There's a lot of things we shouldn't be doing, like breaking into someone else's apartment and stealing his dog."

"If you see Frank around, could you give me a call?"

"If you want. Yeah, maybe. If I'm not too busy. You know, I got things."

"How about if I give you twenty bucks now and fifty more if you see him and call me."

"That might work."

He puts down the bag, pulls out his wallet.

"You got a number, mister?" she says after she takes the twenty. As he gives it, she taps it into her phone. "What's your name?"

"Oliver."

"And your last name?"

"Oliver."

"Oliver Oliver? That's a funny name. Where do you live, Oliver Oliver?"

"Around."

"I get you. I'm Ayana."

"Good, Ayana. I hope to hear from you."

"Oh, for fifty dollars I expect you will. And take good care of the dog."

10

WON'T GET FOOLED AGAIN

The dream world of Avery Road is a fitful, fantastical landscape. Boys and girls in armor ride dragons into battle, adults make love on beaches with high school flames, trains roar across the plain as passengers glimpse from their windows cowboys spinning atop wild broncos, arms flapping. The land is lush, the sky is blue, the clouds so bright they hurt your eyes as they float by like great white turtles. Yet even in this verdant paradise of hope and reverie there are school tests with questions that are impossible to answer, bosses with red eyes and three rows of teeth, ovens left on, clothes that disappear, guns that won't go off. And, of course, there are the money worries, the money worries, the great American fixation on who has what and who has more and what will happen when next month's bills come due.

Yet beneath the simple dreams and frets that build the night gardens of America, on Avery Road there are tendrils of a unique malevolence reaching up from the depths, wrapping ghostly fingers around the sleeping throats of children and adults alike. As boys and girls gambol along storybook paths, monsters lurk. Planes crash into baseball diamonds, transformers slay dragons, beach lovers turn into venomous snakes, and the Angel of Death, looking very much like Aunt Iris, looms. If you follow these dark tendrils back, back, dive with them in and out of the dream earth, trail them to their very root, you will see them rise like living tongues from a puckered mouth of blight in the middle of the landscape. And this malignant maw of darkness and doom has a single address—128 Avery Road—and a single source, a man who sweats feverishly through the night and dreams of death as others dream of Popsicles and trampolines.

Oliver Cross wakes from his howling, growling night dreams to the growls and howls of the dog he stole that very afternoon. Oliver scratches his chest and rubs his head to soothe the disappointment of once again waking into the world of the living. He would shut his eyes tightly and try to return again to the quiet death of sleep, but the dog's yapping makes it impossible.

It has been four years since he had to care for anyone but himself— after the years of daily, hourly care for Helen—and he doesn't like once again being responsible for another creature. What does the damn thing want? To eat? To drink? Most likely just to piss in the yard. Maybe he should let the damn dog out and lock the door behind him. But, truth is, Oliver could go for a piss in the yard himself.

Oliver grunts as he writhes his way off the sodden sheets of the bed, ignoring the screaming from his back. In just a T-shirt and white briefs, he clambers ungainly into the kitchen and turns on the light. The dog is barking at the door, dancing back and forth like a windup doll. Oliver went to the pet store and bought a brush and shampoo and cleaned the thing in the bathtub, so his coat is no longer matted with his own crap, but curly and pert. When he reaches the door, Oliver scratches the dog's side with his foot as he puts his hand on the knob. When he looks up at the door's window, he sees a bearded face staring back at him.

The door smashes open, the dog howls, a sharp blow on the head drives Oliver to his knees. And all along Avery Road, dreams shudder with a darkness darker than black.

◆ ◆ ◆

When Oliver rouses, he is lying on the floor of his living room. The light is on and someone is talking and his stomach is sick. He thinks of sitting up but when he tries his back seizes and the nausea flares, and so he remains lying on the hard floor. He realizes he doesn't hear the dog. What have the bastards done to the dog? He turns his head and sees the leashed animal lying still and contented in the lap of a woman sitting on the floor, a woman whom he vaguely recognizes. Oh yes, now it becomes clear. The girl from the apartment. Ayana.

That explains something, though what he's not yet sure.

He looks around, trying to get his bearings. A tall, beefy man with a bandage around his head is standing by the television, the man whose bearded face he saw in the window before the door smashed open. The bandaged man is drinking one of Oliver's beers. There's also a pale man, round and bald and flabby, sitting in a kitchen chair, and next to him a tall woman with platinum hair. The flabby man is wearing a track-suit and has another of Oliver's beers; the woman has long legs, a skirt the length of a credit card, and high red heels. A young man, with his head shaved up to the tops of his ears and the long brown hair above it gathered into a ponytail, is sitting in Oliver's recliner with a leg slung over the arm. Oliver stares for a bit at the hairstyle. Is that a thing now? Every day there's a new damn thing worse than the old damn thing.

"Which brings up an interesting issue," says the ponytail in the recliner, his voice riding a West Coast wave. "It looks like he's coming around, but I wonder if Sergei here could have been held responsible if the old man died because he has a fragile skull. I mean, look at all the dents in it already. Sergei took a harder blow than that and he's still standing. So is Sergei to blame if a little tap cracks an old man's head in two?"

"Who else would be?" says the platinum-haired woman in a surprisingly deep voice. "The tooth fairy?"

"But Sergei clearly didn't mean to kill the guy."

"I did not, I swear to it," says the man by the television.

"It's just the old man's toddling around with this crazy brittle skull of his," says the ponytail.

Oliver grits his teeth to fight the nausea and sits up with a grunt. His bare legs are stretched before him, his feet are knobby and impossibly ugly, his back is screaming. Everyone looks at him for a moment, before turning back to their discussion.

"I mean, what if the old man's on his lawn," continues the ponytail, "and a kid throws a football and he misses his target and the ball hits the old man on the head and his skull just cracks like an eggshell on the lip of a bowl. Is the kid up on a murder charge?"

"That would not be fair," says Sergei, nodding in approval.

"No siree, it would not. The same thing applies to Sergei."

"He hit him with butt end of revolver," says the flabby, bald man, speaking with a strong Russian accent. His tracksuit is baby blue with gold stripes. The front zipper is mostly down and gold chains glint through the thick black hair of his chest.

"Well, there is that," says the ponytail.

Oliver twists his head to look at the girl with the dog. She is still smiling, the girl, and the dog looks quite content, happier than he's been since Oliver found him.

"You're not getting the fifty," Oliver says to the girl.

"I wouldn't be so certain," says the girl with a sly smile.

"You could use some furniture, old man," says the kid with the ponytail, "and some premium liquor if you want to entertain in style. Get yourself a new pad, a new life. If you're not living large, are you really living?"

"Are you sure this is your dog?" says Ayana.

"It's my dog."

"That's not what the collar says."

"Look, we don't care about the mutt," says the kid in the recliner. "And we don't want any of your crap, I can promise you that. The television is a CRT, are you kidding me? And if you got any hidden stores of cash, well, man, you're hiding that fact pretty damn well."

"What do you want?"

"We want Erica Cross," says the Russian in the tracksuit.

Oliver's stomach turns. He shakes his head with confusion, the joints in his neck crack. "Why?"

"Because she's run away with Frank Cormack, dog's real owner," he says, "and we want Frank."

"Why?"

"Why, why, why," says the kid in the recliner. "The why is none of your business, old man. It's just a distraction. Let's not lose focus here, although I know it's hard at your age." The kid starts shouting. "Maybe it's your hearing. How's your hearing? Is this better?"

"Just because you're young," says Oliver, "doesn't mean you have to be stupid."

"Hit him again," says the kid.

"But what about eggshell thing?" says Sergei.

The ponytail rises from the chair and kicks Oliver in the head, causing an explosion of light that blinds him. When Oliver recovers enough to sense himself in space, he realizes he is lying on his side, bent like a wire hanger, his cheek resting in a pool of vomit. The dog is barking wildly and the kid is leaning over him.

"Can you hear me now, asshole?"

"Sergei," says the Russian.

The bandaged man steps over, grabs Oliver under the arms, and lifts him until Oliver's bare feet make contact with the floor. When he lets go, Oliver is standing, bent forward as if in a low bow, vomit dripping from his chin. Slowly he straightens up as much as he can. The dog quiets and returns to Ayana's lap.

"All you need to know is that we are serious as death about finding Frank Cormack, that son of a bitch," says the ponytail as he walks around Oliver. "And when we do, the shit is going to royally hit the fan."

"It could be dangerous for anyone stupid enough to be with him," says the Russian.

"What is she to you, this Erica girl?" The ponytail is standing behind Oliver now, talking right into his ear. "Same last name, right? Daughter, granddaughter, niece? Or is she just someone you're screwing?"

Oliver raises his hand to rub his head and then slams his elbow into the face of the man behind him, feeling something squash beneath his bone. As the man backs away, hands to his nose, Oliver spins awkwardly. As Oliver falls forward he hits the man again, and this time his fist lands solidly against the man's jaw. The blow sends the man sprawling over the recliner, even as Oliver hits the recliner's arm with his head and flops backward onto the floor, his head bouncing once off the wood. The whole move was as graceful as a hippo dancing with a porpoise in a vat of oil.

Oliver lies there, stunned for a moment, his mind woozy from the thumps on his head, his hand thick with pain. "You touch her," says Oliver to no one in particular, staring at the ceiling, "and I'll smash your nose into your brainpan."

"That might be hard to do, sweetheart, from way down there," says the platinum-haired woman.

The young man, trying to keep the blood in his nose with one of his palms, says in a muffled voice, "I'm going to fillet you like a—"

"Shut up, Kenny boy," says the woman, calmly. "You let an old man sucker punch you. We'll deal with you later. Take him outside, Sergei."

As Sergei lifts Ponytail and helps him toward the kitchen, Oliver picks up his hand and stares at it. His knuckles are oozing blood. His skin is as thin and dry as the husk of an onion, and the Warfarin makes every little cut into a tragedy. Brushing his teeth in the morning is like visiting an abattoir. But for some reason, the sight of the bloody hand calms his stomach and fills him with a strange elation. He popped the little sucker but good, and it was the realest thing he'd felt in years.

"So now that the pleasantries are over," says the woman, "listen carefully to Teddy so we understand one another."

"We don't give shit about law," says the Russian, "eggshells, and such. And we don't give shit about family, at least not about your family. We have embraced great American spirit and care only about money. So it is enough to know Frank Cormack has stolen something from us. We are trying to be good Americans and so we cannot allow such to happen. When we find Frank Cormack there will be blood on floor. Maybe blood of your Erica, too. Maybe we'll even blame her for what happened and make sure that she gets everything Frank Cormack will also get. And then, in your grief, you will try to kill us and then I'll give Ken permission to kill you, and it will all be such a waste."

"Life's a waste."

"You have point. But if you find him first, this Frank Cormack, and you tell us where he is, then we can assure your Erica's safety and we'll be square."

"I don't want to be square."

"Suit yourself. Tell us what we need and, once your Erica is out of way, we can have fun trying to kill each other. They are headed west."

He stands, takes a swig from the beer, tosses the bottle. It hits hard against a wall, bounces without breaking, and rolls, foamy beer spilling onto the floorboards.

"You might want to catch them," says the Russian, "before they reach end of road."

As the Russian heads toward the back door, the platinum-haired woman looks down at Oliver and speaks in that low voice. "Nice shot on Ken, old timer. I've been wanting to see that for the longest time. But he's easy. Teddy's a hard man from a hard land. Give him what he wants and walk away and everyone will end up happy except Frank. And, really now, who the hell cares about Frank?"

After the blonde walks out of the room, her posture model straight and her heels clicking, Ayana brings the dog over to Oliver, stoops down, and hands him the leash. The dog starts licking at his face and the tongue turns red.

"Do you need help getting up?" she says.

"Not from you."

"I'm sorry about this. It didn't need to turn violent."

"Yes it did," says Oliver.

"You talk tough for an old dude. Do you even have a gun?"

"I'm not allowed."

"You might want to break the rules and get one before you head after Frank."

"Is that what I'm doing?"

"If you want to save Erica you will. He has family in Ohio."

"What did he do, anyway?"

"Something stupid," she said.

"Something stupid? Jesus, why don't they just kill us all."

11

SIGNS

Oliver Cross didn't need permission to abandon law school in the fall of 1968 and catch a bus to Philadelphia. And he didn't need permission to wander among the stodgy buildings on the Bryn Mawr campus until he found the green in front of one of the old Gothic dormitories, or then to camp on the green like an old hobo until he saw Helen sauntering up the walk. And he didn't need permission to haunt the campus like Benjamin Braddock for as long as it took to convince Helen to drop all the expectations others had imposed on her life, drop her fiancé, drop out of the future she had seen for herself, as well as out of college, and join him on the hopeful journey west into a radical freedom that would be constrained only by the love they felt for each other. And he didn't need permission to stand with her on the highway and stick out his thumb and hitchhike all the way to the West Coast, bumming rides because they both believed, in their misreading of Kerouac, that hitch-hiking was the purest way to experience the breadth of the American continent along with its people.

Oliver Cross always prided himself on living his life without any-one's damn permission.

But as he stands at the mirror, pressing Band-Aids over the cuts in his scalp, he knows that his freedom to move freely over the surface of the globe is now as dead as Helen. He didn't ask permission before killing his wife and now he can't leave the county without a note from his guardian. He is sixteen again, asking his father if he can borrow the car.

As he stares at the hodgepodge of bruises and cuts on the flesh that hangs slackly from his skull, the dog lies calmly on a bloodstained towel tossed carelessly on the tile floor.

"How do I look?" Oliver says out loud.

The dog doesn't answer but Helen does. "Like my hero," she says. "Like the boy waiting for me outside Denbigh Hall."

"So you're blind as well as dead," he says.

"Are you scared, Oliver?"

"Just for her."

"You'll bring her home, I know you will."

"And if she doesn't want to come home?"

"Then you'll at least make sure she's safe."

"It's easy enough for you to say."

"Do you think it's easy just to watch and fret?"

"Then stop looking."

"Do you think it's easy to see what they've done to you these past few years?"

"You did it to me, too, you know."

"I know that. Who was with you every day in prison?"

"Whether I wanted you there or not."

"Wear a clean shirt."

"Should I also strangle myself with a tie?"

"Do we still have one?"

"No."

"Then just go with the shirt."

He puts clean flannel over his T-shirt and tucks it into his jeans. Into a green duffel bag he tosses shirts, underwear, socks, another pair of jeans, his leather Dopp kit, anything he thinks he might need on the road. He stows the bag in the truck, along with the crap he needs for the dog and the little GPS unit with a dashboard holder he picked up at Best Buy. When he opens the passenger door, Hunter jumps onto the bench seat as if he knows exactly where he is going. That makes one of them.

Before driving to the courthouse, he stops at his son's stone monstrosity. Fletcher will be at the office serving his corporate masters. Oliver grabs a brown bag and climbs gingerly out of the truck. The dog barks, but Oliver leaves him inside as he clambers up the hill to the high house and knocks on the door.

When the door opens and Oliver finds his son on the other side, he steps back at the conflicting rush of emotions that rise within him: love and anger, fear and forgiveness and hate. Somehow his son brings it all to the surface and it's more than he can deal with this morning.

"What happened to your face?" says Fletcher.

"I fell. Where's Petra?"

"Out."

"I thought you'd be at work," says Oliver.

"I took the day off."

"I wouldn't have come if I knew you were home."

"I wouldn't have answered the door if I knew you had knocked."

Oliver throws the bag to his son. "This is Erica's phone. And the phone of the boy she's with."

"Wait a second, what?"

"I thought you should have them."

"Where were they?"

"In the boy's apartment."

"Who the hell is he?"

"His name is Frank Cormack. He's a folk singer."

"Of course he is. And how did you find him?"

"I got off my butt," says Oliver.

Fletcher opens the bag, takes out one of the phones. "She didn't take her phone," he says, staring at the thing with wonder, holding it like it is some sort of divine object, the finger bone of a long-dead saint.

"I found them in a toilet."

Fletcher quickly drops the phone back into the bag. "Where did they go?"

"I don't know."

"What do you know?"

"I know he's in trouble," says Oliver. "And she's with him. That's enough."

Fletcher's expression as Oliver delivers the news is so tragic, Oliver can suddenly find the boy in Fletcher's bloated man-face. Oliver turns and looks down the long lawn and again he can see the three of them in the fields at Seven Suns: Helen tanned and graceful; Oliver tall and lean, still filled with the laughter he lost when he came back into the world; and his son, his son, with his long hair and twisted teeth and his narrow chest bare and nut-brown with sun, the boy a piece of the very land he runs wordlessly across.

"What do I do now?" says Oliver's son.

"Take the phones to the police," says Oliver, still unwilling to look back at what has become of that boy. "Maybe they can grab numbers or texts off the memory."

"What else?"

"Wait."

"I can't just wait. It's killing me. I need to do something. Tell me what to do. You were always so good at that, so don't stop now. Tell me what to do."

"Stay here. If you learn anything let me know."

"How?"

"This is my number," says Oliver, who then recites a series of digits. "Repeat it back."

When Fletcher fails, Oliver gives the digits again.

"But you don't have a cell phone," says Fletcher. "You were always so proud of not being tethered to some crappy piece of technology."

"Of course I have a cell phone. I've had one for years. I just never chose to share the number with anyone other than your mother because there was no one else I ever wanted to talk to. The one I have now is no longer in my name."

"What are you?"

"I'm a convicted felon who doesn't need the government tracking his every step," says Oliver. He repeats the digits a third time, and when Fletcher says them back correctly, Oliver says, "Don't share them. I'll be in touch."

"Where are you going?"

"Where do you think I'm going?"

"But you can't go anywhere, Dad. You're still on parole."

"I'll get permission," says Oliver. "Stay by the phone."

"You're just going to screw things up worse than they are already."

"That seems to be my talent."

"Go back home, Dad. Don't be a fucking hero."

"Don't worry," says Oliver. "The only thing heroic about me anymore is my hemorrhoids. Now I need one more thing from you."

"What's that?"

"Your mother's ashes."

◆ ◆ ◆

Oliver parks the rusted oversize truck at a metered spot in front of the great white courthouse where he was convicted of manslaughter three years before. Sitting in a row alongside a Mercedes, a Volvo, a Prius, and a shiny black-and-red motorcycle with twin exhaust pipes, his truck sticks out like a chewed piece of gristle dropped in the middle of a fancy dinner plate.

He takes the dog out of the truck and walks him around the plaza in front of the pillared entrance. Hunter pees on the bushes behind a bench and continues onto the grass where he squats.

"Good boy," says Oliver. "Don't be stingy."

He puts the dog back in the truck, cracks a window open, and locks him in before heading for the grand entrance with Latin inscribed overhead. The crap stays on the grass, a brown pile of stink and waste that Oliver chooses not to pick up. He considers it a temporary art installation, commenting on the quality and inequality of American justice. Too bad the dog couldn't have dumped it on the judge's chair.

The courtroom where he was tried is wide and domed, with a mural behind the judge's bench representing the settling and taming of the land. The architecture and public art are meant to evoke awe, but all they invoked in Oliver during his trial was disgust. They wanted the grandness itself to settle all arguments about the state's right to regulate the myriad avenues of his love, but to hell with that. When he left law school, he also left fealty to any power higher than his own mores and moral code. He wasn't going to let his father tell him how to live his life, or let the carrots and sticks of capitalism lead him off his path, or let a system of laws riddled with the precepts of someone else's religion define for him what was right and wrong. There is always someone wanting to stick a ring in your nose and pull you forward like an ox.

And yet here he is, walking past that very courtroom and then heading up the stairs to the County Office of Adult Probation and Parole. In prison he had to ask permission for everything; that defined the institution for him. *Please, sir, may I take a crap.* Now he's asking permission to crap outside this crappy little county, which means, in a real way, he is still incarcerated.

"So nice to see you, Oliver," says Jennifer Post, her natural smile muted enough to show it isn't so natural just then. She had to delay an appointment to see him, and her irritation shows. "What happened to your face?"

"I fell."

"And scraped your hand, too, I see. You need to be more careful. How did your impromptu music concert work out? Did the girl give you a name?"

"As a matter of fact."

"My oh my. The power of rock 'n' roll. And did you tell anyone what you found out?"

"I told my son," says Oliver.

"Really," she says, her smile brightening to genuine. "Oh, Oliver, that is wonderful. How did it feel to communicate with your son again?"

"Hard."

"Why?"

"I kept remembering the little boy. And the way we were."

"It's not only the son who has to grow up, Oliver. I assume your father had to go through that, too."

"He never got over it."

"But you might?"

"My wife wants me to."

"I'm sure she would have wanted just that."

"I need to take a trip."

"To where?"

"Ohio."

"Why?"

"To see the Cormacks."

"Who are the Cormacks?"

"Just some people I need to see."

"And they can't visit you here?"

"You want me to get out of my rut," says Oliver. "You want me to start building a life with joy and meaning in it. That's what I'm trying to do."

"In Ohio?"

"Small steps."

"Where did you get the dog, Oliver?"

"You've been spying on me."

"We get reports."

"I just picked him up."

"Why?"

"He needed someone to take care of him."

"And you decided you're the one? That's quite surprising."

"Do I have permission to leave the county?"

"No," says Jennifer.

"No?"

"You know the rules."

"That's why I'm here. You can give me permission."

"I can, but I choose not to. To be honest with you, Oliver, I don't think you're being honest with me."

"Everything I've said is the truth."

"But not the whole truth. Why do you want to go to Ohio? Do you think she's there?"

"Maybe."

"Then tell the police what you know. You also might want to tell them what really happened to your face. But I can't have one of my clients running out of state to chase a runaway."

"She's not a runaway, she's my granddaughter. I haven't asked you for anything before, not even a tissue."

"That's true."

"I'm asking you now."

"I'm sorry, Oliver, but the answer is no. Leaving the county without permission would be a violation of your parole, and would most likely result in your being sent back to Rockview. I know you don't want that."

"No, I don't want that."

"And neither do I. Now I could set up an appointment with the detectives and provide you an opportunity to tell them everything you've learned. They could get in touch with the authorities in Ohio."

"Don't."

"The police are the ones to properly handle a missing-person case." He lifts his hand and rubs the crease in his skull. "Sure they are."

"Oliver, don't doubt that I'll put you back inside if I have to."

"I don't doubt it for a minute, Jennifer. I know exactly what you are."

Oliver stares at her for a moment before lowering his gaze to the scraped and gnarled hands that lay twined on his lap. He rubs his tongue over his teeth and winces as if he has swallowed a load of castor oil.

"Okay then, good," says Jennifer, writing something in his file. "Thank you for coming to see me before you did anything rash. Your caution will be duly noted. I'm very pleased with your progress, Oliver, truly. If I let the prosecutor know how things are going, especially between you and your son, maybe we can work together to shorten your term."

"Jiminy Cricket," he says.

"I'm glad you're pleased." She jots a final note and taps the file with the point of her pen before she flips it closed. "I'll see you next Thursday, Oliver, and we'll talk about all this then."

12

Break on Through
(To the Other Side)

Ayana is leaning against the driver's door of the truck, checking her phone as Oliver leaves the courthouse. He knew he would see her again, the only mysteries were the where and the when. Now those mysteries have been solved. Here. Now. Too bad her timing is crap. She looks up, smiling like they are old friends. There is a backpack on the ground beside her.

"Going somewhere?" she says.

"Home," says Oliver.

"That's why you threw a duffel and a bag of dog food into the back of the cab?"

"Spring cleaning."

"I don't think so, Oliver Oliver."

"It's amazing how little I care about what you think. Get off my truck before I knock you off."

"I want to go with you."

"And I want to dance the rumba."

"What's that?"

"It's a dance."

"What kind of dance?"

"How the hell would I know?"

"But you said you wanted to dance it."

"I just said it, I don't want to do it. I'm no dancing fool."

"Maybe not the dancing part. You going after them, right?"

"I'm on parole," says Oliver. "I'm not allowed to go anywhere except home."

"That doesn't mean you won't."

"Get away from my truck."

"I can help."

"Like you helped by bringing those bastards to me last night."

"I did you a favor."

"It didn't feel like a favor when I was getting kicked in the head."

"But now you know what she's up against. And I can tell you why they're after him."

Oliver starts to say something and then stops. Maybe she does know something, maybe she can help. He hasn't decided yet what to do about his parole. The thought of going back to prison is a shiver in his bones, but, at the same time, what is the point of being out if he can't do something as necessary as saving his granddaughter from the Russian and his mob? He also knows exactly how much he doesn't know: where Erica and Frank are going; why they are going; how to get ahold of them; what to do when he does get ahold of them. Maybe this girl is telling the truth. He shakes his head at the thought. He knows enough to know better, but maybe he can mine just enough truth from her lies to get his bearings.

"Get in," he says, finally, before unlocking the truck.

The girl smiles, grabs her bag, and hops around the front of the vehicle before jumping into the passenger seat. Once there, she hugs the dog, who seems so very happy to be hugged by her, the little traitor.

Oliver growls a bit to himself before he climbs into the driver's seat and inserts the key. The starter whines and the engine sputters before it kicks to life. He backs out into the street and starts away from the courthouse.

"How did you know I'd be here?" he says.

"I guessed."

"Some guess."

"It didn't take much. You weren't at home and the records say you're still on parole. If you were going after her, you'd have to come here first."

"Where do you live?"

"I'm sort of between places."

"What does that mean?"

"Exactly what I said."

"So you're homeless."

"No, I am not homeless. What do you think I am, some flea-bitten bag lady living on the streets? I'm not homeless. I am just . . . between places."

"Homeless."

"My mother's boyfriend couldn't keep his hands off me and my mother didn't like the competition, so I'm sort of bouncing around until I get my bearings."

"And so you bounced around to them."

"They had a couch."

"I'm not dropping you off there."

"I don't want to go there. I want to go with you."

"Not happening."

He drives on, looks into his rearview mirror to see if someone is trailing him, and sees nothing. But what does that matter, she is with him and that's enough. He pulls onto a residential street and parks.

"So what did he steal?" he says. "Drugs or money?"

"Are you going to take me with you?"

Oliver doesn't answer. He isn't going to get swept into promising anything.

"Drugs," she says, finally.

"Was Erica part of it?"

"No, it was just him. They trusted him for a moment and that was enough time for him to screw everyone. Erica's just along for the ride. She probs doesn't even know what he did."

"Where's he going?"

"To a dead end, most likely. They know where he's headed, and when he gets there, bam, bam. But in case he gets wind and goes off route, they wanted someone chasing him, too. That's why they came to you. Right now he's on his way to Santa Monica."

"What's there?"

"A partner named Bongo who they're already on to. Frank's supposed to sell the drugs to Bongo. But I know where Frank's already been. Maybe we can trace him from there, stop him before he gets all the way."

"Tell me."

"I'll show you."

"No you won't."

"Look, man, she might not be part of it, but whatever's coming to him is coming to her, too. I'm her friend, really. She's the only reason I'm here. Frank, he's a loose rocket, and those creeps after him, Ken and Sergei, the Russian, and Madam Bob—"

"Who?"

"The blonde with the legs. Madam Bob. All of them, they're, like, the worst. But Erica, I love Erica, man. Erica and me, we're tight. She helps me see things. And she talks about you, her grandpop the jailbird. I knew who you were the moment I spied you lurking like a fool around Frank's place."

"And still you set them on me like a pack of wolves."

"I had to, they put me there to see who came. They'd bust me up if I held out. But they're assholes. Push comes to shove, I'm with her."

"The only pushing is me shoving you away."

"Then what are you going to do?"

"Go home. Sit. Drink beer." Just saying it hurts his kidneys.

"You got old, didn't you?"

"It happens."

"Yeah, but I don't believe you. If you weren't going after her, I wouldn't have found you. And it doesn't matter what they said in there. Not to you. Erica went on and on about you and Granny. The original rebels. That the two of you just ran away from your lives when you were young, made something new."

"And hasn't it worked out swell."

"She just wanted to do the same. That's probs why she went. She's following in your footsteps. How does that make you feel?"

How does that make him feel? Oliver takes one of his hands off the wheel and presses at the lump in his neck. The only thing he ever inspires now is tragedy. And if this Ayana is telling the truth, the run across the country by Erica, in emulation of him, will end at the Pacific with nothing to show for it but death. The futility of life in one three-thousand-mile jaunt. It is too brutal to truly take in, but even with the specter of Rockview hanging over his head, some decisions are no decision at all.

"Give me your phone," he says.

"I'm not giving you my phone," she says.

"Give me your phone or get out."

"Just chill, ayight. What, you making a call? You don't got one of your own?"

"That's right."

"You need to get a life," she says before taking out her phone, unlocking it, and handing it to him.

He looks at it for a moment before tossing it out the truck window. It lands with a *clack* on the asphalt.

"What the fuck," she shouts as she scrambles to open the passenger door.

"If you're coming with me, you come without your phone."

"You're going to let me come?"

"Without your phone."

"It's my phone, man. I'll turn it off, I promise. I just upgraded."

Oliver raises an eyebrow and waits. He can see the indecision in her, the nervousness rising, and then, in resignation, she slams shut the door. "What am I going to do without my phone?"

"Maybe you'll read a book," he says. "And we can listen to music. I have tapes. You like the Eagles?"

"No."

"Good. Are we done here?"

"We won't even know how to go without Google."

He points to the little screen attached to his fan vent. "I have a GPS."

"Without a phone?"

"That's right."

"They even make those anymore?"

"Some people don't like to be traced."

"Cool that." She hesitates, looks for a moment like she is ready to dart out and pick up the phone, but then leans back and closes her eyes.

"Ayight, then," she says.

"All righty," he repeats. "Did I say that okay?"

"No."

"Where to?"

"He visited his brother, that's all I know."

"Whereabouts?"

"Someplace called something like chilly clothing."

"How do you spell that?"

"How the fuck I know."

He puts on his glasses, starts tapping into the GPS unit, tries a couple spellings until Chillicothe, Ohio, pops onto the screen. When the lady starts talking, he slowly pulls back onto the road.

Following the GPS directions, he merges onto Route 1, driving south on a stretch of road lousy with commerce and traffic. It would have been faster to head to the turnpike that sped west across the state, but he tapped the "no tolls" instruction into the GPS unit. He didn't need tollbooth cameras reading his license plate. With the congestion and the stoplights blinking red every half mile or so, it takes them half an hour to hit Chadds Ford, but then the landscape countrifies and the road turns quick and, before he knows it, they are passing over the swiftly flowing Brandywine Creek.

"Wee haw," he says in a flat voice.

"What?"

"I'm just saying. Wee fucking haw."

"Okay, old man," says Ayana, "don't make a federal case about it."

"State," he says.

"What?"

"It's a state case. It's not going to turn federal until we hit Maryland, but that won't be long."

"Are you okay?"

"Better than ever," says Oliver Cross, and, strangely, he means it. Better than the last few years, anyway. As soon as they crossed the Brandywine he was out of the county and officially an outlaw. It feels good, Oliver thinks, breaking laws and crossing lines, it feels right. He is traveling hopefully once again. He is off and running to save his granddaughter, and that is the right thing to be doing, but there is something else that fills his heart with joy.

He is skipping parole, and they will be after him eventually, surely after he misses his next appointment, probably sooner when Jennifer, alerted by his request, visits the house unannounced to check up on him. But let her check, let them chase. He is on the road again, feeling alive for the first time since his Helen died, free for maybe the first time in decades. *Made it, Ma! Top of the world!* he thinks, and like the grizzled gangster in the old black-and-white, the coppers are never going to take him alive.

II. Cheap Thrills

13

RUNAWAYS

Don't try telling Frank Cormack that the American dream is dead because not only did it dance like a stripper in his heart but he was chasing it full-bore in his baby-blue Camaro with the thick white stripes across the hood, heading west, ever west, where he was surely going to catch her and wrestle her to the ground and make her shout, "Oh, Uncle Frank!"

And don't try telling Frank Cormack that you couldn't change your fate because in one fell swoop he had done just that, turning a stalled music career and a life going downhill fast into something so full of promise that it stole away his breath when he stared straight into its wide green eyes.

And don't try telling Frank Cormack that love won't save you because the proof of that pudding was sleeping in the front seat of his Camaro, her head resting on a sweater pillowed up against the window and a line of drool falling from her pouty lips.

He and Erica had left their cell phones in the toilet and were staying off the interstates so they couldn't be tracked or traced, followed or stopped or hijacked.

Freedom!

The road rushed beneath them like the flow of a mighty river running fast and unobstructed to the sea.

Freedom!

They were Huck and Jim, Bing and Bob, Sal and Dean, Bob and Joan, Joan and Jett, a couple of all-American kids beating out a rhythm of discovery mile by mile on the road first to Santa Monica and then right into the mighty Pacific and beyond. And what were they chasing? That's right, say it together now.

Freedom!

He had to give it to Erica. She wasn't only the object of his adoration and lust, as well as the pivot around which his future would revolve, she was also his prophet. Where he saw obstacles, she saw opportunity. Where he saw obligation and fear, she saw an open road. She had been telling him for weeks that they should just get the hell away from her parents and his failed life, away from the Russian, out of town, out of state, out of Trump's grotesque new America, that they should just breathe deep and go, go, go like a couple of experimental subjects escaping from some bizarre testing facility with a red light blinking over the doors and sirens sounding at the breach.

Erica's call to freedom had been like a hymn playing in his brain, playing in his brain, setting the stage for this breath-gulping sprint into a future of music and art and wine and baguettes slathered with foul-smelling cheese and an attic room with a hissing radiator and sloped ceilings where right in the middle of a long, hard fuck they could turn their heads toward their dormer window to see the spire of the Eiffel Tower rising like life's promise itself above the slate-gray rooftops.

The sky was blue, the road was straight, and Erica's bare legs were curled on the seat beside him as the miles slipped madly past. He dropped his right hand from the wheel and stroked love's ankle.

Between long stretches of rural highway, they herky-jerked through stoplighted stretches of strip malls and pizza joints, chain restaurants, nail salons, discount marts, convenience stores. They even had an Aldi out here.

Before Erica he would have seen it all as part and parcel of the landscape, as natural as the tall grasses and weed trees that grew wild on the side of the road. But now, through eyes unblinkered by love's radicalization, he knew them as the sad service centers of a failing American life. He shared Erica's contempt for all those who tried to fill their holes in such places, all those who felt the key to life was getting enough money to frequent better and more exclusive versions of the very same crapholes. They had sentenced themselves to the chain gang, toiling under the reflective glasses of banker guards as they worked the road in an endless bulimic slog of earning and spending, acquiring, devouring, vomiting up the excess just so they could devour more.

But unlike Erica, who had never worked a day in her privileged life, he felt most strongly about those who were sentenced by fate and misfortune to work in such places, part of a faceless corps of first-name-onlys who bartered their raw freedom for a paycheck, spending their lives in boxes as spare as the cages at a zoo, selling shoes, selling soda, filing nails, serving crap on a bun with a side of fries, restocking shelves picked clean by ravaging hordes, pinching their pennies while extravagantly spending the hours of their lives to satisfy the basest needs of the American consumer. Poor deluded sons of bitches. He had been one of them, but no longer.

Sometimes you had to see exactly where you were coming from so you could appreciate where you were headed, and where he was heading now was to a quaint little development just over the horizon, Freedom's Acre, with plots available to all with the requisite guts and proper financing. And proper financing was exactly what was wedged inside the spare tire resting beneath the floor of his trunk, all the financing he'd need to buy their freedom once and for all.

He wouldn't have had the guts to pull it off without Erica. He would have just gone on going on until time and the drugs squashed him flat.

But Erica had urged him to make a move, so when the moment came and opportunity flashed its shining smile, he bit the lips right off its face and now here they were, he and his great love, on the road to someplace new and glorious. She didn't know what he had done for them, wouldn't ever know if he had his druthers, but she was the reason he had brained Sergei with a tire iron—the Russian always sent teams of two to pick up and drop off—snatched the satchel and the computer, and was now heading to the parking lot on the pier in Santa Monica that stuck out into the ocean like a middle finger.

The deal was all arranged with Bongo, a buddy from his time in Chicago, a roadie with contacts who would buy the merch at premium rates, providing him with the cash that would not only finance their getaway, but also make a sweet go of it as they swished around the world, zigging and zagging, with the requisite bohemian travel stops in Australia, Bali, and Prague, before finding that attic apartment in the City of Light with the Eiffel Tower view, where he could tap out songs on the computer and build on their love. He maybe could have gotten out without stealing from the Russian, but to go globe hopping with Erica Cross there was no other choice; girls like Erica had certain expectations.

It was one of her charms that she never talked about money. Oh, she talked about how money warped, and how money controlled, and how money twisted you this way and that and had the whole country in its sway, but she never talked about what anything cost or how much she needed, or what life was truly like without it, which was why she carried so little on her. But they had left all their credit cards at home, had taken only what cash they could grab and their passports, because to use one of the cards, even once, would put Pops and the Russian right on their asses.

Erica was money innocent in a rich girl's way; she talked about money the way those who never lacked for it talked about money, and that made him want to wrap her in his arms and lick her face. But Frank knew that to keep her happy on the road meant having some money, real money, and that's why Sergei had taken the tire iron to the skull and they were running now. Which was good in its way, because fear was the greatest stimulant ever invented, meth had nothing on fear, fear would keep him moving, charging ever west, fear would keep him from stopping too long to rest here or smell the roses there, fear would keep him out of the Russian's grasp until the deal went down and everything was settled and he and his love were winging their way out over the Pacific toward the new and glorious life they were choosing for themselves.

Freedom!

The only problem was making it all the way to land's end and his rendezvous with Bongo, because even though he might have had close to a quarter of a million dollars' worth of product stuffed into the spare tire, he was woefully short of the hard cash needed to make it all the way to the selling ground. He had thought Sergei would have more cash money on him when he made his move. Truth was, right now he had just enough to maybe fill the tank once or twice more before he fell out flat broke.

And the dashboard arrow was jittering its way straight to E.

"What?" she said, waking up with a jolt when he killed the engine beside a pump at the mini-mart.

"We need some gas," Frank said.

She stretched and wiped her mouth, smiled nervously, looked around at the dumpy little station. Frank's heart filled with hope just watching her move and stretch, watching her legs rub against each other. Sometimes he feared he was just running away, running from himself, from what he had become, which could only end in disaster. But then he saw Erica, her eyes so alive, her body twisting this way and that, and he knew he was running toward something so bright it was blinding.

"So where are we?" she said.

"The great and glorious Circle K."

"I mean what state. Last I remember we were still in Pennsylvania."

"West Virginia," he said. "Mountain momma, take me home, country roads."

"What?"

"John Denver."

"Who?"

"We're just outside Morgantown."

"Is that all?"

"It's a big country, sweet pea, but we're only a couple hundred miles from my brother. You hungry?"

"Not really. All this driving has made me a little nauseous."

"How about a soda to settle your stomach. Ginger ale?"

"Okay, sure. I'll just take a walk, stretch my legs."

He opened the door to the mini-mart and smelled the hot dogs roasting. He'd been driving at speed for hours while Erica slept, and right then he could have gone for a dog, topped with onions and relish, doused with mustard. Man, he could already taste the thing. But he'd be getting no dog, no chips, he'd be getting nothing but the ginger ale for Erica and thirty bucks' worth of gasoline. It felt like putting thirty on his number, hoping the 576 finally hit so that he could make it all the way to his brother in Chillicothe before his wallet emptied and the tank ran dry. Getting to Todd was the surest way to fill up both for the sprint west. Todd had a house, a wife, a kid, a job, Todd had the careful life, which meant he had at least three months' worth of ready cash stored away for emergencies, because that's what they told you to do on all the careful financial websites. What Frank was facing now certainly qualified for a piece of that emergency fund, and a piece would be enough. Once Bongo came through he'd wire Todd back the money, along with a goodbye gift, before hitting the skies.

He picked up a Canada Dry from the cooler and a Slim Jim for himself, a stick of protein for the final sprint, and placed them on the counter. He was about to ask the middle-aged clerk—"Tom," it said on his first-name-only name tag—for thirty bucks on pump three when Erica walked through the door, her shirt loose, her feet bare. He watched the clerk watch her as she made her way through the aisles. The clerk caught Frank glancing at the "No Shirt, No Shoes, No Service" sign. In the mirror behind the counter Frank saw Erica grab a large bag of chips, a box of doughnuts, an iced tea, a magazine, a can of Red Bull, a bottle of Tylenol, and a pack of gum. She came over and dropped the haul on the counter next to the ginger ale and the Slim Jim.

"I thought you were feeling sick," he said.

"I just needed to get out of the car. Something in your engine smells like it's burning. Once I started walking I felt better and then I realized I was hungry." She turned to the clerk. "And can I have a hot dog, please?"

"Sure thing, miss."

"The long one that's well done? No, that one, yeah. Thank you."

When she got the dog she fouled it with ketchup from the counter, took a bite, and then stepped back outside. Frank turned to the clerk, who was still watching Erica. The clerk had a nervous twitch on his mouth. Yeah.

"How much?" said Frank.

The clerk started ringing things up, ringing things up, sweeping the crap into a bag as he rang things up.

"That's twenty-four-oh-one with the tax."

"Take off the Slim Jim."

The clerk hammered at the machine. "Twenty-two sixty-eight."

Frank took out his wallet and fished out the bills one by one. A twenty, two tens, a five, three ones. "Put the rest on pump three."

"Will do," said the clerk as he scooped up the bills. He raised an eyebrow at Frank. "She's a looker, that one."

"Yeah? Tell me, Tom, what kind of look is that?"

The clerk stared back at him flatly, without even the hint of a smile.

14

MILLION BUCKS

"I didn't imagine this would feel so good," she said. "I've been on road trips before, but there was always an expiration date, you know. We need to be back by . . . Got to get home by . . . But this, this is like the greatest drug ever. If we could bottle this, we'd make a fortune. It's like every mile we go, I can feel the hopes for my future falling away like skins being shed from a snake."

"And that's a good thing?" said Frank.

"They weren't my hopes," she said.

The miles were thrumming beneath them as they drove through the wild green landscape of West Virginia. It was about as pretty a place as Frank had ever seen, and for the first time that sappy John Denver song made sense to him. He had about three-quarters of a tank of gas, which should be enough for them to make it to Todd's house. He hadn't told Erica about the money issue, just like he hadn't told her about the drugs in the spare tire—he wanted to take care of that on his own before she had second thoughts about the whole enterprise. All she knew was that they were heading toward a moneymaking proposition in Santa Monica—but still, every time she gurgled her iced tea or loudly chomped a potato chip he couldn't help but wince.

But let her take what she wanted because she was worth her weight in gold, and it wasn't just the love he was talking about. Without her knowing, he had taken a drive to case the granite mansion she lived in with her family, and he could smell the money, as thick as the mortar laid between the stones. Once they got settled, and after the drug money ran out, Daddy wouldn't let her starve. They'd make it on their wits and their wiles, and then they'd make it on Daddy's bank account, but no matter what happened they'd make it all right. It would all be gravy if he could just make it to the coast.

"All year I've been getting the questions," she said as they powered forward. "Where are you going to school, Erica? What are you going to study? Going to be a lawyer like your dad?"

"You'd be a good lawyer," he said. "That we're here just proves you could convince an alligator to give up its teeth."

"Why would I want to be a lawyer? My grandfather told me the only thing he regretted about dropping out of law school was the wasted year."

"He's the one who went to jail, right?"

"Yeah. Good old Gramps. And it's not like being a lawyer has made my father ever so happy. He growls when he gets home and then drinks himself to sleep. You're lucky you have no one resting their hopes on you."

"That's true. I was born just so my family could have someone to disappoint them, and I've played my role to perfection."

"But I'm the eldest daughter of Fletcher and Petra Cross. The expectations are like an anvil on my head, pressing me down every step I take. And it isn't like I couldn't have lived up to them if I wanted to. I mean, high school is just a game, right, and not a hard one at that. Just do a little more than expected and suddenly the teachers start raving. *Oh, oh, Erica.*"

"It sounds like you were doing a lot more than expected."

"Oh, stop it, no. Gross." She took a swallow of the iced tea. "Not that they wouldn't. Every year or so there's a scandal; last year it was the physics teacher. In the middle of the year, gone, rumors swirling. But, yuck. Short-sleeve shirts and ties. And they're so old. Really?"

"My English teacher in high school was pretty hot. She liked me, said I had a poetic soul. I should have done something about that."

"Look her up. We'll stop by on the way."

"But I'm with you now; you're my one and only."

"Isn't that, like, old-fashioned? Aren't we up for anything?"

"Sure, I guess."

"A three-way with your English teacher. Reciting Shakespeare as we go doggie style. I wonder what Shakespeare recited when he gave it from behind. I guess Shakespeare. *Oh yeah, baby, baby, let me do it to you.* Might not be poetic, but coming from him it's still Shakespeare."

"I want to pull over right now and swallow you whole."

"And what's the goal of all this teacher-parent pleasing they wanted me to do? Fill my résumé, battle my way into a top-ten college, find a job that pays more than my friends are pulling down. And all the time looking a certain way and behaving a certain way and laughing at all those who go about it any differently. And what was the pot at the end of the rainbow? A gig at Goldman or Bain?"

"Bane? Isn't that the Batman villain? *I am Bane, you will die.*"

"Bain and Company. A consulting firm. Romney. But see what I mean. Sacks of gold, Goldfinger, Bane. And my father's law firm, Blank, Rome. Really? That's where I want to spend my life, at Blank, Rome? They're like monsters with helmets and sandals and those pleated skirts, and their eyes are all white as they wander zombielike searching for poor people to crucify. *We are from Blank, Rome.* It's like they name themselves just to weed out anyone with a conscience. And what do you end up with? Money, sure, and marriage, and kids, and alcoholism, and adultery, and divorce. And then, in the despair of middle age, you find yourself hiking the Pacific Crest Trail to find yourself, or maybe just stuffing your gut with food and prayer and cheap sex in European hostels."

"So you decided to skip all the other stuff and get right to the cheap sex in European hostels."

"It's a plan."

"I like it," said Frank, and he did.

"So what was her name?"

"Who?"

"Your hot English teacher."

"Mrs. Applethorp."

"Sounds spicy."

"She had this cute overbite."

It was good to hear Erica laugh. The rant he'd heard before, or something much like it. It was like she was trying so hard to convince herself and never quite succeeding, but the laugh, the laugh, hard and guttural and true, that was as real as a drenching rain. That was something he could hang his life on.

"You want to get high?" she said.

He checked his watch.

◆ ◆ ◆

They lolled on a blanket atop the grass by the side of the road. The ground was soft, the air smelled of loam, the tongue of the setting sun licked their faces like a puppy.

It was amazing what you could do with a strip of tinfoil and a straw, as long as you had a lighter and a pill to go with it.

For a moment Frank wasn't being chased, he wasn't afraid, death didn't lie entwined with freedom inside the spare tire of his car. For a moment he and Erica were the only two people in the world and the sun belonged to them as if it could be stuffed into a pocket when they were ready to move on. He believed just then that his love for Erica was so strong, so perfect, it would burst out of his heart like a bottle rocket and flood the world with harmony and peace. In this dark age of madness and hate, his love for Erica might be humanity's last hope.

He turned on his side and nuzzled her sweet, sweaty neck. He wanted to write a song about all this, he needed to, was desperate to. The words began to form like magic puffs of cloud in the sky. "Love." "Above." "Need." "Bleed." "Kill." "Thrill." "Heart." "Apart." It was all there, just waiting to be snatched out of the ether and turned into art.

He always felt so productive when he was stoned, but lately he hadn't done anything about it. Inspiration without follow-through—the story of his life. But tomorrow would be different. There would be follow-through tomorrow, and the next day, and beyond. He wouldn't be pulling out the computer and writing the song just now, there was no time for that, not with the Russian on his trail, but there would be time enough in all the tomorrows on their journey through space and time into the future: Chillicothe, Santa Monica, Sydney, Bali, Prague, Paris. It was all in front of them.

The sun was reaching for the horizon, which meant it would be late when they reached his brother's house, all to the good. The later the better, the darker the better. They would slip in unseen, get the money from his brother, slip out again with nothing to connect him and Erica with his brother's family as they roared ever west.

"Let's go, sweet pea," he said.

"Not yet," she said, her voice a drowsy chime. "Let me sleep a little more."

"Sleep in the car. I want you to be up and chirpy when you meet my brother. I want him to fall in love with you like I did before we say goodbye."

Frank had been in the alley behind the coffeehouse, leaning beneath the single yellow bulb, taking a quick few drags from a reefer after his set, preparing to work the board for the upcoming amateur hour, which just showed how grandly his "career" had been going, when the girl sidled up beside him.

"I thought you were pretty good," she said.

"That's what I aspire to," he said without looking at her, "pretty good."

It had been a crappy set, he knew, a bunch of songs written long ago, delivered with the affect of a terminally bored teen, which was about the best he could muster anymore, considering he hadn't written anything fresh since he left Chicago and was pretty much done with the whole music thing. Working for the Russian was taking all his productive time, but it paid the rent and kept him stocked. He took another drag and then offered it to the girl.

"You want?"

She took the joint and sucked at it so greedily he thought she would smoke it all. About to grab it back, he got a good look at her and his alarm turned to something else. She was so shockingly beautiful that for a moment he forgot to breathe. He had noticed her before, in a pack of high school kids gathered in the back of the room, no doubt to cheer on one of their own playing in the next set. She was pretty in that high-school-girl way—smooth skin, thick mascara, woven bands around her thin wrists—but in the alley, lit by the bulb above them and the glow of the joint, she was otherworldly. Her eyes seemed to glow as the tip of the joint sparked from her inhale.

"You here to watch a friend?" he said.

"I'm singing."

"Really? Your own stuff?"

"Carly writes and plays guitar but she's got the voice of a frog, so I sing for her."

"I'll look forward to that."

"Don't," she said, "I'm not much good either, just better than Carly."

And she was right about not being much good, but it didn't much matter. There was just something about the way she sat on the stool while her friend played. She was self-contained and self-conscious at the same time; it was there in her posture, the spread of her hands, the way her eyes closed as she missed the high notes. Erica sitting on that stool was the very image of the way he had wanted his music to sound when he started out, young and beautiful and fearless and fuck all what anyone else thought. After their set, he stared with regret as she and her friend Carly walked out the door.

It was only a few moments later when he felt a hand on his shoulder while he was still behind the board. "Can you get me anything a little more potent than the grass?"

He turned and saw her and his heart skipped a beat.

"What do you have in mind?"

"Roxies?"

Yes, he had told her, yes he could.

That their relationship had started with and was still largely premised on his supply of the drug was a disappointment to Frank. Erica had become hooked on her pain medicine after her knee operation, and Frank had become hooked on escape as his life teetered, and so it was through the drug that they bonded. This was a failure, he knew; a love such as theirs deserved purity of body and soul.

One goal of their run west was to get them both clean and ready for their glorious futures. The beaches on Bali would be good for that, surely, sweating out the toxins beneath the Eastern sun. And yes, he had felt the tiniest disappointment in Erica when, still barreling west, she asked about getting high (not so much a suggestion as a demand, really, considering the state of things), but damn it had felt good. It had felt real. And truth was, it somehow gave him a renewed confidence.

Sometimes a smidgen of smoke, or more than a smidgen, was just what the doctor ordered.

"You don't talk much about him," said Erica as they roared through the darkness toward his brother's house. "What's he like?"

"Todd? I called him Toddle. He was the perfect son, the perfect big brother. He taught me how to throw a baseball and how to tackle with my head up, and we wrestled like banshees across the living room floor, fighting over this and that. He was bigger and a better athlete, but he was too sweet to hurt me and I was ferocious enough to do damage, so it was almost even. And I was always getting into trouble, which let him play the perfect son all the years we were growing up. Heroic of me, wasn't it?"

"I know the feeling. My little sister will be able to do no wrong."

"Until she follows your path."

"God, I hope she doesn't."

"Why not? You're always going on about how much better it is to strike out on your own than follow lockstep with the masses."

"Not for her. She's too sweet."

"You're sweet."

"No I'm not," she said, looking out the window at the darkness whizzing by. "I'm as sour as a crab apple."

"My brother's sweet. A middle school social studies teacher, what could be sweeter? And he coaches the football team. Not the brightest maybe, but he was always overly protective of me, no matter how much crap I deserved."

"Why?"

"I guess because he's my big brother. And, you know, whatever I got into, and I got into shit, I kept him out of it. I never blamed him for anything, and when he did something bad, I covered up for him when I could. Like the time he spilled ink on the new carpet and I took the blame."

"That was noble."

"I was always in trouble anyway. What difference did it make? It's easier to play along with the roles you've been assigned than to break out and become something new."

"Tell me about it," she said. "It's like I haven't done my daily duty if I don't see the disappointment and worry on my parents' faces. It's like this whole trip is just playing out my role to the end."

"But that's not what we're doing, sweet pea," he said, putting a cheer in his voice as she grew darker. "We're breaking out of those roles, breaking out of the vise of our lives. We're smashing the chains binding us to what we once were and becoming something new, something better and truer."

"It's pretty to think so."

"We're not just thinking it, we're doing it. And that's why I need to see my big brother, the only family I give a damn about. I don't expect I'll ever be this way again, and I need to say goodbye."

15

DNA

It was past midnight and they were driving on fumes when Frank and Erica arrived at Todd's street just above the cemetery. The houses were dark, the roads were quiet, but Frank was buzzing with energy. Maybe it was the upper he had popped when the road started slithering like a snake on him, but most likely it was just the excitement of seeing his brother for the first time in years. His brother was always a tonic for him, and Toddle's very presence made Frank feel protected again, like everything wild was still possible.

The house, a small two-story box with a picket fence and vinyl siding, was dark like the rest; a battered blue sedan, perfectly sedate for his sedated brother, was parked in the drive. He woke up Erica after he popped the Camaro into "Park."

"We're here."

"Oh, okay," she said. "Where?"

"Chillicothe. At my brother's house."

"Okay, good." She wiped her mouth with the back of her hand, pulled at her shirt. "How do I look?"

"Perfect."

"Hardly. Will he have a bed for us?"

"There's a pullout couch in his living room."

"I hate those things. There's always a bar just at the wrong spot."

"It beats sleeping in the car," he said. "Now put on your smile, sweet pea, it's time to charm."

At the front door he knocked lightly and then a little louder when nobody answered. He stepped back, looked up at a second-floor window. "Yo, Toddle," he called out heartily, then stepped forward and knocked again. A moment later, as he felt more than heard the soft footsteps coming closer, he couldn't help himself from knocking some more.

The door opened and Todd's pale face appeared, his blond hair mussed. Frank stepped forward and embraced him tightly. "Toddle, man, look at you," he said, squeezing the breath out of himself.

"Frank. Christ. I've been calling you."

Frank pulled back, ignored the squinty concern on his brother's face. "My phone's dead. You gonna let us in?"

"Sure, yeah, sure," said Todd, looking first at Erica then at Frank, before stepping out and surveying the street. "You parked in front."

"Your piece-of-crap car was in the driveway," said Frank. "What else could I do?"

"Get inside," said Todd, taking one more surveil of the landscape before closing the door behind them all.

It was comforting for the moment being swaddled in his big brother's lower-middle-class nest of mediocrity. The faded living room couch, the coffee table with an actual coffee-table book, the toys in heaps, the very lived-in scent of it all reminded Frank of the choking domesticity of his own childhood. This was what he was running from, had been running from all his life, and yet, for some reason, he was so glad to be right here right now, his mood went into overdrive.

"Toddle, man, I'm so happy to see you. So where's the kid, where's Petey? I need to give my nephew the biggest hug. You'll just love him,

E, he's the cutest thing. The way he runs, like a little penguin with his neck sticking forward. Eeeh, eeeh, eeeh."

"Pete's sleeping," said Todd.

"Well wake him up, man. His uncle's here. Let's have a party. This is Erica. We're on our way west. I don't know when I'll be back and I want to see Petey. I need to see Petey."

"He needs to sleep."

"And what about Kerrie, where is she?"

"Upstairs."

"At least let me say hello to my sister-in-law. Oh man, Todd, man, you look stressed. Lighten up."

"It's after midnight," said Todd.

"That's when all the good stuff happens. Oh all right, I understand. You all got your schedules. Work and stuff. So I'll see them tomorrow. I'll make those pancakes Petey likes, the ones that look like Mickey Mouse, and sing that song. Erica and I can just sack out on the couch. We've been driving all day, man."

"It's Erica, right?" said Todd.

"Yes, that's right," said Erica.

"It's nice to meet you, Erica. You mind if I take a minute with my brother?"

"Go ahead."

"You want a glass of water or something?"

"No, I'm good. I'll just sit." She threw herself down on the green sofa, put her feet on the coffee table, and let her pretty head loll along the back of the couch.

Todd gave Erica a long look, and then nodded for Frank to follow him. Todd led him right through the kitchen and out into the backyard, closing the door behind them. The little lawn was dimly lit by a single light, and the thick trees around it gave them a bit of privacy. When Todd turned to face Frank, his features were firm, almost fierce, the face he undoubtedly gave to those middle-school troublemakers who interrupted his lesson. Frank couldn't help but laugh at his big brother trying to be stern.

"How old is she?" he said.

"Eighteen, man."

"You better hope so."

"Maybe seventeen. But she's amazing, so smart you wouldn't believe. When you get to know her you'll understand. Hang out with us tomorrow and you'll see what I'm talking about."

"You can't stay."

"Wait, what? Just for the night."

"You have to go."

"Is it Kerrie? Man, stand up for yourself, stand up for your family."

"You have to go, Frank. You have to go, now. You can't stay with me. And I can't give you any money, that was made very clear. No money or someone dies. And as soon as you go I have to make a call."

"Wait a second, what?"

"You parked in front of the house. I don't have a choice. They threatened my family. They threatened my son."

"What are you talking about?"

"What did you do?"

"Nothing."

"Don't lie. We've had enough lies, all of us. Stop lying, Frank. What the fuck did you do?"

◆ ◆ ◆

Don't try telling Frank Cormack that you can't change your life, because it's as easy as pie, as easy as one two three, as easy as getting in the car and slapping it into gear and pressing down like a madman on the gas.

And don't try telling Frank Cormack you can't remake your world because he had done just that, blown up everything before racing to a new and light-drenched future with the love of his life, a woman who would exalt him and save him at the same time.

And don't try telling Frank Cormack that you're not in control of your destiny because that's the worst kind of cop-out for those too timid to do what must be done. Sure, you're going to ruffle some feathers and dent some skulls, and sure, parts of your old life are going to end up strewn like garbage along the side of the road, but that's just the price of freedom. Freedom! And don't doubt there's always a price, because the bastards make sure of it.

His brother had hustled him out of that crappy little house in Chillicothe so fast it made Erica's head spin, had pushed them out the front door with a holler and a fight for all the neighbors to see, had told him in no uncertain terms that he was to get the hell out of there and never come back. Ever. Goodbye and get lost.

And Frank had spit back a bellyful of venom at the heavy blond man who was turning his back on his brother and sending him out in the middle of the cold naked night to fend for himself.

But there had been a moment, while they were still inside, when Todd grabbed hold of Frank with both arms. At first Frank thought it was the start of a fight, that Todd was going to wrestle him to the ground like he did when they were kids, but then it turned into a hug, a full-blown teary-eyed hug, and when they finally pushed away from each other, there was a small wad of bills in Frank's palm. It wasn't much, his brother never had much on him, but it was enough to fill the tank full two or three times over and that could get them halfway to where they needed to go, and that was something. That was something.

Damn.

Frank could still feel the explosion in his heart when he recognized what his big brother had done. And the guilt when he realized what his brother was risking. And the determination to do something about it.

So he used his brother's money to fill his empty tank at a self-service Speedway on Main Street, east of his brother's house, where they wouldn't bother to look at the tapes. And then he made his way slowly west searching for a likely spot. When Frank found something that worked, a red-and-black mini-mart on a triangular spit of land still in Chillicothe, he turned right and drove a short way down the darkened side street until he parked in front of a school. He turned off the car lights while leaving the engine running.

"What are we doing?" said Erica. "Do we have a place to stay?"

"Not here," he said. "We need to put some distance between my brother and me before someone gets hurt. We'll drive until dawn, out of this stinking state, and then maybe find someplace to crash."

"I'm not crying about leaving Ohio. From what I can tell this whole state is where cool dies."

"That's why I left in the first place. But I need to get myself a coffee to keep awake. Do you want anything?"

"I'll go with."

"No, stay here in the car. The place looks a little shady."

"I can take care of myself."

"I know you can, but do me a favor and stay, please. I want to keep the car running; something funny's going on with the battery and it needs to charge."

"Okay. Then how about an iced tea and something sweet. See if they have Peeps. I could go for a Peep."

"What's a Peep?"

"Those marshmallow chicks? My dad used to buy them for us when our mother wasn't looking. And the yellow ones, not the blue ones. The blue ones are disgusting."

"Iced tea and yellow Peeps if they have them. Fine. I'll be back."

Frank knew his brother would have already called the Russian by now, and the Russian would have already sent someone out hunting, so Frank didn't have much time. When they didn't find him—and they wouldn't, he'd stay on the back roads to make sure of that—they'd go back to Todd to find out what he had learned and what he had given to

Frank. And the Russian wouldn't believe Todd when he said nothing, nothing; he wouldn't believe Todd because that's just the way he was. Why believe words when there was more truth in blood. So it was up to Frank to convince him that Todd had given Frank not a cent.

Frank slipped out of the car and slammed the door behind him and then went around to the back. He pressed the latch, opened the trunk, and hunted around the crap loaded willy-nilly in his haste to get away from the Russian. In a gym bag beneath his guitar he found the gun.

As he grabbed hold of the grip his ears filled with the throbbing of his blood, each beat of his heart like the sound of a torch bursting into flame, one after the other, bad-a-bim, bad-a-bong, bad-a-boom.

Don't try telling Frank Cormack you can't start new again, that you can't create a future for yourself because he was doing it, one burned bridge at a time, leaving a path of infernos blazing so furiously that there would never be any going back and the path forward would be lit so brightly it would daze him with its beauty. Sometimes you had to see exactly where you were coming from so you could appreciate where you were headed.

He drew the gun out of the trunk and pulled the slide, chambering a round.

Freedom!

16

FORTUNATE SON

Chicago, 1975

Oliver Cross took a commuter train to the tallest building in the world.

On their way back west, after visiting Helen's mother and ailing father outside Philadelphia, Helen and Oliver had stopped off to see one of Helen's friends from Bryn Mawr, who was getting a PhD in anthropology from the University of Chicago. Hyde Park in the fall of 1975 reminded Oliver of Ann Arbor: serious, busy, but with plenty of Frisbee action.

Helen had taken enough courses to complete college and get a masters in art education at Berkeley, and Oliver thought now and then of going back to school himself. Maybe he would finish the law thing, or get a degree in journalism, since he had done a couple pieces for the *Bay Guardian*. But whenever he got down to getting serious about applying, something always came up, an act of political theater, a spiritual awakening he just had to experience, a collective here, a movement there. He and Helen were now headed to the mountains to plant some roots at a commune called Seven Suns, where Helen's friend Gracie was starting to make a life. But if that didn't work out he promised himself he would buckle down and get back to school, guaranteed.

The Frisbees in Hyde Park must have lingered somewhere in the recesses of his thoughts, infecting his emotions, because, after taking the northbound train from the Fifty-Ninth Street Station, as he walked west on Jackson toward the Sears Tower, so solid and black with the twin white towers crowning its top, the astonishing sight filled him with a keen sense of loss. He had been destined to preside in a building like this; he had been destined to convey the same air of hurried importance that was carried, along with their briefcases, by the men and women in suits buzzing around him. He thought of the money he'd be earning, of the sprawling manse or townhouse he'd be living in, of the joy of barking orders to minions over the phone, of the way he'd be looked at as he walked down the street or took lunch at the club, so different from the snuffs he was getting now. He always thought he would have been a crackerjack lawyer and the sight of that high shiny building looming over him pressed a regret into his heart.

But it wouldn't have been his job; it would have been his father's. And the life wouldn't have been the rich multifaceted thing he was creating day by day; it would have been something he picked off the rack, like an ill-fitting suit. He tried to convince himself of the rightness of every choice he had made—even with the big house and high status in the world of business and money as the alternative—and he was doing a pretty good job of it, until he glimpsed his reflection in the shiny window of a passing shop.

The sight stopped him cold.

No briefcase, no power tie, no hundred-dollar haircut or thousand-dollar suit. Instead there were holes in his jeans, his sandals were ragged, his denim shirt was wet with sweat and crusted with salt, his beard was scruffy, and his long hair frizzled out beyond his shoulders. Compared to everyone else in the Loop he looked homeless. And then he realized, traveling from one coast to the other alongside Helen, with just a van to their names, that's exactly what he was.

For a moment he wanted to scream, or to cry, or to do both at once.

The elevator zipped him high up into the tower, where he took a second elevator to the ninety-eighth floor and the lobby of the august law firm of Keck, Mahin & Cate, specializing in all manner of corporate quackery. The receptionist eyed him like he had fallen off a slop car.

"Look at you, the conquering hero," said Finnegan, after coming out to the lobby to rescue Oliver from the receptionist's hostile glare. Finnegan wore a brown suit, a yellow shirt, a wide striped tie, aviator glasses, and had grown the thick mustache of a man on the make. It took Oliver an awkward moment to recognize him. Finnegan had also stared back at Oliver for an uncomfortable span, not sure what he was seeing, before a smile of recognition broke onto his face and they embraced with genuine warmth.

"Let's go to my office."

Finnegan led him out of the lobby and hustled him through the white-walled corridors lined with secretarial desks parked outside endless rows of office doors. The secretaries typed, typed, the phones rang, rang, the fluorescent lights buzzed, buzzed as they painted the frantic scene of commerce in their too-white light. Everyone they passed rushed about as if being chased, everyone but Oliver, who made it a point to stroll casually through these halls of money, exaggerating his saunter, as if he had learned how to walk from Robert Crumb. Finnegan had to stop and wait for him a couple times as passersby gawked at Oliver, before shooing him into a small plain office with one wide window.

"Hold my calls, Debby," said Finnegan before closing the door behind him. "Nice view, huh?"

The window was facing north, and from up so high the northern part of the city spread out like a carpet running toward the John Hancock Center and the lake. Oliver could just make out Wrigley Field in the distance. Well beyond that, as the coast continued up toward Milwaukee, would be his father's house in Highland Park.

"On windy days," said Finnegan, "this whole building shifts back and forth like a ship on the ocean. Get a chick up here at night, put her against the window as the building's heaving, and man, I can tell you from experience that's something."

"Good thing the window glass is thick as a finger," said Oliver.

"You're telling me."

"Are you married, Finn?"

"Not yet, I'm having too much fun. Division Street is like an inexhaustible market of twiff. And the truth is, I've been too busy to get serious about anything but the job. How about you? You still with that girl you met at the demonstration?"

"Yep. She's pregnant."

"Wow, Oliver. Congratulations, man. When did you two get married?"

"We're not. I mean, we had a ceremony of sorts with a Wintu shaman out in the woods, drums banging, sparks rising from the fire, all that, but it wasn't, you know, sanctioned by the state. We're not big on being sanctioned by the state."

"Ah, okay. Is she still as hot as she was?"

"Well, you know, six months pregnant."

Finn made his classic no-ice-cream-for-you face and Oliver laughed.

"I was so glad to hear from you, man," said Finn. "How long has it been? Why did you just disappear?"

"I didn't disappear, I was just doing my own thing. But we're heading cross-country and decided to stop in Chicago on the way. I thought I'd say hello. I didn't even have to look you up, I remembered your mom's number."

"She was so happy to hear from you. She always thought you were going places. She used to call you the senator."

"I thought you said she liked me."

Oliver looked around at the office, as claustrophobic as a coffin. There was the window, sure, and a file cabinet, and cartons filled with ever more files on the floor, and a desk, piled with papers and the kind of law reporters he had lived with as a law student, but that was it. Finn's office was as personal as a rock, so why did it look so cozy and full of possibilities?

"Tell me, Finn, what do you do at this place?"

"Mergers and acquisitions," he said, and Oliver had to turn to hide his expression. How often do you get to see your alternative life playing out in real time? This could have been his office, that caterpillar over Finn's lip could have been his lush mustache, he could have had the bachelor pad in Lincoln Park, he could have been bringing girls in tight dresses up from Division Street to bang from behind at the high window while the tower trembled beneath their feet. If Helen were with him one look would have blunted the dagger of jealousy, but Helen was still in Hyde Park and the dagger was stabbing deep.

"The big time," said Oliver.

"The hours are killer but the issues are really interesting and we make the front page of the *Journal* when the deals are announced. There is more work than we can handle and bigger and bigger deals are coming our way every day."

"So how did a middling student from Loyola land a gig at a high-class joint like Keck, Mahin & Cate?" Oliver asked, a little cruelly.

"Well, you know, I have some charm, along with a sort of runtish ambition," said Finnegan, laughing. "But also, your dad made a call."

"My dad?"

"He's become like a mentor."

"My dad?"

"Yeah. He's been really helpful. He helped get me the job and he's been referring deals his firm can't handle because of conflicts. I don't know where I would be without him."

It took all of Oliver's willpower to put a smile on his face now when facing an old friend who had just died to him.

"Well good for you, Finn. It's what you always wanted. You didn't, like, tell your mentor I was coming, did you?"

"Yeah, I did."

"Finn."

"Man, he helped me. I owed him."

"You shouldn't have done that."

"He's your father."

"I know who the hell he is."

"I thought we could maybe all have lunch together."

"Bad idea, man."

"Yeah, he thought it was a bad idea, too."

"Good."

"He wants to have lunch with you alone."

"What the hell?"

"Twelve thirty at the University Club."

"Finn."

"I'm up for partner in two years, Oliver. You don't know the pressure, man. And where the hell have you been?"

The University Club, housed in a narrow Gothic skyscraper on East Monroe, had been an integral part of Oliver's childhood. When Oliver's mother was still alive, she would often take Oliver and his brother to the Art Institute and the three would invariably lunch at the club. In a formal room overlooking the park, wearing jackets and ties in accordance with the club's strict dress code, Oliver and Fletch would saw at their steaks and sit stiffly with the manners of the well-born as Oliver's mother kept the conversation lightly rolling along in that enthusiastic way of hers. Oliver's grandfather on his mother's side, a graduate of Yale, had been a longtime member of the club, and Oliver's father, a graduate of Northwestern, had been admitted shortly after his marriage. When Oliver had decided to forego his own acceptance at Northwestern to go to Beloit, he assuaged his father's concerns about the lefty reputation of the college by pointing at Beloit's stained-glass window in the club's Cathedral Hall.

But now, in the face of the University Club's Gothic grandeur, Oliver hesitated.

He had thought about not going, had absolutely decided to head back down to Hyde Park and get the hell out of Dodge, leaving his father waiting at the table with his anger and his martinis. Whatever interactions he had had with his father after leaving law school had been like life in the Middle Ages as described by Hobbes: nasty, brutish, and short. There had been a few awkward calls, all of which went very poorly, and a surprise visit by his father to a house squat he and Helen were sharing in San Francisco, a crowded, rat-infested tumbledown that felt like a new world to Oliver but was a sign of squalid mental illness to his father. Oliver hadn't seen or talked to his father in almost four years, and that seemed to suit them both. There was no reason to ruin the good thing they had going.

But the feelings stirred in Oliver by his visit to Finn, the jealousy and a nagging sense of his own failures, forced him to make his way toward the puzzled doorman standing guard under the green awning at the club's entrance.

"This is the University Club, sir. I don't think—"

"I'm expected," said Oliver, brushing right by and striding like Mr. Natural through the front door.

He was building something new with his life, exploring radical freedom, radical love. He was creating a new kind of family, a new way of being in the world, and he wasn't going to let anything, and certainly not the specter of his father or his own newly honed sense of regret, make him feel ashamed about his path. Just showing up was a statement, and Oliver was always one for statements.

When Oliver appeared, finally, at his father's table in the grillroom of the club, a table set discreetly by the tall windows in the corner of the vaulted room, he was wearing a blue blazer with a crest on its pocket and a pair of shined oxfords a size too big. The outfit change had been suggested, or rather insisted on, by the staff at the front desk, and when Oliver tried to make a scene he was frankly told that the only reason he would be allowed to dine, even in the more socially approved outfit, was that his father was a respected member of the club and his grandfather had a plaque in the locker room, which Oliver was urged to visit so he could wash up before his luncheon. "There are razors available at the sink," he was told.

"So you made it," said Oliver's father, glaring at his son with an angry smile from above the sharp lapels of his navy pinstriped suit. His voice was hearty and full of false cheer. "I thought you would chicken out."

"Why would I do that?"

"Because that's what you do, Oliver. Chicken out. And I see you cared enough to dress for the occasion. The generic club jacket always sends the right kind of message. Don't be shy, take a seat."

Oliver pulled out a chair and slumped into it. He always seemed to revert to a rebellious twelve-year-old around his father. His father took a drag from his cigarette before snubbing it out in an ashtray, already well butted, and finishing off his martini. He looked strong, well heeled and well fed, but also older than Oliver remembered. His face had broadened, his hairline had risen, his teeth seemed too big, his forehead was starting to spot, and his eyes, his eyes were narrow slits topped with unruly eyebrows.

Oliver grabbed a menu. "What's good?"

"Nothing," said his father. "That's the way we like it, here. Everything is mediocre. Keeps the frou-frous out."

"Mom always ordered Fletch and me the steak when we came."

"The steak's all right. Unless you don't eat meat anymore, in solidarity with the poor oppressed animals, slain to feed our raging appetites."

"Poultry of the world unite," said Oliver. "You're right. I'll have a salad."

"Why didn't you tell me you were coming to town?"

"I didn't need to, not with Finn around."

"He's a good boy, that Finnegan. I had my doubts when you were palling around with him, I thought he was a bad influence, but I've had to reconsider who was influencing whom. It's nice to see him come into his own."

"With your help."

"I try to be useful." He turned to the waiter who had silently appeared. "I'll have the New York strip, blood rare. My son will have a salad. What kind of salad, Oliver?"

"The salad nicoise," said Oliver.

"There's tuna in that, isn't there?" said Oliver's father.

"Yes, sir," said the waiter.

"Fish okay, then, Oliver?"

"Yes, fish is okay."

"Splendid. I've always said consistency is overrated. Hobgoblins and such. And I'll have another martini. Oliver, something to drink?"

"Gin."

"With tonic?" said Oliver's father.

"No, just gin."

"It's going to be like that, is it?"

"Over ice," said Oliver.

"Very good," said the waiter before sliding away as quietly as he arrived.

"So what are you up to these days, Oliver? What great achievements have you brought back from California?"

"I have a pretty decent tan."

"And I thought you just hadn't bathed. The dean of Northwestern Law School is a friend of mine. Just this morning I was speaking to him about you."

"I wish you hadn't."

"He's intrigued. He believes you could contribute a unique voice to the campus discussion. And he was impressed with your grades at Michigan."

"Aren't those confidential?"

"Just a proud papa bragging about his boy."

"I'm on my way to Colorado."

"Boulder has an acceptable law school, too. I could make some calls."

"There's a farm at the foot of the mountains and some like-minded folk. We're going to try to create something new."

"Farming, is it? Ah, the farming life. Sleep late, soak up the sun for a few hours, flit around the rest of the day like mayflies. That's why people keep running back to the farm. The lifestyle is so leisurely. And you want to create something new, you say? They've only been farming for ten thousand years. I'm sure you'll revolutionize the thing."

"A new type of farm, based on equality of work and reward, of community, of family, of something that's not fouled by the rawness of capitalism or the judgments imposed by false religions. Something clean and free and beautiful."

"It's amazing that hasn't been tried yet. Maybe you ought to call Brezhnev, tell him what you're attempting. Put him on the right path."

"I'm glad you understand."

"How many would give their eyeteeth for what you've turned your back on."

"Talk to the dean about them. I'm living my own life."

"You're throwing it away is what you're doing. Ah, the drinks. Yes, thank you. To your future . . . shoveling cow shit."

As his father tippled the martini, Oliver took a long swallow of the gin. Hard and tart and cold. Just what he needed for a lunch with his father, though to be honest, this was more pleasant than he imagined. His father was almost cheery in his raging disappointment, which added a nice note to the meeting, sort of like the juniper in the gin.

"Helen's pregnant," said Oliver, with a touch of bravery brought on by the bite of the alcohol.

"She's the girl from Bryn Mawr, right, the redhead with all the freckles?"

"That's right."

"Who's the father?"

"I'm the father."

"You sure? I keep on reading about free love in *Time* magazine. It makes one wonder."

"I'm the father."

"Well then, congratulations are in order. I suppose you'll be making an honest woman of her."

"She is an honest woman, the most honest I've ever met."

"Your mother was married when she had Fletcher and you. Something honest about that, wouldn't you say?"

"Mom would have loved Helen. She would have been thrilled to her boots by all this. I can hear her crying with joy."

"Or maybe just crying. So you're going to raise this child on the farm. In the dirt."

"At one with the earth, you mean? Yes, that's the plan."

"I'm sure that will work just dandy."

"Why can't you be happy for me, Dad? I'm going to be a father. You're going to be a grandfather."

"To a bastard."

"If it's a girl we're going to name her Saffron. The color of a Buddhist robe."

"Yes, that will go over well in junior high."

"And if it's a boy, we're going to name him Fletcher," said Oliver, and when he did something cracked in the grotesquery of his father's performance. The smile dimmed, the eyes widened and leaked a sorrow that all the bluster was designed to hide. For a moment he looked like Nixon on the day he resigned, the upper lip stiff in front of a cracking veneer—*Always remember, others may hate you, but those who hate you don't win unless you hate them, and then you destroy yourself*—and suddenly father and son weren't adversaries, apostles of two lives so different they could have been lived on different planets. They were just two men linked by a single loss, neither one yet fully recovered.

"Do you still miss him?" said Oliver's father. "I sometimes miss him so much it takes my breath away. And your mother, too. Never got over that one, I can tell you. Never will."

"Why don't you quit, Dad? Get out of the race."

"You want me to farm? Like a fool."

"Do something else, anything else. Head toward the sun. Hike the Grand Canyon. Hell, hike the Himalayas."

"I can't, boy. I have responsibilities."

"What responsibilities?"

"To the firm. To my love for your mother. To the memory of your brother. To the very order of things. It matters, the life we live, the burdens we take on, it all matters. You don't seem to get that. I tell you, Oliver, I sometimes think the wrong child went to war. You were the one who should have gone."

"Thanks, Dad."

"No, you would have survived. I fully believe that. You have the instinct that would have found a cushy job in Saigon to last your enlistment. Just like you're whiling away your life out of the fray. You wouldn't have rushed to organize a counterattack against an ambush like your brother. The captain said it was an act of bravery above and beyond. I wouldn't have had to worry about that with you. I should have known better."

Oliver caught a flinch from his father, just a slight narrowing of the eyes, but it was enough. "Better than what?"

"Where's our food? How long does it take to cook a steak rare? Not long, that's the point of it."

"Why did Fletcher enlist?" said Oliver. "I was never really clear on that."

"He did it because it was the right thing to do. Because you can't let other people fight your wars."

"Nice bumper sticker. But that can't be all of it. Did you push him to go? Did you set him up for a commission just like you're trying to set me up to return to law school?"

"He enlisted because he was taking control of his future. He had a great future destroyed by a communist bullet. You destroyed your future all on your own."

"It was on your advice, wasn't it?"

"Good cross-examination technique, that. Something got drummed in during your single year."

"Answer the question."

"Fletcher made his own decision."

"And that's what I'm doing," said Oliver, bunching his napkin off his lap before tossing it onto the table. "Thank you for the lunch. Funny thing was that visiting Finn, and then being here in the club, seeing you, I was starting to have regrets. But you solved them for me. This life of yours, what has it gotten you? A big house, a big job, a place at this grotesque club. But who's left to share it with?"

"Just know you get not a penny from me for you and your bastard until you live up to your responsibilities."

"And what are those? Following your lead in all things, like Fletcher did? For you, it all comes down to money, doesn't it? Well I don't want or need your money. I'm off that train."

"You'll come back begging for it. And when you do, you know where to find me."

Oliver stood, kicked off the oxfords, yanked off the jacket and tossed it on the chair. "Let me tell you something, Dad. If I ever become as bitter as you, I'll just shoot myself and get it over with."

As he made his barefooted way out of the grillroom, his father called after him, "What about your salad, Oliver? Think of the poor tuna that gave its life for your salad."

Still retreating, Oliver turned his head and yelled behind him, "Fuck the fish."

"That a boy," yelled back Oliver's father with a broad smile as the other diners looked on with horror on their pasty faces. "Now you're getting it. There might be hope for you yet."

He kept it together, Oliver Cross, kept it together as he rode the elevator down, and grabbed his sandals from the front desk, and stooped to buckle them back on, and walked to the train, and rode it back to Hyde Park and Helen. He kept it together until they were back in the van and Helen was driving them west, past Iowa City on Route 80, when he broke down into tears.

"What?" said Helen in response to the sobs that erupted seemingly out of nowhere. "Oliver, what?"

"We need to make this work," said Oliver. "This has to work."

"It will, darling," she said. "For all of us."

When Helen and Oliver finally arrived at the foothills of the Rockies, they made the turn at the bottom of a hill shaped like a pyramid, as if a marker had been left for just their generation. The van rattled like a broken vase and spewed smoke as they made their way down the pitted drive, flanked by rising hills covered with brush. The road passed a reservoir before opening onto a long magic valley hidden within the comforting arms of the mountain. Helen parked the van by a large juniper tree, its bright branches spreading out like a gorgeous Japanese fan. A thin woman in a long shift, who had been stooping in a field by the end of the road, raised herself to standing.

Gracie.

All around her, amidst the weathered buildings, were well-tended patches of growth, with larger fields and their neat rows of crops stretching out between two running ridges of the mountain. Gracie's back was straight, her long blonde hair was tossed by the breeze. She raised a hand full of carrots streaked with dirt, and positioned the bright-green tops to shield the sun as she peered at their approach. Standing there with her back straight, the wind ruffling her hair, and the sun shining through the gauzy fabric of her loose skirt, she looked to be the very symbol of their rich and fertile futures.

Oliver put his hand on Helen's swelling belly and said to his unborn child, "Wake up, little darling, we're finally home."

17

REBEL REBEL

Oliver Cross has been here before, let loose on the highway, both chasing and running away at the very same time, a king of the road.

He felt the bracing jolt of liberation when he dashed over the county line, and another when he headed out of Pennsylvania, as if he had been signing his own Declaration of Independence—*I hold this truth to be self-evident, that I am finally traveling free and oh so easy, and all the rest of you sons of bitches can suck it*—and that sense of elation has stayed with him. He grew accustomed to staying in one place, with the rootedness of an ancient oak, tied down first by family, later by Helen's illness and his own treatments, and then by the criminal justice system as it twisted its screws into his neck, but here, now, shuddering ever forward as the miles churn beneath him, he is again traveling hopefully—even if his hope is as cratered and singed as a battlefield—and it is as if he is traveling back to himself.

It was the way he felt when he drove with his pregnant wife to make a go of it on Gracie's farm, and before that the way he felt when he hitchhiked west to California the first time with Helen, and before that the way he felt when he boarded the bus on his way to Philadelphia to seize a life of utter freedom with his one true love. And yes, he knows it is illusory, this euphoria, and that the sum total of those other journeys somehow turned to shit, and yet he can't help but revel in the emotions of it. The sheer intoxication of unbounded expectation.

Somehow it makes him want to cry.

Somehow it makes him want to sob out huge honking tears, the kind he hasn't let loose since the moment Helen slipped away from the world like a thief into the eternal night, taking everything he gave a damn about with her. And he would have let loose like a wailing red-faced infant if the girl, Ayana, weren't sitting there in the front seat, with only the dog between them.

The dog barks as if he can sense Oliver's welling emotion. Oliver looks over and sees the dog staring at him like a hypnotist.

"I think he needs to go," says the girl.

"Dog bites man," grunts Oliver.

"Hunter doesn't bite, does he?"

"That's not what I meant."

"Then why did you say it? It was like you were giving him an order. You wouldn't bite me, would you, Hunter? No, you wouldn't, you good little boy."

Oliver doesn't try to educate her on the expression, but the idea of the dog pissing raises the urge in himself. It doesn't take much anymore. He pulls the truck to the shoulder of the road.

"I'll walk him," she says.

"No, stay by the truck," says Oliver. "I'll do it. I could use a little relief myself. This shouldn't take more than ten or twenty minutes. Thirty tops."

She looks at him like he's grown another head.

With his back bent and his feet splayed, Oliver walks the dog across a strip of weeds on the edge of the highway and stands before a stand of trees. Cars scream by as he lowers his fly. He is waiting for something to happen as Hunter squats, pisses, sniffs, and craps, and then goes about sniffing all over again. If there were a bitch around, Hunter would mount her, finish her off, and share a cigarette while Oliver waits for the first dribble. Oliver was feeling good about himself, almost young again, but the dog has set him straight.

When his pathetic splattering is as over as it's going to get, Oliver leads the dog back to the truck, walking right past the pile of crap.

"You're just going to leave it there?" says Ayana, leaning against the passenger door.

"Fertilizer," says Oliver.

"I'm sure the guy who steps in it will agree."

"Then he shouldn't have bought such fancy shoes."

The girl laughs before looking down at the weathered brown boots Oliver wears. "I suppose that's not a problem for you."

"I used to muck the fields with a wheelbarrow, black army boots, and my bare fists."

"Remind me not to shake your hand, old man."

"Now you're learning," says Oliver.

Oliver hears a clatter churning down the road and stops to look. A motorcycle, red and black with twin exhaust pipes and a helmeted rider wearing a jacket of the same colors, roars past and Oliver feels a bout of rebel solidarity. That would have been him fifty years ago, maybe, except motorbikes are always so loud, and the vibrations jangle the bones, and the bugs get caught in your teeth. Yeah, rebel rebel. Slowly and painfully he climbs into the truck and jams the stick shift into gear.

The miles churn beneath them as they bounce along on a rutted asphalt road surrounded by wild green hills. Every so often the speed limit lowers and they hit a little cluster of strip malls, big-box crapereries, fast-food poisonaries. The sight saddens him, as if the great capitalist dog has crapped on the road and no one has bagged it and trashed it. It makes him feel a little guilty about leaving Hunter's leavings all over the place, but only a little. In the congested stretches Oliver dutifully slows down to stay safely within the limits of the law, keeping an eye on any cop he sees in the rearview mirror.

Reminding himself that he is indeed on the run gives Oliver a jolt of joy, until he remembers he's not just running. He is heading into Ohio with a purpose other than escape, and as they grow closer to Frank's brother with every mile, he begins to reconsider his plan. Plan? Truth is, other than chasing after Frank Cormack, overtaking the son of a bitch, and throttling him senseless before sending his granddaughter back home, Oliver doesn't have a plan.

"Do we know the brother's address in Chillicothe?" says Oliver.

"Not now we don't."

"A name?"

"Cormack, probs. It's his brother. Unless it's his half brother. Then we might be screwed."

"When was the asshole there?"

"Right after he stole the shipment and they flew the coop. He didn't stay long."

"Why not?"

"Because Teddy had someone waiting on him, that's why."

"But they didn't get him."

"He slipped through. That's why Teddy came to you."

"Still, he might have spilled his next move before he ran. We need the brother's address."

"We had it before you threw it out the window."

"What's that you say?"

"It was on my phone."

Oliver drives on, nodding silently, chewing his cheek. "And you didn't think," he says finally, "to tell me that before we drove off?"

"My mind went blank from the shock. I couldn't believe you would do anything so stupid."

"You don't know me very well."

"But I'm getting the idea. If I had a phone I could, like, type in the name and the town and Google would spit it out."

"If you had a phone you could call the Russian," says Oliver.

"I'm in this stinking truck with you to get away from that fool. Why would I call him?"

"You tell me."

"I wouldn't. Not even on a bet. You don't trust me."

"Not an inch. Where do you think you're going to end up anyway?"

"I don't know. Frank's headed all the way to California, right? Maybe we'll have to chase him there to find Erica. That would be something. You ever been to California, old man?"

"The name's Oliver."

"Oliver, yeah. Like the movie. 'Please, sir, I want some more.'"

"I never heard that one before," says Oliver.

"It was a line. In the movie."

"I've lived in California. Nothing special, just a place, same as everyplace else."

"Oh, I don't think so, Oliver. Palm trees, surfer movies, In-N-Out Burger, sunsets over the Pacific, Humboldt County."

Oliver snorts. "What do you know about Humboldt County?"

"Nothing but what I smoked. That's the point. I bet you can just get high sitting in the mountains in Humboldt County."

"What you get is wet and cold mostly."

"When were you in California?"

"In my twenties."

"Why'd you leave?"

Oliver shucks up a glob from his throat, rolls down the window and spits. How to answer such a question? He lets the wind wash his face before he rolls the window back up and says, "When I got there the times they were a-changin'. Then they changed."

"I know what you mean."

"No you don't."

"I was in high school, Oliver, it's the same thing."

"Don't be stupid."

"You don't need to jump down my throat all the time. Why are you so mean?"

"I'm old and I don't have time for bullshit."

"I'm just trying to keep the conversation flowing."

"We don't need flow. No flow."

"What about just being nice?"

"You know what nice gets you?"

"I don't know. What?"

"I don't know either."

◆ ◆ ◆

"So who was that Andrew Carnegie?" says Ayana. They are walking along Orchard Street, treed and dark and residential, not far from the Chillicothe Library, where Ayana used the computers to find this address. Oliver thought it best to park around the corner in case neighbors were watching.

"Some rich, dead guy," says Oliver.

"The plaque said he built that library and thousands of others."

"It's easy to be generous on the backs of the working man."

"It's also easy just to drink mai tais."

"He did that, too," says Oliver. "Which one is it?"

"It should be that one."

"Good. Okay. You keep your mouth shut, right?"

"What do you think I'll say?"

"I don't know. That's the point. But I have a story. What do you have?"

"Charm?"

"Stop making jokes."

The house is small, boxy, with a picket fence and a sedan in the driveway. The lights are off, and for a moment, as Oliver knocks on the door, an almost dainty tap for him, he wonders if no one is home, but eventually the living room light switches on. When the door opens, Oliver sees a stout blond man, shoeless in jeans and a T-shirt, with a beer in his fist and a face full of bruises.

"Todd Cormack?" says Oliver.

"What about it?" Cormack says.

"Got a minute?"

"It's late."

"Not too late for a beer."

Cormack looks at Oliver and then at Ayana, giving her a quick and nervous double take before stepping back in resignation and opening the door wide for them to come inside. The house is cheaply built, Oliver can tell, the walls thin, the floor laminate, the furniture distressed and redolent with the faint scent of mold. The American dream in Chillicothe.

"What's it about, this time?" says Cormack before slopping a slug of beer into his mouth.

"What happened to your face?"

"I stepped on a rake."

"We're looking for your brother."

"You and the marines. I've got nothing new for you."

"How about a beer?"

Cormack is about to bark at Oliver, but then he glances at Ayana and his chin drops. "Her too?"

"Sure, thanks," says Ayana.

"How old are you?" says Oliver.

"Nineteen."

"Just me," says Oliver.

"What?"

"Sit down and stay quiet," says Oliver.

The girl pouts as she drops onto a green couch, stretches out her arms on the sofa back, and props her boots onto the edge of the coffee table. Cormack stares at her for a moment before turning and limping into the kitchen.

"He's sweet on me," says Ayana over the sound of the refrigerator opening.

"He's scared of you," says Oliver.

"Why would he be scared of me?"

"I don't know," says Oliver. "But I shouldn't have brought you."

"That's funny, Oliver, I thought I brought you."

Cormack returns with two fresh beers and keeps one for himself. "So you're still looking for him," he says.

"Still?"

"Which means he got away again. Too bad. Like I told you before, I don't know where he is, I don't know where he's going. All I hope is that he never appears in my life again. Is that clear enough? Drink up and then say goodbye."

"Who did you tell all this to before?"

Cormack looks at Oliver and then at the girl. "Who are you again?"

"Ayana," says Ayana.

"When your brother showed up here," says Oliver, "was there a girl with him, about her age?"

"Sitting right there," says Cormack gesturing at the couch with his beer, "with the same snarky smile and her boots muddying up my coffee table just like that."

"That was my granddaughter," says Oliver Cross.

Cormack narrows a swollen eye. "What was her name?"

"Erica," says Oliver. "Erica Cross."

"And who are you?"

"Oliver Cross."

There is a moment when sympathy leaks out of Cormack's swollen expression before he glances again at the girl and his face hardens. "Who's she, then?"

"Ayana," says Ayana.

"A friend of my granddaughter's. Helping me look for Erica."

"Is that a fact," says Cormack. "Well, it's a shame about your granddaughter."

"Why?"

"Because she's messed up with my little brother, and once again he's done something stupid. I don't know all of it, but I know they're both running. It's been like that with him since the day he was born. He was always looking for the big score and trying to get it the easy way. He stole from my parents, he cheated in school. He was a good musician but cared more about the lifestyle than the hard work of banging out songs and plying them on the road. Now I've worked too hard and have too much on the line—a wife and kid, a job, this house, a goddamn life—to get messed up any more in his troubles. That's why I sent him packing when he came, no help, no money, nothing but the door. And when he left, she went with him."

"You didn't give him anything, your own brother?"

"To buy more drugs with? To get in more trouble with? My whole family's learned to say no. So that's what I did. And what did Frank up and do?" Cormack takes another swig of beer. "He robbed a mini-mart in my damn town. My own damn town. And a few hours later the police ended up right where you're standing now."

"Shit," says Oliver Cross.

"That's it right there."

"How long did Frank stay?"

"Long enough for me to tell him to get going and not to come back."

"He say where he was heading? Any clue at all?"

Cormack glances once again at Ayana, as if she is a stand-in for Erica and is just as in over her head. "Not a word," he says finally, shaking his head. "He just asked for money and I told him to go to hell, and that's where they went. Granddaughter. Isn't that a shit pie? I thought you were a little old to be working with them."

"You're talking about the Russian?"

"I don't know who they are, the thugs, but they're looking for him, too. And they didn't like my answers either."

"Thus the rake."

"They finally realized I had nothing to tell them, but they had their fun first. From the bandages on your face it looks like they might have had their fun with you, too."

"I got in a shot of my own."

"Then you did better than me. I just took it. Like I deserved it for even opening the door for Frank one last time. So he's got them on his ass, and the police, and now you. Let's have a toast." He hoists his beer. "My brother. I guess he finally hit the big time after all."

◆ ◆ ◆

Back in the truck, with a darkness descending over his skull far blacker than the Chillicothe night, Oliver slams the steering wheel. The dog yelps and Ayana winces. Whatever elation he was feeling has been swallowed whole by a far more familiar emotion: a sense of abiding futility. The journey to save his granddaughter is getting ever more urgent and ever more hopeless at the same time. He is failing again. Everything he ever touched has turned to shit, and that he thought this little jaunt should have been any different is just a testament to the rabid self-delusion that has scarred his entire life. He slams the steering wheel again, and then a third time. *Yelp, yelp.*

"What do we do now?" says Ayana.

"How the hell should I know?" says Oliver.

"Should we just head on to California?"

"By the time we get there it will all be over."

"Maybe we can fly to Santa Monica?"

"I skipped parole. I can't do shit."

"You want me to call the Russian, find out what they know?"

"If they know where he is they'll pick him up themselves. We have to beat them, not follow them."

"So what do we do?"

"I don't know." Slam. "I don't know." Slam. "I do not fucking know." Slam, slam, slam.

"Do you want to get high?" says Ayana.

Oliver turns to his right, peers past the dog to the girl, and feels the darkness of his depression turn red with anger. His breathing grows short, and what's left of his teeth start to grinding. He tastes the thick stream of rising bile and closes his eyes for a moment. When he opens his eyes again he feels the slight burgeoning of a distant calm. It's not much but it's enough to unclench his teeth.

"Sure," he says. "Let's get fucked up."

18

NIGHT BIRD FLYING

Oliver Cross lies fully clothed on his motel bed, his boots still on, his fingers webbed behind his head, his throat dry, his eyes closed, and his mind twisted in on itself.

He dragged the tape player from the car and now Jimi Hendrix's guitar envelops him in a cloud of nostalgia. There was a moment when everything seemed possible, without any limits on what his life could become, and the soundtrack to that moment was Hendrix. Smoking weed and listening to "Night Bird Flying" with Helen in his arms as they dreamed of a perfected future was as natural then as breathing. He can still feel her lying close, her smooth skin, her bare leg rubbing against his, her back pressed against his chest. He can still smell her, the essence of Helen, mixed with the sweet jasmine candles she used to burn in old Chianti bottles.

After the disappointment at the Cormack house—another dead end in a dead-end life—Oliver found a cheap motel not far away, and rented a single room so he could keep an eye on the girl. He didn't tell the clerk about the dog, but he asked for a first-floor room—for his arthritis, he said—and getting the dog from the truck to the room without being noticed was a breeze. Of course, as soon as Hunter was inside he barked and barked until Oliver filled one metal bowl with water and the other with food. Then Oliver staggered into the bathroom with his Dopp kit to brush his teeth. Blood swirled down the sink like he was jabbing a knife into his gums. He swallowed his night pills and grimaced into the mirror like an ogre.

Ayana was waiting for him when he came out, sitting cross-legged on one of the beds, fiddling with a joint. He sat across from her with an eagerness he didn't recognize.

"When was the last time you got high, Oliver?"

"I don't remember," said Oliver.

"Sure you do." She put the joint in her mouth and pulled it out slowly, wetting it.

"When my wife was dying."

"That must have been hard."

"I bought it for her, for the pain, and when she smoked she wanted me to smoke with her. She wanted the company. And then we pigged out together, which was good because by the end she had no interest in eating. But after a while she got too sick for even that, so we stopped."

"And not since then?"

"No."

"Why not?"

"It didn't seem right, me without her."

"So why now?"

"I'm missing her. Maybe she'll join me."

"It's pretty good shit," Ayana said firing it up, "but not that good."

And with his head now swirling as he lies in the bed, he figures it was some pretty good shit, because he is no longer an old man, or a young man, or anything in between. He is simply Oliver Cross, divorced from time and floating free above the whole of the nation.

The journeys back and forth across the continent conflate into a mosaic of his adventures with Helen: the pickup truck that stops for them outside of Pittsburgh; the deco jukebox in Butte, Montana that winks with the bass line; the strutting funeral procession on Bourbon Street; the diner in Denver that still serves Orange Whip; the jazz combo playing in a field outside Baton Rouge; the great American landscape rushing outside the rattling van's window as if he and Helen are the stillest things on earth. And San Francisco, San Francisco, when they first spy the Pacific from atop one of the city's endless hills and they know with that precious certainty of the young that the life they are beginning together will be nothing less than glorious.

Lying now stoned on the cheap motel bed, Oliver remembers everything. They lived in a ramshackle group house, linked themselves with a community of artists, and moved through that world as if everything under the sun was possible. Helen painted her astonishing freeform canvases, along with rogue murals on crumbling brick walls and great theatrical backdrops for productions all across the city; he wrote and acted, recited his poems, learned guitar and sang songs in the park, organized and protested, danced in leotards. It was perfect freedom, a perfect life, the promise of his breakout perfectly fulfilled.

Even with his eyes closed and his mind whirring across the land and into the past, Oliver can hear the girl puttering around the room, getting ready for bed. The image of her pulling the joint out of her mouth has stayed with him, the eroticism of the act bringing a whole batch of writhing flesh-colored memories to the fore. He licks his lips at the images of his sexual liberation. In the truck on their way to Chillicothe, the girl asked him why he had left California and the answer he gave seemed tersely profound at the time, but now, amidst the memories, proves itself to be weak and glib. Why did they leave California? Why did they walk out of such perfect freedom?

"You know why," Helen whispers to him, and a spurt of joy bursts into his chest at her arrival.

"Where have you been?" he says.

"Watching."

"I missed you."

"I miss you every moment."

"I'm lost, Helen, on the road to nowhere with nothing anymore to go on."

"You're on the road, at least."

"So why did we leave California?"

"It started going wrong," she said. "Remember? Right after Hendrix died."

Yes, that's right. He turns onto his side, away from the second bed and the girl so he can be alone with Helen. Hendrix died, and then Joplin right after, and the war that killed his brother continued churning despite their protests. And, slowly, amidst what seemed like perfect freedom, hard truths started breaking through. With all the choices, he had chosen everything, which meant he had chosen nothing. Helen had her studies and her art, but he had only drifted, which was sweet at first, since his previous life had seemed so stolid and planned, but soon slipped into a depressing purposelessness. And then the tourists came in their buses, gawking at the hippies, which made them feel like exhibits in a zoo. Oliver began searching for a larger truth to hang on to, flirting with all kinds of spirituality and drugs, determined to find the answer. He felt so close to it, so close to something bigger than everything.

And then the universe cracked.

When he recovered enough to see his new world clearly, he realized the great shifting freedom he had found in California solidified into something just as parochial as the suburbs of Chicago. There were just as many tropes to follow, just as much ambition and money hunger. As long as he kept his hair long and wore sandals or Frye boots and rolled a tight joint, he still fit right in, but Oliver never found purpose in fitting right in. His father fit right in, and so did his brother, and where had that gotten them? So they left San Francisco and tried heading north to live with an alternative community in the mountains, but that was more of the same. When Helen became pregnant, they both knew this was not the scene in which to raise their child. It was time again to hit the road.

"Remember the way we felt traveling to Gracie's farm the first time?" he says. "We were going to reinvent ourselves once again by pulling our food and our meaning from Mother Earth."

"What could be truer than finding a new life in the land?" she says.

"It was true for a while."

"But not forever."

"The only forever truth I ever found was in you."

He can feel her arms around him, her lips at his neck. "I've found another one, darling," she says, "and trust me, it can wait."

"At least you don't have to worry about tomorrow."

"I worry about all your tomorrows. And Fletcher's. And Erica's."

"There's nothing I can do for her anymore. I can't return home and there's no way forward. I'm done, I'm finished, I've nowhere to go except to you."

"But he wasn't telling the truth," says Helen, before reaching through the twirl of his high to scratch at his chest.

"Who wasn't telling the truth?"

"The brother. He was lying. He gave Frank help and money and probably knows where Frank and Erica went. Ask him again."

"But if the brother gave him money, then why did Frank hold up the store?"

"To throw off the Russian. How would the police end up at the brother's house right away?"

"Because Frank made sure they got his name," says Oliver.

"To protect his brother."

"Of course he would," says Oliver as he feels Helen pull him onto his back. "It's why they beat the brother bloody but not to death."

"Now you're getting it," she says as she crawls atop him.

He felt wisps of Helen before in their conversations, the breath of a breeze, a twitch in a muscle, but this is more, this is substantial, heavy, blithely erotic. The weed the girl gave him must have been positively supersonic because it is as if, with the help of the drug, the crack in the universe has widened and coming through is not just Helen's voice and Helen's love but her body too, unbuttoning his shirt as she once unzipped his fly long ago, opening to him again like a most precious flower.

He puts his hands on her soft, naked flanks, opens his eyes with a hope so rich, so rich it hurts, and he sees . . . he sees . . .

He pushes the naked girl off with a shout and heave so strong Ayana rolls right off the bed, flopping onto the floor and waking the dog, who yelps and growls before barking as if he has been kicked. Oliver rises from the bed like an avenging ghost with a bent back and stands over the naked girl.

"What the hell, Gracie," he says.

The girl looks up at him, naked and shocked, but not afraid, as if she has been here before, tossed on the floor like a piece of jetsam. "Why'd you do that?" she says. "I was just trying to be nice."

He can't help noticing the smoothness of her dark skin, the swell of her breasts. It's not the sight, but what it does to him that forces him to turn around.

"Put your clothes on," he says staring at the impression he left in the bed and then at the wall and the window beyond.

"You didn't have to get all violent about it. If you don't want me to—"

"Put your clothes on."

"Okay, fine. I was just—"

"Now."

"And who the hell is Gracie?"

"I was confused."

"That makes two of us," she says.

When she steps out of the bathroom, clothed with a T-shirt and a pair of shorts, he is sitting on his bed, his hands clasped before him, ashamed and angry. She stares at him for a moment, as if getting up the nerve to say something, before deciding against it and slipping silently beneath the sheets of her bed.

"I'm sorry," he says.

"Yeah? What for?"

"For not being clear."

"Oh, you were pretty damn clear. Throwing me on the floor like that was clear as a bell."

"No, before that. I must have said something, implied something. Why would you think . . . ?"

"Why wouldn't I? The way you only got one room."

"So I could keep an eye on you."

"The way you looked at me when I lit the joint."

"Maybe I was looking at the joint."

"The way you're a man like every other man. Look, it's no biggie. In my experience it's always expected and I just figured if you're going to take me to California, I'll just do—"

"You figured wrong," he says. "And even if it's always expected, you can always just say piss off. Trust me, it feels good to say piss off."

"I bet."

"Say it."

"Piss off."

"See. Which of the Russian's crew expects your favors when you stay with them?"

"None of your business."

"When push comes to shove, I just want to know which asshole's face to smash in first."

She laughed. "Ken."

"With the haircut?"

"Yeah."

"You don't think much of yourself, do you?"

"What about free love, Mr. Hippie Man?"

"With that asshole, what about it is free?"

"Maybe not all of us can afford to say no. Maybe some of us are just struggling to survive."

"It's easy to find excuses."

"Piss off."

"Good. Now you're getting it. So let's be clear. I'm taking you along to help find my granddaughter. I don't want anything from you except the truth. Got it?"

"Got it."

"If you think I'm after anything else, you know what to say."

"Piss off."

"Good. I'm sorry I wasn't clear before. I didn't think I had to be. Don't you know how old I am?"

"Old."

"Now here." He reaches behind him for a book, a ragged cloth-bound thing with library stamps on its edges. "I saw this in the library and got it for me. But you're the one who should read it."

"What is it?"

"Just a book," he says, handing it to her.

"How'd you take it out from the library? Did you get a card?"

"I didn't say I checked it out."

"Oh, you little thief."

"Back in the day, Abbie Hoffman wrote a thing called *Steal This Book*. It seemed right for this one, too."

"*On the Road* by Jack Kerouac. I heard of him, yeah."

"Read it. But be careful. It's like a bomb waiting to go off."

She laughs, hefts the volume in her hand. "A little like you, hey, Oliver?"

19

PIECE OF MY HEART

Oliver Cross rises from his bed like a dark specter in the thick of the night. The girl is sleeping, but Hunter is restless. Oliver laces up his boots, brushes his teeth, packs his clothes, and puts the leash on the dog, all with as little noise as possible. Even so, the girl awakens.

"What . . . what are you doing?"

"The dog needs a walk," he says.

"Okay. Good." Her head drops back onto her pillow. "Pick up the crap this time."

Outside, he leads the dog to the truck, throws the duffel inside, and drives to a nearby cemetery, where he lets the dog loose among the tombstones to do his business atop the dead.

As Oliver stands by the truck and waits for the dog to return, he hears a motorcycle approach. He turns just as a red-and-black motorcycle drives slowly by, the helmeted rider turning his head to stare at Oliver from behind the dark lens of the visor. Oliver fingers the lump at his neck as he follows the cycle's path until it disappears, leaving the road deserted again.

When Oliver turns his attention back to the cemetery, the dog is out of sight. He wonders for a moment if the dog has run off, maybe he hopes he has—he supposes a dog's life in Chillicothe, Ohio, is about as sweet as it gets for a canine—but the dog is evidently more worried about losing Oliver than Oliver is about losing the dog. Back he comes, his head hanging low, sniffing here and there, studiously ignoring Oliver even as he sacrifices pure freedom to stand by Oliver's side, looking away all the while, too proud to admit what just happened.

"That's all right," says Oliver as he opens the truck door and the dog jumps right in. "We all pretend not to give a damn."

He drives around until he finds an all-night mini-mart, fills up his tank with diesel and then a cardboard cup with coffee. He wonders if this is the same mini-mart stick-jacked by Frank Cormack. He thinks about asking but decides against it when he looks up and sees the camera in the corner. He smiles for his parole officer before paying. The first sip burns his mouth with heat and acid and it feels damn good.

He checks his watch—he doesn't want to be too early or too late—decides the time is right, and drives to the narrow street where Frank Cormack's brother lives. The old blue sedan is still in the drive. There is a no-thruway sign at the mouth of the street so Oliver turns around before parking the truck right in front of the driveway, blocking in the sedan. He turns off the engine and waits, sipping the coffee and letting the bitterness strengthen his disgust.

But he is not disgusted at Frank Cormack's brother. The brother lied, of course he lied; the only puzzle is why Oliver needed Helen to clue him in to that fact. If Oliver ever had the opportunity to lie—say to the draft board—in order to protect his brother, he would have jumped. Jumped! Why wouldn't Todd Cormack think Oliver was a threat? Why wouldn't he lie to Oliver as he had lied to the Russian? Oliver is here to remedy the lie, that is true, but he can't blame the brother for what he did. No, his disgust is for himself.

He knows he is many things—depressed, dour, decrepit, a useless piece of dying flesh—but after his encounter last night with the naked Ayana he knows now he is also a fatuous old fool. As a young man he wanted to change the world—a pathetically banal desire to begin with—and this is where it has led him; he has become a doddering dotard dispensing little bromides mined from a life of utter failure to those who don't give a damn.

But it's not too late to rip the impulse out by its roots. The next time he starts playing the wise old man, he's going to punch himself right in the face. He is smiling bitterly at the image of his own fist flattening his nose when the front door of the Cormack house opens and Todd Cormack appears. As he makes his uneven way down the steps and drags his lame leg along the drive, there is no mark of surprise on his face or in his movements; either he saw Oliver waiting or expected him all along.

Oliver climbs out of the truck, straightens his back as far as he is able, crosses his arms.

"It's time for you to go, Mr. Cross," says Todd. He is about Oliver's height but bulkier, younger, more fit, even with the bruises and the limp. It wouldn't be a fair fight, but when is it ever a fair fight?

"I told you I'm looking for my granddaughter," says Oliver. "What makes you think I won't keep coming back until you stop lying to me?"

"Self-preservation?"

"I've been beaten before. It tastes like licorice. You'll have to kill me to stop me."

"I looked you up," says Cormack. "You made yourself pretty famous. I read the whole tragic story in the Philadelphia newspapers. I can't say I'm not sympathetic."

"Fuck your sympathy."

"But I also learned you're still on parole. I wondered if this little trip out of state was authorized, so I called a friend in the local police force to find out." Cormack makes a show of checking his phone. "He should be here soon. I don't want you to go to jail, again, Mr. Cross. I just want you to go away and leave my family alone."

Oliver lifts a hand and rubs at the dent in his bald head. He hocks up a glop of phlegm that was stuck in his throat and spits it to the side.

"I was just a little younger than you when my brother was murdered," Oliver says. "He was killed by the politicians, by the generals, by the money grabbers keeping the war alive so they could sell more bullets and bombs. I think of him every day. Truth is, I still haven't recovered."

"I'm trying to help my brother."

"But you're not helping him, that's the point. He's in trouble. Bad people are chasing him. And now to protect you, he has the cops after him, too, probably ready to shoot on sight. Without help, he's going to end up dead. I'm the only one who might be able to give it."

"How?"

"Tell me where he went. I'm looking for my granddaughter, but if I find him, I'll help him any way I can."

"And I can trust you?"

"Who else is there? And you tell me, who would you rather have find your brother first? If you read about my case, you know I never denied a single fact. I told the bastards nothing but the truth. I thought it would be enough."

"Learned your lesson, huh?"

"I wouldn't change a thing. When my wife died, all I had left was the truth, no matter how hard to face. And I'm telling you this: your brother's undeserving of anyone's sympathy as far as I'm concerned, but if I find him, I'll help him. Like he was my own brother. Because of what happened to my brother. Do you understand?"

Cormack looks at Oliver for a long moment, then glances at his phone before looking down the street. "I wasn't lying about the cop. He'll be here soon."

"Then it's time to decide."

"I don't think you can help Frank," says Cormack. "I think he's too far gone. But he shouldn't be dragging down that girl with him. If you can save her, that might be enough."

Oliver stands with his arms crossed, saying nothing, since there is nothing to say. The brother licks a swollen lip before continuing.

"Frank had an old girlfriend in Chicago. Marisol. He was going to see her, try to scare up some extra cash before sprinting to the coast."

"You have a last name?"

"No. Just Marisol."

"An address?"

"That's all I have. She sings. Folk and protest songs."

"What's she protesting?"

"Everything."

"I know the type," says Oliver. "I'll be in touch."

"Please don't," says Cormack. "Just go."

And Oliver does go. But first he reaches out and shakes Todd Cormack's hand, one heartbroken brother shaking the hand of another, the handshake itself a sealing of Oliver's pledge.

As he is driving out of the street, a police car, lights dark and siren silent, passes him by. The cop peers into Oliver's truck, Hunter barks, Oliver makes the turn. He considers driving directly west to Illinois, but considers again, and heads back to the motel to wake up the girl.

◆ ◆ ◆

Oliver Cross hobbles around the front of the squat brick diner where they stopped for breakfast before slipping the phone out of his pocket and turning it on. He waits impatiently as it boots. There is a voice message. He presses the screen like he is trying to make a point in an argument with a Republican and then puts the thing tight to his ear.

Uh, Dad, yeah, uh, I assume that's you. So Jennifer came looking for you. She knows you're gone. I thought you were getting her permission. You left the county without permission? How stupid can you get, Dad, really? They're going to lock you up again. We don't need that with everything else going on. Christ.

I turned the phones you found over to the police. Apparently the water killed most of the circuits and the memory—the technicians said they were really foul—but they're trying to get what's left and maybe pull down some information from the cloud. They're especially looking for contacts.

And just so you know, things have taken a turn. That guy you said Erica was with, Frank Cormack? Well, when I gave the name to the detectives, they put it in the computer and it turned out that he's wanted for an armed robbery in Ohio. Yeah. And he gave his name to the clerk like he was some kind of Clyde Barrow, which is really troubling, because we both know how that worked out—you made me sit through that stupid video when I was like ten, remember? There's no telling what this jerk is capable of. But according to the police reports, Erica was not involved, which is something of a relief.

The armed robbery really got to Petra. She's beside herself. And so am I. I hope you're not out there mucking things up for the police. You should come back home, but you won't because that makes too much damn sense, right?

Why do I think I should be with you? Why do you always make me feel guilty? Jesus, Dad, yeah. This is a little rambling, I know. I'll get off. Don't forget to eat and take your pills. Please find her, please.

And Jennifer said you had a dog. What the hell is that all about?

Oliver grins as he listens to the message. He is angry because it has all gone to hell quicker than he ever imagined, but he is grinning because it has all gone to hell quicker than he ever hoped.

But now that he is officially on the run, he wishes he had run a little farther after getting out of Chillicothe. Except the girl had been grumbling that she was hungry, so he asked the GPS for a nearby diner and ended up at this dump in a town called Washington Court House. He considers calling Fletcher and telling him to snap the hell out of it, but he can't imagine the conversation being more productive than exasperating, so instead he decides to punch in a text.

His thumbs slide across the phone like arthritic eels.

"Where'd you go?" says Ayana when he returns to their table in the wide spare dining room and drops with a grunt onto his chair.

"To check on Hunter."

"How is he?"

"Still a dog. Think that's enough food for you?"

"Doubt it," says Ayana. He ordered a bowl of oatmeal and a cup of fruit. Before Ayana sits two plates loaded with fried eggs, a double order of bacon, home fries covered with white gravy thick with sausage, double toast. "Hey, ma'am, yo, lady," she calls out to the waitress.

"What can I do you for, honey?"

"How about a stack of pancakes."

"Short?"

"No, why? Do I look short to you? And do you have whipped cream?"

"We surely do."

"Lots. And more coffee. You too, Oliver?"

Oliver nods.

"Him too."

"Right away, hon."

"I'm sort of famous for my appetite," says Ayana.

As Ayana snaps a rasher of bacon between her teeth, Oliver swallows a spoonful of oatmeal and winces at the tastelessness. He could add sugar, but then he'd be adding sugar and Helen wouldn't approve. He feels bad enough about how their last conversation went so off the rails. Instead he eats a melon square, mushy and sour, and drinks the dregs of his coffee. The taste of freedom.

"When you left I couldn't go back to sleep, so I started that book you gave me," says Ayana as she grabs a forkful of potatoes. She is hunched over her food like there is someone plotting to steal it away. "That Ker-o-whatever guy's not really a very good writer, is he?"

Oliver doesn't look up from what constitutes his breakfast as he eats another spoonful of gruel. Please, sir, I want some less.

"It's just that his sentences are like weird," continues Ayana. "I kept on picking out things that were wrong."

"I suppose they taught you how to write in school."

"I was actually pretty good at it. The teachers always liked my poetry. They said I had a future."

"In what, competitive eating?"

"And now I'm on the way to Santa Monica. Maybe they were right after all." She looks up at him. "That's where we're going, right?"

"Eventually."

"Where are we going now?"

Oliver hasn't told her about his meeting with the brother. "West," he says. "In those English classes, you followed all the rules, right? Thesis statement, logical argument, summary with a kicker at the end, no run-on sentences."

"You're supposed to do all that."

"Yeah, well that Ker-o-whatever didn't give a damn about the rules."

The girl laughs. "You're such a rebel, Oliver."

"Not anymore."

"What are you now?"

"Cantankerous."

"What's the difference?"

"When you're a rebel, you want people to know it. Leather jackets, long hair, attitude. When you're cantankerous, you don't give a damn what anybody thinks."

"I don't give a damn."

"That thing in your nose says you're a liar."

"Piss off," she says.

"Tell me something. Which of the Russian's assholes has a red-and-black motorcycle?"

"Red and black? No one, why?"

"I thought I saw one like it back in Philly and then out here, too."

"I think you're seeing things, Oliver," she says as the waitress brings a stack of pancakes, covered with whipped cream, and a small glass pitcher of syrup. She finds a spot for the plate and pitcher in front of Ayana and refills their coffees. The girl looks at her pancakes and then at Oliver. "You want some?"

"Sure," he says, stabbing his fork into the topmost flapjack covered with all the whipped cream and sliding it into his bowl.

"Dude."

"I'm sick of oatmeal."

"Cantankerous is right."

With her fork she steals a mound of whipped cream from his pancake, and puts it on what's left of her stack. He steals some back with his own fork and puts it in his mouth. He forgot how good whipped cream tastes, like a child's laughter. He scoops another dollop.

"So where are we going?" she says.

He looks up at Ayana, whipped cream still on his fork. "I need to see an old girlfriend."

"Oh, Oliver, that's cute."

"Not mine," he says.

20

ALL MY FRIENDS

It wouldn't be enough for Frank Cormack just to cross America and then the Pacific and then all of Asia and half of Europe in order to breathe in the bracing air of unadulterated freedom, he would have to cross off all the failures of his past, too, one after the other, until his old life was finished off for good, without a vampire's chance of rising from its grave. Now, with its skyline appearing vaguely in the distance, he was headed back to the big town in the middle of everything to scrub it finally and forever off his list. It had been the first stop on his short-lived journey on the music train, the place where he found success and love and disappointment and finally a violence that had scarred his flesh and soul forever. He was coming home one last time to the city by the lake to put a stake in its fucking heart.

"'Hog butcher for the world,'" said Erica as the afternoon sun lit her red hair so bright it looked like a halo. "'Tool maker, stacker of wheat.'"

"What's that, sweet pea?"

"A poem my grandmom used to recite. She made me memorize it when I was a little girl. 'Player with railroads and the nation's freight handler. Stormy, husky, brawling.'"

"What's it called?"

"'Chicago.'"

"Ah, there it is."

"They met in Chicago, my grandmom and my grandfather. At some convention."

"What, like a sales convention?"

"A political convention. During the Vietnam War. There were these demonstrations. My grandfather went with a friend of his, some lawyer called Finnegan, and met my grandmother at the riot. They always said it changed their lives. I don't know what they would have been without the war. Accountants maybe."

"So the war might have been the best thing ever to happen to them."

"In some ways. I wouldn't be here without it, that's for sure. On the other hand, my uncle died in it."

"That sucks."

"They named my father after him. But the city at the time must have been so romantic: the demonstrations, the slogans, tear gas and violence, sex and drugs and rock and roll. Allen Ginsberg was there."

"No shit."

"He was in a circle, chanting by the lake with these little cymbals on his fingers. My grandparents were such hippies, and they fell in love in the middle of a riot in old Chi-Town. 'City of the big shoulders.' I can't wait to see it."

"It's just a town, and we're not going to see the sights. I have a friend I need to meet up with. You know, to set things up for California. One stop and then to the coast. And they don't really call it that. Chi-Town, I mean. Like they don't call San Fran Frisco."

They had stopped at the first rest stop beyond the Ohio state line, parked with their license facing the woods, and slept twisted around each other in the back seat. After waking, weary and sore, they stopped at a Hardee's and paid for the putrid feast with Todd's money. Then they headed west and north, before detouring around Gary, Indiana, to avoid the toll road because who the hell wanted to pay tolls.

"So who's the friend we're seeing?"

"Her name's Marisol. She's a singer, too."

"Marisol. Just a friend?"

"Now she's just a friend. Don't get jealous on me, sweet pea."

"Why would I be jealous?"

"You know. Everyone has a past and sometimes people start imagining things."

"Oh, I'm not imagining anything," said Erica. "And you shouldn't worry about me. You should just do what feels right for you, Frank."

"Listen to you. It touches my heart to know you care."

"And she's probably more your age anyway."

He laughed. "Older, actually. She was twenty-five when I showed up in Chicago, the same age I am now. I liked that she had experience."

"What did you have?"

"Youth."

He looked up at the skyline in the distance. It still had the outlines of hope in its tall towers.

"There was a group of us," he said. "Living in a house on the west side. Humboldt Park. Mostly artists, paying whatever rent we could. We cooked for one another and slept with one another and got high together. But most of all we supported one another. We went to the awful plays Tim was writing and the bars that put up Sheila's paintings. Khalia was working in a bookstore and trying to write her novel. She did poetry slams that we would come to and hoot at. Troy danced in these weird modern dance productions that put me to sleep. Marisol and I, when we weren't playing at this club or that coffeehouse, would sometimes play in the streets and our friends would pass us by like they didn't know us, dropping money in the guitar case to prime the pump. 'Thank you, stranger,' I'd say. And that night at the house, we'd give it all back."

"It sounds dreamy," said Erica.

"It was."

"So what happened?"

"You know, things turn."

"Like they turned in Philly?"

"That's the way life is, there's no fighting it. But not with you. With you I'm going to make sure it stays sweet as honey the whole way through. We're each other's destiny."

"We're each other's something, that's for sure. Can we get a hot dog? My grandfather always said the hot dogs in Chicago are the best in the world."

"Whatever you want. The full works. And I know just the place."

◆ ◆ ◆

They stopped at a squat brick building on a wide commercial strip with the city's skyscrapers looming over its shoulder.

Jimmy's Red Hots.

Below the menu that stretched above the counter, there was a sign with a ketchup bottle X'd out and the words NEVER EVER!! DON'T EVEN ASK ABOUT IT!! Frank laughed as he pointed it out to Erica. It made him miss Chicago, where they didn't take crap from anyone. City of the big shoulders indeed.

They bought three dogs, two orders of fries, and a couple fluorescent-yellow drinks. They stood at the counter beside a big-assed cop as they scarfed, just a couple kids having a late lunch. The cop didn't even look their way as Frank showed Erica how to squeeze the hot peppers that came with the hand-cut fries so that the juice squirted over the semisoggy spuds.

"What's with the whole ketchup thing?" said Erica.

"In this town there's a Chicago way and a wrong way. Ketchup on hot dogs is the wrong way."

"What about on the fries?"

"That's why they give you the peppers. What do you think?"

"Good," she said, wiping mustard off her mouth. "Not great."

"Tough critic. I used to come here constantly. I was such a regular, I even dated one of the girls who worked behind the counter. Deborah. Her skin smelled like hot dogs. I couldn't get enough of her. And of course, she gave me freebies."

"So you were a hot dog whore?"

"You bet your life. And the fries, don't forget the fries."

"I like them crispier. McDonald's-like."

"That's just sad. If you eat these little puppies in your car, they smell up the inside for days and it's like entering heaven every time you slip into the driver's seat. More than once in Philly I thought of just driving out here, buying a dog and fries, and then turning back."

"That would have been something."

"Yeah. But you know, things. When we get to Marisol's house, play it cool. I didn't leave on the greatest terms."

"What happened?"

"There were just issues, you know. Money, love, getting on each other's nerves. Money." He laughed. "But when push comes to shove, which is where we are now, these are the people I trust most."

The house was a narrow two-story pale-stone building with an iron gate and wooden steps, set up next to a small grocery store. To Frank, it looked exactly the same as when he had left it two years before. The trim was still peeling, the steps were still listing, the gate still needed paint and oil. Same stinking suburban landlord. The heat was probably still spotty, too. But even with its flaws, just looking at the pile of stone filled him with an aching nostalgia. What did he miss, the cozy house, the friends, the way he was then in his still aspiring youth? Or was it something else, someone else?

He hesitated for a moment, screwed up his confidence and enthusiasm—he knew he could always bluff his way past a little hesitance with outsize enthusiasm—and then skipped up the stairs.

Knock, knock.

After a few silent minutes, he spun around and kicked at one of the stones in the wall. "There's a place out back we can sit and wait," he said.

"My leg's been hurting," Erica said.

"I suppose that means you want to get high."

"Well, if you're asking."

He should stay straight for this, clearheaded, clean. He needed to look serious as all hell, different in every way from the way he left, but Erica's smile did him in.

There was a small cement patio in the rear of the house with an old grill and some mismatched lawn furniture. Frank and Erica were sprawled on a couple chairs, their feet propped on a rusting fire pit, laughing about nothing, their minds buzzing with the smoked Oxy and the reefer to chase it, when a window on the back side of the house slid open and a heavy woman with long graying hair poked her head through.

"I thought I recognized that heap of crap parked outside," she said.

"Hey, Sheila."

"What's going on, Frank?"

"Just passing through."

"Anyone know you're coming?"

"I thought I'd keep it quiet."

"Good idea. You bring Hunter with you?"

"No. I had to leave him back in Philly."

"That's too bad. He was the sweetest dog in Chicago."

"This is Erica."

"Welcome, Erica. Anything I can get you guys?"

"How about a shower?" said Erica. "We could really use a shower. Especially Frank."

Sheila laughed and said, "Sure. I'll meet you at the front."

The inside was just as he had remembered it. The same sagging couches in the living room with the turreted windows creating a nook, the same paintings by Sheila, the same bookshelf crowded with old paperbacks. Even the battered oak table in the dining alcove was still messy with envelopes and flyers. There was always organizing of one sort or another going on in that house: protest marches, art shows, theater pieces begging for an audience, the vote for one election after another.

"Troy's out with a touring company," said Sheila, "so you can use his room to change. There are towels in the upstairs closet."

"Thanks," said Frank. "I'll show her."

Frank led Erica up the twisting stairway to Troy's bedroom. It looked the same up there too, a time capsule. His room with Marisol had been down the hall. When he gazed at the closed white door he felt something tug at a string of emotion anchored deep.

"You have to wait awhile for the water to heat up," he said as he showed Erica the bathroom. "And don't expect it to get too hot. Tepid is about the best we get."

She looked at him strangely, as if he had shape-shifted the moment he walked in the door. And maybe he had. He left her in the bathroom and went downstairs to talk to Sheila, who was sitting now at the table, shuffling papers.

"What are you trying to save now?" said Frank. "The whales? The trees? The middle class?"

"They're beyond saving," said Sheila, without turning around.

"The whales?"

"The middle class. She's pretty. And quite young."

"About as young as I was when I first came to Chicago."

"You're not staying long, are you, Frank?"

"In and out, Sheila. On our way west."

"Good. Things have changed here a bit."

"For all of us," said Frank. "I was surprised no one was at the house when we showed. At least Khalia was always at home, working on the novel."

"She sold it," said Sheila. "Got herself a teaching job at Northwestern and a place in Evanston."

"Wow. Good for her."

"But the rest of us all have to work. Rent has gone up and we were getting tired of beans for dinner."

"That's easy to do. What about Marisol?"

"What about her?"

"Is she working, too?"

"At some advertising agency. Writing copy. But she still gigs when she can."

"When does she normally get home?"

"She's in a good place now. She's seeing someone. I think it's serious. She seems pretty happy."

"Good for her. We've both moved on. So when does she get home?"

"Why don't you leave her alone, Frank?"

"Why don't you mind your own fucking business?"

Sheila turned around, slowly and without anger. There was something close to pity on her face. "You're in trouble again. I can tell. The pressure changes you and not for the better."

"I just asked a simple question."

"It's like a skittering little bug slips into your eyes. How bad is it?"

"I only want to say hello. That's all."

"I don't believe you. I think you're bringing your new troubles back to her when the old ones aren't even taken care of. What happens when Delaney finds out you're here?"

"He won't. We're on our way west and then overseas. Gone for good. I don't know when I'll be back and I just wanted to say goodbye."

"I'll relay the message for you. I'm sure she'll be touched."

"We'll just wait here, then."

"Is she the problem, Frank? The girl? That Erica?"

"No," said Frank. "She's the solution."

Sheila nodded and turned back to her papers. "Marisol's playing tonight at Armstrong's. She's going straight there. But if you really cared about her, you'd leave her be."

"I'm done," Erica called down the steps. "Shower's free."

Frank turned and shouted up the stairwell, "Thanks, sweet pea. And put on something fresh, we're going out tonight."

21

SHAPE OF YOU

The rise of Frank Cormack's music career was like the trajectory of a rocket ship aimed for the heavens. Only it was the kind of rocket that struggles to rise off the launching pad and hovers just a few feet off the surface of the earth before tilting out of control and exploding in a massive ball of fire and woe.

And the pathetic pinnacle of that disastrous and short-lived flight were beer-sodden backroom bars with bad lighting and crowded tables and a burble of conversation just loud enough to rise above the distraction of the music being played from the stage. There's a circuit of such rooms in Chicago, and it included Armstrong's, an old stone tavern an outfielder's throw from Wrigley Field, with a great red globe carved into the center of its pediment alongside a banner reading SCHLITZ. Classy all the way.

It felt odd and sad being back. Frank and Erica took a table in the rear and ordered a couple beers without being carded. They watched some blond guy with a potato face wailing on the stage.

"You used to play here?" said Erica.

"I confess. They had an open-mike night on Mondays and that's where I started. One day the boss, *June!*—you had to pronounce her name like she did, with fifty years of cigarette smoke curling its edges—*June!* So *June!* called me over. 'I have a slot on Wednesdays if you want it,' she said. 'It doesn't pay much but it's something. What do you say?'"

"What did you say?"

"Hell yes is what I said. It was the greatest moment of my life. I was on my way. Wednesday nights."

"What happened?"

"I never got to Thursdays."

The singer finished his set and the audience gave him scattered applause. The drinks came as a technician started fiddling with the mike, the cords. Erica took a long swallow of beer and looked around, eyes wide. This wasn't much, he knew, but it was enough steps up from the coffeehouse where they had met to mean something to her.

"It must have been pretty cool, though, the whole professional musician thing," she said.

"It gets old fast," said Frank. "You hang out with the same Wednesday night people, drinking up your pay, putting out an EP that no one listens to, working shit jobs just to keep the dream alive. And you begin to resent everyone—those who are working the weekends and aren't as good as you, those who head out to LA even though they have no chance, those who are leagues better and make you feel like shit, even the saps sitting and drinking and talking over your set because they get to go home and have a life that's working for them in a way yours isn't working for you. And there's always one of your fellow performers, maybe with a little gray in her hair, telling you that she wishes she had gone to law school when she had the chance. 'Get out now, before it's too late.' And you're thinking that maybe she's right, except you never went to college yourself and so law school won't work. And then the resentment turns the writing into shit, so you're playing the same crappy songs on the same crappy night in the same crappy room to the same crappy losers, just waiting for *June!* to send you back to open-mike night."

"You're crying so hard," said Erica, "you're making me think of going to law school."

"Welcome to the music biz, birthplace of attorneys," said Frank. But his words didn't match his emotions.

He wanted to taste the bitterness, he wanted to feel so over his old dreams, he wanted to be all about the rush forward toward Freedom!—and that was the way he played it with Erica because he didn't want his doubt to dampen her resolve—but he couldn't shake the ache that had settled within him, eating at his bones.

When he had first played at Armstrong's half a decade ago, he had felt connected to something so rich it snapped the bass strings of his soul. He was a member of a community dedicated to solidarity and to art. He was a creator, tapping into an immortal stream that ran so much deeper than himself, doing work that was the very meat of life. They used to say, all the painters and writers, actors and comedians and musicians who had chosen art over commerce, that no one could make them do anything else.

And yet, here he was, sitting in this very room as an exile.

They hadn't made him give it up, the amorphous yet all-powerful they; he had given it up on his own. Why? How? Jealousy, resentment, bitterness, laziness, the drugs, the money he wasn't making and the disastrous attempt to get it all in one great dare. It was enough to seize his breath and fill his veins with panic. His hands shook as he lifted his beer to his mouth.

And then the next performer was announced and, to a tepid chorus of applause, she walked onto the stage with her guitar.

"Wow," said Erica, with a little laugh. "She's so beautiful."

They ended up back at the house, drinking beer and smoking weed and hanging out, not just Frank and Erica and Marisol, but the housemates, and some others who had come to see the show. And it was just like it had always been, free and calm and comforting, all except for Dan.

"So you're Frank," said Dan.

"That I am."

"I heard a lot about you."

"Most of it bad, I assume."

"Not all of it. You guys were good together up there tonight."

"Thank you. It felt good."

"You still singing?"

"I try."

"Well, keep at it. You never know."

Yeah, thought Frank, fuck you, Dan.

Dan, black and bland, with a rumpled shirt and shifty eyes, was apparently Marisol's new thing. He owned a comic book store, did good old Dan, and the word was he was working on a graphic novel no one had seen but that was supposed to be a piece of genius that would change the entire medium. Frank knew how that worked.

He wandered around the first floor of the house, sucking at a succession of beers. Erica was sitting on one of the couches, chatting with some guy Frank didn't know and who was sitting a little too close. Every once in a while she looked at Frank and smiled and he nodded back.

He usually would have been pissed that some guy was moving in on Erica, and he usually would have done something about it. But at the moment Erica seemed a little young and a little shallow, and the ache of nostalgia had grown ferocious, and regrets were lying heavy on Frank's skull, pressing down his eyelids and sharpening his vision as he scanned the scene as if from miles away.

"Having fun?" said Sheila.

"Like old times."

"Marisol says you're staying for the night."

"Troy's room is open, right?"

"I'm not sure it's such a good idea."

"Good old Troy wouldn't mind. And you know me, Sheila. If there's a bad idea, I'm all over it."

"You won't believe it, Frank, but that's what I always liked about you."

"You're right," said Frank. "I don't believe it."

As he spoke with Sheila, Frank scanned the party, looking for Marisol, with a dark and shining purpose in his soul. Talk about bad ideas.

Something had snapped in him and he couldn't stop remembering the feel of her skin, the tang of her sweat, the way she laughed in bed when he was inside her, the way they sang together way back then, and the way they had sung together that very night.

It had been a surprise when Marisol gave him a shout-out during her set. He hadn't even known she had seen him sitting there in the back. And it had been a bigger surprise when she called him up to join her in one of the songs they had written together. He hemmed and hawed but Marisol insisted, and there was even some polite clapping from the crowd, as if one or two people actually remembered him. With Erica's urging he made his way to the stage to stand beside Marisol and lean toward the microphone.

The song was a ballad called "Torn Hearts," with bittersweet lyrics and a simple chord structure that went dark in the bridge. For a moment he was stumped on the opening verse, but as soon as Marisol started in on the first chord change the song blossomed for him like a flower, and they sang it together with an easy familiarity, complicated harmonies and all. Just being up there, with the dark swing of the music, the sadness of the verse, the plaintive note in Marisol's sweet voice, the scent of her hair, all of it had left Frank with a profound sense of loss.

And the ache told him, with the simple clarity of an old folk tune, that what had been lost was Marisol.

As he made small talk in the house with one old friend here, an old acquaintance there, some woman he had never seen before named Frieda who had taken Khalia's bedroom, his gaze kept shifting back to Marisol. Tall and thin, gawky almost, the way her elbows bent and her head bobbed, with that smile that was as genuine as gold.

He wanted to rush over to her, to wrap his arms around her waist, to take her upstairs, or outside, or anywhere where they could be alone and talk, just talk. And maybe kiss along with the talk. It's amazing where kissing and talking could lead.

What he needed was some alone time with her, but at the club there was Erica hanging around, suddenly wan in comparison with the shining Marisol, suddenly more millstone than life preserver, and then here, in the kitchen or the dining alcove, there were always other people within earshot. And Dan was eyeing him like a hawk. And Erica was sitting on that couch. And every time he made a move to get close, to maybe talk a bit one-on-one, Marisol had that scared squint in her eye before pulling away and escaping to chat with someone else.

So he stood there in purgatory, staring with his sharp gaze and wondering how he could fix this whole damn thing to get back to where he suddenly hungered to be, to where he had been just a few years ago, living with a true partner in love and art, singing for paying crowds, making real music, to get back to the perfect life he had created before he took the stupid risk with Delaney and blew it all. But there was no way to get back. He couldn't think of any way to fix it.

Yet.

The party slowly petered out, until there was just a handful of them sitting on the couches, sharing a bag of Doritos, laughing about nothing and too tired to really talk about anything. One by one they rose to go to bed: first Frieda, then Dan, heading home but not before giving Marisol one of those Dan looks that had become so annoying in the few hours Frank had known the guy, and finally Erica, with an expression Frank hadn't cared enough to read, until it was only Marisol and Sheila and Frank, talking about nothing.

"It's all right, Sheila," said Marisol, finally. "You can go on upstairs. We don't need a chaperone."

"That's not what I was doing, it's just that—"

"Go to bed, Sheila."

"I think I'll go to bed," said Sheila.

And then, finally, it was just the two of them, along with an unexpected awkwardness born of past intimacy and sorrows.

◆ ◆ ◆

Frank would have one chance to get this right, one chance to change all their destinies. "So," he said after a long moment. "Advertising."

Marisol nodded as if she had been expecting to hear exactly that. "Tell me about Erica. She seems nice."

"Yeah, she's great. We're on our way west, to do some business in LA and then head overseas. I'm going to try it over there. Maybe they'll be more receptive to my sound."

"You think so?"

"Sure. Why not?"

"Maybe because your sound is from here. You look thin, Frank."

"I'm keeping in shape."

"By running?"

"And other things."

"What are you running from this time?"

"Advertising."

Marisol laughed. "It's good to see you, too."

He leaned toward her, lowered his voice. "Thank you for letting me bust your set. I forgot what it felt like to sing with you."

"It would have been churlish to play that song alone with you sitting in the audience. I think it went over."

"Hell yes it went over. It reminded me of how good we were together. It reminded me of other things, too. The work, the emotions, what it was like to be beside you day and night. I felt like I was home."

"Why did you come back, Frank?"

He played it a bit; she would expect him to. He pulled back, lowered his eyes, fiddled with his thumbs. "I came back for you."

She laughed at the line-ness of the line, and he laughed too, defensively. But in the moment that line seemed to be the truest thing in his life and the words almost caught in his throat. He had thought he had come back to Chicago for a hot dog and some quick cash, but just the sight of Marisol had changed everything.

"I mean it," he said. "And truth is, I didn't know it when I was driving here. I was coming just to pick up enough money to get me all the way west. But seeing the shape of you, your eyes, the glow of your skin. And your scent. God, you smell so good. You smell like you. I don't know. As soon as I saw you I knew why I had come back to Chicago."

"It's a little late for all this, don't you think?"

"No, I don't. Or yes, it is, late but not too late. I don't know. All I know is the moment I saw you on that stage again everything changed."

"For you, maybe."

"And yet you're down here, alone with me, after avoiding me all night."

"You looked like trouble."

"I've always looked like trouble," he said. "That's my charm." He leaned in to kiss her and she let him. She tasted like cigarettes and sex and spice, like his youth and his future. He pressed a little harder with his tongue and she pulled back.

"So what's your plan, Frank?"

"Taking you with me."

"You're kidnapping me?"

"I would if I could."

"Where would you take me?"

"Away." He kissed her again, quickly. "West." And again. "California and Bali and Paris. We'll sing together, we'll make art, we'll drink cheap wine and screw all night."

He tried to kiss her again but she put a hand flat on his face and pushed.

"Don't be stupid," she said.

"Flying to the stars is not stupid. What's stupid is staying in a life that's sucking you dry. Is this what you want, working in an office selling crap to the masses?"

"It's not what I expected, true. But you want to know a secret? I'm good at it."

"Why wouldn't you be?" Frank said. "You're pitching the same crap to yourself and buying it hook, line, and sinker."

"Maybe I am. But maybe it was time to do something different. I'd been at it long enough to know that Clive Davis wasn't calling and the fill-in gigs at Armstrong's weren't covering the rent. But the truth is, now that I got the day job, I sort of like it. The office chatter, the way I have to focus on something other than myself, the free coffee. The money."

"The selling out."

"Why not that, too? It feels better than I thought it would. It's nice to have some change in my pocket and a bit of status in the world."

"And settling for Dan with the beady eyes and mumbled platitudes. He told me to keep at the singing thing, like he had any idea."

"Oh, Dan's not so bad. He's sweet, and he's reliable, and I get free comics."

"He's never going to finish that amazing graphic novel everyone says he's working on."

"And you know that after one night?"

"That's all it took."

"Yeah, well, I think you're right."

"Come with me."

"I'm not coming with you, Frank. This is my home. And what about the girl?"

"Erica."

"What about her? Is she coming, too? Does baby make three?"

"I'll send her away, send her back to daddy. It would be the best thing that ever happened to her. She'll have a story to tell at that fancy college her parents will pay for."

"You'll give her up that easily?"

"She was the dream, you're the reality."

Marisol laughed. "You really know how to charm a girl."

"What I mean is, when I saw you again, I realized that what I hoped Erica and I would end up with is what I had and screwed up with you. Come with me. We'll make it work this time. I'll make sure of it. Be wild again."

Marisol was about to say something and then she stopped, and pulled back into herself. She was thinking about it. My God, she was thinking about it. His blood started bubbling with hope. He took her hand and she let him. He rubbed her knuckles like they were a rosary.

"You said you came for money, Frank. Where were you intending to get it?"

"I don't know. Friends, maybe. That's not the point."

"Let's make it the point." She jerked her hand from his. "Were you getting it from me? Is that what this is all about? You came back here to tap me for cash like an ATM?"

"No, not you, no. I didn't even know you were working. I thought maybe, I don't know, maybe you could hook me up again with your cousin Jorge."

"Jorge? What the hell do you want with Jorge?"

"I have some stuff he might want. I don't need to sell much. Just a little."

"This again? After what happened last time?"

"In and out, Marisol. That's all. In and out."

"And where'd you get it, Frank? The little bit of stuff for Jorge?"

"I just did."

"You are such a fucking biscuit. Delaney's still hunting you and you have merch for Jorge? Stolen I'd bet, which is why you're running. But why not, running is your goddamn specialty. And I bet your Erica doesn't even know. Sheila told me something was dirty about you."

"That girl needs to mind her own business."

"You need to get the hell out of Chicago."

"I will, as soon as I talk to Jorge. Can you set it up for me, Marisol?"

"Fuck you, Frank."

"Yeah. But can you? Please?"

22

BLOOD // WATER

The idea came to Frank on the Red Line, heading south.

The train buzzed through the west side of the city before diving into the Loop, where he transferred at Washington from the Blue to the Red. He wasn't about to drive to South Chicago in the Camaro, with its full load in the spare tire. In his backpack he had brought only a quarter kilo, which was more than enough to get him to Santa Monica if he made the sale. He hugged the backpack in front of him as he sat in the plastic yellow seat.

The hard cityscape flew by outside the windows—first Chinatown and then Sox Park just beyond the highway—and as it passed he wondered whether it would be Marisol or Erica flying with him over the Pacific to a new life. One moment he was sure he could convince Marisol to take the leap and renew their love on the other side of the world, and the thought filled him with peace. Marisol had owned his heart, she knew his soul, she was the one person who could make him the artist he once believed he could be. But in the next moment he was pining for Erica, her youth and beauty, her boldness and her lack of shits to give. In that moment he was certain that she was the necessary catalyst for living the brave and roguish life he so craved.

Marisol. Erica. Freedom! Fuck.

As the train rumbled south, he thought of the next step, the ride west, the hard miles driven while being chased by all manner of demon: the Russian, Delaney, maybe even some deranged detective hired by Erica's parents. He thought how the squabbles and deprivations that came from life on the road could leave him making the trip alone, a prospect that frightened him to his bones. He needed a muse, someone to push him and guide him and love him, someone to cure the abject loneliness that periodically came over him like an illness and sent him spiraling into depression and ever more drugs. Marisol or Erica, it didn't much matter as long as there was someone; but would there still be someone by the time he arrived in Santa Monica?

Then the idea came in a swift and beautiful rush, like all the best ideas do.

Maybe he didn't need to drive all the way to California to make the final sale. Bongo was fun, sure, but never the most reliable; it was always a crapshoot with Bongo. Maybe there was another answer. After enough begging the night before, Marisol had finally made the call to set up the meet with her cousin Jorge. Frank had always gotten along with Jorge before the thing with Delaney blew everything sky-high. Good old Jorge, who sure as hell owed him big time. Maybe Jorge could do more than give him a fair price for the quarter kilo. Maybe Jorge could give him a fair price for all of it. Maybe Frank could complete the sale in the here and the now. Maybe he could be winging out from O'Hare by nightfall, tomorrow night at the latest.

He began to shake with a fevered excitement, so close to everything, so close to true freedom, when the train lumbered into his stop. Garfield, just west of Hyde Park. It was only a few blocks to Green Street.

The house was just like his old house in Humboldt Park, a Chicago-style single with a covered entranceway and a jutting alcove beside the door. It had probably been a fine house at a different time, but now the lawn was uncut and its next-door neighbor, an identical structure, was boarded up. Across the street was a weedy lot with a lone tree. On the steps, a burly young man tapped on his phone.

Frank bobbed his head as he stood there, getting into business mode, before he headed up the stairs.

◆ ◆ ◆

He had been here before, not at this house in this run-down neighborhood, but on the edge of a life-changing deal.

About two years before, toward the end of his time in Chicago, sick of the stasis that had overcome his life and feeling middle-aged defeat in his early twenties, he had taken a risk, stepped out of his lane, made his move. If it had worked out, Frank would have made enough money to build that recording studio he had been incessantly talking about, the one that could have started his producing career and finally taken him to the stars.

At the time, as a side hustle, he had been working for an Irish motorcycle maniac turned drug kingpin, Delaney, delivering product to customers in Humboldt Park, Garfield Park, West Town, and Logan Square. There wasn't much to it, and as his music career stalled the money was enough to pay for his room, and his drugs, and keep his car gassed. Then Marisol's cousin Jorge told him of a contact who was looking for some serious merch. And Frank knew about a shipment that Delaney had been having a hard time unloading. Delaney's stranded shipment and Jorge's contact seemed like a match made in heaven.

He should have run the details by Delaney first, but then the profit would have been Delaney's profit, and the contact would have ended up as Delaney's contact. So, at Jorge's urging, Frank told Delaney he'd take care of it all on his own. Delaney had raised an eyebrow to let him know he was on the hook if things turned south, before he okayed the move.

Of course it all went to shit. The contact was sketchier than Jorge had let on. The arrangements were sketchier than Frank wanted to admit. And then Frank wasn't smart enough to catch the briefcase switcheroo. Really? Yeah. So what should have been a triumph turned into a disaster.

When Delaney found out, he ripped Frank's face apart and gave him a week to get it back, all of it, the money or the drugs. A week. Three days later, without a word to anyone, including Marisol, Frank was in Philadelphia, bunking with an old friend from high school, waiting for the hammer to fall. But though Delaney hadn't found him, all that waiting only led to despair and defeat and a rampant bit of drug use to quell the swell of loneliness and fear, which led Frank to falling in with the Russian, like he had fallen in with Delaney.

Frank had a habit of falling in with the worst.

But this was the end of that. He had sworn to himself this would be the last deal. Take the money and run, baby, run from Chicago, run from America, run from every failure he had ever had into the waiting arms of Freedom!

"Yo, what's up?" said the man on the stairs. He was still looking at his phone.

"Is Jorge in?"

"What's in the bag?"

"Nothing much."

The man put aside the phone and wiggled his fingers. Frank handed the backpack over.

After a quick look, the man stood wearily, handed Frank back the pack, and patted Frank down, tracing his palms over Frank's legs and ankles and crotch, across his sides, around his belt. Frank had left the gun in the car, along with the rest of the stash. Sometimes carrying a gun only showed fear, not confidence, and this play was all about confidence.

When he was done, the burly man dropped back down onto the stoop and picked up his phone. "Go on," he said.

"The name's Frank."

"Who gives a shit," he said.

"Good answer," said Frank on his way up the stairs.

It wasn't an encouraging scene inside the house. A television was on, and a pack of men and women with hard, blank expressions were sprawled on the couch and the floor, watching explosions going off on the screen. One of the men eyed Frank and called out, "That dude's here."

A moment later a woman with blue hair and a tight T-shirt pushed open a swinging door that led to a kitchen and waved Frank inside.

Jorge sat at a linoleum table in the crappy little kitchen. He smoked a cigarette and held on to a beer. On the table in front of him was an ashtray and a gun. Jorge was tall and lanky, like Marisol, but butt ugly. He smiled weakly at Frank, his face not so much lighting up as cracking, as if the meeting wasn't his idea of fun.

The woman with the blue hair sat down next to Jorge, leaned back in her chair, crossed her legs, took the cigarette from Jorge's fingers. Jorge didn't invite Frank to sit. Instead, Frank remained standing, like a peasant before a king. Fuck that, Frank thought. He grabbed a chair, pulled it from the table, and sat like it was nothing.

"Your ass shouldn't be here, Frankie man," said Jorge with his little lisp that could be endearing or threatening, depending.

"In and out," said Frank.

"You better be right. Where's your boy Hunter?"

"I left him with a friend in Philly."

"Too bad. I always liked that dog. You know, I wouldn't see you at all if it wasn't for Marisol making the ask. I can't believe she's still giving you a lift after what you did on her. She was so worried, you leaving like you did, and not a word from you."

"I'm trying to make it up to her."

"Maybe you could make it up to her by leaving again."

"I'm leaving as soon as our business is done. I'm just here to make a deal."

"Okay then. What you got for me?"

"This," said Frank as he pulled a small packet wrapped with gray tape out of his backpack and tossed it onto the table. It landed with a *thud.*

"What is it?"

"H. Prime. Strong as shit."

"Where'd you get it?"

"I got it, what does it matter?"

"It's nice to know you didn't get no smarter."

Jorge grabbed hold of the packet, weighed it in his hand, gave it a sniff, and then put it on the table in front of the woman. She kept smoking for a bit before she squashed the cigarette into the ashtray, grabbed the packet, and headed down a set of stairs to the basement.

"You still singing?" said Jorge.

"Sure."

"Where?"

"Philadelphia."

"You going back?"

"Nope."

"Then where you headed now?"

"LA. Santa Monica. You ever been to the beach at Santa Monica?"

"Nah, man."

"It's like miles wide and white as cocaine."

"You been?"

"Not yet, but I'll be there soon."

"That's good. I was sorry how that other thing turned out. But you know, my cousin, she's working now."

"Advertising," said Frank.

"She's making pretty decent bank. And she's got this boyfriend who's got himself a business. She's in a good place now, my cousin, and my aunt, well she's talking about a baby. You know she only had the one daughter, which means she's been waiting. And it wasn't like you were gonna get it done. So I got to say, I wasn't so happy to hear you was back."

"Like I said . . ."

"Yeah, like you said."

Just then the girl came back with the packet, a blue piece of tape now over the gray. She sat down and tossed it onto the table.

"How much?" said Jorge.

"A quarter."

"Any good?"

"Too good."

"All right, Frankie man. Five thou."

"Fifteen."

"Now you're making jokes."

"Ten then, and let's say a hundred forties."

"Cotton?"

"For a friend."

"Go home, bucko."

"This is pure. You'll be cutting it every which way before it hits the street or you'll be losing customers, if you know what I mean. It's a bargain at ten. And if you go with that, I can get you more. Same quality."

"How much more?"

"I could load you up, man."

"How much more?"

"A full five k."

"That's like, two hundred."

"It's not like anything," said Frank. "It is what it is."

"Wow. Frankie, man. You hit the mother lode, didn't you, motherfucker. Maybe my cousin missed a good bet with you after all. Wait, two hundred, that's about how much you owe Delaney, isn't it?"

"Fuck Delaney," said Frank.

"Yeah, I get you. Sorry about how that turned out. Your face don't look so bad, you want to know the truth. So when could you get it?"

"Tonight if you want."

"It's in the city?"

"We can arrange a meet."

"I bet you'll be a little more careful with the briefcases this time."

Frank waited for the laughter to die. He was so close to closing the deal he could taste the marmalade on the croissant.

"So, Jorge," said Frank, "are you big enough to handle it all?"

"Am I big enough?"

"I'm just asking. I don't want to waste my time."

"Maybe I wasn't before," said Jorge. "Back then I'd be stretched to buy the quarter, you know what I mean? But things have changed. I'm flusher than I was, and I got me a new partner."

Frank felt a sense of unease at that last word, "partner." That meant someone else had entered the equation. But Frank didn't realize all of what was happening until Jorge went and picked up the gun.

When he heard the footsteps climbing the basement stairs, it came to him, the truth of things.

"Sorry about this, Frankie man," said Jorge, waving the gun loosely. "Except, you know, my aunt, she so wants that little baby, and I had to think of her in this whole messed-up situation."

Frank bolted out of his seat and tried to smash his way through the swinging kitchen door, but the door bashed back, hitting him like a right hook to the face and knocking him off his feet. He was sitting on the floor, holding the blood back from his smashed-in nose, when the person who had been waiting in the basement finished climbing the steps and stood in the doorway.

"Well now, what a sweet thing this is," said Delaney, broad as a bull, a gold hoop in his ear, and his smile a smear of malevolence. "Frankie boy has finally come home."

When Delaney's boot stamped down on Frank's knee, releasing a kaleidoscope of pain, the crack of the blow and Frank's own scream combined into a death knell for all the unrequited yearnings of Frank Cormack's pathetic little life.

23

Fast Car

The skyline of the city appears like a ghost in the distance. As he drives toward it, the shape and rhythm pull a complicated longing from Oliver, even as it mocks the very emotions it evokes. And right in the middle of the jagged cityscape, rising above all the other massive obelisks, is the Sears Tower, standing tall like his father, staring down with stark disappointment at his younger son.

Was it worth it? his father demands. *Was leaving your life for some utopian fantasy everything you ever hoped?*

"No."

What have you achieved, Oliver?

"Nothing."

What do you regret?

"Everything."

What gift have you bequeathed to humanity?

"Grief."

Where is the girl you threw it all away for?

"Dead."

How did she die?

"I killed her."

Just as I always knew, the old man says. *The wrong son died and the world has paid the price.*

"Go to hell," says Oliver Cross in his imagined dialogue with what was once the tallest building in the world, but the dialogue might not have been so imagined after all.

"What did I do now?" says Ayana. The dog looks up at him as if to echo the girl's question.

"I didn't say anything," says Oliver.

"You just told me to go to hell."

"That wasn't directed at you. But save it anyway. I'm sure it will come in handy."

"Then who were you talking to?"

"A dead man."

"Do you often talk to the dead?"

"Whenever I can."

"Because they don't talk back, I suppose."

"Wrong," says Oliver. "Talking back is all they do. But these days I have more in common with the dead than the living."

"And yet here you sit."

"Don't remind me."

"You're just so sad, Oliver. You'd bring me to tears if I didn't know you."

"There," he says. "That thing I said you should save. Use it there. But it could be worse. I could be nineteen again and think I'm something. I'm pulling over. Give the dog a walk before we hit the city."

"Does he have to go already?"

"He's a dog. He always has to go."

As Ayana walks Hunter along a ditch, Oliver climbs out of the car, steps to the road, and looks to the left. A few cars slide by, a van, a pickup, nothing he recognizes. He took a few turns this way and that as they passed through small towns on the way to Chicago, and he saw no motorcycle behind him. Maybe it was nothing after all and the dope had made him paranoid; it had been known to happen.

While he stands by the road he slips the phone out of the inside pocket of his jacket. He asked Fletcher to see if the police had found a list of contacts on Frank Cormack's phone or from the cloud. He told his son not to ask for anything specific, just request a look at the names and numbers to see if anything rang a bell. And then to find an entry for some Marisol. This is the third time he's checked to see if Fletcher has come through.

Nothing. Not a thing. But what else could Oliver expect from his son? So many unions to bust, so little time.

When the girl and the dog are back in the truck, they start again toward the big city that was his home. Returning once more as an exile, he remembers the poem Helen used to recite to the girls. *Hog butcher for the world. Tool maker. Stacker of wheat.* Helen always thought it was so romantic; to Oliver, now, it sounds like a Costco.

"I've never been to Chicago before," says the girl.

"It's just another city."

"What fabulous things are there to see?"

"Buildings," says Oliver. "Crowds. Traffic. Sewers."

"You're such a romantic."

"What's wrong with sewers? Where would we be without sewers? Sitting in crap, that's where we'd be."

"Like this truck, for instance."

He drove on for a moment, thinking. "In Chicago," he says, finally, "they have the best hot dogs in the world."

"Really?"

"Scout's honor, though I'm no Scout."

"The best hot dogs in the world. Now that sounds like something. I'm all for that. Let's eat a dog, no offense there, Hunter."

"Sure," says Oliver. "We'll find us a dog. But first, we need to do some shopping."

◆　◆　◆

"Act natural," says Oliver as he and the girl walk toward the store. "And don't go blabbing about all nervously, or more nervously than you normally blab about."

"Why would I be nervous?" says Ayana.

"That's it exactly. You shouldn't be. So play it just like that. We're thinking of buying a guitar. You're going to try some out, strum a little. I'll look on like the loving grandfather."

"You're not that good an actor, Oliver."

"I'll look on like the angry grandfather bitter about having to fork over his hard-earned cash to buy a piece-of-crap guitar for the talentless child of his worthless son."

"Better," says Ayana, laughing. "That you can pull off."

"And then you'll slip the question."

"I got it. Jesus, chill. I can play a scene with the best of them."

"I just want to be sure."

"I got your number, didn't I?"

"When?"

"Outside Frank's apartment. I played that smooth enough, didn't I?"

Oliver thinks for a moment. "Yeah, you did. And it got the hell beat out of me."

"But even after that, I got you to take me west, didn't I?"

"As a matter of fact."

"And after this you're going to buy me a hot dog, right?"

"Shut up."

"So if I'm playing you like a violin, Oliver, maybe I can handle a guitar-store jockey. But it's probs better if you just keep your own mouth shut."

"It usually is," says Oliver.

Oliver got the name and address of the music store from his GPS. A number of hits came up, but he was looking for a place on the north side, where, from his memory of the city, he figured someone like Frank Cormack, white and scheming, would have lived and sung his bullshit songs. This store, southwest of Wrigley on Lincoln Avenue, seemed to be at the epicenter of that scene.

"Any idea what kind of guitar you're looking for?" asks the woman at the front desk. They have entered some sort of fancy guitar emporium with dark wooden shelves behind the counter and what look to be thousands of guitars hanging from its whitewashed walls.

"Just something I can play anywhere," says Ayana.

"What kind of music do you play?"

"I'm just learning. But like folk and stuff?"

"And not too expensive," adds Oliver. Ayana gives him the stink eye. Nice touch, that, Oliver thinks. Like a happy fucking family.

"Why don't you check out the acoustic room. Let me know your name and I'll set you up with Karl. He's our resident folkie."

"Perfect," says Ayana. "I'm Ayana."

The acoustic room, behind a glass door, is long and white with a pile of guitars in the center like some deranged Christmas tree and three rows of guitars dripping off the high walls like tinsel. Ayana walks along one of the rows, brushing each guitar she passes with her fingertips, leaving marks on the buffed wood. Oliver takes one off the wall, big and dark brown. He presses down on the fretboard and flicks the strings with his thumb; the sound is rich and deep.

"Do you actually play, Oliver?"

"I used to," he says. "Just happy little love songs, you know. 'Eve of Destruction,' 'A Hard Rain's A-Gonna Fall,' and that old classic 'Shut Up Already and Die.'"

She laughs. "I never heard of that last one."

"I wrote it."

"I should have known."

Oliver turns the guitar over and checks the price. Almost two thousand dollars. What the hell? When did it become so damn expensive to strum a few chords and complain about the world? Even the simplest pleasures now have the moneyman's stamp on them. Next thing you know they'll be pulling bills from your wallet just to let you pee. Oh yeah, Flomax.

He has the sudden urge to make like Hendrix and burn the goddamn guitar, to burn the whole damn place down. He is watching the flames leap in his imagination when a man strolls into the room with a chin beard and a salesman's smile. "Hey, guys," he says with the voice of an earnest kindergarten teacher. "I'm Karl, and I hear you're looking for a guitar."

"You don't make sandwiches here, do you?" says Ayana.

"No, we don't."

"Then I guess a guitar will do."

"It's Ayana, right? So what are we looking for, Ayana?"

"I don't know, something. Just to play."

"That narrows it down." Karl turns to Oliver. "Do you know what you're willing to spend? That could narrow it down some more."

"Not two thousand dollars, I'll tell you that," says Oliver, as he returns the guitar he strummed to its hook on the wall.

"That guitar is a Martin Dreadnought, a beautiful piece, a true classic, but a little pricey and probably too big for her. Have you played much, Ayana?"

"A little."

"Okay, good. A little is better than not at all. Take a seat," he says, gesturing to one of the couches in the center of the room.

Ayana sits as this Karl walks along the rows of guitars before he stops at something pale and not so big, a little small, actually. He pulls the instrument off the wall and tunes it before he props a leg on a stool and plays a bluesy riff, his fingers sliding expertly up and down the fretboard. The guitar sounds clean, strong, like it could play anything, which means that Karl can play anything. That's a trick, Oliver knows, to make a buyer believe she could sound that good. Even though he has no intention of shelling out actual cash for a guitar, somehow the trick pisses Oliver off.

"This is an Eastman acoustic, three-quarter size made for travel," says the salesman. "It's used but in really good shape, and the price is about a third lower than the price for the same guitar new. Why don't you give it a try?"

He hands the guitar to Ayana, who looks at it for a moment like she is looking at a pineapple.

"Show her how to hold it," says Oliver.

"Oh, I think she knows how to hold it just fine," says this Karl. "Do you want a pick, Ayana?"

"No," she says as she crosses her legs and fits the guitar on her thigh. "I'll just fiddle around."

The first few burps she tickles from the guitar are discordant scraps of sound that scratch the ear, but some notes start to emerge that are less jarring and her grip on the guitar becomes more sure. Before long, actual chords slip out from her fingers, chords that build on each other until something close to a melody emerges. And then this girl, whom Oliver thought he had figured out, a little schemer scheming her way west as she lies to him about motorcycles and the Russian, begins to sing in an uncertain voice with eyes trained on the floor before her. The song is vaguely familiar to Oliver, a classic about being trapped in life and a plea to be taken somewhere, anywhere, away in a fast car, along with the feeling that she could be someone, be someone, be someone.

But it is her voice that slays him. Ayana's voice is as soft and textured as velvet, with a rough edge that bites and a sweet innocence that transports him into his past. About an hour north of where they are now is the house where he grew up with his mother and father and brother and all the expectations of his class. About two miles southeast is the center of the '68 demonstrations where he met the love of his life. And now this girl, with a barely whispered voice almost unearthly in its beauty, is breathing back into his regret-laden soul the emotions of his youth, when he needed to break away, to get away, to be someone, be someone, be someone of his own creation, not some clone of his father but his own strutting self, no matter the cost.

As the girl's fingers pluck at the strings, the power of her voice fills his eyes. He turns away and wipes his face with the back of his hand. When he turns back, she is someone new, someone he has never seen before. When was the last time he took off his blinders?

"That was really good," says Karl when the girl doesn't so much finish the song as let it peter out. "Your voice is lovely. Where did you learn to play?"

"Around," says the girl. "And I took some lessons with a singer I knew. Marisol Something? She lives around here, I think, and plays in some of the clubs. She mentioned this place."

"The Marisol who performs sometimes at Armstrong's?"

"I suppose. My brother knew this guy Frank who set up the lessons."

"Yeah, Marisol Sosa. I've played with her. She's great, and she comes in now and then just to look around. She really did a job with you. Your voice, I have to tell you, is something special. How did the guitar feel?"

"A little light, smaller than I'm used to. I don't know. I haven't played in a while."

"How much does it cost?" says Oliver.

"Three hundred. Two ninety-five, actually. It will come fully set up, with a gig bag. We'll even throw in a strap. We can set up a payment plan if you want. It would be like . . ."

As Karl searches the tag for the monthly payment Oliver says, "We'll take it."

"What?" says Ayana.

"Do you like it?" says Oliver.

"I guess, yeah."

"You said this is a travel guitar, right?" says Oliver.

"That's right," says Karl. "From Eastman. A very good maker. Spruce top, rosewood fingerboard. A nice bone saddle."

"And we're traveling, right?" says Oliver.

"I guess so," says Ayana.

"And I like my saddles made of bone. Where do I pay?"

Karl smiles. "Is that cash or credit?"

"Cash," says Oliver.

◆ ◆ ◆

The Vienna Beef frank is grilled, the poppy seed bun is steamed, the relish is the same radioactive green Oliver remembers. Onions, sport peppers, tomato wedges, and a pickle spear, all sprinkled with a dash of celery salt and topped with mustard.

"This is good, Oliver," says the girl, her mouth full as she wipes a smear of relish off her cheek.

"Good?" says Oliver. "Mama's boys are good. A B-minus is good. A Chicago dog is the pinnacle of Western culture. Everything else is second-rate. And all you've got to say is good?"

"Really good."

"Better."

They are sitting at one of the red wooden tables outside a hot dog stand on Clark Street south of the ballpark. Hunter is taut on the leash, staring like a wolfhound at the passersby. The dog joint, called the Weiners Circle, wasn't here when Oliver was last in the city, but the GPS spit out the location, and it was sort of on the way to Marisol Sosa's address, which guitar store Kyle, as a special favor, had given them from the customer list so Ayana could start up again on her fictional lessons. When they drove by the stand in the rattling truck he saw nothing more than a shack and a sign, which seemed right. What more do you need?

Oliver hasn't touched his unadorned hot dog, but he is enjoying the hell out of watching the girl polish off the first of her two loaded franks.

"So tell me something, Oliver," says Ayana after she finishes the first dog and is fiddling with her cheddar fries. "Why did you buy me that guitar?"

"It was part of the act," says Oliver. "A cover for getting the address."

"Oh, I could have gotten hipster Kyle to spill without you spending a dime, and you know it."

"Yeah, probably. He was an eager beaver."

"I think you're getting soft on me."

"Piss off. It'll also be a good prop for when we meet this Marisol whatever."

"She'll know she didn't give me lessons."

"Yeah, but with the guitar you'll look like one of the tribe."

"What tribe is that?"

"The lost singers of the stockyards."

"And what the hell do I do with a stinking guitar after we get what we need?"

"Whatever you want."

"Maybe I should pawn it."

"Maybe you should. At least then someone who knows how to play the thing could own it," says Oliver, before he snaps off half the dog in front of him and feeds it to Hunter, who nearly takes off Oliver's fingers as he lunges for the gift.

"My playing was that bad?" says Ayana.

"You were good."

"Good, huh?"

"Yeah."

"B-minus. I'll take it. So what do we do now?"

"Head on over to that address and find out what this Marisol knows."

"How do I play it?"

"Silently, that's how you play it. The guitar will say everything you need to say. I'll do the talking."

"And I'll step in when you screw up."

"Yeah, I suppose, something like that."

◆　◆　◆

Marisol's house is in the Humboldt Park section of the city, a light-gray stone structure with a listing porch and a rusting iron fence. Oliver parks a bit down the road.

While Ayana waits outside the truck, Oliver takes Hunter for a quick walk. As the dog squats, Oliver appraises the condition of the house. The rotting front stairs need to be replaced, the porch probably, too. It would be a couple days' work, not much more. It is the kind of job Oliver used to like, taking something ruined and fixing it sweet. Sort of the reverse of what he has done to his life. When Hunter is finished, Oliver takes out a blue bag and bends his already bent back to pick up the crap. If anyone is looking from behind the curtains of the gray stone house, it's time to playact being a civic-minded dog owner. Standing almost straight again, Oliver clasps the leash beneath his arm in order to tie the bag closed.

Suddenly the dog barks and charges forward. Oliver spins and the leash yanks free. As the crap bag goes flying, Hunter dashes toward a woman walking down the street.

The woman is tall and thick with long graying hair. For a moment Oliver fears her face is about to be eaten off, but then, as the dog leaps about in some strange dance of the ecstatic, the woman kneels down and grabs Hunter by the scruff of his neck.

"Hunter?" she says as the dog licks her chin. "Oh, Hunter, where have you been, you bad boy? We missed you so much."

24

RESCUE ME

Oliver Cross sits in the truck with the dog, keeping watch on an old stone house in South Chicago. A man kicks back on the front steps, a kid really, not much older than Erica, big and young, fiddling with his phone. The kid has looked up enough to eye the truck sitting halfway down the street, but he isn't concerned enough to do anything about it. Which means, as best as Oliver can figure, there's more muscle inside.

"This won't go well," says Oliver out loud. Hunter raises his head, but it is Helen who answers.

"Probably not," she says. "But you know what I used to tell my students: if it was easy, anyone could do it."

"But that's exactly who I am, just anyone."

"No you're not, darling. You're the man who charged the big blue line in Chicago."

"We all make mistakes. They won't tell me anything."

"Of course they will," she says. "Because you'll ask politely. And because people like you."

"People don't like me. People run away as soon as they see me. I make strangers puke from across the street."

"I liked you on first sight."

"That's a lie. You didn't like me until I got my head bashed in."

"You were so dashing with the blood pouring out."

"Maybe that's my superpower, being dashing when I get my head bashed in."

"Let's find out," says Helen.

This is where the path has led, to this old house on this forlorn street in this forgotten part of the city. Frank asked his old lover Marisol to set him up with her cousin Jorge so he could make a deal, and this is where she sent him. And the fact that she hasn't heard from Frank since bodes ill for him, and not too well for Erica either.

"Frank went alone," said Marisol after she came home from work, let the dog lovingly jump all over her, and learned who Oliver was and what he was after. "He left the car and took the el. Later the girl, your granddaughter, Erica? She got a phone call from someone at this number, and she left right after with the Camaro."

"Did she say what she was told?"

"No. Just asked us to help her find a lawyer. Then she left."

"A lawyer?"

"We didn't get it either. We never heard from either of them afterward."

"No calls? No word from your cousin?"

"I asked him, of course," said Marisol. "All he said was, '*Primita*, don't ask.'"

That was the extent of the information Marisol had for him. A crumb, nothing more. But after giving it, Marisol was gracious enough to invite them both to dinner.

Oliver and Ayana joined Marisol, along with Sheila, the woman whose face Hunter had tried to lick off, and some of the other residents at the dining table. Papers were stacked up at one end and the food laid out on the other: kale salad with nuts and dried cranberries, lentil soup, thick and black, and then some curried potato and cauliflower stew, along with a bitter red wine. Ayana ate like the hot dogs had been no hot dogs, but Oliver only picked. It all tasted so familiar, so much like the past that it caught in his throat. As they ate, Hunter roamed around the house, sniffing here and there, searching, Oliver supposed, for traces of Frank, and maybe Erica, too.

But Oliver did some sniffing of his own. The house smelled like false dreams and blighted hopes and fairy tales gone all to hell. How many vegan meals just like this, at a communal table just like this, in a community of lost souls just like this, had he suffered through? He knew the story, knew it in his bones: the group house; artists just trying to find themselves; all for one and one for all until money or sex or failure or, even worse, success gets between them and it all goes to hell. Which, considering the condition of the ramshackle house, was where it seemed to be going.

"We share most things," said Sheila at the dinner. "The work, the rent, the political cause of the hour. And we support one another creatively."

"That sounds close to perfect," said Ayana.

"It is. It's like we're living with a family we chose instead of the one we got stuck with."

"Dysfunction is dysfunction," said Oliver.

"We seem to get along okay," said Sheila.

"Give it time."

"How long have you been playing guitar?" said Marisol to Ayana.

"Not long. I'm not very good."

"She sings," said Oliver.

"Not really. B-minus."

"Maybe we can play together some, a little later."

"That would be . . . But I don't know. Oliver?"

"Knock yourself out."

"You can stay the night if you like. There's an open room. Troy is still on the road and we can put some fresh sheets on. It's where Erica and Frank stayed when they were here."

"Go ahead," Oliver said. "You've bunked out on worse."

"We could find a place for you, too, Oliver," said Marisol. "There's always a couch."

"I'll take the couch," said Ayana.

"I'll find a motel," said Oliver. "Something crappy and cheap to fit my mood. You said Erica wanted to find a lawyer?"

"That's right," said Sheila. "Someone specific. Something Finnerman, or Fingerman, or something. She didn't say why. I showed her a bar association list online."

He pushed his chair out, stood as straight as he was able, and threw his napkin on the table. "I have things to do."

"I'll go with," said Ayana.

"Stay. Play your little toy. I'll pick you up sometime tomorrow. You guys got a knife I can borrow?"

"A pen knife?" said Sheila.

"More like a cleaver."

"Where are you going, Oliver?" said the girl, a note in her voice like worry. As if she cared, the little actress.

"Out," said Oliver, and that's where he is now, in his truck, out: out of Humboldt Park, out of any zone of sanity, out of his fucking mind.

He takes the phone from his pocket, turns it on, and waits for it to reboot. He has a message. From his son. Marisol's address. A little late, but it's something. When was the last time he received anything from his son, other than his dead wife's ashes? He does a little search and makes a call, leaves a message with the switchboard, closes up the phone, and looks again at the house. He has more than an inkling that he's going to die tonight and, of all the places in the world to do it, that craphole house isn't where he would choose. But then who the hell ever got to choose, other than his wife?

"Don't worry so much," says Helen. "You won't die tonight. I won't let you."

"You might not have much to say in the matter."

"Oh, Oliver, don't bet on that. We'll be together, soon, I promise, but not yet. Not until you find her."

"There might not be anything left to find."

"She's not here with me, Oliver. What does that tell you?"

He doesn't respond. What is there to say? That her vision of the afterlife is as narrow as his father's? Wings, harps, clouds, Christ. Or worse, that she is just a figment of his psychosis, an aftereffect of the universe cracking under drugs too pure for his brittle brain? But real or false, he never could refuse Helen, even at the end, even after the end. He opens the door of the truck and climbs down to the pitted street. He grabs ahold of the dog's leash and Hunter raises his head, as if he, like Oliver, would rather stay in the truck.

"Let's go, dog," he says. "The master has spoken."

"Oh, and Oliver," says Helen, after the dog jumps down but before Oliver can shut the door on her. "Don't forget the knife."

◆ ◆ ◆

He meanders up the sidewalk toward the house, the dog sniffing here and there, before taking a quick piss to impart his scent on the scene. It's cute that the dog still thinks leaving his mark on the world matters. For Oliver that fiction died long ago. When he gets to the house, he starts climbing the steps as if the big kid isn't even there. The kid, still looking at his phone, kicks out a leg like a tollgate.

"What you want, old man?"

"Jorge. He in?"

"You the one he's waiting on?"

"I doubt it."

"Then he not here."

"Maybe I am the one he's waiting on."

"Then he still ain't here." As he says this, while looking at his phone, the kid lifts his T-shirt to show the fat handle of a gun sticking out of his belt.

"Mommy must be so proud," says Oliver.

"Leave her out of it," says the kid as he stands, pockets the phone, and then reaches for his gun.

Before Oliver can react, the gun is out and waving at his chest, the hole in its fat barrel as black as all eternity, growing larger and more inviting as Oliver stares. It looks like a licorice taffy: you either like licorice or you don't. The sight of the hollowness makes Oliver smile even as the dog starts to growl.

The kid's gaze darts to the dog, and as it does, the aim of the gun slips to Oliver's right. Oliver drops the leash, reaches to pull the cleaver from behind his back, and smashes the flat of the blade hard against the gun, which flies out of the kid's hand.

The kid and Oliver both turn their heads to look at the gun as it bounces twice down the stone steps, smack and then another smack, before spinning onto the cement of the walk.

The dog howls.

The kid turns toward Oliver as Oliver reverses the swing of his arm and backhands the flat of the cleaver into the kid's jaw, sending him sprawling onto the level stone by the door. The force of the blow sends Oliver tumbling down after him, his shoulder landing painfully atop the kid's stomach, forcing a loud exhale. Oliver scrambles forward and lays the knife blade at the kid's gasping throat.

The dog barks and growls. Oliver's back shrieks. "Let's try this again," he says.

The kid's eyes widen and he looks at Oliver as if at some kind of monster looming over him, a half-human, half-goat thing with big yellow teeth and gray hairs sprouting from its ears.

"I'm here to see Jorge," says Oliver between gritted teeth, with his back seizing and his blood boiling.

It is all so stirring and painful and life-affirming in its own violent way that Oliver barely notices the front door opening until the dog stops his howling, growling.

With the blade still against the kid's neck, Oliver turns his head to see Hunter dancing all over a tall, thin man with tattoos up his arms and neck. The man is kneeling down, scratching the dog's ears. Behind this tender scene stand two men with guns trained at Oliver's face.

"Look at you, such a good dog," says the kneeling man, in a lispy accent. "I've missed you, Mr. Hunter. How have you been? Has this old buzzard been treating you nice?"

The dog, in the midst of his love dance, turns his snout to Oliver and appears to grin.

"Ungrateful cur," sneers Oliver.

"You talking to me?" says the man.

"To the dog."

"Yeah, well, what else do you expect from a dog?"

"Are you Jorge?"

"I am. And you, I suppose, are the geezer my cousin said was probably stopping by. She says I'm not allowed to kill you, which is a pity. Now why don't you get off my boy Rami before you accidentally lop off his head?"

"I can't," says Oliver.

"Why the hell not?"

"Because my back went out."

A woman appears, standing behind the two men with guns. She's pretty, with blue hair and bad teeth, and she laughs brightly.

"Get him up," says Jorge.

The men with the guns step forward, grab Oliver by the armpits, and raise him to standing. It feels like his vertebrae are connected only by pain, and the pain itself is snapping. The agony takes his breath away.

"Go pick up your piece, Rami," says Jorge, "and be more damn careful next time."

As Rami rolls over and pushes himself to his feet, Oliver says, "You know what you need, kid?"

"What's that?" says Rami.

"A bigger gun."

The woman laughs. Jorge takes hold of the leash and heads into the house, the dog trotting happily beside him. Oliver, back bowed, follows.

◆ ◆ ◆

They are sitting at the kitchen table, Jorge, the blue-haired woman, and Oliver, who once again has a hold of the dog's leash. There are beers, there's a joint, there's the cleaver, and there is a gun. The nausea from the violence is settling nicely with the beer in Oliver's stomach.

Oliver doesn't care about the gun, but he looks at the joint longingly. It would help his screeching back, so it would be medicinal, *Really, Officer,* but he needs his wits about him, so he lets it pass when offered and sticks to the beer and the handful of Advil the blue-haired woman gave him.

"Marisol told me about your granddaughter," says Jorge as he holds the smoldering joint. "It's a shame she mixed up with that Frank. I never liked nothing about Frank except the dog. The dog I liked. Smarter than Frank, you ask me."

"And just as loyal," says Oliver.

"There you go."

"Was she here? My granddaughter?"

"Nah, man. Just Frank." Jorge takes a hit. "He said he needed a quick infusion of cash to keep him on the road." Exhale. "He had some stuff, good quality. Theresa here checked it out. It was good, pure. We made a deal and that was that."

"That was that?"

"Simple as stone, man."

"I'm trying to track him down before it all goes to shit. This was the last place I knew he had been to. Did he say where he was headed?"

"California is what he said. The sun, the sand. Truth was, I would have paid him just to get him out of town and away from Marisol. He was no damn good for her. She's family, right? You do what you need to do for family. You know what I'm talking about, you riding out here like the Lone Ranger on a broken-down horse, looking for your grand-daughter with nothing but a cleaver and a dog. I admire that. And what you did to Rami, man, he won't be living that shit down for years. For years." Another hit. "The things we do for family. Am I right?"

"Are you?" says Oliver before he takes a swallow of beer. He thinks about grabbing the cleaver and taking off one of Jorge's hands, just for the fuck of it. Teach the lying bastard a lesson about lying. He makes a quick calculation about whether he could get away with it. Probably not, but he bets blue-haired Theresa would be amused. He can tell right off she's too good for him.

"I got an aunt, Marisol's mother," says Jorge, droning on like he's got to get something off his tattooed chest. "Auntie Alejandra. She's one of them women who is forever mourning the man who was no damn good for her in the first place. Pepito, that son of a bitch. Gave her Marisol and then the clap and then he died in a knife fight in Pilsen. It's more than twenty years later and Alejandra, she still wears black. Hasn't been laid in decades, drying up like a raisin. But that Marisol, she is her sweet little princess."

Oliver is sort of listening. There's something to digest here, he knows, but his back is hurting and the beer tastes good and the dog is acting strangely. There's an open door leading down to the basement and the dog is facing it at the end of a taut leash, his body tensed, one front leg reaching out and his nose pressing forward as if against a piece of glass. What's down there, a brace of pheasants?

"And now there's not a Sunday dinner that don't go by without Auntie Alejandra going on and on about how Marisol is wasting her life with her guitar and this no-good *idioto* or that no-good *idioto*. And Frank was the worst of all the *idiotos*, man. It got to the point where *mi madre*, she told me I had to do something just to shut her big sister up, you know what I mean. So I convinced him to make a move and then made sure it all went to fuck. Family. Shit. The messes they make. Am I right?"

Oliver takes another swallow of beer and nods, like this is all as fascinating as the northern lights, like Jorge is another Allen Ginsberg spouting Buddhist truths with his poetry and finger cymbals. Oliver nods and nods as he gently lets go of the leash.

It takes a moment for the dog to realize he is free. Feeling the leash slack, he looks at Oliver as if to say, *Hold me back, don't let me go,* but then he's off, charging at the door and down the stairs, the leash rattling after him.

Jorge is blathering on about something or other to do with his sour aunt Alejandra when he stops, mercifully, in midsentence and looks at the doorway the dog just darted into. Oliver slams down the beer and raises himself to what almost qualifies as standing.

"I'll get the little bastard," says Oliver as he grabs the cleaver off the table.

The moment it takes Jorge and Theresa to react is long enough for Oliver to stagger to the doorway, flick on the light, and start down the rickety wooden stairs. Jorge shouts after him, but Oliver keeps heading down. Until his boot hits the wet cement of the basement floor and a shock reverberates up his spine, along with a pathetic disappointment.

For a moment he thought Hunter might have found her, finally, Erica, bound and gagged in that foul basement. For a moment he thought he would be the hero of the day with the dog and his cleaver— slash, slash. For a moment his hope soared, but reality has a way of always slapping him straight.

The basement is empty, except for a furnace, the rusting hulks of a washer and a dryer, and a metal table in the middle, with a couple chairs. Empty. Like his hope, his life, his prospects, his leads for ever finding his granddaughter.

But the dog is having none of Oliver's melancholic self-pity. Hunter is deep in sniff, as if there is something precious buried among the crap. Hunter barks and sniffs, scampers to the table, to a corner, and back to the table, where Oliver spies stains on the cement floor.

Oliver totters over to the stains, toes them with his boot. Blood? Hunter pushes Oliver's leg away as he gets another sniff. Frank Cormack's blood? The stairs shudder with pursuers. His back cracks as he reaches down to finger one of the stains. Nothing smears. He can't tell the age. New? Days or weeks old? What the hell does he know about stains? When he straightens up as much as he is able, he turns to face the wooden stairway with the cleaver in his hand.

Jorge stares at him from the bottom of the steps. Theresa stands above Jorge with the gun.

"Where is he?" says Oliver.

"I told you already, old man. We made a deal, I gave him cash, he left for the coast."

"And every word a lie."

"Yeah, well, what else did you expect? Frank never should have come back. I save his ass last time, set it up so he gets gone without being killed. That was the deal. And Auntie Alejandra was so grateful, *mi madre* so happy with me for once."

"My heart bleeds," says Oliver.

"But then he comes back? Hitting up Marisol all over again? What the hell was I going to do? And it wasn't like Frank left square. He owed big time still. He knew what was waiting for him in this town. What you care about him anyhow? He just doing with your granddaughter what he do to Marisol. Taking her for a ride to nowhere. You should be thanking me. You should be kissing my ring."

"I should be putting this cleaver in your face."

"You got spit for an old man, I'll give you that."

"It's bile," says Oliver. "At your fucking gall."

Oliver imagines it all just then, the hurl of the cleaver, the purity of violence, bone on flesh, the cleansing spray of blood, the flash of the gun, the taste of licorice. It is so inviting, so soul thrilling, so soul filling, that the temptation shakes him in his boots.

It is the sight of the blue-haired woman on the stairs that brings him out of his reverie and into the world where his desire for self-immolation will do nothing to help find Frank Cormack or his grand-daughter. He never fails to disappoint himself, and this little jaunt to South Chicago is no exception. But what is that there, right there, on the woman's pretty lips: a malicious sneer or the hint of an encouraging smile? It matters because she's the one with the gun.

He lets out a grunt as he pulls back the chair beside the stains on the floor. He sits down hard, tosses the cleaver onto the table. It bangs and then rattles, metal on metal. He realizes he's going to have to talk his way out of this one. Fuck.

"You make me so goddamn weary, Jorge," says Oliver in a slow, calm voice as he rubs his huge hand over his skull. "No matter how shit your life is, and I know a shit life when I see one, you still think it's your duty to protect cousin Marisol, whose life is not shit, whose life is pretty damn sweet from what I can see. And why are you stepping in? Because of Aunt Alejandra, a desiccated witch, who wants only to squeeze the balls of the entire world in her shriveled little fist. And she's sure as hell squeezing yours."

The blue-haired woman laughs, something rich and personal, as if she's had a run-in with Jorge's dear old aunty.

"I am so sick of this goddamn country and its fucking tribes," continues Oliver. "You're in or you're out, and if you're out, fuck you. Frank Cormack wasn't in your tribe, so you sold him out twice. All for your wretched aunt Alejandra? Who's next to go? Who else are you going to sacrifice on the altar of that witch's sexual deprivation? If I was you, I'd take the cleaver and slice my own goddamn throat."

"Careful, old man."

"I'm tired. Are you tired? I could sleep right here. I think I might, except that someone needs to save the son of a bitch you set up to die."

"And you think you're the one?"

"Who else is there?"

"Why would you even try?" says the woman on the steps.

Oliver looks at her. "Because no one else wants to. And because I made a promise. And because the only tribe I know is the tribe of the tribeless, and Frank Cormack belongs."

"Go back to the nut farm," says Jorge.

"At least he's trying," says the woman. "And he's right, Jorge. What you did to Frank was wrong, egging him on to do that deal and setting him up to fail. That was low."

"It was a family thing."

"You and your family," she says. "Fuck your family. There's a man named Delaney."

"Shut up."

"He's the one Frank owed. He has a place on the west side, an abandoned factory where he keeps everything, his motorcycles, his drugs. Jorge gave Frank to him. He's the next stop on your trail."

"What the hell are you doing, Theresa?"

"It wasn't right what you did, Jorge. I don't know what this old man is going to do about it, but what you did wasn't right. And this way it's Delaney who has to kill him, not us. It's cleaner that way. I got the address. You want me to write it down?"

Oliver nods.

"And you're right," says Theresa, "his little auntie is a bitch. But I'll tell you something else. Jorge's mother, she's worse."

Out of that house and back in the truck with the dog, Oliver lets the GPS take him to Delaney.

The address Theresa gave Oliver is to an abandoned factory in a deserted western sector of the city. Oliver is not yet ready to make a move. The night has grown late and there are things to figure out before he again wields the cleaver. How should he enter? How should he behave? Is there a bribe that might work? And what the hell did Erica want with Finnegan? Tonight is merely about scouting the terrain.

But the sight of Delaney's ruined factory, with its smashed windows and great steel ducts slithering in and out of its walls like a ravening serpent, tells Oliver exactly what he's up against. Oliver sees the jerry-rigged ugliness of the building—a foreboding landscape out of some dystopian nightmare—as a place where nothing matters but the money, where scores are kept and fates are tallied only in dollars and cents.

He is facing the most merciless of forces, stone-cold capitalism, and not just in the figure of Delaney, but also in Jorge, and the Russian with his pack of brutes, and everyone else who has flayed Frank Cormack with the knife of Cormack's own ambition.

Oliver has faced it before, every day of his goddamn life as a matter of fact. It has been Oliver's fight from that first moment in Chicago when he kissed Helen and saw the possibility of a future different from what he had ever before imagined. Every step of the way since then, no matter how misguided or futile, from San Francisco to the farm to his working-class life on Avery Road, was always an attempt to free himself from the shackles not just of this brutal overseer but of his own wanting and greed. So maybe he failed and failed again, but the fight always continued.

And now, here, he realizes that he is in that same battle once more, this time not for his own fate, but for the fate of his granddaughter and a man he has never met. It's a battle that won't end well, he knows, but it's a battle that brings a song to his heart.

As he drives away, and the city night paints his face with streaks of light, the dog looks up and tilts his head in confusion. What's that on the man's lips as he heads in search of a bed to sleep on that night? It is something new, something the dog hasn't seen on the man's ugly features before.

It scares the dog to see it, this strange and bitter smile, and the dog is right to be scared.

25

FOUNTAIN OF LIFE

Like a haughty society matron, Oliver Cross leads his dog to the plush environs of the University Club.

Oliver is wearing jeans and a flannel shirt, both still firmly against the club's dress code. The dog is naked, which is even better, and Oliver considers following suit. He is looking forward to the inevitable brouhaha when he passes by the doorman beneath the green awning and tries to get past the front desk. He imagines the lackeys shouting about his problematic jeans; he imagines himself saying, "I'll take them off if that's what you want," and stripping right there in the lobby. His bare red ass would let them know exactly what he thinks of them all. Oh, he is ready to huff and puff. He feels almost young and fresh again, full of piss and vinegar. Well, the piss for sure.

But when he rounds the corner and sees the tall Gothic cathedral of wealth and privilege towering above him, his spirits turn. There stands his father, once again peering down at him. *What have you made of yourself, Oliver? Certainly not something worthy of this citadel. So pray tell, boy, where do you belong?* But the voice he hears has none of his father's flat Midwest matter-of-factness; the voice he hears is mysteriously his own, full of bitterness and regret.

And with that voice now burning in his ears, the University Club and all it represents are suddenly not something he spurned, but something he lost. He considers the life he could have had behind those stained glass windows, a life of wealth and consequence. He would have been listened to in corporate boardrooms, he would have been honored at charity balls, he would have run for the statehouse, the Senate, he would have fulfilled, maybe even exceeded, his brother's destiny. The world would have known his name.

And everyone would have been so fucking proud.

His walk is now no longer assured; every step forward becomes arthritic and full of regret. He would stop, turn around, badger Delaney and end up with a bullet in his head, anything rather than go through this whole dog and pony show with his alternate life, but something keeps him moving forward, as if it is actually Hunter doing the leading. Stinking dog.

"Yes, sir," says the uniformed woman at the desk, young and blonde and smooth as silk. "How can I help you?"

"Lunch," grunts Oliver.

"Are you meeting someone?"

"Would I come to a craphole like this if I weren't?"

"Perhaps not," says the woman, her smile soft with pity. "But we do have a dress code, sir. Jeans are not allowed. And neither are dogs, I'm afraid."

"I'll take the jeans off and put them on the dog, if you want. Is there a rule against dogs with jeans?"

"I would assume so, yes. And skivvies aren't permitted either."

"At least that won't be a problem then."

"If you let me know the member you were intending to meet, sir, I'll run up a message."

"Excuse me, Mr. Cross?"

Oliver turns to see walking toward them a dark-skinned young man in a ridiculously tight blue suit, with light-brown shoes, gelled hair, and shining teeth.

"Mr. Prakash?" says the woman behind the desk. "Was this man supposed to be your guest today?"

"Not my guest, Cecilia," says Prakash with a slight British accent. "Mr. Finnegan's guest. This is Oliver Cross. The famous Oliver Cross. His father was a longtime member, Gerald Cross?"

"Oh, yes, of course. Mr. Cross was a fine old gentleman, from what I hear," says the woman.

"One out of three," says Oliver.

"We assumed Mr. Cross might not remember the dress code," says Prakash.

"Oh, I remember it all too well," says Oliver.

"And so we asked Mr. Pederson to waive it in this special case, out of respect for Mr. Cross's father, and he agreed. I have a note here confirming." Prakash pulls a letter from his pocket and hands it to the woman.

"Yes, I see," says Cecilia, as she reads. "But there is still the matter of the dog."

"It's a service dog. Isn't that right, Mr. Cross?"

"If service means crapping all over the place."

"We would give you the specifics of the medical condition the presence of the dog ameliorates but that could open the club to HIPAA liability, and we wouldn't want that, would we, Cecilia?"

"Uh, no, certainly not, Mr. Prakash."

"I'll take Mr. Cross up to Mr. Finnegan, if that's all right. Thank you for your assistance. We'll let Mr. Pederson know how helpful you've been."

"Are you going to let him bamboozle you like that?" says Oliver to the woman.

"Evidently," she says cheerfully.

"You'll go far."

"We can only hope. Enjoy your lunch, Mr. Cross."

In the elevator with the very capable Mr. Prakash, Oliver says, "When did I become so famous?"

"Mr. Finnegan talks about you all the time, Mr. Cross. He admires you so. Whenever he grows wistful, which happens more and more often these days, he inevitably brings up your name."

"You work for him?"

"I work for you, too, Mr. Cross," says Prakash. "I'm a senior associate in the Trust and Estates section of the firm. Ah, here we are. This way, in case you don't remember."

On their parade through the vaulted grillroom, Hunter pulls at the leash, angling toward this table and that, smelling the steak, the salmon, the lamb chops with their rib bones waiting to be snapped in his sharp yellow teeth. Oliver keeps yanking him toward the table in the corner where a handsome gray-haired man with a blue suit and a smooth, oily face waits at a table set for two. The man looks like a senator who has been surgically made up for the cameras.

Finnegan smiles as Oliver approaches, stands, reaches out both arms to give Oliver a hug. Oliver lets Hunter sniff and jump, putting the kibosh on the deranged hug idea.

"You look good, Oliver," says Finnegan as he backs away from the dog's affections.

"No I don't."

"You're not dead yet, at least."

"Give it time."

"And who is this little fellow?"

"He's a rescue."

"Nice touch bringing him into the club. We all need companions in these later years. Sit, sit," says Finnegan addressing not the dog but Oliver as he takes his seat and gestures to the chair across from him. "How about a drink? Something festive to celebrate our reunion? Champagne, or is that a bit too festive?"

Oliver, still standing, says, "Did you see her?"

"Maybe Scotch? That always works." He motions for a waiter. "How are you readjusting after prison? It can be difficult, I am told. I suppose the dog helps."

"Did you see her, Finn?"

"Yes, I saw her. Ah, Wesley. I'll have a Scotch. What about the Macallan Rare Cask, with ice."

"Very good," says the waiter.

"And you, Oliver? The Scotch is a bit oaky, but otherwise quite brilliant and fiendishly expensive."

"Beer," says Oliver as he drops into the chair.

"Oh come on, this is my treat. Live a little."

"Beer."

"We have some wonderful IPAs on tap," says the waiter.

"Old Style."

"Coming right up."

"And two bowls," says Oliver. "One with water, one with meat."

"Give him the aged New York strip," says Finnegan. "Rare. It's a nice cut. Please slice it into small pieces, Wesley, we wouldn't want the old thing to choke. And we might want to get some food and drink for the dog, too."

"Very good, sir," says the waiter.

"How did she look?" says Oliver when the waiter has departed.

"You have a lovely granddaughter. And she reveres you."

"Don't lie to me."

"Well, 'revere' might have been a bit strong."

"What did she want?"

"She asked for help. I gave it."

"When was this?"

"A few days ago. Right here, as a matter of fact."

"What kind of help?"

"If she wanted you to know, Oliver, don't you think she would have asked you for the help?"

"Don't fuck with me, Finn."

"I'm just trying to be polite. You called me, remember?"

"Okay. Let's be polite. How's life?"

"Grand."

"What number wife are you on, now?"

"Four. And they keep getting younger. How does that happen? But it's really not my fault. You have to catch them while they still want to have sex. When they reach a certain age they just don't care anymore. And the older I get, the younger they need to be to still want to have it with me. Have you dated since Helen? I mean other than in prison."

"What did Erica want?"

"Money."

"And you gave it? Without asking me?"

"It wasn't your money I gave to her. I drew it out of my personal account. Believe it or not, even after the divorces there was still something left."

"I'll pay you back."

"Of course you will. In fact I brought an estate check. Ah, the drinks."

They stay quiet as Wesley places the glasses before them, an amber liquid surrounding a great ball of ice in Finn's cut crystal rock, a tall tapered pilsner filled with cheap Wisconsin beer for Oliver. He puts a bowl of water on the ground for the dog, who ignores it.

Finn takes a sip, lets out a satisfied sigh. "You know what it tastes like, Oliver? It tastes like money, limned with sex. A taste that never gets old. I hope you don't mind meeting at the club with all its tender familial echoes, but I so love it here. It was everything I aspired to when I was young. Your father sponsored me, and brought the other two nominators on board. I've always appreciated that. Pretty heady stuff for a Loyola grad. I've tried to pay it back. What do you think of Divit over there?"

"Prakash? His suit is too tight."

"The young these days have their own ways. But he's quite a brilliant lawyer, and such a people person. Divit Prakash will be a partner in two years and running the firm in seven. Who knows after that. Mayor, perhaps? I wouldn't put it past him. I sponsored him here. So it goes. One passes on the life."

"Tell me, Finn, when did you become such a pretentious asshole?"

Finn leans forward, stares into the glass as if it were a magic eight ball. "I don't know," he says, finally. "One day it was like a switch turned. I think it's something the club puts in the water, not that I drink too much of it."

For a moment Finn looks so stricken, Oliver doesn't know how to react, until something unbidden and unfamiliar rises from his chest and startles him. And then Oliver Cross begins to laugh, for the first time in how long he doesn't remember. And the dog, hearing an unfamiliar sound, yelps twice before he stands and starts tonguing the water bowl. And then Oliver's old friend Finn begins to laugh with him, ruefully at first, and then more openly. And as the two old men laugh, years melt away like drying tears.

They order, they eat: filet for Finn, a mushroom soup and salad for Oliver, the cut-up strip steak for Hunter. And the two men remember together the years long ago when everything seemed possible, when everything was possible. And now here they are. So, how was it? Not like I expected. Another drink? Sure, what the hell. Would you do it again? Fuck no, except, well, you know. Yeah, I know. And they both think, at least I didn't turn out like you.

And then, in the middle of some inconsequential memory that makes them both shake their heads at the stupidity of the young, Finn leans forward and says, "What the hell are you doing, Oliver?"

"Eating lunch?"

"I mean here, in Chicago. I mean breaking parole to chase after your granddaughter who obviously doesn't want to be found."

"She's in trouble."

"Of course she's in trouble, she's on the road with a folk singer. That's the definition of 'trouble.' I'm sure Helen's parents thought the same thing about you, even though you had the voice of a frog."

"It's worse than that, Finn. Trust me."

"She said you had spoken of me fondly, your old friend Finnegan. I was touched."

"Did she say why she needed the money?"

"She didn't want to say exactly, but I asked enough questions to learn that she intended to buy back her boyfriend from some thug he owed money to from his last time in the city."

"And you gave her the money and let her go? Just like that?"

"Calm down, Oliver. I didn't let her go at all. She's the granddaughter of my oldest friend. What kind of animal do you take me for? I sent Divit instead."

"Prakash? With the gelled hair?"

"Of course. It was a negotiation and Divit is a crackerjack negotiator. In fact, he already spoke to your lawyer in Philadelphia about this parole violation."

"What? Prakash spoke to Don?"

"Your lawyer said Divit could speak to the DA if he wanted to, and so he did."

"I'm not going back."

"Divit also talked to your parole officer. Who is it, a Jennifer Post? He put me on with her. She sounded nice."

"Nice as a pitchfork in the neck."

"She says if you go back right away she'll speak up for you at the hearing. And the DA is inclined to follow her recommendation. Divit doesn't think you'll be sent back to prison."

"I'm not going back."

"Go home. Enjoy your money. Buy some wine, some hookers. Three's a good number. One's good but three tastes like the Scotch."

"I'm never going back."

"Then what are you going to do?"

"Go forward. Like always. So? What happened, Finn? Finish the story."

"Divit worked it out."

Oliver turns in his seat and spies the young man in the tight suit lunching with a pretty woman. He is leaning back, regaling her with an anecdote. His ease makes Oliver feel so very old.

"He made a deal with a man named Delaney. From what he says he had to turn over a spare tire filled with something illicit and some additional money for the vig, so to speak, but the boy was released. A bit worse for wear, I can tell you. When Erica and I saw him, finally, it was like he had been in a twelve rounder with Sonny Liston. Remember Sonny Liston? No one else does."

"Christ. You couldn't have told me all this right off? So they're out of the city?"

"After a quick visit to the hospital so a doctor could look at one of the boy's legs, which wasn't quite working anymore, I gave Erica some more money, not too much mind you, but enough to travel on. So yes, they're gone. And you're welcome, Oliver."

"Where'd they go?"

"Away. Don't you think it's best to let them work it out for themselves? My guess, from the looks of it, is she'll be home within a few weeks. This has all been more than she bargained for and she wasn't quite looking at him with goo-goo eyes when Divit brought him around."

"They're still being chased."

"I assumed. He was anxious to get back on the road."

"And he robbed a convenience store."

"Kids these days."

"It's easy to be cavalier when it's not your granddaughter."

"Here's the thing, Oliver. You want to save her, I know you do, but I don't know if she wants to be saved. At least not yet."

"Doesn't matter."

"Your father tried to save you from a life among the rabble. How'd that work out?"

"Look at me."

"I am, Oliver. I see a man who lived his dream with the woman he loved."

"It wasn't all sweet tea and flowers."

"Helen was a disappointment?"

"No, never. She was magnificent to the end. I was the disappointment."

"Ah, there's the rub. Everything's possible until we screw it up ourselves. You need to learn to live without her, Oliver."

"Why?"

"It's the only way to live with what you did. The only way to give it meaning."

"I don't need it to have meaning."

"I understand, but—"

"You don't. You can't."

"You're right. Sorry. This club does terrible things to its members. We become insufferable."

"What, you mean you detest this place, too?"

"I love it, so help me. It is somehow more satisfying than the wives, the children I spoiled and then left, the pack of hyenas at the firm whom I call my partners. All I ever wanted to be was a member of the club and here I am, without regret."

"Well, you pursued it with an admirable relentlessness, I'll give you that." Oliver takes a long drink from his beer. "You've been a good friend, Finn."

"I stole your birthright."

"Birthright? Do I look like Esau?"

"Once, maybe, but you don't have the hair for it anymore."

"You gave my father someone to take care of, and you took care of him at the end. Whatever he granted you, you earned, and I'm grateful."

"I actually loved him."

"Me too. Where'd they go, Finn?"

"I don't know for sure, but she asked about the farm where her father was born."

"The farm? Seven Suns?"

"She said she needed a safe place for Frank to recover. I hope you won't be cross—well, you can't help that—but I told her where it was."

"The farm. Hell. Isn't that a peach? Does she have any idea who owns it?"

"No."

"Good."

"So, what now, Oliver?"

"It's time to get the hell out of here. But first I need to settle up my estate. I might have some changes to make."

"Good idea. Let me call over Divit, that's his bailiwick. You don't mind if I sit in and have another Scotch?"

"Knock yourself out."

"I'll be billing for it, too. You know, it really is good to see you again, Oliver."

"Why?"

"That, right there. That's why. Oh, Wesley. Another round. And, please, let Mr. Prakash know we'd like to see him."

26

Ballad of a Thin Man

There is a moment on the road to the farm, somewhere on a dead flat expanse with the mountains appearing like a mirage in the distance, when Oliver Cross senses this entire irrational chase will be as fruitless as his life. All his noble impulses and clever wiles will once again be for naught. Maybe it has something to do with the farm itself, which for Oliver continues to hold an air of loss and tragedy. Or maybe it has something to do with the way Chicago ended, how he crossed a line after his meeting with Finn that he needs to pay for. Or maybe it is the general sullenness of the girl, sitting as far from him as possible on the bench seat, staring out at the dreary prairie as if its very monotony is a foretelling of a numb future. But something has gone wrong and the bitterness of failure has already slicked itself on his tongue.

"I'm so bored I could grind my teeth to dust just for sport," says the girl.

"We're getting there."

"Where? You still haven't told me."

"What's that on the horizon?" says Oliver.

"Nothing but clouds."

"Those aren't clouds."

"Then what are they?"

"The Rockies."

"And you think Frank and Erica might be somewhere in the mountains?"

"In the foothills."

"What makes you think that's where they went?"

"Just a hunch. The Rockies are the beginning of the west. California's somewhere beyond. Turn on the radio if you want."

"It's all preachers and country music. It's enough to make me puke."

"That would be entertaining at least."

"For you."

"The dog would like it, too. It's almost feeding time. I could play a tape if you wanted."

"Your old crap gives me the creeps. You don't have anything made since I was born. I mean really, Oliver, that's just sad. Your music is so old and white it should be in the Senate."

"I have Hendrix."

"Wow. Now I'm impressed. You're like every other old white dude. Look how radical I am, I dig Hendrix. Hendrix. Jesus, Oliver. He's playing your music, not ours. It's still just guitars and psychedelic shit with that same old beat."

"He was a genius."

"Sure, but if Hendrix rapped you'd throw him out with yesterday's garbage."

"Maybe that's where he would belong."

"Didn't you hear? Kendrick Lamar won a Pulitzer."

"Who?"

"Now that's just embarrassing."

He thinks on that a bit. "Truth is," he says, finally, "I embarrass myself. I also have Jimmy Cliff."

"Rock's dead."

"Reggae."

"Doesn't matter. All your music's dead. And good riddance."

"Why the hell are you in such a twist?"

"Forget it."

"Fine," says Oliver. "Consider it forgotten." But it isn't forgotten, it is a thorn in his shin, and he has a pretty firm sense of what it is all about.

When he had returned to the house in Humboldt Park after a long meeting with Finnegan and Prakash in a private room at the University Club, Ayana was shining. She had spent the night before playing guitar with Marisol, and the next day working on the songs and pick patterns her host had taught her. She was bursting with stories about how nice everyone was, how they had a little party for her that night, how she nervously sang her Tracy Chapman song for the group and everybody oohed and aahed.

"Marisol said if I learned a few more songs and tightened up my guitar work she could get me some gigs here or there."

"We have to go," said Oliver.

"She said I could be really good."

"Get your stuff."

"Can we wait at least just to say goodbye? Sheila said Marisol would be back soon."

"We're going."

"Oliver, please?"

"Now," he said.

But before they left the city, he drove the girl to that abandoned factory in the deserted western sector. The cracked windows, the snaking metal ducts, the air of treacherous neglect. There were motorcycles in the lot, and light behind some of the windows. Two henchmen henched at the entrance. Oliver slowly passed it once, turned around, and parked a ways down the street. The factory was visible through the windshield.

"What's here?" she asked.

"Death," said Oliver.

"What the hell?"

"It's being used by a gangster named Delaney. Marisol's cousin gave Frank to Delaney because Frank owed Delaney money. Lots of money. I thought I was going to have to go in and get him out. I probably wouldn't have survived. I was almost looking forward to it. But someone got here before me and bought Frank's freedom. Do you want to know the price?"

The girl just turned and looked at Oliver.

"The Russian's drugs."

"Wow."

"Well said."

"That's that, I suppose."

"Not yet. Have you been in touch with the Russian since we left Pennsylvania?"

"No. How could I? You threw away my phone, remember?"

"There are enough phones in the world to choke the Mississippi. Every diner has a phone, every stranger we pass. Marisol has a phone, too. Did you call the Russian? Did you check in with your handler?"

"Handler? Oliver? No, I swear. Truth is, I'm thrilled to be away from those assholes. I'm going west, man. California, right? Or someplace on the way. Fuck them and their bullshit. No, I haven't. I don't want to. Ever again."

She was looking at him with some sort of pleading in her eyes. Whether she wanted him to believe a lie or the truth he couldn't figure, but just then it didn't much matter. From out of his jacket he pulled the phone and a paper with the address that the blue-haired woman had given him.

"You had a cell all this time?"

"Of course I did," he said, turning it on.

"Who were you calling?"

"That's not what's important. What's important is who you're calling now. You're calling the Russian or one of his people."

"Wait a second. What?"

"You're going to tell him you're outside the hideout where his drugs are sitting. You're going to describe it, tell him the name Delaney, and give him this address."

"I don't get it. Why?"

"He needs to know that Frank doesn't have his precious cargo anymore. He needs to know where it is. Maybe he'll give up the chase. Maybe he'll barge in here and try to get it back. Let these assholes kill each other instead of chasing Frank."

"Oliver?"

"Do it," he said.

"I don't want—"

"Do it."

She did it. He stayed silent as she made the call and gave the information. Then he listened to the cursing and threats from the other side. That was the line he had crossed, forcing her back into that world, and he knew it even as he was crossing it. But what else was he going to do? If it came from him, they wouldn't believe it. It had to come from the girl. When she finished, he pulled the truck away from that stinking place with a hard piece of hope lodged in his heart.

Let the blood flow.

It wasn't long before the spires of the city flashed in the rearview mirror. Oliver suspected then it would be the last time he ever saw the royal skyline of his hometown. You would think he would have shed a tear, but the hell with sentimentality. Finn was old, and his father was a ghost, and except for a few paintings in the Art Institute there was nothing there for him anymore. His home now was in his love for Helen, and what was left of Helen was behind the bench seat, and so he was homeless, finally, and glad for it.

So long and good riddance. Westward ho!

But his race to the farm hadn't gone smoothly, as if he was being made to pay for his transgression. To cheer up a suddenly quiet Ayana, he had taken her to a barbecue joint in Moline. Beautiful Moline, not exactly the barbecue capital of the world.

"What are you getting?" she said.

"Potato salad. Beans, maybe."

"No brisket? No pulled pork? The beef ribs look big."

"Is there an animal you won't roast and chew?"

"Stringy old men. Though with the right barbecue sauce, you never know."

"Funny."

The beans were good, and he had seconds, suddenly not caring about the chunks of smoked pork stirred into the mess. But his stomach cared, turning as soon as they hit the Iowa-Illinois Memorial Bridge over the Mississippi. Whatever he had eaten in Moline he ended up crapping out in a gush in a motel room east of Des Moines. He thought he could make it all the way to the farm the next day, stopping only to fill up with diesel and to feed and walk the dog, but his truck disagreed, having its own kind of intestinal distress outside of a place called Salina.

"Your belt's worn and your radiator hose is collapsed," said the mechanic, wiping his filthy hands on a filthier rag. "It's an old truck you got, mister. We need a get the parts in from Topeka."

That cost them another night, staying at the Starlight Motel with its fabulous neon sign, its aerosol scent, its pink walls and stiff sheets, with a microwave sitting atop the fridge so you could eat like a king while you waited for the parts to come in from Topeka. The television was on, tuned to some piece of trash the girl picked out.

"Turn this shit off and walk the dog," said Oliver over the celebrity groaning. "I need to get to sleep."

"I'm watching this. You walk the dog."

"I know you're watching. I can smell your brain rot. Why don't you read the book I got you?"

"Fuck your book."

"What the hell's got into you?"

"I think the truck is telling us something. I think the truck is saying give it up."

"Why would I listen to a truck?"

"Because maybe it's smarter than you are. Maybe it's time to call the whole thing off."

"What are you talking about?"

"You made me call the Russian. You made me tell him Frank's got nothing anymore. What makes you think Teddy's still hunting him? Maybe the danger's over. Maybe Erica and Frank are off on some great adventure. Maybe they're already gone from where you think they are."

"Maybe they're not."

"Maybe they don't want to be found."

"Maybe I don't give a shit."

"Maybe you're doing this for some other reason."

"Like what?"

"I don't know, Oliver. I'm no psychiatrist. But you sure as hell need one."

"Probably."

"Let's go home."

"Now you want to go back?"

"You already sent me back."

"Freedom's hard, isn't it?"

"Let's let them be and go home, Oliver."

"This is my home, now."

"Where, here? This crappy motel in this crappy town in this crappy state?"

"On the road."

"You and that stupid book."

"It's a good book. Respect the book."

"Fuck the book. I read a little more in Chicago when I was waiting on you. I got to the part where he meets a girl on a bus, and falls in love, and screws her silly."

"Terry, yeah. Sweet Terry. I was always a little in love with Terry."

"Then he runs away because he was a college boy, and she was a migrant, and he didn't want to spend his life picking cotton. He went back home to his college boy life in New York and the girl was left flat. Maybe even pregnant. But what did he care. I mean, she was a Mexican, right?"

"It wasn't like that."

"No."

"Well, maybe it was."

"Your Ker-o-what-the-fuck would have voted Trump for sure."

"Not when he was young. He wouldn't have voted at all when he was young. But when he became an old drunk, yeah. There's film of him complaining about dirty hippies to Buckley that makes me sick."

"Who's Buckley?"

"Some old fascist with a Brahman accent. But still, what the hell's gotten into you?"

"We need to look after our own, right?"

"That's what I'm doing."

"Then do it. I mean, Oliver, he's your fucking dog."

Oliver walked the dog.

And as he did, all his fatuous little explanations rose like pin bones to gouge his throat. She was right about the book, Ayana, damn right; he was a fool to even try. Every generation finds the voices that call it to order. Oliver's mother was making Oliver and his brother sit down and listen to Gene Krupa even as Chuck Berry and Little Richard were tearing the face off anything she could have understood. Why should Kerouac's riff on Thomas Wolfe have any call to the children of today's insanity? And with the mash he'd made of everything in his life, what standing did Oliver have to push anything on anyone, a book, an idea, a cynicism or an idealism, a political view, a poem, a way of life. It was all illusion, the only truth of things was in the urn tucked behind the seat of the truck. The girl was nineteen and utterly lost yet still she saw Kerouac more clearly than he ever had.

Before they picked up the truck the next morning, he mailed the book back to the library in Chillicothe.

◆ ◆ ◆

And now, with the cab of the truck fetid with the stink of an animosity of his own dealing and with the sense of everything gone wrong, the girl, the dog, and Oliver are rumbling ever closer to the great ridge of mountain.

Somewhere in a hollow beneath two high hills leading to Blue Mountain lies the farm. Seven Suns. A place of blood and ghosts. Oliver remembers making this same journey all those years ago, with a desperate hope that the three passengers in his VW van, one still unborn, would find a new and brilliant life there based on principles pulled from the heart and the earth instead of from the balance sheet of a bank.

But this trip is made with clearer eyes.

He slides off the interstate and rolls through the commercial crap of small-town America in the shadow of Pike's Peak, the little airport, the holes strip-mined into the hills, the Walmart and Sam's Club and fast-food burrito joints. They continue past the turnoff for Pueblo, until he hits old Route 115, now called the Vietnam Veterans Memorial Highway. It should bring fond thoughts of his brother, but all it does is piss him off. They lied to him and killed him and all he ended up with is this beaten stretch of rural road.

"Did I ever tell you about my brother?" he says to the girl.

"No."

"He's dead" is all he says.

The earth starts bulging with muscle as he heads south. And then things start to look familiar: a water tank, like half a barbell stuck into the ground, along with the mountainous rise on the right. There's more development than he remembers, a tract of houses here, a strip mall and trailer park there, but even with the surface changes, the landscape is as ingrained in his memory as the venous back of his dying wife's hand.

They used to take this road up to Manitoba Springs, where they had a Mardi Gras–type fair that brought in good folk from up and down the Rockies. After the dancing, the drinking, the reefer and 'shrooms, the laughing and protesting, the organic tomatoes eaten by hand—sweet as cotton candy with juice and seeds dripping down chin and forearm—they would ride back down old Route 115 in their trucks and jalopies, and that pyramid-shaped hill of rock right there, just there, told them when it was time to take the right; a pyramid, like a noble grave for all the hopes that died in that spot of the foothills.

Even before the GPS starts chirping he spots the familiar mailbox at the mouth of the farm's driveway. The mailbox lists on a rotting post; the drive runs over a steep ravine and then is flanked by bushes and tall weedy trees so overgrown it is impossible to see where the drive leads. It is a dusty dirt path to nowhere. He pulls to the side of the road and stops the truck.

"Is this it?" asks Ayana.

"This was it."

He leans over the back of the seat and pushes away this bag and that piece of garbage until he finds the urn. He hands it to the girl.

"Hold this."

"What is it?"

"My wife."

"What?"

"Just hold it," he says.

"Why?"

"Because I need a psychiatrist."

She looks at him, at the dog, and then puts the urn atop one of her thighs. With a grunt of satisfaction, Oliver grinds the truck into gear and starts down the rutted dirt path into the mountains.

He is waiting for the vista to open up from the wild scrub so he can see, wedged within the valley, the long flat expanse of green that constitutes the working part of the farm. But the brush obscures everything except the rocky hills on either side. Stray branches, reaching for the sunlight-baked road, brush against the side of the truck. The sound is like unintelligible warnings from the past.

Finally they pass the reservoir on the left, the grand old swimming hole, its banks overgrown and untended. In the distance there is an opening in the bushy barrier, and in that gap he spies a familiar tree, the old juniper, twisted now and worn, half its rising trunks shorn of any green at all. He parks in the tree's uneven shadow, next to a baby-blue Camaro with two stripes down the middle of its hood.

"This place doesn't look like much," says Ayana.

"It never really did. Piece-of-shit land farmed by idiots."

Ayana leaves the urn on the bench seat and steps out of the truck; the dog leaps after her and starts running. Oliver sits there for a moment, taking in the scene.

The fertile expanse he expected within the high hills on either side, the flat fields of corn and wheat and soy and hay are gone; what's left is weedy and wild and worthless, planted with bits of strange decoration that make the land look like a junkyard curated by the mad. The orchard in the distance, once so fertile, has become a nest of twisted branches reaching leaflessly to the sky. It's as if the farm hasn't been cultivated for years, for decades, except for a small patch of dirt in front of one of the cabins, crossed with scraggly rows of vegetables. The place is a ghost of what it was.

An old woman, long gray hair falling from a wide straw hat, is sitting in a wooden chair in the middle of the vegetable field. One hand holds a trowel, one hand a thick sheaf of useless weed. She lifts her head, peers at him, and then struggles to stand.

Beside the woman is a girl who looks like a memory. She holds a hoe and takes a step forward.

The dog sprints past the two women and jumps around a skinny young man with long hair streaming from beneath a backward baseball cap. He stands stiffly with a metal crutch under one of his tattooed arms. His chest is concave, his chin is pointy, his narrow face is a swollen mess. The dog dances, spins. The man takes the crutch from beneath his arm and bends to grab at Hunter's snout. A long tongue licks the man's wrist.

"Do you see it?" asks Helen. "Do you see it all, my love?"

"I see it," grunts Oliver.

"What do you see?"

"Desolation."

"Oh no, that's not it, not it at all," says his dead wife. "It's a chance, a final chance to make everything right again. To grab hold of life again. To heal the world and make something new."

Oliver groans. He was right, dead right; it is all turning to shit.

III. Electric Ladyland

27

Astral Weeks

He was a boy who knew nothing but freedom.

He ran naked through the fields beneath the harvest moon. He swung through the orchard trees like an ape-man and jumped into the reservoir before he could swim, thrashing his wild way to the surface. Sometimes he even crapped in the bushes like one of the coyotes that snickered across the fields and terrorized the chickens. His face was dark with sun and dirt, his ruddy hair long and tangled, his teeth twisted like the trunks of the juniper tree at the mouth of the road. At night he would crawl into bed beside his mother and roll his naked body into a ball like a dog as she hugged him tight and sang him to sleep. He smelled like a feral creature of the foothills, and he didn't talk.

He could talk, certainly. He had been a jabbermouth as a toddler, poking his voice into every crevice of every conversation. But two years before, at age five or so, he just stopped, as if within the crucible of his freedom he was devolving, or evolving, depending on your view, into a species of his own.

Hominis bestia.

The boy was still alert, still listened and understood, still made himself understood, still read picture books from the makeshift schoolroom in the main house, his lips silently mouthing the words.

"He'll talk when he's ready," said his mother as she painted, daubing a light cerulean blue onto a wild abstract canvas set just outside the old stable the boy's parents had taken for their home. "We don't want to force him into inane social chitchat."

"What about school?" said Angie, her dark face creased with concern. Angie managed the farm's homeschool. "He never participates. He just draws with crayons or scratches designs into the floorboards with scissors. I can't bring him into any of the discussions."

"Are they good?"

"The discussions?"

"The designs?"

"Yes, actually. He has an artist's eye, like his mother. But he could be doing so much more."

"He'll do more when he's ready."

"Like he'll speak when he's ready? This isn't normal."

"Is that what we aspire to now?" said the boy's mother, looking away from the canvas for a moment to gaze at her son. The boy squatted in the dirt under the portico that stretched across the front of the stable. Wearing his paisley tunic and ripped cotton pants, he wasn't paying attention to the conversation as he used one of his father's chisels to gouge at the spare piece of wood he was carving into a frog.

"I've been asking around during market day," said Angie. "There's a child psychologist who people say good things about."

"He's just a boy. And we don't have the money."

"His grandfather has money."

"That's not what we do."

"Maybe you should start. Or why don't you let Lucius work with him? He is great with the children. His therapies are very spiritual."

"Whatever that therapy is, it is not spiritual."

"I think your son needs to see somebody."

"He sees me," said his mother. "And his father. And his friends. Maybe he just doesn't have anything to say. Maybe he's waiting until he does. And maybe then his words will change the world."

"You think he's a poet?"

"Or a seer. One never knows."

The boy licked the side of his mouth as he gouged out a frog's eye.

There was a clutch of children at the farm, but it was Arlo and Sunrise who held the boy's heart.

Arlo, twelve years old, was big for his age, with huge rounded shoulders. He talked so slowly you could go to sleep between his words. Sunrise was twice the boy's age, slender and blonde, and she spoke in a voice so flat and lacking in emotion that it squeezed at the boy's heart. Sunrise's father had run off back to the world. Some days the girl would sit for hours in the juniper tree waiting for her father to come back and take her away with him.

The three friends would play together, adventure together, swim together in the reservoir. After swimming they would lie quietly side by side on the reservoir's banks, staring at the clouds as gnats and dragonflies flitted about them. Sometimes they would hold hands in a chain, with the boy in the middle, and crack whips across the fields. The boy, with a grip as tenacious as an ironworker, would let go only when the force was threatening to tear out his little arms.

"Let's go see Crazy Bob," said Sunrise to Arlo and the boy on the day when everything changed, and off they went.

The three friends started running together beside the dirt road on the southern edge of the farm that passed the cabins and ran around the orchard before heading for the rise at the far end of the valley. They ran whenever they could, as if running across the surface of the earth was as natural as breathing. As they ran two of the dogs, Skipper and Moonstone, joined them. The sun was high, the air had a snap to it, the ground felt warm under their feet. The three children spun with their arms stretched as the dogs loped around them, barking and keeping pace with ease. They were five now, running wild, as much creatures of the mountains as the striped chipmunks that darted around the edges of the cabins and the peregrine falcons that swooped down to grab the chipmunks in their claws.

Crazy Bob lived with Toby, who had been in the war, in a small cabin at the westernmost point of the farm where he would make caramels for the children on a wood-burning stove. Crazy Bob had his own special field that he tended, ringed by a post-and-rail fence the boy's father had built, and a shop behind his cabin for his science work. He didn't let the children inside his shop but they had spied the whole setup through the window: the white plastic jugs, the oil lanterns, the racks of glasses filled with bubbling liquids.

"Well, well, well," said Crazy Bob, wild haired and long bearded with the face of a samurai. He sat on a rocking chair in the dirt in front of his cabin, fiddling with some little machine. "If it isn't the three Mouseketeers. Come to spy on Crazy Bob, did you?"

"What's that you're playing with, Crazy Bob?" said Sunrise.

"It's called a carburetor."

"What's—what's," said Arlo.

"A carburetor is a thingamajig in an engine that never seems to work right," said Crazy Bob. "This is from that motorcycle over there."

"That's a big motorcycle," said Sunrise.

"It's a Harley."

"What's its last name?" said Sunrise.

"Davidson. Harley Davidson. I dated his sister Tina back in the day."

It was not strange to see a motorcycle on the farm. They came a lot, the motorcycle people, with their black jackets and vests with pictures of skulls on the back. They were friends with Lucius and Crazy Bob and they always came to the cabin back here when they thundered down the dirt road. The sound of the motorcycles was so loud and throbbing that it scared the boy, especially when they came in the middle of the night, like monsters from another world.

"Why—handles—so—" said Arlo.

"Why are those handles so high?" said Crazy Bob. "Because some people are damn fools. You children want some caramels? Course you do, why else would you have come. Other than the spying thing. Here, Fletcher, you hold this for me."

Crazy Bob handed the machine to the boy. It was heavy and felt oily and smelled like gasoline, but it had a little flippery thing that was fun to play with. Arlo leaned over and poked at it with a thick finger.

When he came back, Crazy Bob's head was wreathed in the smoke of an uneven cigarette that smelled as sweetly sticky as the candy he handed out. Two caramels for each and a couple extra for Wendy if they saw her.

"But none for them boys with the boots," said Crazy Bob as he took the machine from the boy and sat back down in his rocking chair. "I don't want to ruin their pretty white teeth. Fire would pull out my beard by the handfuls, she would."

"Thanks, Crazy Bob," said Sunrise.

"You kids are welcome anytime. Just so's you don't step in my field. I don't want you crushing any of the tender little shoots. It's the little shoots that grow so rich."

The three children walked back along the northern edge of the farm, chewing on their candies. Even after wiping his hands on his shift, the boy thought the caramels tasted strange, like he had licked the machine. Sunrise couldn't resist giving Wendy's caramels to the dogs.

"Don't tell," said Sunrise.

"We—won't," said Arlo. "Promise."

While walking through a field of still green hay, letting the blades tickle their faces, they saw Flit riding on a tractor. Arlo let out his famous hoot, like the night call of an owl, and Flit waved. In the distance, Toby and Gracie were working the cornfield. The children climbed through the fence around the cow pasture and walked past the beasts with their heavy udders and their eyes as black and dull as Crazy Bob's. The cows were chewing, chewing like they had caramels of their own. Sunrise petted one, who ignored her. The dogs loped along outside the fence, while Sam, the farm's peacock, ambled over and pecked at the ground.

"Hello there, Sam," said Sunrise. "Want to put on a show?"

The kids danced around the peacock urging it to display its feathers. The dance sometimes worked and the peacock would flash his tail, but this time he kept pecking, so they moved on.

On the other side of the pasture, beyond the barn and next to the little plot of land where Arlo's mom was buried, the boy's father was working on the chicken coop.

"Hello, Oliver," said Sunrise. "What'cha doing?"

"Just changing some of the boards that have started going to rot," said the boy's father. "I've been meaning to get to them for a while, but last night Toby said he saw a coyote trying to paw his way in. The chickens weren't so happy about that. Hey, Fletcher, you want to help?"

The boy looked at his father for a moment and then turned away.

"Come on, Fletcher, don't be like that. I'll let you use the plane. You like using the plane. Or we could have a catch after. You want to have a catch? Take some swings with the bat I brought back from Chicago? Just talk to me."

But what could the boy say? There was too much to say. The words caught one on the next before they reached his throat. The flatness of Sunrise's speech thrilled him because everything she said was bleached of emotion. But for the boy, words were emotions and he was so filled with words that they jammed up against each other, like the bits of ice on the creek leading to the reservoir on the coldest winter days. He looked once more at his father, felt something press at his eyes, and then he walked away.

The boy joined Sunrise and Arlo, sitting on the ground with Wendy, who was holding a black-feathered chicken in her lap. The dogs were looking on with something sharp in their faces. "Down," said Wendy, and the dogs lay right down, but their eyes stayed trained on the chicken.

Wendy was the boy's friend, too. She was three years older and spent all her time with the cows and chickens, the frogs by the reservoir, the three dogs that roamed free. She even left food out for the coyotes and waited in the weeds with the boy so they could see the creatures up close and give them names. Savage. Lucky. Notail. The coyotes, knowing where their bread was buttered, sometimes followed her as she walked across the fields.

"She's not feeling well," said Wendy about the chicken. "She was just lying on the ground breathing so hard. I think something's wrong."

"What are you going to do?" said Sunrise.

"Hold her, kiss her. That's what Mommy does to me when I don't feel good."

"Will—she—let—you?" said Arlo.

"Of course. She loves me." Wendy gave the chicken a big kiss on her neck and the hen turned her red-combed head back and forth without any upset, like Wendy's kiss was as natural as a breath of air. It was strange that the chickens took to her, since the kids had often seen Wendy wring the neck of a chicken when it was time to cook. She would hold its wrinkled little feet and yank down on the head before twisting it upward, fast and hard until the neck gave a snap like Lucius's knuckles when he cracked them. And afterward, as the dead chicken kept flapping its wings, Wendy would hug it close and say, "Oh little baby, sweet little baby."

"Can—I—hold—it?" said Arlo reaching his hands out for the chicken.

"Sure you can," said Wendy, but when she tried to give over the chicken, the hen started fussing and squawking, batting its wings with such fear that Wendy pulled her back again. "Sorry."

Just then Lucius appeared.

He tended to do that, Lucius, just appearing as if out of a puff of Crazy Bob's smoke.

He was tall and thin with a long mournful face that seemed to never smile. It was Lucius who, with Gracie, had leased the old unused piece of ranch land from Mr. Oates, brought in the other farm members, and ran the meetings that managed to keep the members fed, the rent paid, and the electricity on. He often had articles printed in the local paper spouting off about this or that. The boy's father said Lucius was becoming a thing, as if to become a thing was like crapping on the dinner table. Whenever Lucius leaned down to rustle the boy's hair, the boy would jerk away as if Lucius had fingers made of cactus.

"I'm glad you finally got to that, Oliver," said Lucius.

"It wasn't really a big deal," said the boy's father.

"Until the chickens started going missing again."

"I said I'd get to it."

"You say a lot of things, that's the problem." Lucius leaned over the circle and rubbed Wendy's shoulder. "Shouldn't you children be with Angie?"

"She gave us the afternoon off," said Wendy, hugging her chicken, who continued acting as if a predator were near. "It's laundry day."

"How are you feeling, Sunrise?"

Sunrise looked down at the ground, rubbing a finger in the dirt.

"Since you have the afternoon off, why don't we have another session? Did you think on what we talked about?"

"I suppose," she said.

"Okay, good. I'll see you in the dakhma."

They watched as Lucius made his bowlegged way to the main house, where he lived with Desire and the baby Tamara, who liked to touch the boy's red hair. Desire and the baby were off visiting Desire's folks in Iowa, so the only one sleeping in the main house just then was Lucius. The main house also held the kitchen, the communal dining room, the little library that also acted as the school, and Lucius's dakhma, what he called his sacred space. The main building had been the ranch house when the farm was still a ranch and was the only structure on the farm made with stone. Behind the house Angie and Fire were hanging clothes, wet from the washing barrel, on the line.

When Lucius disappeared inside, Sunrise waited a long moment before silently standing and following. She walked slowly toward the cabin and they all looked at her go, even the boy's father, even the chicken and the dogs, and no one said a word.

After a while the boy and Arlo left Wendy and her chicken and walked to the hill overlooking the main house. The two sat on the slope, leaning against scrub trees, and waited. Sunrise had told them about the sessions in Lucius's office. Lucius would make her hit pillows with a baseball bat, shout and scream and vomit and cry.

"Is—it—fun?" Arlo once asked about the sessions.

"It's not supposed to be fun," said Sunrise. "He says he's trying to help me remember."

"Remember—what?"

"If I knew, I wouldn't need his help, now would I?"

On the hill overlooking the house Arlo picked at the sparse grass, putting the blades between his thumbs and trying to create a whistle. He mostly failed. The boy scratched designs into the dirt with a stick, little crowns and curlicues, smoothed the dirt with his hand, and scratched something more. Together, like brothers, they felt no pressure to do anything in each other's presence. The minutes passed like the clouds floating above, slow and quiet.

"Waiting on your girlfriend, boys?" said Victor from the bottom of the hill. He was holding a shovel.

"You'll be a while," said Hugo, a little shorter than his older brother but with longer hair.

Hugo and Victor were a few years older than the boy and had perfect teeth. Their mother, Fire, had family money and they saw a dentist in Colorado Springs. The two were rough and liked to give orders and when the boy was around them he would clamp his lips closed and refuse to smile. Both brothers wore boots, where the rest of the children went barefoot. The buckles on their boots were shiny, like their teeth.

The boy picked up a rock and threw it at the two brothers, missing badly. The brothers laughed.

"We saw you up at Crazy Bob's cabin," said Hugo. "Did he give you any caramels?"

"No," said Arlo.

"We're digging for gold in the hills. Flit told us where to find a lucky strike. You want to come? We'd let you do the digging if you want."

The boy shook his head.

"Suit yourselves. But we're not sharing when we get rich."

"There's—there's—nothing—"

"Spit it out," said Hugo.

The boy threw another rock that got a little closer.

"Well, ask Sunrise when she gets out of her little powwow with Lucius," said Victor. "She might want to help."

"If she's not too tired," said Hugo.

The two brothers went off, snickering. The boy threw another rock that skipped at their feet. They didn't even turn around.

"Ignore—them," said Arlo.

The boy just shrugged. That's all he ever did, ignore the two of them, but his lips still covered his teeth.

A while later Sunrise left the main house and headed to the reservoir. The boy and Arlo followed. She was already swimming when they reached the water. They took off their clothes and joined her and no one said anything. After a while she climbed out of the reservoir and put her shift back on and headed to the juniper at the mouth of the drive.

That night the boy was sleeping in the big bed, drugged by the warmth of his mother's arms and her breath, by her heartbeat, when he was startled awake by the loud hoot of an owl in his dream. Or he only dreamed it was in his dream, because when it came again in his awakening he knew it for what it was.

The boy crawled from his mother's arms, slipped off the bed, and ducked around the curtain. He put on his pants and tunic and slipped outside. The moon was bright. When the call came again, he followed the sound. Arlo was hiding in the cornfield. The boy grasped the hands of his friend. Arlo's skin was dark and sticky and he was crying.

"I—need," Arlo said between deep sobs. "I—need."

The boy hugged Arlo and let Arlo's sobs shake his heart. The boy could feel the trembling, the fear, and it made him afraid.

"I—need—you . . ."

The boy nodded, took one of Arlo's damp, sticky hands and let himself be led across the farm. The cows stood silent as ghosts but the chickens were all aflutter inside their hutch. There were still coals glowing in the fire pit surrounded by a ring of rocks and logs where the adults sat at night, but the yard behind the house was empty and the back door was open.

Arlo stopped abruptly by the dying fire. He wouldn't go forward no matter how hard the boy pulled. So the boy went by himself, creeping up the wooden stairs to the ranch house and then slipping into the open door. In the dark corridor he leaned his back against a wall and listened.

The sound, when it came, was slight and strange, so soft it barely registered. The boy closed his eyes, listened: a pulling, a slurpy snarl, with something fast and halting beneath them both. He wasn't sure from where the sounds were coming, but when he started sliding down the corridor, silently, on bare feet, the noises grew louder, just the tiniest bit, then the tiniest bit more.

A door was open. It led to a private room that the boy had never entered. He had wandered most every inch of the farm, including within the ranch house, but that door had always been locked. Lucius's dakhma, he had been told, was used for meditation, therapy, work, prayer, and was absolutely private. But now the door was open, and the sounds were growing louder. As the boy drew closer, a scent like rotted peaches in cow dung encircled him.

He hesitated at the doorway, his own breath growing shallow, his own little heart beating faster, before he stepped inside.

The scent turned into a stink and the sounds were louder, closer. His feet touched a wetness on the floor, something thick and alive. The shades were drawn and all the boy could see in the darkness were shadows. All he could smell was the sweet, sickening rot. All he could hear was the halting breath and the pulling and the growling. All he could feel was a sense of something evil.

And then the pulling quieted and the faint impression of two yellow eyes, low and hateful, turned on him.

He retreated into a wall, reached up for the light switch. Found it, flicked it.

Light flooded the room and the sight seared his eyeballs. He couldn't take it in, all of it—the colors swirled crazily about him: the red across the floor and bed, the walls, the pale flesh of the naked girl on the floor with her back to a wall, the white baseball bat with blood on its barrel, the scraggly gray of the coyote's fur, the mauled and smashed head of, head of . . .

He couldn't take it all in; it was too much to process. But some actions don't need processing.

A *Hominis bestia* lives on instinct.

When the coyote with a missing tail turned toward the boy and exposed its bloodstained teeth, the boy lurched for the bloody bat. He grabbed the bat's handle, recognized it as his own, and raised it high with two hands. He growled loudly, growled again, and then took a step forward, swinging the bat through the air.

Swish.

The coyote squinted its eyes for a moment, before lowering its muzzle.

The boy kept the bat raised and his gaze hard on the coyote while stooping by the naked girl. It was Sunrise, his Sunrise. She was sitting with her legs pulled up tight and her head buried in her knees. He took a hand off the bat and tugged gently at her arm.

"Go away," she said.

He tugged again and she lifted her face and he turned his head to stare at her. She was bruised and bloody and as close to him as his own heart. When she saw it was him in that hellish room, the girl widened her eyes.

He stood again and pulled at her arm and she stood with him, raised by the power of his very presence. Together, slowly, with the bat held before him in one hand and his other hand grasping her arm, the boy backed out of the room, taking the girl with him.

In the corridor, he growled once more before tossing the bat at the coyote and bolting toward the outside door, pulling the girl along. He slipped once from the slick on his foot, his free arm wheeling to maintain his balance, but he kept pulling Sunrise, until they reached the outside door.

He gently led her down the stairs to where Arlo waited. Without letting go of Sunrise, he grabbed hold of Arlo's hand with his own bloodied paw.

And then they were cracking the whip on their way across the farm, the boy holding tight, pulling the bigger children on each side along with him. They raced straight across the farm to the stable where the boy had been sleeping just moments before.

He stopped and gestured for Sunrise and Arlo to go inside, to sit safely with his mother, who was the safest thing in the entire world. When he was sure Sunrise and Arlo had stepped through the door, the boy took off toward the mouth of the farm.

As he sprinted alongside the road, he let his instinct take control. There was so much he didn't know about what had happened in the dakhma, but he knew enough. He knew Sunrise and Arlo were too gentle, each of them and both together, to have used the bat on Lucius's head. And he knew who Lucius had been touching more and more around the farm, and who could make the coyotes follow her when she wanted, and who had asked him just that afternoon to borrow his baseball bat.

Past the fields and the row of cabins, running in the moonlight, his feet kicking up dirt and leaves as the high grass whipped his legs, the boy ran like a coyote himself, until he reached the cabin closest to the juniper and the road, just across from the vegetable garden with its neat rows glowing dully in the moonlight. There was so much love in the boy just then, and hurt, and sadness, and fear, but no uncertainty. He would do whatever was necessary to protect those he loved, whatever the price. And he knew who would do the same for him.

He didn't knock, just barreled up the stairs and barged through the door and rushed to the bed, where a man and woman slept together like a knot. He shouted out as he pulled at his father's arm.

"What, what?" said Oliver.

"Who is it?" said Gracie.

"I don't know," said Oliver as he switched on a light. "Fletcher?"

Oliver Cross sat up, naked, staring at his boy, who was marked with blood on his arms, his chest, his feet. Overcome with the sight and some fierce emotion, Oliver crushed his son in a hug.

"What is it, Fletcher?" he said. "What?"

"Daddy, Daddy, a coyote killed Lucius," said the boy. "There's blood everywhere. And it was the coyote. Notail. Daddy. I saw him. It was the coyote, I swear. I swear. I swear."

28

BLACKBIRD

When he finally leaves the truck and stands beneath the ragged old juniper, Oliver Cross can sense the anxiety his presence stirs.

The old lady sees a stranger with something familiar in his eye and undoubtedly realizes that a dark force has returned to the farm.

Frank Cormack sees an avenging demon come to make him pay for his sins, because that is what he has been searching for in the rearview mirror during his entire run west.

Erica Cross, the only one certain of Oliver's identity, is perhaps most alarmed as she sees, coming for her, the man who killed her beloved grandmother.

"Oliver?" says the old woman. "Is that you? It is, isn't it?" She puts the trowel down on the chair and picks her way toward him through the rows of vegetables. "My Lord, what a surprise." She glances back at Erica. "Well, maybe not a total surprise."

Gracie. Her long, loose dress flows with her movements, and her hair streams silkily out of her straw hat, just like old times, but not like old times. Her body now is thick, her face lined deeply by the sun, the hair streaming behind her is gray and thin, and she walks with a hitch that raises her elbows with each step.

"Well now," says Helen. "She's surely aged well."

"Be nice," says Oliver.

"Why?"

"Oliver," says the old lady standing now in front of him. "My God, look at you." She puts a hand to his cheek as she stares, as if she is staring into his sadness, and then wraps him in an unwelcome hug. She smells of sweat and pollen and tiger balm.

"You've come home," she says. "How long are you staying?"

"Not long."

She lets go, steps back, tilts her head, and widens her eyes. "We'll have a party for you tonight."

"Don't," says Oliver.

"Everyone will be so happy to see you, at least everyone who's left. Crazy Bob came back, can you believe that? And Toby never left. Flit too. And some others. We'll have a homecoming celebration."

"I need to talk to my granddaughter," says Oliver.

"Of course. Erica told me about Helen. She was a heavenly light, Oliver, pure and bright, and we all loved her."

"Tell her to piss off," says Helen, sweetly.

"I'm so sorry, Oliver," says Gracie.

"Everyone's sorry," says Oliver.

"And how it ended was so horrible. I can't imagine you in prison."

"Neither could I," Oliver says, "and then poof. I need to talk to Erica."

He turns away from Gracie and walks toward his granddaughter. Erica flinches at his approach, and the instinctive rebuke pokes at his heart. It hurts to be so close to her. She is something precious that vanished from his life when Helen died, and now she looks so much like his dead wife, so much like the young woman for whom he changed his life, that he has to look away.

"Funny seeing you here," she says.

"I was in the neighborhood," says Oliver.

She laughs. "No one's in this neighborhood. But I knew when I went to Mr. Finnegan, someone would come. I'm supposed to hate you."

"It's a big club," says Oliver, "and I'm a charter member. Let's take a walk."

Oliver strides along the dirt path toward the stable that had long ago been his home. Erica hesitates for a moment, but when Frank takes a crutched step forward, as if to offer his protection, she puts a hand out to stop him and follows her grandfather. As Oliver passes Frank he gives the boy a stone stare and then looks at the dog.

"You happy now?" says Oliver to Hunter.

The wagging tail would be answer enough, but the little bastard has to shift his hind legs back and forth, too. Just to rub it in.

Oliver stifles a bark at the dog and moves on. He and Erica walk quietly together, grandfather in front and granddaughter trailing like the teenager she is, past a row of cabins in various states of disrepair, weeds like a plague all around.

"Be gentle with her," says Helen. "Tell her you love her."

"That would go over well," says Oliver.

"What's that, Grandpop?" says the girl from behind him.

"Nothing," he says, staying quiet even as Helen keeps hectoring him on how to play it, how to be the kind, loving grandfather she needs.

Now, before the old bleached stable on the edge of collapse, Oliver and Erica stand side by side, looking at the ruin. To her, he knows, it is just a ramshackle heap of wood and iron, but to Oliver it is a living, breathing thing, with its foundation buried deep in the land and its smoky tendrils reaching out to latch on to his heart.

"That's where your grandmother and I lived with your father when he was small," says Oliver to the girl.

"High living, Gramps."

He thinks of defending the old stable as if the structure represents the very life he and Helen chose, but the reality of the thing chokes off his defensiveness. Strips of tin have fallen off the roof, leaving the exposed purlins to rot. The old portico roof is half-collapsed, and two of the barn shutters have fallen off their rusted hinges. The windows Oliver put in all those years ago are now just shards of glass in peeling frames.

"It was collapsing back then, too, before I went to work on it," he says. "Your mother was worried about you when you ran off. Your grandmother too. I told them both I'd find you and see if you were okay."

"You promised Grandmom?"

"I still talk to her."

"Isn't that, like, weird?"

"That's not weird. That she talks back is weird."

"Are you trying to be hurtful?" says Helen.

"I brought her ashes along hoping it would finally shut her up."

"Oliver!" says Helen.

"Grandpop?" says Erica.

"If I scatter them here, on our old homestead, she might finally be happy enough to leave me alone."

"Don't count on it," says Helen.

"They didn't belong in your father's creepy stone monstrosity anyway," says Oliver.

"Okay, so you found me," says Erica. "Now what?"

"Are you okay?"

She hesitates a bit. "I think so. I don't know."

"That's comforting."

"It's gotten confusing."

"It tends to do that."

"But yeah. I'm okay."

"Good."

"I remember you talking about your run west with Grandmom. It sounded so romantic."

"Only a fool takes me as a role model."

"Maybe that's my problem. You brought Hunter."

"I went to Cormack's apartment looking for you. The dog was there, hungry and covered in shit."

"Frank said he arranged for a friend to pick him up."

"I suppose he says a lot of things."

"Yes, he does. How did you even find us?"

"I made like Marlowe and played detective."

"Who's Marlowe?"

"Words on a page. And the girl helped."

"Ayana? I always liked Ayana. Frank says he loves me. He wants us to go around the world. Asia. Prague. He wants us to make a new life for ourselves in Paris."

"Most new lives are just like the old lives."

"Yeah, I'm learning that. But Paris does sound nice, better than some stupid college. You heard what happened in Chicago."

"I heard."

"Mr. Finnegan saved us both."

"Have you ever seen a more unlikely superhero?"

She laughs. "So what are you going to do? Kidnap me and take me back to my life of wealth and privilege?"

"Do you want me to?"

"No. God, no."

"Then I won't."

"So instead you'll try to convince me how big a mistake I'm making. How I'm too young to run off like this. How bad he is for me. How much I need my education. How my future is hanging in the balance. How I'm about to ruin my life."

"Are you?"

"What?"

"Ruining your life."

"Maybe."

"Good. From what I could tell it could use some ruining."

She turns to look at him, a squint of incomprehension in her eye. "Then I don't get it. Why were you chasing me?"

"I told you. I promised I'd see if you were okay. Are you okay?"

"Yes."

"Then I'm done."

And he realizes, as soon as he says it, that he truly is. He isn't using reverse psychology to convince her to make the right decision on her own—he isn't that clever— and he doesn't know what the right decision is anyway. All he knows is that this jaunt is over, and he has no idea what to do with the remaining nub of his life.

He is looking at the stable, as if it might supply the answer, when, in an act as sudden and surprising as a seizure, Erica hugs him. His granddaughter, who resembles so much his dear dead wife it hurts to even look at her, hugs him. And it feels so pure and rich that he can't hug her back for fear of the sensation dissolving under the slightest bar of his pressure.

"I knew you would understand," she says softly.

He shakes his head. "I don't understand anything anymore."

They walk back to the mouth of the road together, side by side now, as if something has been resolved between them.

"You couldn't have mentioned school?" says Helen.

"I seem to remember you dropped out," says Oliver.

Erica turns to him, her head tilted in confusion but a smile on her face, and she grabs hold of his arm. As they walk together Oliver notices a slight jaunt in his bent-back, splayfooted step. And why wouldn't he have such a jaunt? He found her after all, and didn't screw it up when he did, at least not as of yet. It is only the sight of Frank Cormack, standing next to Ayana and peering at the two of them from a distance, that brings him back to himself.

What is he going to do about that piece of shit?

"Stay calm, dear," says Helen.

"The hell with that," says Oliver under his breath.

"Frank, sweetie," says Erica when they reach the battered boy, "this is my grandfather, Oliver." She holds Oliver's arm tight enough to keep him from lurching forward to strangle the reprobate son of a bitch. "He came all this way to make sure I'm okay."

"I heard a lot about you," says Frank. "Erica talks about her old hippie grandfather all the time. And thanks, man, for bringing Hunter. Ayana told me where you found him and how you took care of him."

"You can pick up his crap from here on in."

"Like you ever did," says Ayana with a laugh.

"And call your brother," says Oliver. "Tell him you're still alive. He'll be surprised."

"He won't want to hear from me."

"Don't be so sure. He asked me to look out for you. I told him I would. Which means you and I have some hard talking to do."

"Yes, sir."

"Don't be such a fucking idiot all the time."

"I'll try."

"And don't call me sir."

"Grandpop," says Erica.

"What?"

"Can you try to be nice?"

"Next you'll have me swinging on a trapeze," says Oliver. "A man needs to know his limitations."

◆ ◆ ◆

Oliver Cross surveys the ruinous inside of the old stable, filthy with cobwebs, with leaves and trash and animal droppings. The front door is wide-open and the wheels on its track are so rusted he can't budge it closed. An abandoned bird's nest sits high and ragged in the rafters, beyond which he can see spots of the sky. He wonders what Helen thinks of the decrepit state of the place, but for some reason she is quiet, as if the life forces emanating from this building are so powerful they still her voice.

Finally. He could use the silence.

He knows he should do some rudimentary cleaning, yet the idea is so wearying that he decides instead to take a nap. Napping is one of the great pleasures of old age, that and being a cantankerous old fool. And lucky him, he can do both at the same time, as long as he's not chewing gum.

Oliver finds an old bed frame in the stable and rolls out a sleeping bag atop the rusted springs, but he lies uneasily atop the quilted bag and naps fitfully. His sleep is attacked by psychedelic shaped wisps of memory that rise from the land and out of the wood, assaulting him like wraiths: fights and kisses, work, sex, a smile from his wife. They trouble his sleep, these remembrances, until one, when it rises, snaps open his eyes. He is besieged by the memory of a gory night in that very space, a night of candles and chanting and the foulest of odors, the night when, with a scream and a spurt of unseemly blood, his baby was born.

Angie midwifed and Gracie and Fire both assisted, their faces lit by candles set about the bed as they hovered over his writhing wife. Oliver had wanted to take Helen to the hospital in Colorado Springs for the birth, but Helen insisted on delivering at the farm, in their new home, in the arms of their new community, and as usual she had gotten her way.

As the woman clutched Helen's hands and mopped Helen's brow and urged her on with song and chant, Oliver paced the dirt within the stable. It was all happening at a disconcerting remove. He wanted to be part of the moment, the second greatest moment of his life, but he felt elbowed out, somehow, by female solidarity.

His wife screamed, the women chanted, Oliver paced.

Then Helen shrieked so loudly it sounded like she was splitting in two. Oliver couldn't take the separation any longer and leaped onto the raised floor beneath the bed. That's when he first saw the thing, the bloody creature with the squashed head and writhing limbs, emerging like a sickness from the well of his wife. He couldn't help himself from reaching for it like a baseball catcher. It all happened so quickly, the splat of blood, the slide and catch, Angie lifting the child from his arms, and then the slap, the howl, the biting of the cord, the placing of the baby atop its beaming, crying mother.

"Come close, Oliver. Closer," said Helen. "Come and see baby Fletcher."

◆　◆　◆

When Oliver leaves the stable after his fitful nap, more exhausted than when he first lay down, he finds, to his dismay, that preparations for his grand homecoming party have begun.

A fire has been built in the pit next to the stone ruins of the old ranch house. On a grill atop the fire, cast-iron pots are bubbling away, releasing burps of spice: cumin, cardamom, cinnamon, clove. A wooden table has been set with plates and pitchers, loaves of peasant bread, garlands of wildflowers, handmade candles. Music is playing over a jerry-rigged set of speakers, a playlist of the old stuff: Stevie Wonder, Neil Young, Gladys Knight, Dylan. Four dogs are running about in a pack, one of which is Hunter, dog-grinning ear to ear as his tongue lolls over his teeth.

"Looky, looky," says a short bearded Japanese man in a ragged voice, his eyes glowing as he slams Oliver in the shoulder. "A sight for stoned eyes. You're the one prodigal I thought would never come home."

"Crazy Bob," says Oliver. "You got old."

"Beats the alternative," says Crazy Bob. "And you lost your hair. You always had a good head of hair, it was your best feature. Now you look like a pissed-off turtle peering out of the soup pot."

"I thought you'd be somewhere in the bay, making tech, counting your money."

"I went," says Crazy Bob, "but it didn't take. I like building and fixing, fiddling, but here it's a hobby. There it's like a death march. Truth is, Oliver, I never was much one for work."

"I always admired that about you."

"I mean any idiot can work himself to death."

"And you're not just any idiot."

"That's my motto. Not just any idiot. Put it on my tombstone. So I came back to the farm. I like the pace. Not the winters, the winters are getting too hard to bear, but the pace is just right."

"What pace is that?"

"No pace. That's just it. The money was good, though. I liked the money. I liked shoving it in their faces. That's what it's really all about anyway, that and the planes. The planes are gravy, baby. Give the working man a few rides in those private planes and you'd have your revolution. So how you doing in the world? Killing it?"

"Hardly."

"Not from what I heard. Sorry about Helen. I loved that girl."

"You shouldn't have come back," says a squat old man with a long gray ponytail standing behind Crazy Bob. "You had no call to come back."

"Flit?" says Oliver.

"You killed the farm, ruined us all."

"Oh, leave him be," says Crazy Bob.

"I didn't think you'd have the nerve to come back."

"You thought wrong," says Oliver. "All I've got is nerve."

"Toby, get him a drink," says Gracie, looking on from the table with concern on her face.

"Oliver," says Toby, standing behind Flit, tall and thin, his afro now gray, though still in his green fatigues as if the war ended only yesterday.

"Toby."

Toby winks as he puts an arm around Flit and pulls him toward the fire.

"Sometimes it's hard to bury the past," says Crazy Bob.

"Is that Oliver?" says a wiry middle-aged woman as she wedges her way between Oliver and Crazy Bob. Oliver would have sworn he has never seen her before. "Yes, it is," she says. "Give me a hug."

"No," he says, backing away.

"Oh, Oliver," she says, tromping forward in her heavy boots and giving him one anyway. "It's good to see you again. Tell me all about Fletcher."

"Who are you?"

"You don't remember?"

"I have no idea."

"Wendy."

"Animal girl?"

"That's right."

"Wendy? What are you still doing here?"

"I returned a couple years back, after my marriage died and the rat race got too damn ratty. I run a goat farm on one of the back fields. Completely organic. I sell the milk and cheese. Award-winning cheese, I might add. The key to a great cheese is keeping the goats happy."

"Lucky goats."

"Except when we eat them." She laughs. "You'll be having some tonight if you haven't stayed vegan. There's wild herbs growing in the field and you can taste them in the meat. So tell me about Fletcher."

"What's to tell? He's a lawyer."

"Funny job for someone who didn't talk. Did he grow up handsome?"

"He grew up fat."

She laughs again. "You have a lovely granddaughter. And she looks so much like Helen it took my breath away."

"I've noticed."

"I'm glad you're back, Oliver."

"Why."

"Because we're always needing someone to fix the chicken coop. Are you staying long?"

"No."

"Too bad."

When he looks around he sees Erica staring at him from a distance. She's looking at him strangely, like there is some bizarre creature perched on his head. He rubs his skull and then moves the hand down his face. What's that he feels there? A smile?

Gracie slips by his side and grabs hold of his arm. "It's time to eat, Oliver. Hungry?"

"Not in years," he says.

"Don't worry, Crazy Bob will take care of that."

After a boisterous dinner of a beetroot salad from the vegetable garden, bread and cheese, grains, tempeh, Indian-style mashed eggplant, roasted goat leg, and wine from a jug, with which they all toasted Oliver's return, the celebrants have repaired to sitting by the fire.

Frank Cormack is playing his guitar, singing something soft and stupid, while Ayana and Wendy look on. Gracie is talking to Erica as if they are confidantes of long standing, while Angie, yes, old Angie, now withered like a dying dogwood, sits beside them. Crazy Bob, Toby, and Flit sit on rocking chairs like old men at the cracker barrel, drinking beers and chortling. Every now and then Flit eyes Oliver like he is a plague returned, but then Crazy Bob cracks another joke and Toby laughs and Flit turns away. The dogs are scattered about, including

Hunter, who is curled on the ground beside Frank's chair, his head lying on his paws, contented as only a dog can be contented. There are a few other folks around the fire whom Oliver doesn't know, earnest fools trying to find a new life on an old farm.

Amidst this scene of bonhomie and animosity and grace, Oliver stares into the fire and broods.

For a moment, in the midst of his homecoming party, he felt himself cloaked in the comforting robe of self-satisfaction. He was back on the farm, back at the site of his still burning youth, with friends of yore and Helen in an urn by his side. He had achieved the goal of his mad dash west and was thinking, just for a moment, that maybe this remaining bit of life might not be so empty after all.

And then it came to him, a revelation that burned the self-satisfaction right out of him like a flaming arrow in the gut.

It had been a setup, this whole road trip piece of crap, a conspiracy among his dead wife and his granddaughter and Gracie. They had created a slapstick farce to force him to start his life over again here on the farm with purpose renewed. They had played on his pathetic need to save the world by giving him a world to save: Erica, Frank, Ayana, the farm itself, which these sloths had turned into a weed-infested wreck. The route to salvation is so clear, so easy even. A hug here, a dollop of advice there, a new tractor to plow the overgrown fields. They had even given him a goddamn dog.

They are forcing redemption down his throat.

"The hell with that," he mumbles quietly enough so that no one notices.

"The hell with what, dearest?" says Helen.

"The hell with all your scheming. The hell with you. I don't want to save the world anymore. I'm too old to start again and the thought of handing out advice like after-dinner mints makes me want to vomit."

"Don't be a stick in the mud, Oliver," says his wife. "You should be happy, you should feel renewed."

"You can stuff your renewal where it will do the most good," he mumbles, loud enough for some to look his way, but he doesn't care. "All I want anymore is for you to shut up and for my life to be over and done with, finally, Oliver out."

He considers standing up, walking to the fire, lying down amidst the coals, and letting the bright-orange flames wrap themselves around him like a cloak, warming his soul as they devour his body. It seems so perfect to do it here, in this spot where it all went to hell in a gash of fire, to use the same magical substance to turn himself into the same ash as his precious wife in the urn perched next to him on an overturned log. That would serve her right. And he would do it, honestly, lay himself gently down among the embers, if he didn't have to stand up first, because the way his mind is swirling from the joints that Crazy Bob passed around earlier, he doesn't think he could manage that.

So instead he continues to stare into the fire and continues to brood.

He suddenly misses the sacred solitude of 128 Avery Road. He was left to his own devices there. He could hate cleanly and happily there, without any temptations to do anything about it. His suburban piece-of-crap house was a worthy place to wither and die. It had sufficed for his wife, why shouldn't it have sufficed for him?

But no, they had to plot and plan in this world and the next to save his life for him. Talk about a conspiracy of dunces. And sure, his paranoia might be an outgrowth of the weed—under the influence he had been known to envision gossamer conspiracies reaching to the very sky—but it doesn't really matter because the truth of the situation is so evident that he can hear their goddamn voices relating it straight to him, with Helen leading the charge.

Come on, Oliver. Get up, get going; rah, rah sis boom bah. Who around this fire can't benefit from your wisdom? Your healing hand? Step up, Oliver, step in and be the man you always planned to be.

"The hell with that," he shouts again to his dead wife sitting next to him. The music stops, the babble of conversations stills, faces lit by the firelight turn toward him. "I don't need your fucking redemption. I don't need these fucking voices in my head anymore. The hell with all of them. The hell with you."

And then, despite the swirl within his skull, he grunts himself to standing and heads for the fire before wheeling around. He grabs the urn and turns to face them all.

"Piss off, all of you. Especially you, Flit. Nice fucking ponytail."

Ayana lets out a burst of laughter as Oliver lurches away from them all, the little conspirators, lurches away like Frankenstein's monster, heading toward the unkempt environs of the deserted stable with its tendrils of memory and the spiders ready to eat him alive.

29

I Took a Pill in Ibiza

Frank Cormack didn't need a map to know where this whole ragged lurch to freedom had landed him.

Welcome to Shitsville, USA.

He was on the run from the law and the lawless, stuck on a crappy scrap of overgrown farmland inhabited by packs of old hippies and baby goats, and he had no money, no family he could count on, no friends who gave a damn, no road forward, no money, no money, and on top of it all, besides having no money, he was losing Erica.

He could see it in her eyes when she looked at him now, the three Ds: disappointment, disillusionment, doubt. He had first seen hints that night in Chicago, when she glanced at him before heading up the stairs at the house in Humboldt Park, leaving him alone with Marisol—not totally alone, Sheila was there, but Erica knew, she knew—and just then, with the intoxication of Marisol in his blood, he hadn't really cared. But the triple Ds were full borne two nights later after that smooth-talking lawyer bought him out of Delaney's clutches, giving over not just all the merch he had stolen from the Russian, but a load of cash Erica had somehow picked up to go with it.

Afterward, when the lawyer brought him back to Erica and that weird old man Finnegan, he tried to thank her, he tried to smooth it over with his smooth-sounding words, but she could barely glance his way. All she could manage was a "Shut up, Frank."

Truth was he had failed her, repeatedly, like he had failed Marisol and his brother and his parents and everyone else in his life, including, ironically, the Russian himself. So at the hospital, where they had x-rayed his knee and then given him the crutch, when Erica came up with the lamebrain idea of coming here, to this wasteland, he hadn't stood in her way. And with his knee filled with pain after Delaney stomped on it like he was stomping on a cockroach, there wasn't much standing he could do anyway. She had talked the place up as she drove them west from Chicago: her father had been raised there; the lawyer said some of the old commune members were still living on the land; and Erica was certain they would take care of her as one of their own. It would be a place to recover, to gather themselves, a quiet refuge where they could figure out their next move. And all the time he knew what her next move would be.

Bye-bye, Frank, you penniless fuck-up.

The farm, though more ragged than expected, had been pretty much just what she had promised. They had been warmly welcomed after Erica told their story. They were fed and put up in one of the rotting old cabins. They had even been given a bit of work to do to keep them busy. "It is a commune after all," said the old lady. It was all as friendly as preschool.

And then they waited. For what? For his leg to heal? For the scant amount of pills he still had to run out? For Erica to find a way to abandon him without losing her fake rebel edge? For him to be left here without a penny or a purpose and the whole fucking world breathing down his neck?

It was certainly heading that way, Frank could feel it, when, like a bolt of no-damn-good out of the blue, that ragged rattling truck appeared, coming at them as if there was hot vengeance roiling through the engine's crankshaft. It jammed to a stop beside his Camaro, vibrating on its axels with a back-and-forth rhythm that matched the rabid, fearful beating of Frank's heart.

When Ayana stepped out of the truck, Frank blanched with terror, certain that he was already dead. Ayana was a figure in the Russian's orbit, a homeless waif hanging with Ken and his hipster ponytail. Frank didn't recognize the man in the front seat, but he assumed he was a killer who had come to cut out Frank's febrile little liver; the geezer sure had the face for it. Frank would have run right then, but with his leg still a wreck and only the crutch to aid his flight, any attempt at an escape would have been more humiliating than successful.

So he stayed stock-still, waiting for the inevitable, when a beast leaped out of the truck, an animal that turned out not to be a hound from hell but instead a dog, his dog, Hunter, who should have been idling like a spoiled prince at Javier's place in Philly.

What was Hunter doing here?

The dog tore at him and leaped in the air. Frank instinctively bent as low as his leg would allow and rubbed his dog's head as Hunter's tongue swiped across his wrist. It was a touching reunion, until the bald piece of jerky stepped out of the driver's side of the truck.

Sour, that's what his face was, sour as a sour drop, sour as a Chinese soup without the sweet, sour as a corpse.

Frank glanced around to see if the others saw it too, Erica and the old lady, but instead of fear there was something other on their faces. Erica was almost smiling, and the old lady was looking on with a puzzled expression, as if the world had gone awry. And then the old lady put down her tools and stepped across her vegetable patch.

"How'd he find us?" he asked Erica, later, when they were alone in the cabin. Erica was fiddling around, straightening up for some reason.

"He says he followed our trail. We sure left one."

"You called him, didn't you?" he said, lumbering behind her with his crutch.

"No."

"Then how?"

"I don't know, Frank. When I went to the lawyer to get you out of that trouble in Chicago, I figured someone might follow."

"But how did he know about here? And he said something about my brother. How did he talk to my brother?"

"Ayana, maybe? He said she helped him."

"So you're saying he chased us all the way out here from Philadelphia? In that old beater of a truck? Just on Ayana's word? I wouldn't buy that crap in a thrift store. What is he after?"

"He just wanted to find out if I was okay. He said my mother asked him. And my grandmother too."

"Your grandmother? The one he killed?"

"He says they still talk."

"Well isn't that something. Isn't that just some damn thing."

"Don't you think it's romantic, Frank? A love that transcends the grave."

"No, it's creepy. Ghosts and ghouls and shit. What did you tell him when he asked if you were okay?"

"I told him I didn't know anymore."

"Jesus, Erica. Throw me under the bus, why don't you."

"I was just trying to be honest. I'm still trying to process Chicago. It's been hard so far."

"I know, baby. Look at me, I know. It will get easier. I'll make sure of it. I got plans for us, still. But we need to leave and fast."

"Why?"

"Because if an old man who talks to dead people can find us, anyone can. And because of Ayana. I don't trust her. She's probably given us up to the Russian already."

"Oh, Ayana's okay. She helped Grandpop, and we talked already. She's so happy to be away from the rest of them."

"It doesn't matter. We have to get going."

"Then go, Frank. No one's stopping you."

"You're not coming?"

"Not right now. And not just because you say so. I want to stay for a bit."

"Why? What's here?"

"My grandfather. We're on the road to freedom, right? That means freedom to go, yes, but also freedom to stay if there are things to stay for. I haven't seen my grandfather in a couple years. We've been kept apart. I sort of want to get to know him all over again."

"You're going to get us killed, sweet pea."

"No one's after me, Frank."

And there it was, Erica stepping away from him as clearly as a slap in the face. Separate threats, separate futures, suck on that. He should have seen it coming; he did see it coming. It was what the heist from the Russian was all about in the first place. The only way to keep someone like Erica has always been the only way. He needed to get some bank and quick. He needed to get off the farm and find enough cash to get them out of the country and off to Paris. He needed to find some money, real money, or their life together was dead.

In a fit of frustration he threw the crutch across the room. It slammed loudly against the wooden wall and Erica jumped.

"Fuck this," he said, keeping his leg stiff as he banged, crutchless, out the door.

It was always the same, always the same, there was never enough and it was always the same. His leg burned and his breath was fast and when the dog came up to him he pushed him away with his lame leg and sent him scurrying. What was he going to do? What the hell could he do? He buzzed with a bitter deprivation. This day was like every other day of his fucking life—he was always short of the one thing that could solve everything.

He looked up and saw the old man in his battered work boots lumbering toward the ruined stable with the dog, Frank's dog, trailing behind, and something started clicking in his head.

Erica hadn't had a spot of trouble getting the extra cash from the lawyer friend of her grandfather to pay off Delaney. Why was that? Apparently she had met the lawyer at some fancy club in the city, a place where her great-grandfather used to belong. That meant there had been some money there, at least once. With the one brother dying in Vietnam, old man Cross would be the only heir. He wasn't living high like some rich suck-up daddy's boy, that was for sure, but that didn't mean much; these old hippies were batshit crazy. And the lawyer who came with Erica to buy him out was as slick as they come. Lawyers like that don't work for old men with nothing to their name but a ratty old truck. Lawyers like that work for high-balling squillionaires.

Maybe Erica was right. Maybe they should spend some time getting to know the old goat.

30

Our House

Oliver Cross is lying on his back, his ankles and chest stippled with spider bites, his nose clogged and his mouth dry, when the dog licks his face.

He pushes the mongrel away, squints at the sun shafting through the gaps in the stable's ceiling, and rolls heavily onto his side. He hopes to drift back to his dream of youth and vigor but it is too late. He rises slowly, he walks stiffly, his bladder is heavy, his neck is stiff, and his back is screaming. He has done this three times already through the night. The dog bounds around him like an idiot.

He steps through the open front door and surveys the sun-blessed earth shimmering before him, wild and weedy and green. Yesterday it looked like a junked-up scrap of abandoned land, but now there is something of Elysium in the view. He presses the swollen nodule on his neck, twice the size that it was when he left Pennsylvania, which explains the stiffness. The dog sprints past him, stops, turns, bows, barks; his posture says, "Let's play."

Let's not.

Oliver steps from beneath the sagging portico roof, blocks one nostril and blows half his nose crust onto the packed dirt, blocks the second nostril and finishes it off. Then he strides toward a bush and starts to peeing, right there. Watching his own pathetic spatter, he feels like a lion being served an avocado.

"Jesus, Oliver, put on some clothes." Ayana is leaning against one of the portico's pillars, facing away to avoid the sight of him. "That's disgusting," she says.

"Welcome to Seven Suns."

"What the hell got into you last night?"

"Other than Crazy Bob's reefer?"

"I'll admit it, Oliver, that bud should be wrapped with a bow and sold on TV. But when you sort of went loco, everyone looked around, wondering what the hell you were going on about."

"I saw a piece of truth."

"So did I, just now, when you stepped naked out of the door. Truth is overrated."

"No one told you to stalk me."

"I'm not stalking you. I'm just trying to figure things out. Like, okay, we found Erica, and everything's fine. And maybe you knocked the Russian off Frank's trail. Yay. But what happens now?"

"Who the hell knows?"

"I need to get back."

"I thought you were going west."

"Plans changed, I told you. How do I get home?"

"Maybe ask someone who cares." All he wants to do is relieve himself in peace, and here he is, facing the world in the raw, getting neither peace nor relief.

"You brought me here," she says.

"You hitched a ride. I let you come. The rest is up to you."

"What are you doing, Oliver?"

"Turning over a new leaf. And it feels sweet. Here on in, I'm out of the helping business. You want advice, check an almanac."

"What's an almanac?"

"Yeah," he says as he turns around and heads back inside.

◆ ◆ ◆

He steps again out of the barn, this time clothed in his boots, jeans, and flannel shirt. Ayana is gone and Helen has been quiet since his outburst at the fire last night and so he is blessedly alone.

He scratches at the bug bites on his chest and looks at the ruined orchard. The sight of it hurts his heart; he can almost hear the dead trees weeping. He turns away and surveys the wreckage of the stable. The old place is in better shape than the orchard, but not by much. Staring at what's left of the building he pulls out a memory of this place, a memory he has kept close all these years, holding it in his pocket like a coin, a hedge for when the failures of his life ricochet dangerously about him.

He rubs his fingers over the coin's delicate contours.

A winter's day, the snow blanketing the earth is bright and endless. The stable's wood-fired stove is doing its best, but inside the walls there is still a bite in the air. Sunlight streams through the windows, along with a draft. Fletcher is swaddled and gurgling in a wooden bassinet Oliver built. Helen has set her easel by one of the windows. She is wearing three sweaters, a woolen hat, woolen gloves with the fingers cut off. Her hair is pulled back, a smear of white paint rises like a flare on her cheek.

He is working on a piece of a Ponderosa pine that had come down in a windstorm on the slope of Mount Blue. A lumberman friend had milled a burled slab and Oliver is in the process of using a hand plane to smooth its surface. The curls of wood that roll out beneath the blade are almost thin enough to see through. And with each pass of the plane it is as if the soul of the wood is becoming clearer.

He looks up and sees Helen by the window. The sunlight highlights her cheekbone and the lines around her eye. She is no longer the Bryn Mawr junior he first fell in love with eight years before; it is as if their time together, all their experiences and experiments and love, is etched now into her face. The sight of her takes away his breath. She doesn't look back; instead she is absorbed in her work, her art. She is the cause, she is the result. With each push of the plane and stroke of the brush they are growing closer to the source of all things. It feels just then so very near. He lowers his gaze, lays his tool carefully on the wood, grips the bulb and presses forward.

He is still fingering the memory, lost in his losses, when he spies Gracie making her hitching way up to the stable from her cabin. At the sight of her, he puts the memory back into his pocket to protect it. She almost stole it once.

"Good morning there, Oliver," says Gracie as she approaches. "I wondered when you were getting up."

"I've been getting up all night," he says.

"Quite a performance out there by the fire. Reminded me of old times. You were always one for raging at the ghosts. There's coffee if you want it. And some breakfast. Oatmeal with molasses and fruit."

"The old stable has gone to crap."

"It has, yes. Some people tried living in it for a bit after you and Helen left, but it's tough to heat in the winter. And then the upkeep got away from us."

"It appears the upkeep of the entire farm got away from you. What happened to the orchard is a crime."

"You were the one who took care of the trees, Oliver. Some of us ran and some of us stayed; those who stayed did the best we could. For a time it was a struggle just to keep feeding the chickens and finding enough to eat."

"You look like you did okay."

Gracie smiles tightly. "You used to admire my appetites," she says, and then, as if she can't help herself, she lets her mouth twitch.

"I was young and stupid," he says, turning away from her to look out over the fallow fields.

"So you were the one. What's your plan, Oliver?"

"I don't have a plan."

"If you're thinking of staying awhile and fixing up the old place, you should maybe think again. We're trying to sell."

"You're selling the stable?"

"The farm. We've been making do with what we can, Social Security, some trusts we've inherited, the vegetables we grow, the chickens and goats. But you can see it's not working. And the area's changing. Development has come and we got an offer that's hard to refuse."

He turns to face her. "But you don't own the place, Gracie."

"That's not so clear. It turns out Oates sold the land a while ago. And we haven't been paying rent in all the years after, and the new owner never came around to tell us to start paying. There's a lawyer the developer brought in who says we might actually have a right to the land because of that. It's called adverse possession. You went to law school, didn't you, Oliver?"

"For a time."

"Then you might have heard of it."

"And you might want to look up the word 'hostile.'"

"The lawyer says it could work, and he actually got his degree. Those of us who stayed would get a piece. Wendy, too, since she'd have to relocate the goats. But only those of us who stayed."

"Not me, you mean."

"Not you, yes. We hate to do it, but it's time. Toby and Crazy Bob say they're ready to move to Florida. Flit too. Remember how hard the winters are? And those old men, they like to eat early. Angie has grandkids in Oakland. As for me, Sunrise is out in San Bernardino, now. Three kids. I'd like to get to know them better."

"What does she do out there, Sunrise?"

"She's a venture capitalist. Calls herself Susan. And Fletcher, I hear from Erica, has become a corporate lawyer."

"We did a hell of a job with them, didn't we?"

They stand together quietly, not laughing.

"Sunrise went to live with Juba's mother right after you left," says Gracie.

"And you stayed without her?"

"It made sense at the time. Juba's mother had some money but she never had much use for me, so I thought it was better for Sunrise to be there without me. I had my own issues then, remember?"

"I remember."

"I visited as often as I could, but I regret not moving out there now."

"What would we have if we didn't have our regrets?"

"Memories. Fond memories. At least some of them are. I missed you, Oliver."

"No you didn't."

"Maybe I didn't, but I would have if I ever gave you much thought."

"You know," says Oliver, "I think I will work on the old stable. Give me something to do."

"Of course you will. It's a stupid and futile gesture."

"The only kind I like."

At that she smiled. "Same old Oliver."

He is scavenging in a pile of crap behind the stable, searching for building materials, finding a few cinder blocks, some twisted metal fencing, rotting planks of wood among the weeds. He is trying to lift a steel beam when he looks up and sees his granddaughter, and a blade of ice slips into his heart. He can deal with Ayana and Gracie, sure, but with

Erica he is so afraid of making a mistake he is paralyzed. For a moment he wishes his wife would pipe up, but she remains obstinately silent.

"Hey, Grandpop," says Erica. "What are you doing?"

Still gripping the beam, Oliver says, "Looking for something useful in this pile of crap."

"Gracie says you're thinking of fixing up the stable."

"I did it once, I can do it again."

"It's a wreck."

"So?"

"Wouldn't it be easier to knock it down and build something new?"

"What would be the point in that?"

"You'd end up with a nicer place."

"But it wouldn't be this place."

"I get it," she says, nodding her head, though he doubts that she does. "My father talked about the farm more than you would think. It's why I decided that Frank and I would hide out here. What was it like, living in the stable with him and Grandmom?"

He drops the beam, stands as straight as he is able, and claps the rust off his hands. "It was as sweet as honey cake," he says. "Different than out in the world."

"How so?"

"What mattered in the stable were love and art, family and community, the land and the sky. What matters in the world are money, status, power, domination. Where would you rather live?"

"I don't know."

"Get back to me when you figure it out."

"Do you think I made a mistake?"

"Leaving home?"

"Or leaving with Frank."

"Where would we be without our mistakes?"

"Back in AP chem, I suppose."

"I never much cared for chemistry," says Oliver, "although Crazy Bob could teach you a thing or two."

"It must have been dreamy here back in the day."

"It was something, all right."

"Maybe I should stay for a bit."

"Here?"

"Sure."

"Why?"

"I don't know. I needed to get away to clear things in my head; maybe I can do it here. And it might be safer than being on the road with Frank, which hasn't been a picnic, let me tell you. Instead of just leaving, like I should have, I convinced him to go with me, you know, because I was scared to be alone. And when you went you had Grandmom."

"I only went because of her. She was what I was running to."

"The farm is so peaceful. Things might be able to calm down for me here."

"Doubtful."

"You know, every stupid thing Frank did he did because of me. Somehow I feel responsible."

"Maybe you are."

"What do I do about it?"

"It's your story; write it yourself."

"Aren't you, like, supposed to give me sage advice?"

"It's good with millet."

"What?"

"It's not easy, that's all I can tell you. Living your own life is hard. It's easier just going along, doing what they tell you to do."

"Was it worth it, though, running off on your own? Do you regret it?"

"You'll regret it either way. That's Kierkegaard."

"Who?"

"Maybe college wouldn't be the worst thing. Look, Erica, living your own life means living your own life. The rest is dicta."

"What's dicta?"

"Useless crap."

"You don't have anything to tell me?"

"Your mother and father love you."

"I know that."

"And your grandmother too."

"If she was here, what would she say?"

"She'd say she never liked millet."

When the girl goes off, he can feel her disappointment. They all want answers when they don't even know the questions. They read Robert Frost to decide which path to take without realizing the poet is talking about fatuous old fools justifying their own lives with false flashes of bravery. What could Oliver tell her about the beauty or costs of the life he chose? He tries to finger again the memory of the perfect winter's day with his wife and child, but that's not what comes to him now. It is as if the stable itself has raised a memory of its own, a shadow cast on the side of the building, the shadow of a man, tall and dour, with all hunger and no hope in his heart.

"You weren't at the assembly last night," said Lucius.

Oliver was working on a maple bowl, slamming the curved blade of his adze into the meat of the thick wooden disk, when Lucius appeared. Oliver took two more shots before putting down the tool. He had always felt uneasy around Lucius. There was something of a street preacher about him. San Francisco had been rife with the type, peddlers of the true and only faith, selling it to those searching for any piece of hype to hang on to in the storms of their lives.

"The assemblies are an important part of our democratic process here," said Lucius. "It hurts the whole community when we're not all together."

"Do you have a point?"

"The point is, we're running short of money, which you would know if you attended last night. We have rent to pay, electricity. And the food we're growing isn't enough to keep us fed year-round. We're in danger of losing the farm."

"I'm not much for meetings."

"You're not much for fieldwork either."

"I put my time in at the orchard. And when I'm out there in the spring I don't see you plowing. But I can be of more use in here."

"Making bowls? We can't eat bowls."

"They sell at the market."

"For how much, Oliver? Helen's art brings more than your little pieces, but together it's still not enough to keep you in wood and paint, water and food."

"It's nice you're keeping such careful track of our earnings, since we don't see a penny of it."

"Some of us talked it over, without Helen, and we thought you might want to ask your father for help."

"Some of you talked it over, did you?"

"The farm's in trouble. We're not going to make it through the winter without making some changes."

"If you want to give me a helper, I could boost production. More bowls, bigger pieces of furniture."

"Let's be honest, Oliver. Bowls aren't going to save us."

"Neither will my father."

"Why do you think you're here? How do you think you ended up with such a sweet setup in the stable? When she put you up for inclusion, Gracie said you had money. Fire gets some from her family and that helps. You need to step up, too. It's only fair."

"If I wanted to live off my father's money, I'd be back in Chicago, drinking martinis at the club."

"Just ask him."

"No."

"Oliver."

Oliver lifted the adze high before slamming it down, chewing out a thick shiver of wood and splitting the roughed-out bowl at the same time.

"That's not going to be worth much now," said Lucius.

It wasn't time that killed this place, it was the world. It creeps in like fog—the money cares, the corruption and politics—and fills the air with a noisome mist that devours flesh like acid. Oliver is standing now behind the ruin it has wreaked, still with his eyes closed, counting the losses, when he hears sounds approaching, a grunt, a swing step.

"You got a minute?" says Frank Cormack, limping toward him without his crutch, his injured leg stiff as pine.

"No."

"Too busy standing around a pile of crap with your eyes closed?"

"I'm thinking," says Oliver. "I'm crafting a plan of action. Something you might consider."

"That's exactly what I came to talk to you about."

"The answer is no."

"You don't even know what I'm going to say."

"It doesn't matter. Whatever plan you came up with, you're not asking my opinion or looking for my permission. What you want is money."

"You think you can read me that easily?"

"Like a cheap paperback. You're a money-mad dog, that's all you are, rushing here or there in a desperate attempt to fill the holes they tell you need to be filled."

"If I was looking for money, would I be coming to someone tooling around in a truck like yours? I was just thinking, I don't know, about Erica."

"Jesus, the two of you."

"You know this whole get-out-on-the-road thing was her idea. She wanted us to follow your example."

"That's funny, I don't remember stealing heroin from a Russian drug lord before my wife and I headed west. And I sure as hell don't remember sticking up a mini-mart on the road."

"Yeah, I screwed up. I was trying to get a stake for our trip. And Erica had nothing to do with any of it. But the way it worked out has gotten me thinking about everything."

"Good luck with that."

"I don't know what to do from here on in. I can't go back, I know that. But I'm not sure how to move forward. All I want to do is what's best for her."

"Then do it."

"But I don't know what that is. She wants to be free, man, she wants to see the world, chart her own path, all the jive you put into her head. That's what I thought I was giving her."

"And now?"

"Now I see I'm giving her nothing but trouble."

"So you decided to blame me."

"All I want is some advice or something. You said you were going to help me."

"I lied."

"I want to do the right thing."

"No one wants to do the right thing. They want to do the easy thing and be convinced it's the right thing."

"You're a boiled old peanut, aren't you? The word is you're thinking of fixing up the stable?"

"I thought I'd try."

"You want some help?"

"You're a fuck-up with a bum leg who knows nothing about carpentry. Why would I want your help?"

"Because no one else is offering?"

"Well," says Oliver Cross, before hocking up a wad of phlegm from his throat and spitting it onto the ground. "There is that."

Oliver surveys what's left of his workshop as the injured boy awkwardly sweeps the leaves and garbage from the stable's wooden floor, the little dead animals, the shivers of roof timbers that have fallen to the boards that Oliver laid over the dirt decades ago.

The workbench is in place with the vises still bolted onto the surface, the big hunks of metal a deep maroon from the rust, but what's left of the tool set is scattered on the floor: planes and saws, adzes, an ax, a set square, a brace, scattered auger bits. One by one he picks up the precious tools, brushes off the crust of dirt and loose rust. Each piece holds the memory of the trees whose wood it gouged, the force of his hands on their grips. He lifts his old spokeshave, brushes dirt off the handles, takes hold. Still balanced, still ready to shape another fucking bowl.

He wonders for a moment why he left all his precious tools here to rot, and then, with a wince, he remembers.

"Well now, what a nice little coffee klatch," says Erica from the open door of the stable. She is standing next to Ayana, looking in at the two men working quietly on opposite ends of the building.

"I'm helping your grandpa resurrect his old homestead," says Frank.

"Really? Why?"

"He's trying to wile money from me," says Oliver.

"Trust me, Frank, that won't work," says Ayana. "Like getting blood from a stone, which is what Oliver's heart is made of."

"My father was born in here," says Erica. "Isn't that right, Grandpop?"

"Right there," he says, nodding to the corner where the bed had been.

"What do you remember of the day he was born?"

"It was night," says Oliver. "And there was blood."

"Such a romantic, Oliver," says Ayana. "What about the joy of seeing your baby boy for the first time? What about sharing the moment of birth with your wife?"

"It also stank," says Oliver.

"How did somebody born here end up like my dad?" says Erica.

"You were in my father's club in Chicago, right?"

"Such a snooty place."

"How did somebody born to that," says Oliver, "end up here?"

Erica thinks on that for a moment and then smiles.

"We were going to go swimming in the reservoir, Frank," says Ayana. "You want to come?"

"Maybe I should keep working," says Frank before looking over at Oliver.

"Just go," says Oliver. "I see you hop around on that bad leg anymore I'm going to get seasick."

"You're still not getting any money," says Ayana before the three head out to the reservoir. "I can promise you that."

After they all leave, Oliver puts the spokeshave on the workbench with the rest of the tools and walks over to the part of the stable Frank started cleaning. The kid worked a bit, not too well considering his leg and his lack of interest, but he tried, at least. No one else came in to lend a hand.

On the floor, Oliver can finally see the splintery surface of the wood. From the workbench he grabs a rusted chisel, returns to where Frank swept, stoops down, and slams the blade into one of the boards. Fibers separate like chewed-over pieces of string. The roof gives out, the rains fall, the insects come from underneath. Ruin cascades.

"I think it's time," said Helen, one night in their bed, with the boy asleep between them. "It feels here like it felt in San Francisco."

"It's not the same," said Oliver. "It's just something the farm is passing through on its way to its next evolution."

"And what will that be, Oliver?"

"We don't know, that's the point. Maybe something brilliantly spiritual. Something to give hope to all humanity."

"Or something dead. It feels played out. It feels like it's time to leave."

"And go back to the world? For what?"

"Maybe to take care of our son."

"Fletcher loves it here. He has nature, he has friends. He is becoming his true self."

"He's not speaking."

"He'll speak when he wants to."

"And his teeth, Oliver. We need to fix his teeth."

"Can we not talk about his fucking teeth anymore? I can't go back. I can't fail again."

"It's not failure to know when to move on."

"Tell that to my father. I need to make this work."

"Where we are is not important. Wherever we are we'll have each other."

"Easy for you to say. You grew up in a split-level in Havertown. You're not a Cross. You're not living in the shadow of the perfect life the perfect brother was not allowed to live."

"Oh, Oliver."

She reached out to caress his cheek and he slapped her hand away.

They decided they needed a break. They decided that without a break something irreversible would happen between them. And within that break he fell into the embrace of Crazy Bob's pharmaceuticals and Gracie's slender arms. Even as he once again felt the universe cracking above him, he could imagine that he was finally leading the life that was supposed to be his destiny, a brilliant life of pure freedom that held the possibility of changing a world that desperately needed changing.

He knows things now he didn't know then. He knows freedom isn't in a drug, or on a road, or in a snarl of defiance. Instead, it lives in the bones of your relationships. He knows he was always free with Helen because Helen never wanted chains on his body or his soul. And he knows the goddamn world is well satisfied with what it is and will knock the crap out of anyone who tries to change it. But back then he still hadn't learned those truths, and so he ran around the farm like a jackass with his tail on fire, at least until Fletcher showed up at Gracie's cabin, jabbering about a coyote and Lucius and the blood—a searing moment that brought him back to himself.

A day later, with the ruins of the main house still smoldering from the fire he had set to destroy a crime scene he didn't understand but that he knew held only misery for him and his kin, he and Helen and the boy pulled away in the same van in which they had arrived seven years before. They left with the fiction that they were visiting Helen's ill mother and had every intention of coming back. No one needed to know they were fleeing for good; no one needed to read the guilt and fear that were sending them back to the world.

And as they prepared to flee, to keep his cover, Oliver left his precious tools in the stable, consigned with all his outsize dreams of creating a new kind of life to the dustheap of his history.

31

FINAL MASQUERADE

"Aren't you coming in?" called out Erica from the reservoir.

Frank Cormack sat on the bank, among the weedy grasses, facing one of the high hills that framed the farm. Erica was swimming with Ayana, two naked women, young as spring, with the sun shining off their slicked hair and soft shoulders, kicking their long legs in the swimming hole. Why wouldn't he be in? Well, the pain for one reason. And he was tired after working all morning on that stupid stable for another. And then he wondered what the old goat would think if he saw Frank skinny-dipping with his granddaughter, even though he had to know that Frank was banging her silly. It pissed him off that Erica's grandfather had wormed his way into his head, but if he was going to make this hustle work, every move had to be right.

"I can't," he called back. "My leg."

"Oh come on. A little water aerobics will do it good. And the water's beautiful."

"Really, no. I can't."

"Coward," she said.

"Coward?"

The taunt was enough to force him to his feet, to strip off his shoes and pants, boxers, and shirt, to send him limping and flopping like a three-legged dog until he fell into the water with a grunt and a shout. Because if he ever had a hope of keeping her as part of his future, it would take more than the old man's money. He'd have to show some spit and initiative, too, and if this wasn't it, at least it was something.

But the water was cold, unbelievably cold—Erica had kindly left that out of her exhortations—and the shock of it squeezed his body and shrank his testicles even as it numbed his brain. But this last thing wasn't entirely unwelcome.

While the girls swam and dived to the bottom, laughing and chatting, he turned onto his back and floated, letting the sun paint his face and chest with warmth as the water buoyed him with its frigid fingers. Breezes danced across the surface, tugging him here and there. He maybe should have been up at that falling-down stable, continuing to wile his way into the old man's graces, or still clothed at least, but this, just now, the warmth and the cold together, the swirl of the breezes, this was something new and peaceful. For a moment he lost the buzz of anxiety and felt something else, a kind of peace rising from the depths of the reservoir to pierce his heart with calm.

"Uh-oh," said Erica softly.

"What's wrong?" said Ayana.

"My grandfather's coming down and we're not wearing anything."

Frank's peaceful heart seized in him, and he rolled off his back to go vertical in the water, moving his arms to keep his shoulders above the surface and his junk below. Erica's grandfather was trundling down the path as the dog trailed behind. With his back bent like it was, the old man looked like a walking pretzel.

"Don't worry about him," said Ayana. "Most old men are pervs, they can't help themselves, but Oliver's not like that. Definitely not."

"Why do you say that?" said Frank. "What happened on your little road trip? Anything we should know about?"

"Nothing. That's it. Not a thing. Just gentleman stuff is all. Except that he stole the whipped cream from my pancakes, if you can imagine that."

"The little thief," said Erica. "I thought he was vegan."

"He took me to a barbecue joint. All he had was the potato salad and beans, but there was definitely pork in the beans. He paid for it, too."

"You almost sound like you like him, Ayana," said Frank.

"Well, he goes on and on about the stupidest things, and he curses too much for an old guy, and his taste in music is the worst."

"I know, right?"

"But he bought me a guitar."

"Why did he do that?" said Frank, perking.

"I don't know. He heard me sing."

"He didn't seem to like my voice much last night."

"The man knows quality," said Ayana. "And you know, he actually listens when you talk, which is strange for someone who watches Fox News."

"He watches Fox News?" said Frank.

"Yeah, in the motels, with the sound off. He stares and grinds his teeth. He says it keeps him seething, which is the way he likes it."

"Hey, Grandpop," called out Erica. "You coming swimming?"

"In that sewer?" the old man called back as he tromped down the path. "Not on a bet."

"Is anything wrong with the water?" said Frank.

"It's open season on rivers and streams again. Who knows what the strip mines in the mountains are dumping into the creek. You're likely to come out with three eyes."

"Is that what happened to you, Oliver?" said Ayana.

"It was clean as soap back in the day. Your father learned to swim in that reservoir."

"It must have been sweet," said Erica, "you teaching little Fletcher the backstroke in the old swimming hole."

"No one taught your father anything," said the old man. "He just jumped in and did it."

"I didn't know he was such a wild kid."

"There's a lot about him you don't know," said the old man, collapsing in slow motion until his butt hit the ground. "Lot I don't know either."

The dog ran to the lip of the water and barked at Frank. Frank swam slowly to the shore, limping forward once he could stand on the soft muddy reservoir bed. On dry ground he leaned down to ruffle the dog's neck before, without drying off, he turned away from the old man and put on his shirt and boxers. He dropped to the weedy dirt to slide his pants over the lame leg. Then he lay in the sun on a patch of grass not too far away from the old man. The dog paced around for a bit before dropping onto his stomach between them.

"What are we doing next?" Frank said, like a good little suck-up.

"I'm going to try to raise the portico roof," said the old man. "I don't know what you're going to do."

"I can help," said Frank. "We have some time before we have to get back on the road."

"On the road to where?"

"Away. We'll be safe overseas."

"Maybe, if you get there. But that's the trick with an open warrant."

"We'll be flying out from California."

"Yeah, that might work. I hear they don't have computers out there in California."

"Then what am I supposed to do?"

"Face what you did."

"Like you, old man?"

"Exactly."

"How was prison?"

"Lonely. Anxious. Shitty food. A boredom so brutal it squeezes your eyes. Sort of like running."

"I'd rather run."

"But you might not have to. I made sure the Russian knew you had given up his stuff, and I told him where it was."

"You put him on Delaney?"

"Maybe they'll fry each other's asses. My guess is he's off the chase. And a lawyer might be able to talk to the DA in Ohio. Maybe work out a deal."

"I'd rather run."

"If you tell the whole story, it won't be as much time as you think. And you'll know the deal before you give yourself up."

"You have all the answers, don't you?"

"What do you have, Frank, other than a bum leg and price on your ass?"

"Love?"

The old man laughed. "If you're going to stake your life on love, it better not be a question."

"She's a complicated girl."

"She's her grandmother's granddaughter."

A howl came from the distance, like the call of a wolf, and Hunter's head lifted. A moment later the dog was up and sprinting away from them both.

"So," said Frank. "The portico roof."

"The posts on the end look solid enough, it's just the bases that rotted out. I found a metal beam the right size. We could use the jack from my truck to raise the roof and then slip the posts onto new bases and bang in some supports."

"I'm game if you're game."

"But now that I'm down I won't be able to get up for a while. And then after all that getting up I might need a nap. Maybe this afternoon."

"I'll be there," said Frank. "Anything you need you can count on me."

◆ ◆ ◆

"In the end," said Crazy Bob, "they pinned it on the coyote."

"It's always the coyote," said Erica's grandfather.

"He must have knocked over one of the candles when he was snacking on Lucius's guts," said Gracie. "The fire destroyed most of the evidence."

"Wily bastard," said the old man.

Frank was sitting in the circle around the fire, just beyond the stone ruins of the ranch house. He wasn't really paying attention—he didn't have much interest in anything that happened yesterday, not to mention forty years ago—but the oldsters were talking as if it sure had meant something to them. And he noticed that Erica was listening as if it mattered to her, too.

There hadn't been a party like the night before. Instead it had been a normal evening of exquisite boredom on the farm. There was a plain mash of beans and squash to go with the salad, and now it was seven of them wiling the night away with loose talk about old times, a bucket of Blue Moons, and Crazy Bob's crazy shit. Wendy, Angie, and Toby had gone with some of the others to a country and western bar across the hills in Fountain. Frank had been thirsting to get away from the farm and maybe guzzle a bellyful of whiskey, but he decided he was better off staying close to Grandpa Moneybags. The dog pack, with Hunter included, was sitting just outside the firelight.

"It doesn't matter what the fuzz said, we knew the truth of it," said Flit. "It was a crime, and not just against Lucius. The farm's never been the same for any of us."

"How not?" said Erica.

"The spirit went out of it," said Gracie. "We were here to raise a living from out of the ground, yes, but also to explore our way of being, to create something new in this world. We thought changing one piece of the landscape could change every other piece. It was a political act, being here."

"Everything's political," said Crazy Bob. "Buying into the capitalist fantasy is political, just as turning away from it is political. And preparing for the inevitable backlash from the capitalist overlords and their money slaves was political, too. And we were prepared, weren't we, Oliver? All across the valley, and even up as far as Manitoba Springs, we were a militia of our own, ready to beat back the invasion."

"You were always the feisty one," said Erica's grandfather.

"We're still ready, all of us who are left. No one gives up power and money without a battle. Revolutions are all about the might."

"And the spiritual, too," said Gracie. "Let's not forget that. That's where Lucius came in."

"He was as spiritual as a cobra," said old man Cross.

"That's sweet of you to say," said Gracie with an indulgent smile, "since cobras are worshipped as gods in India. Lucius believed he had the answers while the rest of us were still trying to figure out the questions, but there was something there, Oliver, you can't deny it. And when he went like that, in blood and fire, the spiritual part of the farm seemed to get burned away along with the ranch house. Of course, Erica, then your grandmother and grandfather left. And not too long after that Fire left with her boys."

"And then the peacock died," said Crazy Bob.

"The peacock?"

"Sam we called him. Majestic bird. Another coyote took him down. That was like the gods telling us the golden age was over. We should have given it up right then, but it's tough, sometimes, to admit defeat."

Yeah, tell Frank about it. It had been a hard afternoon, shoring up the portico roof of that crumbling stable. The old man had made Frank do most of the work, even with his bum leg. Jamming the rusting metal beam between the roof and a plank set up on the jack, pumping the jack handle as the roof rose the barest of intervals with each pump, then slipping the weathered wooden post between a loose cinder block and the roof. As he lowered the jack enough so that the post took the weight, he kept waiting for the whole thing to blow apart. And he certainly noticed that the old man stood behind him, so that Frank would take the shards if the wooden post exploded into failure.

Except the post didn't explode, it held, and the roof started to look almost level.

"All right," said the old man. No smile, no word of thanks. "Let's do the next one."

Now, even after a hot shower, Frank's muscles radiated ache as he sat by the fire with his sore leg extended. Manual labor was a thing for the first-name-onlys, and they could have it.

Truth was, he should have been high as a cloud right now, but the old man had passed the joint and stuck with a beer, as if still recovering from his crazy outburst the night before, and so Frank had decided it was best to do so himself. He didn't even know if the old man had noticed, but Erica had given him a strange look when he passed the blunt. He just shrugged, grabbed a bottle from the bucket, and twisted off the cap. She didn't have to know the game he was playing, though she could probably figure it out.

"Why did you leave the farm, Oliver?" said Ayana.

"Helen's mother took sick. We went on a run to visit." The old man, staring into the fire, gave a shrug and took a slug of his beer. "And then we just sort of stayed."

"That was the story, at least," said Flit. "The sick mother. The short visit. Just a few weeks you said. But you left the day after the fire and we all knew you weren't coming back."

The old man didn't say anything, just kept staring, like it was as true as the night, all of it. In the darkness, the eyes of the dogs glowed.

"Why wouldn't they come back?" said Erica.

The quiet stoked Frank's curiosity. He noticed Gracie looking at Crazy Bob, as if there were a secret buried somewhere in the past.

"The boy," said Gracie, finally, after a long and uncomfortable silence. "Your grandmother was worried about your father."

"My father?" said Erica, curled with interest in her chair. "What about him?"

"She wanted to get him to a real school," said Gracie. "Fletcher had stopped participating in Angie's lessons. And for a long time he refused to talk."

"Daddy wouldn't talk? I can't imagine that. Why not?"

"Maybe because he felt more like an animal than a kid," said the old man.

"My father?"

"He used to run wild across this land, as wild as the coyotes. And then there were his teeth. Helen wanted to get them fixed."

"Oh those teeth," said Gracie with a laugh.

"They were a spilled box of Chiclets, they were," said Crazy Bob. "And Fire's boys had such grills, like picket fences, white and straight enough to make a movie star green."

"But it wasn't just the teeth, was it, Oliver?" said Flit.

"Stop it, Flit," said Gracie, with a warning snap in her voice. "It wasn't Oliver."

"It wasn't the coyote, that's for sure. There was enough of the skull left after the fire to know that."

"I'm telling you the facts," said Gracie. "And I know."

"How do you know so sudden like?"

"Because he was with me when it happened."

"Middle of the night like that?" spit out Flit, and then he quieted when he realized what he said and everyone, Frank included, turned to the old man, who kept staring at the fire. One of the dogs yawned loudly.

"Convenient," said Flit, finally and abashedly, "coming up now after we been mashing it between our teeth like cud all these years."

"Maybe she's been protecting someone else, you old fool," said Crazy Bob.

"Aah, I don't buy it," said Flit. "I know what I know, and I know Oliver ran like a scared dog after the killing and the fire."

"That's just Oliver," said Gracie. "He always runs when things get hard."

Frank would have thought old man Cross would have spoken up after that, spit out some sharp barb defending himself, but all he did was hold his beer in both hands and continue gazing into the fire, as if some answer were there in the flames. Frank turned from the old man to Erica, and realized she was staring at her grandfather with a look of shock. Then she turned her face to Frank and he cringed.

"How'd it finally all work out for you in the world there, Oliver?" said Crazy Bob. "You fix them teeth?"

"They're so bright and flat now," said the old man, "you can shave by them."

"I bet it burns your britches," said Crazy Bob with a yelp.

"And Helen?" said Gracie. "How did Helen do?"

"Better than me. She taught art, got a rep for her work, doted on the boy, and then the grandkids."

"Grandmom was really something," said Erica. "She painted a zebra on a carousel in my room. She did it when I was a baby and I still won't let my mom paint over it. She's such a part of my heart."

"Helen was fine in the world," said the old man. "I was the trouble. Being out there was like living in someone else's delusion."

"Most of us left the farm at one point or another," said Crazy Bob. "But unlike you, we came back."

"Yeah, well, it was a marriage, not a dictatorship. Helen couldn't be shoved one way or the other. Ever. Even at the end."

Frank knew what the old man was talking about. Everyone did. When Erica showed up at the farm it was one of the first things she blurted. *"How's your grandfather?" "I don't really know. I haven't seen him since he killed my grandmother."* That put a halt on the old conversation. But there were secrets here, and lies too, maybe, material to mine and use. Frank wanted to keep the old man talking.

"That must have been hard, what you did," said Frank, putting an edge of sympathy in his voice. "I can't imagine that."

"Good for you," said old man Cross, "because I can't forget it. I keep living it over and over."

"Daddy never forgave you," said Erica.

"I knew he wouldn't. But it wasn't up to him." The old man stared into the fire. "If you ask the court, it wasn't up to me or her, either."

"Well, it's not like you didn't have practice," said Flit.

"Shut up, Flit," said Gracie.

"It would have been legal in Oregon," said Crazy Bob. "You should have gone to Oregon. They know how to run things up there. And a slice of marionberry pie might have changed her mind."

"She wasn't eating at the end. She was just hurting. And we weren't running off to Oregon to do something as natural as dying. She wanted to go out on her own terms and she had earned that right. It wasn't about being legal or not. Fuck legal. It was about the doing of it, and I did it, and it still fills me with regret every minute of every day."

"So it was a mistake?" said Ayana.

"I didn't say that."

"But you said you regret it."

"Life is choice," said the old man slowly, carefully, like he had chewed on this same piece of gristle for years now. "For every path you take, there are three you piss on. If you're not living in a dream world, then the regrets pile up like corpses in a war. The only thing I never regretted was her. But sometimes, when you love so hard, you have no choice but to let go. So I let her go."

The old man continued staring at the fire, as his words settled over them like a cold mist. Then, with eyes glistening like marbles in the firelight, the old man lifted his gaze until it locked tight onto Frank's.

!Snap!

A spark flicked in Frank's brain, right behind his eyeball, and it felt like a jagged piece of electricity had jumped right from the old man into Frank's skull. And even as Frank jerked his head back the old man kept staring, as if to say, *It hurts, doesn't it?* But he knew right then what he had to do to get in the old man's pocket.

The dogs stirred, a couple barked as a light painted Gracie's cabin, her field, and the scrub brush beyond. As the dogs bounced up and bounded toward the juniper tree, Frank heard a vehicle pulling slowly into the mouth of the drive.

"They're back early," said Crazy Bob. "That's strange. The dancing probably hasn't even started yet at Anchors. Wendy does love her line dancing."

As the light died and doors slammed, Frank waited for the sound of revelry from the returners, the burble of laughter and alcohol-fueled high spirits. But instead his neck bristled at the barking of the dogs, and a low murmur of voices he didn't recognize. He looked around. No one seemed worried or perplexed, no one but Erica, whose head swiveled to a whistle only her ears could detect.

Frank tried to rise but a fear pressed him down in his chair, pressed him down even as Erica stood. Frank was expecting the worst when a little girl, blonde and barely hip high, ran out of the darkness right up to Erica and gave her a hug.

It took him a moment to realize what was happening, but when it came to him it was dizzyingly clear. That was Erica's sister, the perfect little sister she talked about all the time. And there, standing just outside the fire's circle, with the shifting light giving them the aura of ghosts, were a big-bellied red-haired man and a woman, thin and blonde, with a gold necklace hanging over her white silk shirt, a hand over her mouth, and tears catching bits of firelight.

Frank wondered for a moment how Erica's family had gotten here, until he spied, coming from behind the parents, a dark man in a suit. A suit. On the farm. It was the lawyer, of course, the slick, high-class mouthpiece who showed up everywhere and was working, somehow, for Oliver Cross. Son of a bitch. When he turned to look at the old man, the old man was looking right back with a crooked grin. All this time who had been playing whom?

The lawyer stepped around Erica's parents and went up to the old man.

"Good to see you again, Mr. Cross," said the lawyer.

"Prakash," said the old man without getting out of his chair. "About time you got here. Have yourself a beer."

"Yes," said the lawyer. "I don't mind if I do."

And just that fast, Frank Cormack knew his manic run to Freedom! with Erica Cross had finally come to an end.

32

THE HIPPY HIPPY SHAKE

Oliver Cross is lying on his back, his ankles and chest once again stippled with spider bites, his nose once again clogged with crust. It's déjà vu all over his face. So where the hell's the dog?

He rolls over and sees the beast lying stretched on his side atop a blanket on the hard stable floor, facing away from the bed. The dog's head perks at the sound of Oliver rustling behind him, and then falls back down on the blanket. Beyond the dog lies another cur, on his side, sleeping atop a pad on the floor: Frank Cormack. Maybe the two of them could eat out of the same bowl, Oliver thinks. It would save on the washing up.

Oliver cranks his back until he is sitting, stretching the bedsprings with a *cronk*, and then grunts to a rise. The dog jumps up in a startle as if a marching band has barged through the open door. Frank doesn't stir.

Back bent, bare feet splayed, neck stiff, naked as the dog who bounds crazily about him, Oliver shuffles through the gaping front door and from underneath the cover of the newly leveled portico roof. The green, the blue, the white, the song of the birds and the hum of the insects, the hot yellow sun peering over the ridges to his right. And still no Helen. He clears his nostrils, one then the next, and breathes in the crisp morning air before heading to the bush.

"You've been waiting on me," he grunts.

Ayana, leaning on one of the pillars, studiously looks away. "Have you seen Frank?"

"He's sleeping on the floor inside."

"Poor Frank. You really screwed him to a post, Oliver."

"I gave him a chance."

"By bringing in the family to whisk her away?"

"Is love worth fighting for?"

"Sure, I suppose."

"Then I gave him a chance to fight," says Oliver.

"I don't think he sees it that way."

"That's his problem."

"I'm leaving."

"Goodbye."

"That's all you got?"

"What do you want, a brass band?"

"I need a ride to the bus station in Colorado Springs."

"Okay."

"And bus fare."

"Okay."

"And maybe some food money."

"Fine."

"Do you want to know why I'm leaving or where I'm going?"

Oliver lifts a hand and rubs his skull. She is here to talk. She has something to say, and wants him to say something back. But just then, in the crisp morning air, he doesn't want to hear her mewings or his own, especially his own.

"I don't give a shit," he says.

"Your concern always leaves me dazed, Oliver."

"I could fake it if that would make you happy."

"Don't put yourself out for me, old man. Just let me know when we're leaving."

"Sure," he says, giving a final shake before turning around and heading back to the stable.

"Hey, Oliver," says Ayana before he disappears through the door. "Why do you act like a crazy bird out here, wandering around naked, peeing in public, not giving a damn about anything? What the hell's gotten into you?"

"This place brings me back to myself."

"I don't want to burst your bubble, but maybe, you know, that's something to avoid."

"Too late," says Oliver.

After he dresses, he gently kicks at the sleeping corpse on his floor with a battered boot. Frank squirms but stays unconscious and Oliver kicks a little harder.

"What?" says Frank, pissed.

"We need to fix the roof and then the floors," says Oliver. "For that we'll need wood."

"What do you want me to do about it?"

"I'll bring you an ax."

"What the hell?"

"Wake up, Frank. The birds are singing your song. I'm going into town to buy some wood and maybe some power tools."

"Power tools?"

"I thought we'd saw the wood by hand, but you'd collapse after two boards. You want to come?"

"Anything to get out of this place."

"We'll also be taking Ayana to the bus station. We leave in a couple hours. I'll feed the dog."

"Good. Now let me sleep."

Oliver fills a bowl with kibble and a bowl with water and leaves them outside the front of the stable. Hunter starts chomping, glancing once at Oliver as a warning that he's not sharing.

"Capitalist swine," says Oliver.

He didn't stay around long enough the night before to see the results of the reunion he had engineered. He had set it all up with Prakash at his father's club in Chicago, told him to get Fletcher out to the farm in three days' time unless Prakash heard from Oliver first. And now there Prakash and Fletcher were, along with the rest of the family, which Oliver didn't anticipate but understood. Fletcher might have been his son, but Petra was the fierce figure in that family. She wasn't going to be shunted aside.

Petra had actually come over to him by the fire and tried to give him a hug, which Oliver was able to avoid with awkward thrusts and feints, but he couldn't avoid her profuse thanks.

"Just be calm with her," Oliver said softly. "No orders."

Petra nodded tearfully. Oliver was sure Prakash had given the same advice on the ride down from Denver, because he and Prakash had discussed that very thing, including the legal freedom of Erica's majority. But still he knew how hard it could be. While Petra kept mumbling her thanks, Oliver caught Fletcher staring at him from the other side of the fire, his face slack with complicated emotion. Parents are such fools sometimes.

But that was enough family time just then for Oliver. He took a fresh beer from the bucket and headed out into the darkness to fill in Helen on the goings-on. But Helen stayed quiet, as if still angry at his stoned accusation the night before. Or maybe she was just pissed at the tone of his voice. Whatever, he spent the night alone with his beer and the stars, before heading into the stable to sleep.

Now as he approaches Erica's cabin he sees the strangest sight: his blobby middle-aged son in khaki shorts and a pink golf shirt, doing deep knee bends, skinny white legs flexing, arms thrusting forward from the bulbous torso with every dip like little pale pistons.

"What the hell are you doing?" says Oliver.

Fletcher stops his dipping and pistoning, takes a deep breath, wipes at his sweat-dripped face with the bottom of his shirt. "I'm working out."

"Is that what that was? It looked like you were having a fit."

"I've gotten fat."

"It happens."

"Not to you. You never got fat."

"I worked for a living."

"I work, too."

"In boardrooms? At swanky corporate retreats? Is that work?"

"Can we not do this?"

"What else do we have?"

"It's just being back kind of invigorates me. I barely remember the place, but still. I want to get strong again. I want to race like a coyote again. The firm sponsors a five K. You think I should start running?"

"Who from?"

"Daddy?" came a soft voice from behind a tree. Fletcher turns and the little girl comes forward and leans herself against her father's hip. Blonde hair, scared eyes, thin arms as pale as her father's. Elisa. Somewhere Helen's heart is swelling.

"Say good morning to your grandfather," says Fletcher.

"Morning."

Oliver, speechless in the face of such innocence, nods.

"Mommy said you were going to try to find Erica and then you found her. Was it hard?"

"Not really," says Oliver.

"You made Mommy so happy. If I run away will you find me, too?"

"Not if you're better at hiding than your sister."

The girl laughs and moves slightly away from her father. "I am better at hiding. I'm the best. In hide-and-seek Daddy never finds me."

"Is he trying?"

"Of course I'm trying," says Fletcher. "Usually trying to sleep."

"Where did you take my grandmom?" says the girl.

Oliver's tongue is immediately tied. How can he possibly answer this? How can he explain to this little person what really happened to her grandmother and why he did what he did? What answer can he give her that isn't a sugarcoated denial of everything?

Before Oliver can mumble some platitude that would make him sick, the little girl goes on. "We liked talking to her."

"We all did."

"We would go to the fireplace, Daddy and me, and tell her things. You know, when we had news or something."

"Ah, I see," says Oliver. "And what did she say?"

"She didn't talk back, silly. She was in the jar. But we still liked talking to her."

Oliver closes his eyes and rubs his skull. Even dead she is a bigger part of their lives than he could ever be. Some things can't be recovered.

"Come with me," he says and he starts off for the stable. He glances back and sees father and daughter, his son and granddaughter, standing together for a moment, hesitating, before following behind. He slows to let them catch up and the three walk together. When they reach the stable he stops in front of the portico.

"We used to live in this building," says Fletcher to his daughter. There is a note of pride in his voice that surprises Oliver. "We all slept in one big bed."

"That sounds like fun," says the girl.

"Don't get any ideas."

"Why does it smell like pee out here?"

"It's the cows," Oliver says.

"They got out of their pen?"

"Or the squirrels. Wait here a minute."

He goes inside and when he comes out again he is holding the urn. The girl claps when she sees it.

"The Grandmom jar," she says. "Is she still in there?"

"Still in there," says Oliver. "I thought your grandmother would like to be part of this place. We were happy here, for a time at least, and it seemed fitting. 'I bequeath myself to the dirt to grow from the grass I love. If you want me again, look for me under your boot-soles.' That's from Uncle Walt."

"Who's Uncle Walt?" says the girl. "Do we have an Uncle Walt?"

"No," says Fletcher.

"I was going to scatter her ashes here," Oliver says, "but your grandmother would be happier hearing you telling her all the good things that happen to you and your sister and your mother and father."

"And you?" says the girl.

"She already knows what's happening to me, good and bad. Here." He bends over and hands the urn to his granddaughter and the girl takes it with a fierce solemnity before smiling wildly and hugging the urn tight like a teddy bear.

"Thank you, Grandpop."

"And when you get tired of her," says Oliver, "she liked the Pacific Ocean, too."

"Why don't you go show your mother and sister what your grandfather gave you?" says Fletcher.

"Okay, bye-bye," says the girl before wheeling and running off, stiff legged, back toward the cabin.

The two men stare at the girl as she runs from them.

"That was almost sweet," said Fletcher.

"I'm slipping."

"Where's the son of a bitch?"

"Inside the stable, pretending to sleep." Oliver grinds his teeth, looks out over the ragged remains of the farm. "Let's take a walk before you do something stupid."

◆ ◆ ◆

They walk quietly across the land, letting the earth speak to them. Memories twist and rise from the dirt like blades of grass beneath their shoes. This place was a crucible in both their lives, though in very different ways, and so as father and son cross the valley, they do so quietly. Can the father remember the way the son held tightly to his friends' hands as they cracked the whip across these fields? Can the son remember the way the mountain wood came to life for the father beneath the soft rush of the plane, or the intentness of his wife's eyes as she wrestled a canvas into purity? As soon as they talk they will fight, that is what has become of them, so for a time they walk across the land without words.

"Why did we ever leave this place?" the son says, finally.

Oliver gives Fletcher a sideways glance. "Your grandmother took sick," Oliver says, using the simple excuse he has used ever since they drove off the land for the final time.

"But we could have come back."

"We have."

"With Mom dead and you on parole, you figured now was the time? Erica said that some of the people here think you killed Lucius. She said you didn't deny it."

"I don't care what they think."

"We never talked about any of it."

"There's nothing to talk about."

"Okay," says the boy. "Good. So what are your thoughts about the future? Are you coming back home?"

"I busted parole. They'll put me in jail again. Hell with that. Maybe I'll stay here. Frank is helping me fix up the stable."

"Frank? Mighty chummy with the scumball who kidnapped my daughter."

"No one kidnapped anyone."

"It is so like you to defend him. He should be in jail. He was dealing drugs before he stole from his drug-dealing boss. He absconded with my daughter, who is barely of age, and took her over state lines for immoral purposes. Isn't the Mann Act still something? And he robbed a mini-mart with a gun. Not to mention the crap in Chicago that Divit told us about. If I had a shovel I'd knock his head off and bury both pieces right here."

"I don't doubt it for a minute."

"What does that mean?"

"Frank's a young idiot who made mistakes, but it's a big club."

"This is so typical. He's a criminal who almost got my daughter killed and should be in jail, but he's on the road, chasing America with a gun and a Camaro, a goddamn Jack Kerouac on steroids, and so he's a hero. And me? Well, I work in a suit and tie, which means I'm just a piece of shit."

"Ah, good," says Oliver. "So you do get it."

Fletcher stops cold and stares, before he starts laughing. "Piss off, Dad."

"Good boy," says Oliver without turning around.

"What's with your neck?"

"It's a little stiff."

"Is it your nodes again?"

"The bed in the stable is not a bed."

"You've got to take care of yourself."

"Why?"

"Don't."

"Just come on."

They walk on together in quiet again, moving west toward the end of the valley, choking down the anger they still feel one for the other.

They are both puzzled at its origin, both saddened by the losses, both forever in its grip. Somehow the river of their lives together that had sprung on this very land has been rerouted to a fetid pool of muck neither can escape.

"Chicken coop's still up," says Fletcher. "And there are still cows in the pasture. Not very vegan of them."

"Purity is overrated," says Oliver.

"And Gracie's still here. She gives me the chills, like some old harpy with loose stringy hair. But I was happy to see some of the others, Angie, Toby, and Crazy Bob. I always liked Crazy Bob. He used to give the kids caramels."

"The caramels without the acid, hopefully."

Fletcher trudges on in silence before he starts laughing. "I do remember he had this chemistry set bubbling away in the back of his cabin. Jesus, you guys were so cracked, all of you high as kites, dancing like waterfalls in the moonlight. No wonder it all went to hell. But the goats are new. Look at them all."

"They're Wendy's."

"I saw her last night when she came back from some bar."

"Tearful reunion?"

"Once I realized who she was. I didn't recognize her at first, it was just some strange stringy lady. But she remembered me. She hugged and hugged."

"She got me, too."

"Every time she clutched me close I felt like one of her chickens and my neck started tensing. I can't believe she came back. Of all the kids, she was the one I was sure would leave for good."

"Why?"

"Because, well, you know. You don't know?"

"Know what?"

"I mean, who else could get Notail to follow her? She was pretty amazing like that."

"Notail?"

"The coyote with the missing tail."

"Wendy?"

"She was getting old enough. It was going to be her turn. Sunrise told her to run, but she had a different idea that would protect them both. Why, what did you think?"

"It was your bat."

"Wendy asked to borrow it. But wait, you didn't think . . . ?"

"I bought you that bat."

"I was only seven, Dad."

"But you were a wild seven."

"Well, I wish I had done it. That son of a bitch had it coming. What do you hear about Sunrise?"

"She's a venture capitalist."

"Good for her. It's not easy bucking the craziness, let me tell you. I bet it put Gracie's back up."

"Yeah." Pause. "Wendy, huh?"

"Wait a second. Is that why you never bought me another bat?"

"Didn't I?"

"In Little League I always had to use one from the team bag."

"I didn't notice."

"Were you scared of me?"

"Don't be silly," says Oliver.

But thinking about it, he wonders: Was that it, the night of blood and fire, when everything between them changed? Had Oliver ever looked at his son again without seeing the smashed head, the intestines ripped out by the coyote's teeth? Or was it his own sense of failure that was looking for an excuse and seeing it somehow in his son? He is still considering it when they reach the three-railed wooden fence surrounding Crazy Bob's field. The fence is so old, and in such poor condition, it might still have some of the wood Oliver put in himself when he built it. Oliver rests his arms on one of the top rails. Fletcher leans on the fence beside him. The two men look forward so they don't have to look at each other.

"It's nice to see some things never change," says Fletcher.

"It's legal now in Colorado," says Oliver. "Growing it, selling it. And no one knows those plants like Crazy Bob."

"I guess there's money to be made, huh? But you couldn't do it without consent of the land's owner."

"That won't be a problem."

"Why not."

"I consent."

"Wait, what?"

"When my father died, I had Finnegan have the estate buy the farm from old man Oates. I didn't know what to do with the money, but keeping my friends from being evicted off the land seemed like an okay deal. And maybe I had some guilt for leaving like we did."

"How much money was there in the estate?"

"Enough to ruin us all."

"Did Mom know?"

"Of course she knew. She always knew everything. But she also knew my father tried to hold his money over our heads like a whip. We didn't want it when he was alive and we sure didn't want it when he was dead."

"So you bought the farm with it instead."

"With some of it."

"And with the rest?"

"I told Finnegan to do with it what he wanted. I figured he'd siphon it into nothing."

"And?"

"Finnegan was cleverer than I gave him credit for."

"How much is there?"

"Does it matter?"

"Hell yes it matters. Money always matters. Why did we live poor all those years if you inherited this big estate?"

"We didn't live poor. We had a roof we paid for with work, food we paid for with work. We went to the beach when we wanted to swim, camped out when we wanted to drink in the stars. If I lived in some snooty stone mansion I'd have drunken myself to death."

Fletcher stays quiet for a while, letting it sink in. "Did you ever think the reason I chose the path I did was because I wanted better for my kids than I had?"

"And how's that working?"

"Yeah. Did you ever use your dad's money?"

"To get your teeth fixed before my father died. Going to Chicago and asking for that was fun, but your mom insisted. And then that college you chose up in Vermont."

"I thought you got aid."

"It didn't seem right to take from a kid who didn't have the backstop we had. And we paid for some of the second opinions for your mother that the insurance sons of bitches wouldn't cover. We always knew we had it if we needed it, which is a lot, but we didn't want it to dominate our lives."

"Grabbing it by the fistful or refusing it out of pride doesn't seem so very different."

"Don't get too wise, it's unbecoming."

"Why don't you buy a new truck or something?"

"I like my truck."

"It's a wreck."

"So am I."

"We finally agree on something," says Fletcher.

They lean together on the fence, looking out over the field. The plants are still young, not yet bushed to the max, but there is a pleasant sweetness in the air.

"There is money now in weed, I must admit," says Fletcher.

"There always was."

"The problem is there are so many regulations for a legal cannabis farm. It's not easy complying, even out here. And the price of entry is high on purpose. They make it hard so they can keep it under control."

"Regulations and money. Too bad that's not anything you have experience handling. Maybe Sunrise can help."

"And can you imagine my partners' reaction if I started representing a pot farm. They'd go apoplectic."

"Win-win."

"Truth is, it could be a whole new practice area. Maybe we'd have to open a Denver office. And you'll want to include Crazy Bob and Gracie and the rest in the operations, I assume."

"And Frank too."

"Hell no."

"Think about it, Fletcher."

"I don't need to think about it. He's a wanted felon. He's a punk who can't be trusted other than to screw up everything he ever touched. And he stole my daughter from me."

"How's it going with Erica?"

"Not well. She says she wants us to leave her alone. She says it's her life and she'll do what she wants with it."

"I always liked that song."

"I don't know what to do."

"Maybe start by taking care of the kid."

"So it's a strategic gambit?"

"He's in trouble. Give him a hand. He doesn't deserve it, but he needs it. That's gambit enough. The world sometimes opens up when you step out of your narrow path. Besides, I promised his brother."

"Ah, so that explains it."

"And he reminds me of my brother."

"He's nothing like your brother. Your brother was a hero."

"They're both lost in someone else's war."

"I look at my daughter, Dad, and my throat just constricts in panic."

"Trust me, I know what it is to lose someone more important than your own heartbeat."

"I know you do. I still think of Mom all the time."

"Yeah, the old bat too," says Oliver.

33

PRETTY VACANT

If you asked Frank Cormack then, right then, what ticked him off most about Erica's family showing up unexpectedly at the farm, he would have told you it was that, for some insane reason, he hadn't been expecting them to show up at all.

What kind of dupe had he been? The same kind of dupe he had always been. Anyone looking at the thing with a clear eye would have known they were on the way as soon as the old man showed up in his ratty old truck, but Frank was too wrapped up in his own little hustle to see it. So when they appeared like ghosts in the shifting light of the fire, it felt like a kick in the gut.

He shrank in his seat when they appeared. He had never seen them but had heard all about them in Erica's late-night rants as the remnants of the sex and the drugs licked their jaws: the perfect little sister; the cold and demanding mother whose status depended on her daughter's achievements; the work-obsessed father who stormed about with a Scotch in his hand, wondering what went wrong with his life. It sounded like a nightmare, something absolutely to flee, and he had believed when he started this run that he had been breaking Erica out of some sort of prison.

But here, now, in the fire's glow, they didn't seem so god-awful. They hadn't given up on her the way his family had given up on him. And when they looked at him, first the mother, then the father, picking him out as the problem right off—*troublemaker* had been written across Frank's face from the time he was five—the anger in their stares showed only how much of a shit they gave.

"Mom, Dad, this is Frank," said Erica in a grotesque playact of a high school girl introducing the 'rents to her prom date.

They wanted to wring his neck, especially the fat ruddy father—Frank could see his lips tighten and his fists clench—but all the father did was nod, curtly. When the women and the little girl slipped to the other side of the fire, the father held down the volume of his voice, though not of his anger.

"Nice night," said the father.

"It sure is," said Frank. "How was the ride down?"

"Uneventful."

"We didn't have it so easy."

"I heard."

"I figured the lawyer might have filled you in."

"What are your plans?"

"Stay here for a bit, maybe. I need to rest the leg. Then Europe if we can swing it. Paris eventually, depending on the money."

"Right now I want to break your jaw so bad you'll spend your life in Paris eating onion soup out of a straw."

"I don't doubt it."

"I could do it, too. It wouldn't take much with a druggy piece of string like you. But Erica's looking over here with a worried gaze. And the sight of my daughter ministering to your broken body with tears in her eyes would have me projectile vomiting."

"I'll keep her close, then."

"But know that if anything happens to her you'll be answering to me and it won't be pretty."

"Get in line, Pops," said Frank, and they both smiled as if they were enjoying getting to know one another, and in a way they were.

"My family's staying in the cabin with me tonight," Erica said to Frank when they had a moment together.

"Why don't they get a room in town like the lawyer?"

"I can't do that to them. They want to stay. And my father has history here."

"What about me, sweet pea? Where am I supposed to sleep?"

"I don't know. The stable?"

"You're killing me. You know how bad that place smells. And they leave tomorrow?"

"God I hope so."

"Either they leave or we leave."

"Yes," she said, and then she kissed him and the kiss was so sweet it almost choked him. "Either they leave or we leave."

"I don't think they're leaving without you."

"I think you might be right," she said, already looking away to her sister and mother. "If I'm going to get through a night with my family, I'm going to definitely need some medication."

"That can be arranged," he said.

When she trundled back to her mommy and daddy and little sis, Frank bummed a joint from Crazy Bob and headed away from the ruined old farmhouse. The old man had already disappeared, as had the lawyer, and there was nothing anymore keeping him at the fire. By the light of the low crescent moon he picked his way past the vegetable garden and Gracie's cabin, around the Camaro and the old man's truck, and along the path to the reservoir. When he reached the slope leading down to the water he sat on a mat of grass.

The moonlight danced on the calm surface of the pool. He lit the joint, lay back, grooved on the stars as he smoked. They were so sharp and bright, paving a shining path across the heavens.

Marisol told him once that everyone was formed from stardust. Which meant those stars overhead might be relatives, parents or cousins. That one there might be his uncle Ernest. Hey, Ernie, how's it hanging? He couldn't help but admire them, the stars, so cold and brilliant, so impassive. There was something punk rock about them, all bright eyes and dead affect, all simple chords and snarling riffs, not giving a crap what you thought of them, just glowing, glowing. They were the goddamn Sex Pistols of the universe, oh so pretty, and oh so vacant. He closed his eyes and saw the startling array beneath his lids. And then he imagined what kind of star he'd be up there.

Skittering, desperate, shifty and red, rushing here and there like a mad dog, like a money-mad dog, as the old man would have it.

He snapped his eyes open, desperate to again see the cold brilliant stars with their utter lack of concern. How had he ended up like this? How had he lost his way so brutally?

Somehow he had always felt like he was being left behind, like a truer life was being lived elsewhere. Like all would be well if he could only make it to Thursday nights at the club. Like all would be well with one big score. Like all would be well if he could get Marisol back. Like all would be well in Paris. He had never been to Paris, had no idea what it really was like, but the pictures were so beautiful. The pictures. His life would be perfect if only he could get there. Until he saw another picture of another place to skitter off to.

Truth was, he just wasn't big enough and that made him sad. Uncle Ernest was up there burning bright, not giving a fuck, and he was down here spinning like a top.

When he felt the earth itself heave beneath him like it was somehow alive and trying to shuck him off, he took a last draw from the joint and flicked away the nub. Enough of that. Thinking too much only caused trouble. There was something about the old man and this place that chewed at him, like an infection. And Crazy Bob's weed, having been grown right here, had the same disease.

He didn't remember how he got up from the reservoir and into the stable, but the boards beneath him continued to heave even as the old man kicked him awake and started talking about wood. He tried to go back to sleep, lay curled on the floor beneath a thin blanket hoping the day would slip away from him, but his leg hurt and his side ached and his life sucked and there was nothing to do for it but to rise. When he finally stumbled out of the stable, dressed but still a bit wacked from the weed, Erica was waiting for him.

"I brought you a muffin," she said.

"Bran I assume," he said.

"Sadly, you assume right."

Even though it was dry and medicinal, he still tore at it. "How was your night?"

"My dad snores. I guess I knew this, but sometimes you don't really know a thing until it's shaking the timbers of a cabin in the foothill of the Rockies. The coyotes were coming up to the front door asking him to keep it down. No wonder my mom drinks."

"Other than the snoring how was it?"

"Can we go?" she said. "Can we get out of here? Please. Let's just go."

"Are you sure?"

"I've never been more sure of anything in my life."

"Okay, okay, yes," he said, the cavern in his chest filling with hope as the brochures of their next stops played like a slideshow in his mind. LA, Bali, Prague . . . The image of the Eiffel Tower sparkling in the perfect Parisian night slowed him down.

"It's just, being with them, right now in my life, it's impossible. They're trying so hard, being so careful. It's like I'm a little porcelain vase that they're afraid of breaking. But I can see in their eyes what they're thinking, how much of a disappointment I am, how much of a problem. All they want to do is solve me, but I don't want to be solved."

"They care. You can't fault them for that."

"But it's not me they care about, don't you see? They care about their plans for me, which is something very different. They care about what they'll say to their friends about me, how they'll explain me. I'm another totem on their status pole. But as for what I want or need, all they want for me is not to be a burden anymore."

"I've heard this before, sweet pea. Maybe they just care."

"What, you're on their side now? I saw you chatting gaily with my dad. Best buds now, huh? But you've seen them for one night around the campfire, I've lived with them all my life and I can't do it one more day. Your stuff's in the stable and I can pack up and be ready to go in like five minutes. My dad's off with my grandfather somewhere. I'll say goodbye to my sister, tell my mom we're going into town—she won't try to stop me—and that will be that."

"What about money?" he said between bites. "Can you get us any money?"

"No, I'm sorry, baby, no. I can't ask them, I just can't. But I don't care about their money. Fuck their money."

"We don't have enough for the airplane tickets."

"Sell the car."

"It won't be enough; the car's a piece of shit. It's my piece of shit, and I love it, but it's still a piece of shit."

"Then we'll drive down to Mexico and make our own money. You don't have to do that drug mule shit you were doing in Philadelphia. I'll waitress or something. You'll sing in a café. We'll make do. We don't need much down there. And we'll be free. Don't you want to be free?"

"Yeah, sure, of course I do," he said.

"The beaches, the street food. That corn with the cheese and spice you like so much. And if we get bored we could keep going south. Belize, Colombia, Peru."

"Machu Picchu," said Frank, his eyes widening. "I always wanted to do Machu Picchu."

"We'll get clean down there, both of us, I'll make sure of it. I'll make it all up to you, baby. We'll make it happen. Real freedom. All we have to do is get out of here, now. Get away from them. What do you say?"

What would he say? What do you think he would say? The siren call of freedom and adventure rocked like Johnny Rotten in his skull.

He could see the destinations flash like someone else's Instagram feed in his consciousness, the kind of feed that turned you bitter with envy: striding down the sordid streets of Juarez, making love on a pristine beach in Puerto Vallarta, devouring a pork taco from a cart in Mexico City, playing his songs in a laid-back beach bar in Belize and the wild streets of Colombia, reverently climbing the steep rocky path to mystical ruins atop a great Peruvian mountain. And all of it with Erica, all of it drenched with love and possibility. *Hell yes* is what he would say.

But even as the travel photographs flashed through his consciousness he could see the other pictures, too, the inevitable flip side of all that freedom. Hustling for drugs, turning to cheaper alternatives when the pills got too expensive, sordid hotel rooms shooting up shit, stealing what they could, selling what they had of spirit and body just to get enough to keep going, keep going, so they could steal more, sell more, and keep going.

It would end badly—everything he touched turned to shit—but still the jolt of it sang to him. Maybe the exhilaration of the first few hours, the first few days or weeks if he were lucky, would make it worth it. That had been his skittering red-shifted life, an exhilarating run leading to disaster. Maybe that was the trade-off he had made with fate, and maybe that was the most he could ever expect for himself, the most anyone could expect.

He closed his eyes and saw the stars of the night before still burning heroically beneath his lids, cold, bright, indifferent, vacant. And then he heard the gruff, ruined voice of the old man talking about loving so hard and still letting go as if it was now coming not from the old man's scarred throat but from the stars themselves, and when he heard it some living, squirming thing died in Frank's soul.

"What's wrong, Frank?" said Erica, his last hope on this damn spinning top. "What's happening?"

In the old man's truck just a few hours later, he was still trying to figure it all out: what he had done; what he would do now; how he could get his life back on a track, any damn track but the down-bound one he had been on. They were driving into Colorado Springs, the old man and Ayana and Frank, heading for the bus depot to drop off Ayana—goodbye, Ayana—and then buy some wood and tools and run a few other errands, when Oliver pointed out a cyclist perched atop a black-and-red motorcycle parked on the street across from the transit center. The cycle was big; the cyclist was thin and tall with platinum hair, wearing a red-and-black leather jacket with "V-ROD" spelled across the back.

"Do you see her?" said the old man.

"Uh-oh," said Ayana.

"What did you do, Ayana?" said the old man as he accelerated the truck past the cyclist and then past the bus station itself. "What the hell did you do?"

As the truck roared forward, Frank's head spun to take in the rider and this is what the face he spied told him:

Frank Cormack, you lame-legged, pathetic son of a bitch, you're going to die.

And all he could think, even as fear shot through his heart like a spear, was that it was about fucking time.

34

SURFING SAFARI

Oliver Cross used to lean against the railing on the pier at Fort Point in San Francisco and watch the surfers ride waves beside the rust-colored towers of the bridge. The surfers balanced on their boards like sovereigns of the sea as the ocean's high glassy walls propelled them forward.

Ever since the epochal events in 1968, Oliver's life has been all about fighting the current, swimming against the flow, battling complacency and the status quo. The struggle, ah, the struggle. But letting oneself not only accept the flow, but ride it while standing like royalty atop a narrow board, seemed to Oliver like a brilliant act of alchemy. Surrender turning to mastery, submission as a means to power.

He should have bought a cheap board and jumped into the water and paddled out to where the waves rose like unbroken beasts and given it a go when he was still young enough to have had a chance. He should have submitted to the current, time after time, letting the waves overwhelm him, smashing him into the rocky surface of the seafloor over and again, until once, with just a bit of luck and a shocking outbreak of balance, he had ridden one of those monsters and felt the power of the universe working with him instead of against him. For once he might have lived within the flow instead of outside it. For once he might have been a king.

Except the inevitability of repeated failure in front of an audience of snot-nosed kids who had been surfing since they were grade-schoolers had killed any idea of trying it on his own. His self-image was too fragile, his self-consciousness too strong. So he never tried, never failed, never surfed.

Regrets, who will rid him of these meddlesome regrets?

But as soon as he spies the familiar motorcycle in front of the transit center in Colorado Springs and recognizes the platinum-haired rider, he knows the Russian is coming. The Russian is coming. Maybe the son of a bitch is already here. And he is bringing, along with his weapons and lackeys, violence and death. But Oliver isn't fighting it anymore. He's not slapping against the current in some desperate attempt to peel himself away from the wave. He's not hiding, hoping the thing breaks over his head and leaves him whole. Screw that. Whatever is coming, Oliver decides he is going to face it as if he's on a longboard riding death like a brute wave breaking beneath the Golden Gate.

After passing the motorcyclist, and spotting Madam Bob's leer, Oliver takes the first right, then the first left, then the first right again, checking all the while the rearview mirror. She had to have spotted the truck, had to, but she isn't following to see where the truck ends up. She's at the transit center waiting for someone. And quick as that Oliver knows that the Russian knows everything.

"Let me out," says Ayana.

"Piss off," says Oliver as he spins the truck back toward the highway.

"If she's here, then they're all here," says Frank. "They've come to kill me."

"They're going to try."

"Where are we going now?" says Ayana.

"We need to get back to the farm," says Oliver. "We need to pass the word." He doesn't say that he fears it may be too late.

"I'll get out here," says Ayana.

"Be my guest, but I'm not slowing down," says Oliver. "No bag, no guitar, just the asphalt making you pay for your betrayal."

"I didn't have a choice."

"All we have are choices."

"Remember in Chicago, at that factory place you dragged me to? I didn't want to call but you made me. Remember that, Oliver, you son of a bitch? Yeah. Well on the call they made a threat."

"Boo-hoo."

"If I didn't give them Frank they were going to kill my mother. She's a rat but she's my mother. And they would have done it, too. You didn't leave me a choice."

"But why are they still chasing Frank?" says Oliver. "We made sure they knew he didn't have the stuff anymore. What else did you take?"

"Nothing," says Frank.

"The computer," says Ayana. "He took a computer from Sergei when he bashed his skull."

"So what?" says Frank. "A stupid MacBook. It was in the bag with the shit."

"They want it back."

"Why?" says Oliver. "What's on it?"

"Something they need," says Ayana.

"Evidence?" says Oliver.

"A wallet or something."

"I didn't know," says Frank.

"A wallet, huh?" says Oliver with a bitter laugh.

"We're so screwed," says Ayana.

"Maybe not, if it's what I think it is," says Oliver, veering left onto the entrance ramp. With the window open and the wide white cement of the highway rattling the truck, Oliver can hear the roaring call of the ocean.

Surf's up, motherfuckers.

When they arrive at the pyramid, Oliver turns at the mailbox and speeds over the ravine while Frank and the girl sit frozen, sullen with fear, each of them expecting the worst. But when they reach the farm, all is calm, all is as if this was just an ordinary day at Seven Suns. Oliver wonders if that's the way it always is before hell drops in your lap.

He doesn't park under the juniper but keeps driving, past the parked cars and the lawyer's rented van, onto the bumpy dirt road that heads into the hills, until he gets to the cabin where Erica and the family are staying. He slams the truck into "Park," scuttles out of the still rocking vehicle as fast as his bones allow, and storms the cabin.

Empty.

When he steps outside again, he looks around. Frank and Ayana are also out of the truck, searching the emptiness. The birds twitter, the insects buzz, the heavy sun bathes the empty fields as his stomach anxiously contracts. Then he hears a spark of laughter riding on a soft breeze.

"Come with me," he says.

Oliver finds them at the reservoir. Fletcher is in his old swimming hole, clowning in the water with Oliver's two granddaughters. Petra is sitting primly on the bank with Prakash, who is in jeans and a T-shirt. Prakash waves cheerfully when he sees Oliver barreling down the path. It's enough, all of it, to still Oliver's beating heart. He stops on the path; Frank and Ayana halt, too, standing on either side of him. It is as if the land and the water of this place are wrapping their arms around his family. He wants to call back Helen from whatever hole she disappeared into and show her this. If he could freeze time, right now, freeze time and let this vision soak into his bones, he would.

But time marches, ticktock, and death is on its way. He starts again down the path to relay the terrible news.

There is no time for heartfelt confessions and familial break-throughs, there is no time to counteract decades of animosity and disappointment. There is no time for a happy ending. There is just time to leave.

"Oliver," says Petra after the van is packed. Her hair is stiff as wire even as her head shakes. "Oliver."

"Yeah," says Oliver, taking a hug because it's quicker than avoiding it.

"Thank you," she whispers. "I know you're not coming home, but wherever you end up, we'll visit. I promise."

"Just not too often," he says before pushing her to the van's door.

The little girl, still clutching at the urn, turns her head, smiles, and gives a little wave before following her mother into the van. She's the only one who knows how to do this.

"Come home with us, Dad," says Fletcher, eyes red behind his glasses.

"Take care of your family," says Oliver.

"Don't worry about the parole thing. Prakash has already talked to Jennifer. I'll talk to her, too."

"Give her my regards."

"Maybe I should stay with you. I feel like I should stay."

"Don't be a fool."

"Why do you always make me feel guilty?"

"It's my gift."

Fletcher turns and looks at his daughter, standing off, talking to Frank, and Oliver turns with him. "I told her she had to come with us. No choice."

"I'm sure that worked well," says Oliver.

"I didn't know what else to do."

"My father tried to browbeat me, and I tried to browbeat you. Fat good it did either of us."

"So I'm part of a long tradition of failed Cross fathers."

"My grandfather voted for Eugene Debs."

They stand there for a moment, watching the discussion between Erica and Frank play out. There are hesitations, there is anger, Frank says something and Erica whips out a response, and then Frank starts singing something, too low for them to hear. They talk more before Frank turns away and Erica, with tears in her eyes, heads toward them.

She looks at Fletcher and says not a word before spinning around to face Oliver. She leans forward until her forehead rests on Oliver's chest. Fletcher nods at Oliver before heading off to stand by the van door, giving them a moment alone.

Erica stays quiet for a couple heartbeats before she says, "He won't let me help him."

"Maybe he's helping you."

"To do what?"

"Whatever."

"I'm not ready to go home."

"Just get away from here. Promise me you'll get away."

"I promise."

"Good. Go."

"Say hi to Grandmom for me," she says. As she passes Fletcher on her way into the van, Fletcher gives Oliver a look, a helpless, thankful look, a look that suddenly reminds the father of his own emotions so many years ago, before Fletcher follows his daughter inside.

"It was a pleasure to see you again, Mr. Cross," says Prakash. "Especially in more convivial circumstances."

"What's wrong with the University Club?"

"Don't get me started, I might surprise."

"I don't doubt it." Oliver looks up and sees Ayana standing hesitantly off to the side, her bag and guitar on the ground beside her. "Ayana, get in the fucking van."

"Maybe I'll go with Frank," she says.

"Don't be stupid," says Oliver. "Get in the van."

"Piss off, Oliver."

He looks at Prakash and smiles. "Our time together wasn't a total waste."

"They're not going to stop chasing him," she says.

"Oh, I think they will, one way or the other. But no matter what happens, it will be better for you and your mother if you're not involved. Mr. Prakash will take you wherever you want to go."

She hesitates before picking up her bags and heading for the van. "Anywhere that's not here."

"Good motto."

She goes to the rear of the van and throws in her bags. Then she slams it shut. On the way to the door she stops in front of him for a moment.

"I'm sorry."

"That and a quarter will get you a cup of coffee."

She laughs. "What century are you living in? You know, Oliver, you could be a halfway decent human being if you ever let yourself try."

"That's what I'm afraid of."

"See you on the far side," she says, before she climbs in.

Still looking inside the van, Oliver says, "How is the real estate purchase going?"

"We offered," says Prakash. "They countered. We laughed. They sulked. It's as good as done."

"You'll take Ayana back to Chicago with you."

"Whatever she wants."

"Convince her. Tell her I'm buying the house. Tell her she can live rent free as caretaker and also get a piece of the rent in salary."

"How generous a piece?"

"Up to you. But a room of her own, enough to eat, and medical insurance is what anyone deserves. Make sure she has it all. And keep your eye on her."

"Of course."

"There's something there, more than she knows. It'll turn to crap, it always does, but still."

"I'll do my best for her."

"Drive carefully."

"And fast."

"Yes," says Oliver, "and fast. Now get the hell out of here."

He watches the van as it backs up, turns around, heads off along the long, overgrown road. When it disappears from his view, he turns and watches Frank stare down the selfsame road, his eyes red, his hands trembling.

"Well that's that," says Frank, wiping his nose with a sleeve-tattooed forearm.

"Yep," says Oliver. "You got a password to open the laptop you stole?"

"Putinrocks293."

"Good. Now get the fucking computer and follow me."

"Where we taking it?"

"To Crazy Bob," says Oliver.

35

HURT

Frank Cormack's life had finally hit rock bottom, there was no denying it, and when someone like Frank hit rock bottom, it was not like a fall from great heights where Icarus McMoneybags ended up in some springy little rehab on the coast with ocean views and daily massages from Sven. Hell no, rock bottom for someone like Frank Cormack was low, baby, lower than low. Falling out of the shit into the Shinola. And it wasn't the drugs that sent him down this time, or the perpetual lack of cash, it wasn't his audacity or stupidity, though he had both in abundance, and it wasn't his usual desperate need to do something, anything to clear the murk of his life. No, what finally toppled Frank into the lower depths was the vile spark of decency.

Where the hell had that come from?

Not once but twice he had sent Erica away. Not once but twice he had told her no, no, even though what he wanted to say was yes, yes, yes. Not once but twice he had thrown away the key to the magical life he had imagined for himself, an odyssey of travel and love and music and sex.

Now, instead of roaring south to Mexico, his Camaro was still parked under the juniper tree, like a sign. Come and get me. And instead of barreling to freedom with love by his side, Frank Cormack lay sprawled beneath a mess of bush with his pistol in his belt and a rifle in his grip, waiting. Waiting for them to come and get him. Waiting for them to put a bullet in his heart. But he wasn't waiting alone.

Gracie was squatting within her cabin with a gun. Toby and Flit were holed up behind another. Wendy was high in a tree with a rifle. And the old man's truck was parked squat in Gracie's vegetable patch, facing the road. Oliver Cross sat in a chair in the truck bed, a slab of wood over the rear window and a rifle of his own propped on the top of the cab. It would have been almost heroic, the sight, except his chin was on his chest, his eyes were closed, and he was taking a nap. Yeah, a nap. The old man looked like a crazed geezer getting in his rest before a night of scaring Halloween trick-or-treaters off his lawn.

The rest of the farm had been cleared out, except for Crazy Bob, who was in his cabin, working on the computer, trying to break past whatever safeguards had been built into the operating system. If he succeeded before the Russian and his soldiers showed up, the old man thought they might have a bargaining chip to exchange for Frank's life. Otherwise Frank would be running until he was dead.

It promised to be a short run.

"I don't understand," Erica had said when he turned her down for the second time. "Why are you doing this to me? What did I do?"

"Nothing, baby. You did nothing. You're perfect."

"I'm trying to help you, to take care of you."

"But it's not enough, don't you see? I'm no good, not like I am. I'm killing myself, running so hard I can't stop from tripping over my own damn feet, and there's nothing you can do about it. I keep falling, sweet pea, and I can deal with that. I am what I am, and might always be. But I'm not any more willing to drag you along just so I don't die alone."

"You won't die, I won't let you."

"It's not up to you, is it?"

"And you're not dragging me, I'm coming because I want to. It's my choice. Freedom, right?"

"Is this freedom, really, running from disaster to disaster, waiting for it all to come crashing down? It's getting old, baby. I need something different, I need to be something different." And then he had begun singing in a low voice, with dark hopeless tones, about starting over again a million miles away and this time not losing himself along the way.

"That song always makes me cry," she said.

"I used to think it was just another addict's line, but I don't know anymore."

"I don't want to go back to the way it was, either."

"Then don't. Be what you want to be. Whatever you want to be. Get a million miles away and make it different. And when you get there," he said, turning away so she wouldn't see his tears, "look me up."

That was about right, ending things on a pipe dream, that was about as perfect as it could get. And he had thought, maybe, she'd fight a little harder, and maybe he would have given in, and maybe they'd be on their way now to that glorious fire of destruction waiting for them south or west or wherever the hell they'd run to. But that she didn't fight a little harder was the answer right there, and he knew that answer was coming in the way she had looked at him, and kept looking at him, after he lost everything in Chicago.

So maybe it wasn't decency that propelled him after all, maybe it was just the flat reality of the thing, along with the still living hope of digging his hand into the old man's wallet. And those motives comforted him some as he waited beneath the bush with the rifle in his grip and the pistol in his belt, gave him the hope as he lay there that he was still conniving enough for some sort of future.

He awoke from his self-pitying reverie to the sound of an engine roaring down the drive. He lifted a hand and wiped his face as his heart churned like an engine of its own.

The same red-and-black motorcycle they had seen in Colorado Springs slid to a stop behind Frank's car. Madam Bob pulled off her helmet, shook her hair, and yanked the bike onto its stand as a rental sedan pulled in behind. She walked around Frank's Camaro, not paying the truck in the vegetable patch any heed as she examined the vehicle. Then she pulled a knife from her boot and stooped down and stabbed the car's rear tire.

Frank had to swallow a shout of outrage as two men stepped out of either side of the sedan: Ken and Sergei. This was far less a force than he thought would come, three soldiers, but surely enough against the old hippies and a damaged piece of crap like himself. Sergei still had a bandage on his head where Frank had whupped him with the butt end of his gun. That at least was satisfying. And Ken had something wrong with his nose: it was swollen and a little bent. Who had done that?

"Frank?" called out Ken. "You there, Frank? We have business to discuss, little Frank."

"The nose looks good," grunted the old man from the truck, awake now with his rifle pointed at Ken's head. "One more shot and it'd be perfect."

Ken smiled at that. "Oh, we can have our dance, old man, though I'd worry about that eggshell skull if I were you. But we've got business to get through first. We're looking for our friend Frank. We need him and the computer he stole, that's all. Give them up and we can do this without violence."

"What good is that?" said the old man.

"How was traveling with my Ayana? I sure missed that sweet thing. I sent her to you because I figured over time you'd grow sweet on her, too. Nothing beats the young stuff, am I right or am I right? Did she take care of you as sweetly as she takes care of me?"

A shot rang just then, a spurt of fire from the old man's rifle and a simultaneous kick of dust from the dirt beside Ken's boot. While

Madam Bob and Sergei, pulling out pistols, ducked behind Frank's car and the old man chambered another round, Ken stayed admirably still.

"I guess that means yes. She's a talent all right. Now tell me, did you miss on purpose, or are you just a bad shot?"

Another shot rang out, busting the dirt on the other side of Ken. Frank trained his rifle on Madam Bob and Sergei. He had them smack in his sights, but actually pulling the trigger while his heart was thrumming was another thing entirely.

"Take it easy there, old man. We don't want to kill everybody and burn this place to the ground. We will if we have to, that's what we do, but all we're asking for is what we're entitled to. Think of us as an advance party giving you a friendly way out of your predicament."

"My trigger can do the same thing," said the old man.

"Kill me and what do you get?"

"Joy."

"But you know it's not just the three of us. We brought the whole gang. And that's not all. You sent word through Ayana about the thing in Chicago without knowing that Delaney's an old friend of ours. In fact, he's in town right now, having a few brewskis, getting ready for a brawl. And you know, he's looking for Frank, too."

Frank's rifle went off at that, the fear pressed his trigger for him. He hadn't been aiming anymore and the bullet passed through a tree, but it drew an unwanted barrage of attention as Madam Bob and Sergei both aimed their guns in his general direction.

"Oops," said Ken. "Someone got a little anxious." He turned toward Frank's hiding place. "How's it going there, Frank? Throat getting a little tight? Delaney wasn't so happy learning that the drugs you gave him were stolen. A typically boneheaded move."

"Just say what you need to say," said the old man, "and get the fuck off my land."

"Let me show you something."

He took a piece of cloth out of his belt, waved it around like a towel. It took Frank a moment to figure out what it was, and when he did his breath stopped. Ken twirled the vest that Erica had been wearing a final time and then let it go, flinging it toward the old man's truck.

"We found your granddaughter in the bus station," said Ken. "Buying a ticket to California. That trip will be delayed, but give us what we're asking for and she can be freely on her way. What, it's one o'clock now? We'll be back at six sharp with the girl. If Frank and the computer are waiting for us, we'll make a trade, and you and this farm and your precious little granddaughter will never hear from us again. But hold out, old man, and trust me, blood will flow."

36

ALL ALONG THE
WATCHTOWER

Oliver Cross manages to wait until the bastards leave before he leans over the bed of the truck and vomits.

He doesn't have the stomach for games of threat and violence. He thought he did—watching Fox News with the sound off is enough to make anyone believe they have the intestinal fortitude to choke a goat—but this ragged journey west has convinced him otherwise. Every time he is forced into a bout of violence his stomach betrays him, and so it is now. He probably never had the stomach for surfing either.

He is wiping his mouth with the back of his hand as Gracie, Toby, Flit, and Frank leave their hiding places and Wendy climbs down from her tree. Frank picks the vest off the ground and presses it to his nose, and there is a moment when Oliver tries to justify the trade, simple and straight-up, this stranger, who is a perpetual fuck-up, in exchange for his precious granddaughter. On its face, it seems more than fair. As a carpenter married to a teacher, he spent enough time at Value City to know a bargain when he sees one.

"That's some vile shit there," says Flit. "Is that really Erica's vest?"

Oliver looks at Frank, who nods.

"I should have known she wasn't going home," says Frank. "She wanted to keep going west. I guess she left the van and went off on her own. They probably had someone at the station, waiting."

"You shouldn't have shot at the dirt, Oliver," says Wendy. "You should have shot the bastard in the chest."

"I was trying."

"Is that a joke?" says Flit. "Because I'm not laughing."

"They sure have the hots for you, young man," says Wendy to Frank. "What did you do to them?"

"My usual," says Frank. "But, I didn't mean to bring this to you or her, I swear."

"But you did, didn't you?" says Gracie. "And now we don't have a choice, do we?"

"There's always a choice," says Oliver. "First, Gracie, you need to get out of here, you and Wendy, Toby, anyone who can. They'll let you go out the road. Less people to fight."

"We're not leaving you here alone," says Toby.

"And Frank's our guest," says Wendy. "That means something. I say we prepare a table for him in the presence of his enemies."

"We're going to eat?" says Flit.

"Hell no, we're going to fight," says Wendy. "They'll find out why they call this the blood farm."

"Who calls it that?" says Oliver.

"The coyotes," says Wendy with a laugh.

"And the people in town," says Gracie. "For a long time after Lucius they thought it was haunted."

"If you try to fight they'll kill Erica," says Frank. "I can't let them do that."

"It's not up to you, is it?" says Wendy.

"Maybe it is," says Frank.

"Get in the truck," grunts Oliver.

"They want the computer and they want me in exchange for Erica. It seems fair. What else is there to do?"

"Get in the fucking truck," says Oliver. "We're not deciding anything until we talk to Crazy Bob."

As the truck trundles along the rutted path to Crazy Bob's cabin at the west end of the farm, Oliver takes sidelong glances at Frank. The four others are in the bed, letting the air blow their hair, their chins out in defiance. But there is something defeated about the way the boy sits beside him, the way he stares out the window. He has climbed out of himself.

"That must have been tough," says Oliver. "Pushing Erica away like you did."

"Fat lot of good it did. It would have been better if we hit the road."

"They would have had you already, along with Erica and the computer. They've been at the mouth of the road the whole time, waiting on the Camaro."

Frank looks down at his hands twisting on his lap. "Saying no to her was like getting hit in the gut with a baseball bat."

"But I bet somewhere it felt good and right, too," says Oliver as the boy nods distractedly. "I bet somewhere it warmed your heart."

"Maybe it did."

"That's the problem."

"What does that mean?"

"You did something selfless, for maybe the first time in your crappy little life. But you lost a part of yourself doing it."

"Tell me about it."

"And you can get used to it, the selflessness of losing yourself. It gets easier the more you do it. It can be its own drug. You start thinking that's the only way without noticing how much of yourself you're giving away piece by piece. Next thing you know you're killing armored truck guards and blowing up townhouses."

"What the hell are you talking about?"

"Old friends."

"I thought it was good to do good."

"It is, sure. But what you're talking about is something else. It's like giving a kidney and then giving another one. You think you need to give yourself over to those bastards. You think that's what I want."

"Maybe."

"Stop thinking it."

"It's the only way."

"It's the easy way," says Oliver. "The selfless way."

"I stole from them. She doesn't need to pay the price, I do."

"But you don't have to pay their price."

"Just drive."

They ramble on in quiet for a moment, neither knowing what to say, until Oliver breaks the silence.

"Anyone ever accuse you of being too damn selfless?"

"No."

"Me neither," says Oliver.

There's a moment of quiet in the rattling truck and then they both start laughing.

Crazy Bob is sitting on a rocking chair on the dirt in front of his cabin, smoking a pipe with a rifle on his lap. Four dogs, including Hunter, are leashed to ropes bound around one of the cabin's posts to keep them out of the fight. Open on a table to the side is the laptop computer, its screen quiet, a cord snaking from its side into the cabin. Crazy Bob eyes the truck as Oliver and the five passengers climb down.

"Well?"

"They have Erica," says Toby.

"That's not good," says Crazy Bob.

"They're coming back at six. They want the computer and the boy."

"Why do they want the boy?"

"They want the boy because they're killers," says Wendy, "and they want to kill him."

"Well, there you go," says Crazy Bob. "That just makes too much sense."

"But that's not the question," says Oliver. "The question is, Why do they want the computer?"

"Well that's a little simpler," says Crazy Bob. "They want the computer because they're the worst kind of fools."

"What kind of fools is that, Crazy Bob?" says Wendy.

"Cryptocurrency fools," says Crazy Bob with a grin.

Instead of following Crazy Bob's convoluted technological explanation, Oliver's mind wanders, as it tends to do in his dotage. He thinks back to the beginning of all things, when in the midst of a clash of generations he charged an injustice like a bull and saved the day while getting brained by a billy club. He doesn't remember the actual moment, only Helen's retelling of it, but the fact of his minor heroism remains seared in his consciousness, as well as marked on his skull. It is what gives him hope that he can rise to the moment here and now, when it might be needed most.

"So they have the passwords," Oliver hears Crazy Bob say when Oliver snaps back to attention, "but apparently we have their only wallet."

"Wallet?" says Oliver.

"Their Bitcoin wallet," says Crazy Bob. "Haven't you been listening?"

"No," says Oliver, though Bitcoin is exactly what Oliver thought might be involved, or some other such nonsense, when he gave the computer to Crazy Bob in the first place.

"They wouldn't be after the computer so hard if they had properly backed up the wallet," says Crazy Bob, "but cryptocurrency fools always find a way. My guess is that when the computer went missing they checked their backup and found it corrupted. And then they found their other backup disappeared. And they were up shit's creek. Which means this little piece of crap MacBook is the key to all their money."

"Well, well, well," says Wendy.

"I didn't know," says Frank. "I just thought it would be useful in Paris, you know. Emailing, recording songs. It was better than what I had so I took it with the stash."

"Can we get their bitcoins with the wallet?" says Gracie, eyes wide.

"Wouldn't that be nice, what with the run-up lately," says Crazy Bob, "but without the passwords we're SOL. If we had a supercomputing system and a couple hundred years, we might have a shot at brute forcing our way through, but that's it. And I don't have the patience or the liver for that."

"Why don't we just trade the computer for Erica and call it square," says Gracie.

"What about the kid?" says Wendy.

"Maybe they'll take the computer and forget the kid."

"And if they don't?" says Toby.

"I don't know," says Gracie. "We'll talk about it then."

"We're not talking," says Oliver.

"Maybe we should just call the police," says Gracie.

"No police," says Oliver. "They have my granddaughter. She's evidence now. The police come, the evidence gets destroyed. I busted parole to come out here and make sure she's okay. And it's going to end here. We've all been through the wars, Toby for sure, but the rest of us in battles of our own. We might be hobbled by time, but we don't run and we don't beg."

"I missed you, Oliver," says Wendy.

"I know these sons of bitches," continues Oliver. "I've known them all my life. They're about money and power and leeching the blood off those too weak or too filled with their bullshit to fight back, like Frank was before he got the balls to turn the table on the sons of bitches."

"We've seen their like before, that's for sure," says Crazy Bob.

"Vampires," says Flit.

"The same vampires who sent Toby to Vietnam," says Oliver. "The same vampires who killed my brother. The same vampires who are stealing the country right under our noses. They have money and might and the will to kill. The young like Erica and Frank are just loose change to them, not worth stooping over and picking up off the asphalt. Their deaths won't register on their profit sheets so their lives don't matter. But like every bully, deep down they're afraid, and what they're afraid of is us."

"What do we have?" says Gracie.

"We have each other, and we don't give a shit about their money, and we're too old to be scared of dying. We're going to get Erica back our way, without giving up anybody because we don't give up on anybody. What are they going to do, kill us? Do us the fucking favor."

"I can put out a call," says Crazy Bob. "There's still a network of the old-timers ready to raise their fists and start the revolution."

"Defend the farm."

"Defend the cause."

"Resist."

"Defy."

"Ho, Ho, Ho Chi Minh."

"Who?"

"Fascist pig bastards."

"Hell no, we won't go."

"This farm belongs to us."

"Well," says Oliver, breaking the spell, "technically to me and then to Fletcher."

"What? Oliver?"

"I bought it with my dad's money to stop old man Oates from kicking you guys off. And we have plans for it."

"Development?"

"Weed."

"Really?"

"Crazy Bob's special crop."

"I always wanted to be an icon," says Crazy Bob.

"Put out the call."

"We'll need more guns."

"And some explosives."

"And Advil."

"Those bastards won't know what hit them once we get the Advil."

"I tell you, I feel twenty-five again."

"Whoa, whoa, whoa," says Oliver. "Let's not get carried away."

"Hey, who's that?" says Flit, and the group's attention and guns whip around to see a pale, stolid figure jogging heavily toward them along the northern edge of the valley.

"Crap," says Oliver when he recognizes the pink golf shirt and realizes who it is.

It takes a few minutes for a gasping Fletcher to make his ungainly way to the crew. He stops running, puts his hands on his hips, bends over, and takes off his glasses. Sweat cascades across his face in a sheet.

"So," gasps Fletcher as he catches his breath. "What's up?"

◆ ◆ ◆

After Fletcher is brought up to speed on the events of the morning, and while the others are figuring out a plan of action, Oliver grabs his son by the collar of his golf shirt and pulls him to the side. "Get the hell out of here," he says. "Get off the farm before it all blows to hell."

"They have my daughter."

"And you still have a wife and another child to take care of. Let me handle this."

"Would you run? Would you even think of running?"

"Don't start suddenly using me as an example. Why did you let her go anyway?"

"She said we had to. She said she'd jump out of the van if we didn't let her out. So I took her to the station. I even gave her money so she wouldn't starve. What else was I going to do?"

"Maybe just say no. You're her father, you could have stopped her."

"Did your father ever stop you? Did Mom's father ever stop her?"

"That man hated on me so hard," says Oliver, "it kept him alive for ten years after his stroke."

"Did you ever think of just giving the bastards what they want?" says Fletcher.

"They want Frank."

"It seems a fair trade."

"He's somebody's son, somebody's brother. As a lawyer, is that what you would have us do?"

"No."

"And as a father who doesn't want his daughter to call him a murderer the rest of his life, is that what you would have us do?"

"You're right, you're right, you're always right. Happy?"

"Yes."

"Jeez, you're almost smiling. It looks weird. Stop it."

"I've been looking for a fight for the past fifty years and here it is. But you don't have to be part of it."

"Why do you always do this to me? When you fixed my teeth, when I quit guitar lessons, when I went to the wrong college, when you took care of Mom without letting me help, and then when you went off after Erica without me, you've always made me feel like I'm letting you down."

"That's on me, not you. I had a father, too, who let me know exactly whose shoes I could never fill."

"I often wondered what your brother would have thought of me carrying his name."

Oliver looks at his son, then looks away. "If he was here right now he would look at us both and think us the worst kind of fools."

Fletcher laughs.

"But he would stand with us," says Oliver. "I have no doubt."

"And I will, too."

"Okay. But you do as I say. Follow my lead and I'll deliver Erica into your arms. I promise."

"And then you'll come home? You'll come home and get that thing in your neck looked at? And you'll let me handle the legal things? You'll let me take care of you?"

"Sure, yeah. If that's what you want."

"It's what I want."

"Done."

"So what now?"

"Now?" says Oliver, rubbing his head. "Now I need to take a nap."

Oliver leaves his son and heads toward the truck. "Where are you going?" says Gracie.

"To the stable," says Oliver.

"For your afternoon siesta, old man?" says Frank, who stands there grinning, awaiting some flippant witticism as a response.

"Shut up, grab hold of Hunter, and get in the truck," says Oliver.

The boy, the dog, and Oliver drive quietly toward the stable but then Oliver passes it and keeps going, toward the mouth of the road before dodging around Gracie's cabin to the edge of the southern hill of the valley. There he stops the truck.

"What are we doing here?" says Frank.

"Saying goodbye," says Oliver, before he opens the door and climbs down. As Frank follows, Oliver walks around to the side of the truck and unlocks the aluminum toolbox at the front of the bed. He pulls out a hammer, a T square, a box of nails, a bundle of cash bills, and another bundle of cash bills. He can hear Frank's intake of breath.

"You can't take your car, because they're waiting for you at the end of the drive," says Oliver as he pulls out still another bundle.

"What are you doing?" says Frank.

"I'm giving you enough to buy another when you can. You only need to get to an airport anyway, preferably in Mexico. You could just take a bus and keep the extra cash."

"I don't understand."

Oliver closes the lid of the toolbox, stacks the bundles one on top of the other. "This is what you were after all along, isn't it? A stake for your new life. A bankroll to freedom."

Frank looks at him until his eyes are drawn back to the money.

"You did everything I could have asked for," says Oliver. "You let her go for her sake, not for yours."

"I didn't say no to Erica for the fucking money."

"It doesn't matter, though, does it? If you stick around they're probably going to kill you, and the hell with that. Over that hill is your road to freedom."

Frank turns to look at the hill and the path over it, then turns back to look at the money.

"Take the money, take the dog, and go."

"I don't know what to say."

"Say goodbye," says Oliver.

The dog barks and Oliver rubs Hunter's side with his boot. "You I might miss," says Oliver to the dog, "but probably not." Then Oliver looks at Frank flatly. "Try to figure out a better way to live."

There's a hesitation in the boy, something Oliver didn't expect, but it doesn't last long. Frank Cormack grabs at the money like a hungry man grabbing at a pie.

It feels like Oliver is melting into the seat of his truck as he drives along the rutted path back to the stable. It feels like his consciousness is leaking out through his ears. Weariness has come upon him like a sickness. He staggers beneath the stable's portico and through the wide front door. He expects to fall into sleep the moment he collapses onto the bed, but instead he falls into memory.

He is surprised that sleep is evading him, but not that the memories arise. This place has been a memory dispenser since he first stepped into it upon returning to the farm. He sees again the fight with his wife, the visit from Lucius, but new memories, too: teaching his son at the workbench how to hold a hammer and a chisel; sitting on the bed, peeling an orange while Helen sleeps naked beside him, her ribs rising with each breath. Images of sex and love and anger and work, all in this place, ascend and overlap and twist into new images that take away his breath.

It reminds him of the way his mind bent after drinking the potion in the sweat lodge in the New Mexican mountains. That night the images rose in front of him like sand paintings floating in the air, dissolving one into the next. And that memory, from outside this place, brings new ones without any connection to the heap of rot and rust in which he lies.

Protest songs in Buena Vista Park.

Football with his school pals by the lake.

Spinning wildly at a music festival in Monterey.

His mother staring at the famous diner painting at the Art Institute with tears in her eyes.

Teaching little Fletcher how to hold his new bat in the fields of the farm, and Oliver's brother, Fletcher, teaching little Oliver the same thing when he was only five.

A birthday party in Highland Park when he turned seven with candles on a white cake and a piñata.

A birthday party at 128 Avery Road when his son turned nine with candles on a blue cake and a piñata and Oliver wearing clown's makeup and juggling for all the little kiddies, laughter bursting out each time an orange fell with a wet slap onto the ground.

And those aren't the only memories from his time after the farm. Doing construction work on the developments to keep his family fed. Watching his son graduate from middle school, high school, college, his white teeth gleaming as he was handed his diplomas. Giving out Halloween candy to the kids on Avery Road as Helen exclaimed at the costumes. *You are such a beautiful princess.* Waiting outside the hospital room when Erica was born.

They rise, these memories, one after another, a stream of images so painful and pure they turn his stomach. He can't keep track of them all as they fill the space around him and above him until the inside of the stable has become a galaxy of memory, each recollection a pinprick of light piercing the darkness. And the brightest of the stars, the red giants and supernovas that guide his eyes from one sector to the next, all include her, yes, the one true thing, the very North Star of his life. A dam cracks in his heart and the overflow fills him with tears.

"Don't get misty eyed, you old fraud," says Helen.

"You're back," he says, wiping at his face with the back of his big old hand. "I didn't know if you'd make it in time."

"I couldn't miss the big finish."

"Where did you go?"

"Where I always go when you get too full of yourself."

"To that speed addict Dereck, with the blond hair and the leather hat who was always hitting on you in the Haight?"

"Death has mellowed him."

"One can only hope. I missed your hectoring."

"I know you did."

"They have Erica."

"Which makes it a good thing that you are here."

"You sent me here."

"Then good for me."

"What am I going to do about it?"

"I don't know, dear. That's out of my realm. Like dealing with Fletcher is out of yours."

"I tried."

"I know. Remember what I used to tell my art students who were devoid of any talent?"

"Good effort."

"And it was, darling."

"You're heading back east in the urn. Little Elisa insisted. So we'll be separated, finally. She says she talks to you."

"Sweet thing."

"But you don't talk back to her."

"Only to you."

"Just my luck. I think I make you up. I think you're a figment of my fancy."

"You've finally figured it out."

"Now you're playing with me."

"Why were you crying?"

"Memories. They say your life flashes before your eyes in the moments before your death."

"And that's why you're sad, because you think you're going to die?"

"My dying will be nobody's tragedy, especially not my own. No, because of what I saw, what my life had been. Did the memories come for you at the end?"

"Some."

"Did they make you happy?"

"Joyful."

"What did you see?"

"Only you."

"That's what I want, too, but everything has come back. All the failures, the wrong turns, the thwarted plans and missed trains. I was given everything and accomplished nothing."

"What did you expect? To cure cancer? To save the world?"

"Why not? If I had put my heart into something, if I had taken up my brother's mantle, there's no telling . . ."

"You put your heart into me, into the boy, into our life."

"That's not enough for a Cross."

"I hear your father talking from the grave."

"He'd be the first to tell me I didn't cure cancer, I didn't save the world."

"You saved my world, you cured my cancer. Wasn't that enough?"

"No."

"Well then, you're in luck, dear heart. You get to save Erica, too."

37

OLD MAN

They had come for him, the Russian and his minions, Delaney and a crew, even Jorge with his gang, including the kid from outside that house in South Chicago, all the frightening figures of Frank Cormack's past had come for him, as was inevitable from the start. And this henchman army, twenty strong, had brought with them their guns, their ill will, and Erica, held tight by that asshole Ken with his stupid ponytail in case she had the deranged notion to run. They had also come for the computer, and they had also come to rape and pillage, but most of all they had come to put Frank Cormack, who had betrayed them all, out of his misery.

And in a way, in this primary purpose, they had succeeded.

Years after the battle of the blood farm, it is difficult for Frank to remember the way he was before he returned to live at Seven Suns for good. Life on the farm is hard for a boy who only wanted to wander, but he knows each day what needs to be done and finds comfort in the doing of it. There are the cows to milk twice a day, and the chickens to care for, and the vegetable garden to plant and weed and harvest. He had even found another peacock to strut around the grounds and unfurl his iridescent shield, like a superhero whose only power is beauty. The old folk want to keep these parts of the farm alive so they can stay in touch with the land and their pasts, and who is he to argue?

But the rest of the farm, the great expanse from the juniper to the west end of the valley, is now rich with Crazy Bob's Special Blend. That's what they call it since that's what it is. A whole new irrigation system had to be put in, with feeder lines running from the reservoir across the fields, and greenhouses were raised to start the seedlings, and a great wooden barn was built next to the cow pasture where the plants are hung to dry. It is not an easy business—all their competitors are big agra concerns or the pet projects of billionaires from the Bay—but they have found their niche, hiring workers from as far south as Pueblo to keep things humming, under Frank's direction.

What the hell had Frank known about running a farm when he took control four years ago? Nothing, that's what. But Fletcher Cross, the farm's owner, had told him he needed to learn everything he could about the legal cannabis business, and that's what he did, with the help of some business and agricultural courses at the University of Colorado–Colorado Springs.

Now Crazy Bob's Special Blend is a big seller, with a high reputation all across the west. They put Crazy Bob's picture on the label, and that seems to have done the trick. There is Ben and Jerry, there is Famous Amos and Mrs. Fields, there is Orville and his popcorn, there is Burt and his bees, and now there is Crazy Bob. These days everyone wants bud from Crazy Bob, and Frank Cormack is the man who makes it happen. Too bad Crazy Bob himself didn't make it past that day of blood, because he would have loved the hell out of what he has become.

When the Russian came calling, his makeshift army arrived with their trucks and their cycles and their heavy boots, ready for a war. But when they looked around, they saw nothing arrayed against them other than the old man's truck, sitting in the middle of a vegetable garden with Crazy Bob behind the wheel and Oliver Cross sitting atop the hood. A laptop computer rested on the hood beside the old man and a pump-action shotgun was cradled in his arms. And it looked as if . . . No, it couldn't be . . . But it was, yes, the old man was napping.

The Russian nodded, a shot rang out, the old man twitched his eyes open.

"Sorry to disturb," said the Russian as he and Delaney walked together toward the truck. "But we come to finish deal."

Delaney was wearing a black leather jacket and heavy boots. A rifle was slung over his shoulder like a guitar. His earring shone in the sun. The Russian was wearing a baby-blue tracksuit with three lines running down the side. His sneakers were white and high, his jacket was halfway open, the gold chains on his fat hairy chest glistened like his bald head in the setting sun. As they stepped forward, Ken turned Erica over to Madam Bob and followed behind. At the same time, the henchman army divided into three, with Delaney's crew heading to one flank and Jorge leading his gang to the other, creating a semicircle of potential fire with Oliver Cross and his truck smack in the middle.

"You did good, old man," said the Russian, "exactly what we told you do. It would have been better you made call, but we can't have everything."

"Piss off," said Oliver, slipping down off the hood and giving the shotgun a pull.

The Russian and Delaney stopped their approach. "The name's Delaney," said Delaney.

"I don't care," said Oliver.

"Where's Frank?"

"Waiting."

"I hope the boy's not waiting alone. He's a runner, don't you know, and runners run."

"Is that my computer?" said the Russian.

"Let my granddaughter go and you can find out."

"This is like old days of Soviet Union on bridge of spies, no?" said the Russian. "You have, we have: crisscross. But first I need check that is not some useless clone from Best Buy."

"As long as you can do it with my shotgun at your head."

"Ken can do it with shotgun at his head," said the Russian, and Delaney laughed.

The Russian gave a tsk along with a head tilt and Ken, with the busted nose and his arms raised, walked past the Russian and Delaney to the front of the truck. Oliver trained the shotgun on him for the whole of his little walk.

"I won't be long," said Ken as he took hold of the laptop.

"I told you what I'd do if you touched my granddaughter," growled Oliver lowly. "You touched my granddaughter."

"Don't be so prickly, old man, everything's copacetic. We're going to work this out and she'll be in your loving arms in no time. What you do with her then is up to you. Now just let me check the device. Is it charged?"

With the shotgun barrel aimed at Ken's head, Oliver nodded. Ken opened the laptop, waited, tap-tapped, waited some more, tap-tapped again. "You guys got wireless?"

"Shut up," said Oliver.

Ken took out a cell phone, checked it for service, frowned as he put it back in his pocket. Closing the lid, he took hold of the computer and turned to the Russian. "This is it, and the wallet's still active. I couldn't check the connection because there's no fucking internet and I only got a single bar. But I don't see anything messed up and he's not clever enough to have done something without me catching it."

"This is good," said the Russian.

"Leave the computer and step back," said Oliver, wagging the gun. "And then release the girl."

"What I think we'll do is take the computer now," said Delaney, "and when you give up Frank, we'll turn over your precious granddaughter."

"You can trust us," said Ken with a wink at Oliver, his hands still gripping the laptop.

Oliver spun the shotgun and jammed the stock into Ken's face once, twice: *crack, crack.*

Ken dropped to the ground like a sack of onions spurting blood.

As the rustle of guns rose from the semicircle, Oliver spun the shotgun again and pointed it at the Russian and Delaney. The Russian raised his hands, Delaney grinned. Oliver stooped down, knees popping, and lifted the computer off the ground. He kept the gun aimed at the two for a moment before he turned and jammed the barrel against the computer's side.

A gasp rose, and not just from the Russian.

"Send over my granddaughter," said the old man, "or the laptop gets it."

◆ ◆ ◆

True to form, with the old man's money in his pocket and Hunter by his side, Frank had resumed his run to freedom. Freedom! He hitchhiked to a car lot in Colorado Springs and then drove a battered old pickup over the mountains and across the desert to the coast, actually making it to the end of the pier in Santa Monica, where the fishermen were sitting with their lines dipping into the water, sitting and waiting, waiting. He understood: Who knew when a fresh bag of cash would rise up on the end of that line?

He could have kept on keeping on, could have found somewhere new to play his game of hustle and pain, a fresh place to screw things up enough so that he'd have to be off and running again within a few months. He could have gone back to his life, Frank Cormack's wonderful life of footloose shittery, but the time he spent on the farm had altered something in him.

It was the old man, it was the stars, it was Crazy Bob's special weed, it was the warm welcome he had received and the camaraderie around the fire, it was the land itself with its tendrils of memory and loss, but it wasn't only that. There was also a spirit from a time before he was born, a spirit that sought fights worth fighting and didn't hesitate to wade into the fray, a spirit that exalted things other than possessions and position and power, a spirit that made money itself seem something ill and infectious, a yellow fever that boiled you from the inside. He saw that spirit in Crazy Bob; he saw it in Wendy with her goats; he saw it in Toby, who still wore his army greens like he owed it to the dead; and he saw it in those who had answered Crazy Bob's call and risen to join the upcoming battle.

From the knoll where he had been hiding with the dog and the stacks of bills he had just been given by the old man, he spied them climbing down the hills in ones and twos and fives, a gray army marching to the fight with their hunting rifles and shotguns and pistols. They smoked reefer and chewed flaxseed and hobbled on ruined knees and hugged each other and spoke a language of their own, born of fire and loss and the music of a dying generation. And they came not for the cash or for the kicks of it or to gain for themselves a place in the world; they came because one of their own had asked.

All of it, somehow, put Frank Cormack outside himself. Even as he could feel the fear and the wanting, the greed and the need twist his body and soul like a wet rag, outside of himself he was filled with something as clean and fresh as the mountain air of the farm, as cool as the water trickling from the creek into the reservoir, as bright as the stars he had seen in the sky above, as pure as Crazy Bob's herb.

It took him a moment to recognize it, this new thing, this calm, so strange it was and unfamiliar. But it was a calm that allowed him to see the world and his life with a clarity that stunned. He saw his skittering madness within the beauty and serenity of the natural world. He saw his unquenchable need for more matched against the infinite vacuums that lived between the stars. He saw his utter selfishness contrasted with the determined selflessness of the gray-haired and poorly regulated militia that poured down the mountainsides. And it was that newly acquired vision that convinced Frank to stash the money beneath a rock, come down off that hill where he was hiding for his life, and join the fight.

He thought the old man would at least smile when he saw him, but the old man didn't smile. He just shook his head as if shaking it at a fool, and then told Frank with a scowl to put the dog safely with the others and get himself a gun.

But here's the thing. After the battle had been waged, after the bombast and blood, and after Frank Cormack had headed back onto the endless road, hitching that ride to Colorado Springs and buying that pickup and driving west, ever west, he had finally, after far too many months, had his gutful of running. And the Frank Cormack who came back to the farm was the one who had been on the outside looking in, the calm one with a vision of searing, shaming clarity.

The calm hadn't yet left him, and that was a surprise. Every day he woke up with the serenity in his heart he was thankful, and every day he knew whom to thank.

◆ ◆ ◆

With Oliver's shotgun now aimed at his precious computer, the Russian ordered Madam Bob to let Erica go. Erica, when she was freed, ran straight to her grandfather, as if to give him a great hug.

"Get in the truck," he grunted at her, halting her in her tracks. "Crazy Bob will drive you to the stable and bring back Frank."

"What?" she said. "You can't give over—"

"I told you not to come back," said the old man. "Trust me this time and do what I tell you."

She looked at her grandfather for a moment, this crazed old man in his crazed posture, and then lowered her head and slipped into the passenger seat of the truck. Crazy Bob put the truck into gear and backed away before he turned around and headed for the stable.

"Now that your pretty little granddaughter is safe, why not give Teddy boy his computer," said Delaney, "so we can avoid any accident that will only cause much needless destruction and death."

"Get off my lawn," said the old man.

"That's not going to happen," said the Russian, "until we have everything we come for."

"That's exactly what you're going to get," said Oliver.

When the truck reached the stable, Erica left the cab and hurried under the portico where her father waited. He took hold and pulled her through the front door into the stable, and then brought out a figure in Frank's jeans and jacket, his head covered by a white hood, his hands bound behind him. Fletcher Cross led the hooded figure to the truck and placed him inside.

"You took no chances on the little bastard escaping," said Delaney. "I'm impressed."

"I told you he'd be reasonable," said the Russian. "I told you there be no problem."

The truck, in the distance, slowly, made a U-turn and started rumbling back to the mouth of the farm. At that exact moment the music started, distorted and loud, coming from speakers hooked up at the ruins of the ranch house and the cabins across the way, echoing crazily across the landscape, four bass-heavy riffs, down and up, up and down, followed by a snarling guitar. It was unmistakably Hendrix, rough and ragged and oh so beautiful.

As the truck made its slow way back to the Russian, and Hendrix started singing an adventure story written by Dylan, the invaders looked around disconcertedly, uncertain where to aim their guns.

The truck grew closer, the music grew wilder, Hendrix spun his magic as the truck kept coming, slowly, inexorably. The soldiers were still looking around, distracted by the music, when the truck doors opened on either side of the cab and the figures behind the windshield disappeared even as the truck kept coming, kept slowly coming.

The gunshots started from the Russian's army, staccato snaps of a snare aimed at the engine of the truck, shots that seemed to have no effect as the truck kept trundling forward, rumbling forward. The soldiers easily avoided the slow-moving vehicle, like bullfighters swishing away from an arthritic cow.

Then came the explosion.

Frank spied all the action from his vantage within the ruins of the old ranch house, protected by one of the stone walls, a speaker blaring just above his head. He saw the exchange, the rumble forward of the truck, the explosion that took out a handful of fighters, including Madam Bob, and the fighting that broke loose after as the smoke billowed. And at that point he should have been firing, madly, crazily, loading and shooting like a wild man out to protect his own damn hide, that was the plan all along. But instead he was frozen behind the stone, transfixed by the most extraordinary sight.

Frank Cormack can still see Oliver Cross as clearly as if he were again right in front of him, standing sideways before an unyielding force, feet splayed, knees and back bent, chin high, holding a shotgun against the body of an Apple laptop as if ready to blast the present-state things into smithereens just for the sheer anarchy of it. And if Frank squints just a bit, yes, in the old man's gritted teeth Frank might just see a grin, and in the old man's sideways stance and bent posture he can almost imagine the old man surfing some monster wave into the shoals of destiny.

Frank is married now, not to Erica, who is off somewhere in Africa building wells and trying to save the world, but to Loretta, whom he met one night when he was out drinking at the cowboy bar with Wendy. They have a daughter, Olivia. Olivia laughs and spins and totters around the farm with Hunter, who keeps the coyotes at bay. And Frank's brother, Todd, comes west summers with his wife, Kerrie, and son, Peter, to visit. And whatever roots he has in this world are now buried deep into this land.

They live in the stable, Frank and Loretta and Olivia. Frank set up a small studio within the remains of Oliver's workshop where he writes and records his music. The acoustics are only okay, but he cut a few EPs he can sell when he performs at the local joints. It is less of a music career than he dreamed, but probably more than his talent deserves. On one of the EPs there is even a song he recorded with Ayana, and that EP, understandably, sells better than the others.

Ayana has become a thing. After playing at Armstrong's for a couple years she was accepted for one of the TV singing game shows, and though she didn't win—some white country singer took the top prize like they always do—she made a name for herself and ended up signing with a small frisky label that squeezed out a couple hits. Then she found a role in an indie film, scored an award nomination, and is now looking down the barrel of an acting career. Her success should have jittered Frank up and sent him back on the road, desperate to claim his rightful spot in the limelight. It should have tainted what he had built here, but all it does is make him happy for Ayana.

It isn't that he has become a saint—no one is further from sainthood than Frank Cormack, as his six-month stint in the pen in Ohio, negotiated by Mr. Prakash, had proven—but whenever he feels himself grow sick with envy, which he still does, or when the walls close in on him as he thinks about all he is missing in the world, which they still do, he closes his eyes and summons a singular image that calms his heart, a sight he spied that day of violence from behind the ruined stone wall.

Bullets were flying, raining down from the hills, from the ruins, and from behind the cabins where the gray-hairs hid as they fired and fired, even as the invaders shot back from whatever cover they could grab. But in all that carnage, none of the firing was aimed at Oliver Cross, for fear of what might happen to the most valuable of hostages. They hobbled Toby, they shot Crazy Bob in the throat, a wound from which he never recovered, they laid down withering blasts into the hills and pinged a few against the ruined stone wall behind which Frank hid, but the old man raged unharmed.

Then there came a moment when the fire slackened against the Russian's army and Delaney was able to lead his gang to more advantageous ground, a moment when two of the gray-hairs were hit and the battle seemed to turn. It was there, at the crux, when Oliver Cross, still in his crazed bent-knee, bent-back surfing stance, grinned wildly and cursed one last time, before he pulled the trigger of his shotgun.

Shards of the computer's shell and its innards burst forward like a great party popper shooting celebratory streamers into the air.

The sight shocked the battle into quiet as the truth of what the crazy old man had done began to sink in. And in that moment all that could be heard, other than the howls of the Russian, were the glorious strains of Hendrix's savage, psychedelic guitar in a loop that promised nothing less than eternal salvation.

It is this image that Frank Cormack holds close as he walks across the farm through the seasons, carrying his daughter and smelling the fragrant air of his own freedom, while Hunter leads the way. In the hopeful springs, in the fruitful summers of growth and green, in the autumns of celebration, and in the white frigid winters whenever the sirens sing to him their sweet and bitter songs of worldly things, it is this image that he carries in his pocket like a lucky penny to quiet the yearnings of his still hungry heart. This image. This.

Oliver Cross, holding the shards of a shattered laptop as if they were the cracked remains of his mortal bonds, standing like a giant, triumphant and transcendent, upon the smoldering ruins of his past.

38

TIME IN A BOTTLE

Oliver Cross has lived this day too often to keep track of the number. Before it happened, he lived it over and again in dread; after it happened, he relived it over and again in torture. Time is less an arrow than the tonearm of a turntable, seemingly moving ever forward until, upon reaching a fault in the vinyl, it repeats on itself mercilessly until someone knocks the needle out of its insane loop. This day is the fault.

As always, he doesn't so much wake into the morning as decide in his sleeplessness that it is time, finally, to rise from the bed he still shares with his wife. He gets his sleep when the hospice nurse arrives, goes into the boy's room and honks out a few snores as Helen is cleaned and dressed, medicated, comforted with ice chips, and fed teaspoons of broth. But at night, lying by her side, he stays mostly awake, listening to her breathing and sensing the tiny tremors as she makes slight alterations in her body position. She is too far gone now to make the side-to-side shifts that shake the bed, but her legs bend and straighten, her arms twitch, her head turns on its castle of pillows. Each movement brings him to alertness. And then, through the night, her breath catches and stops for a moment and he lies there wondering if this is it, hoping and dreading it all the same, before the labored breathing starts anew.

Usually, when he arises, she is still asleep, as worn out by her difficult night as he. But this morning, as always in the skip of time, her eyes are open, her muscles are stiff, her skin is dark and grotesquely taut over the bones of her face, her green eyes, dulled by time, shine strangely, and she is smiling with the purse-lipped smile that she can barely still manage. And already he knows. He has been here before and he knows.

"Love," she says slowly, with a struggle, her greeting no more than a whisper. "Today."

"Not today," he says, matching the true smile of her chapped lips with a pallid imitation of his own. "Tomorrow maybe, but not today."

"Soon, I won't be talking." Her tongue moves within her mouth like an awkward toad. "Soon, it will be too late."

He sits on the edge of the bed, takes her hand. As always it is thin and gray, venous and spotted and as lovely as the moon. "That's not for a while yet. And don't worry, I can read your eyes like a paperback. There's time. Tomorrow."

"Today."

He looks around, sees the sunlight slanting through the window. On this day the sun is always shining, one of the universe's better jokes. "It's too nice a day, today. I'll take you outside. We'll sit in the fresh air."

"And then."

"We'll see."

"You promised."

"I did."

"My decision."

"It is."

"Don't be weak."

"I'm good at being weak. That's all I've ever been good at."

"Stronger than you know."

"But not today."

She lifts her hand and points. "Ox."

As always, when Eleanor arrives with her blue coat and steady hands she checks the morphine ledger and the amount remaining in the bottle. As Eleanor holds the brown bottle up to the light, she gives Oliver a sideways look. How many times has he seen that warning glance, how many times has he chosen to ignore it? If character is destiny, his whole life can be read in that glance, as well as in his reaction to it.

"Did she wake in the middle of the night and ask for a dose?" says Eleanor.

"She was restless. I could tell she was in pain. I woke her."

"The protocol is very specific, Mr. Cross. Maybe it's time for a night nurse. It would be covered by the insurance. And it is a shame if her restlessness keeps you awake."

"I handle the nights."

"You know the rules. You can only administer the prescribed amount on demand and only after four hours from the last dosage. You need to stay within the protocol. Have you been keeping the written record?"

"Her tea is ready," he says.

"Not too hot," she calls out to him as he heads for the kitchen.

Later as Eleanor eats her lunch, Oliver takes his wife outside. There is a wheelchair, but she prefers to go on her own power, wearing her dusky red robe and pilled slippers, balancing heavily on the walker as Oliver holds tight to her elbow and she makes her interminable way. Through the kitchen door, down the steps. Two chairs and a little table are set up on the ragged lawn behind the house. She collapses from weariness into one of the chairs, breathes heavily. He holds her hand while they sit. As always in this moment, the sun slips through the old dogwood, dappling her cadaverous face with light from the heavens.

There is a ring from inside the house and then Eleanor appears within the frame of the back door. "Your son is on the phone."

"Later," says Helen, her face remaining tilted toward the light.

"He'll be so sad," says Oliver when Eleanor retreats into the kitchen.

"He's sad now."

"He says there's a new study opening in Dallas."

"No more. Look at me."

"You're too lovely for words."

"Look at me, Oliver."

"He'll never forgive me."

"Then you'll be even."

"What will I do without you?"

She raises her hand from his grip and puts it on his cheek, as she always does. "I won't let you find out."

Fletcher comes for a visit after Eleanor leaves for the day. He is still in his white shirt and red tie, his suit pants and shiny black shoes. Fletcher starts talking about the doctor in Dallas he wants her to meet. He's already set up the appointment, he says. In the middle, Oliver leaves the bedroom to sit in his recliner. He turns on the television with the sound off. It's his favorite way of stretching time. There is a baseball game. A batter claps his hands together, spits, takes his stance, calls for time, backs out of the box, tightens his gloves, claps his hands together, spits.

"She looks good," says Fletcher when he leaves the bedroom. "She seems happier today, stronger. I want her to meet this doctor."

"She doesn't want to go to Dallas," says Oliver without looking at his son.

"My client says this doctor performs miracles. There's a new immunotherapy study she's beginning. Mom might qualify. Talk to her, please."

"It won't do any good."

"Why am I the only one who's still fighting here, Dad? Why aren't you helping? All you do is sit in front of the damn television."

"I wouldn't want to miss the game."

"Why? You always said baseball went to hell when Ernie Banks retired. And you don't even like the Phillies."

"They lose so much they're growing on me."

"Look, I'm going to make an appointment. I just need you to get her there."

"She doesn't want to go to Dallas."

"Dammit, Dad. Can you step up, please, for once?"

"Can I?"

"I guess not. I'll have my secretary make the travel plans. I'll take her. You can stay here in your chair and watch the Phillies lose. I'll be back tomorrow."

"Good," says Oliver, like he says every time Fletcher visits on this day. "And maybe we'll play Parcheesi."

It's not a good line, but he's stuck with it. He would rather rise and hug his son and let their individual trails of tears melt into one stream of misery and loss, but he can't. Nothing ever changes, time after time, and he's left with the Parcheesi line that makes him cringe every time it slips out of his mouth. And so his son leaves without an embrace, leaves by slamming the door, *slam, slam, slam* through all eternity.

Later, with the dusk making its sly approach outside their window, he is lying next to her in their bedroom when he hears her sigh. He hoped she might fall asleep until the morning, allow them both another day, but the sigh gives her away.

He rolls over and she is staring at him. He waits for her to say something, but she says nothing, or rather she lets her eyes say what she needs to say, and what they say is, *Thank you, my love.*

He puts a hand on her cheek and lightly kisses lips pulled taut by impending death. Then he rises for a final time from beside her. He moves about their room in silence. She doesn't talk and neither does he, though she follows all his movements with those eyes. Everything to be said has already been said, every declaration has already been declared. There is nothing else to do but the doing.

He reaches up and pulls down the bottle from the high shelf where Eleanor put it, takes the syringe from a bureau drawer. He walks to the side of the bed and sits. Her eyes grow wide as she watches him fill the barrel.

She takes the syringe from him. With heavy arms and shaking hands she squirts the morphine into her mouth. He fills the syringe and she takes it again. And then again. She is too weak to put the last bit from the bottle into her mouth and so, as he does each time he lives this day, he gives her the final dose. Then he takes her hand and sits by her side as those marvelous green eyes, the eyes that could have launched a thousand ships but chose to launch only his, close for the final time.

Her breathing slows, catches, starts again, as it always does. It lasts longer than he remembers. Each time he is taken aback by the length of the wait. Each time he wonders if there was enough of the drug left. Each time he wishes he could go with her. Each time he holds his position and holds her hand until, mercifully, her breathing catches, this time never to start again. He puts his head on her chest. Nothing. He puts his ear to her mouth. Nothing. He kisses her forehead, still warm, and kisses her hand, still warm, before letting her go.

The emotions overwhelm him and for a moment he is frozen in pain; he is reliving the worst of his days, and no day since has been worth a damn. The sobs don't last long; the huge tears come and go leaving him simply empty.

He stands, wipes at his eyes with the backs of his hands, and heads for the bathroom. He needed to go for the longest time, all the while he was holding her hand he needed to go, but he held off so she wouldn't be alone in those last few moments. Now within the blue-painted room he stands over the toilet like he does within each loop, and each time the spatter is as disappointing as the last.

But today, now, the spatter forms into a trickle, at first barely drooping into the bowl before strengthening into a pleasurable stream that slaps at the water so that bubbles form. And then the stream widens until it surges out of him, filling the room with its ripe scent even as it empties his bladder, pulling age and bile from his body, releasing his pain. It is the dream flow of a young man, of an army of the young, bold, and pure, the torrent of a generation ready to piss on all the delusions of the deluded world.

That's when he realizes how it ended for him on the blood farm. The needle has been jostled from its loop by the violence. He stands before the toilet and lets it go, lets the years pour out of him until he is emptied of all his ache and all his losses. And as he washes his hands of the regrets of the life he chose, he realizes what now might be waiting for him in the bedroom.

With the raw excitement of his youth, standing once again before a wall of blue, he flings open the bathroom door.

ABOUT THE AUTHOR

Photo © Sigrid Estrada

William Lashner is the *New York Times* bestselling author of *A Filthy Business* and *The Barkeep*, as well as the Victor Carl legal thrillers, which have been translated into more than a dozen languages and sold across the globe. *The Barkeep*, nominated for an Edgar Award, was an Amazon and Digital Book World #1 bestseller. Lashner, a graduate of the New York University School of Law as well as the Iowa Writers' Workshop, was a prosecutor with the Department of Justice in Washington, DC, before taking off his tie to write full-time.

Listen to Oliver Cross's Final Fatal Freedom Road Playlist at https://open.spotify.com/user/wlashner.